THE LOST PORTAL

A Quest to Save Olympus and the Underworld

By Raymond R. Mann

ABOUT THE AUTHOR

Raymond R. Mann is a published playwright (*The Petition*) who lives in Seattle with his wife Kathryn, an aspiring cellist. His other works include a three-part family memoir (*War, Romance, and a Life Together*) and a chronicle of his service in Vietnam as an Infantry platoon leader and company commander (*Candles in the Wind*). His combat experiences, including extensive operations in the Plain of Reeds, where the action of *The Lost Portal* takes place, have informed all of his writings as a compelling storyteller.

DEDICATION

To Kathryn, my very own goddess.

ACKNOWLEDGEMENTS

Writing a novel is rarely, if ever, a product of one person's "genius." It is a project that, beyond all else, requires people that believe in you. People that share your vision but are not afraid to offer an honest critique. I am fortunate to have a family and friends that shared the journey of *The Lost Portal* through every twist and turn.

First is Kathryn, my wife of fifty-eight years super-researcher, typist, editor, and coach. There is little doubt that without her efforts, this book would not have been published. Donn Wonnell is a cherished friend, co-author of our play *The Petition*, author of the '*290*' series on the Civil War, and a constant source of input and encouragement. Thanks, old friend! Our daughter, Lisa Woodley, is an aspiring author and has been a terrific sounding board during all that I write. Thanks for the help, and thanks for the love we all share.

Dr. Susan Myers of Seattle University shepherded the entire manuscript through development and line editing. She believed in the story from the beginning and never failed to keep me on course. Her coaching helped me to develop the character Alagon as the storyteller. Good news, Susan, Alagon returns in the sequel!

We met Dimitra Stesioti at our hotel in Plaka, just steps from the Acropolis. Many times, I would go to her office in the evening and read portions of the book to her. She was an instant believer in me and the story, which continues as this book goes to publication. We love you, Dimitra, and your precious son, George.

Debby and Jim MacSwain are best friends who have read and enjoyed almost everything I have written for the last decade. Debby served with the Red Cross in Vietnam. Her unique perspective on the war and the history of Vietnam has been a welcome and valuable asset.

As he might put it, here's a shout-out to fifteen-year-old Lynx Beauregard, a family friend with a keen interest in Greek mythology and the patience to read the manuscript and provide comments from a young reader's perspective. Good luck with your piloting.

An editor is someone who takes on your publishing project and puts up with rewrites and a thousand changes along the way, but whose principal contribution is getting the book and the author across the finish line. Maya has done all that and more. We are grateful for your persistence and championing spirit. Sorry for all of those Greek names and places!

This final acknowledgment is in a different category. It is a tribute to all of the officers and men I served with in Vietnam in 1968–Alpha Company and 3ᵈ Platoon of 2nd Battalion, 39th Infantry. We shared some tough times in the Plain of Reeds, the backdrop for The Lost Portal. There was a real Battle of the Plain of Reeds, where we lost too many good soldiers and friends, but our own band of brothers still stands ready to "saddle up" when any of us needs help. These are the men who put their lives in my hands. They will always be Mann's Marauders!

PRINCIPAL CHARACTERS

The Six

Ares: Son of Zeus, the fierce god of war, brother of Athena and Hermes

Athena: Daughter of Zeus, the goddess of war and strategic thinking, sister of Ares and Hermes

Hermes: Son of Zeus, winged god, herald of the Olympians, brother of Ares and Athena

Castor: Twin brother of Pollux, the deity of voyages and travel

Pollux: Twin brother of Castor, the deity of voyages and travel

Damon: Deity known for loyalty and true friendship as told in the story *Damon and Pythias*

<u>The Olympians</u>

The Immortals: The gods and goddesses of Olympus, deities the world (Cosmos) and different aspects of the lives of humans and mortals, including Zeus, Hades, Poseidon, Apollo, Ares and Athena and Hermes.

Zeus: Son of Cronus, ruler of the world (Cosmos) and Olympus, brother of Poseidon and Hades, god of the sky and constellations, married to Hera, one of the immortals.

Hera: Goddess of marriage and family, protector of women, sister and wife of Zeus.

Poseidon: Ruler of the Kingdom of the Sea, brother of Zeus and Hades.

Hades: Ruler of the Underworld, married to Persephone, the daughter of Zeus, brother of Poseidon and Zeus.

Ares: God of War.

Athena: Goddess of War.

Hermes: Herald to the Olympians.

Demeter: Sister of Zeus, goddess of harvest and agriculture, mother of Persephone.

Persephone: Daughter of Zeus and Demeter, goddess of seasons and vegetation, Queen of the Underworld, wife of Hades.

43^d Special Forces Operational Detachment Alpha (A-Team)
Unit Roster

Captain Antonio "Tony" Galanis, Detachment Commander (DC)

Chief Warrant Officer 2 Thomas Fredricks, Assistant Detachment Commander (ADC)

Master Sergeant (MSG) Bobby Travis, Operations Sergeant

Sergeant First Class (SFC) Robert "Rob" Salinas, Assistant Operations and Intelligence Non-Commissioned Officer (NCO)

Staff Sergeant (SSG) Arthur Gage, Senior Weapons Sergeant

Staff Sergeant (SSG) Vincent "Vince" Taylor, Weapons Sergeant

Staff Sergeant (SSG) Manuel "Manny" Perez, Senior Communications Sergeant

Sergeant (SGT) Carson "Kit" Rogers, Communications Sergeant

Master Sergeant (MSG) George Santini, Senior Medical Sergeant

Staff Sergeant (SSG) Stacey Diggs, Medical Sergeant

Sergeant First Class (SFC) Dennis "Hoppy" Hopkins, Senior Engineering Sergeant

Sergeant (SGT) Mason "Brick" Osbourne, Engineering Sergeant

<u>Other Characters of Mythology</u>

Pythia: The high priestess of the Temple of Apollo at Delphi, known as the Oracle of Delphi. She was consulted by the gods and mortals alike to hear her prophecies and predictions.

Pygmaioi: Tribe of diminutive (1 ½ foot tall) men who lived on the earth encircling Oceanus, engaged in an endless war with flocks of migrating cranes, also known for unsuccessfully attacking Hercules.

Gerana: Goddess of the pygmaioi who despised the goddesses of Olympus and claimed she was more beautiful than any of them. As punishment, she was metamorphosed into a crane by Hera.

Voltera: King of the pygmaioi and leader in battles against the cranes.

Spartoi: The "sown men" who sprang from the teeth of the dead Colchian Dragon, they became fierce warriors who disappeared as a result of internecine wars.

Titans: The pre-Olympian gods of the Cosmos. They were the twelve children of Uranus and Hesiod. Cronus was ruler of the Titans until they were overthrown by Zeus and the Olympians.

Cronus: Cronus became the ruler of the Titans and the Cosmos after he killed his father, Uranus. He led the Titans in a ten-year war against the Olympians (The Titanomachy), who were led by his son Zeus. The Titans were defeated, and

Cronus was sent to Tartarus (the 'abyss') in the Underworld as punishment. Later, he was freed by Zeus and given the Kingdom of Elysium.

<u>Fictitious Characters</u>

<u>Artineus and Tarellus</u>: Officiant priests of the Temple of Apollo at Delphi, devoted to Pythia.

<u>Adecius</u>: A false deity and rebel leader, made a god by Cronus. He became the military commander of "Operation Chimera," the plan to overthrow the Olympians.

<u>Alagon</u>: A traveler, master thief and trickster, friend of Hermes and messenger from Zeus to the Underworld. Demigod son of Zeus and his mortal mother Dimitria.

<u>Ephesis</u>: Father of Alagon residing in the Elysian Fields.

<u>Heleron</u>: Warrior and commander of Greek legions at Troy, hero granted eternal life in the Elysian Fields, made a deity by Hades and appointed as commander of the Legion of Aeneas in the battle against Cronus.

<u>Tanaurus and Arcelium</u>: Two principal commanders of the Legion of Aeneas under Heleron.

Pataurus: Soldier in the Legion of Aeneas captured by guards of Cronus' temple fortress. He escaped and later returned to the fortress to spy on Adecius and his soldiers.

Cerenia: Wife of Pataurus, a servant girl in Cronus' palace. She spies on Cronus and Adecius and reports to Hades and Persephone.

The Underworld

The Underworld: Commonly known as "Hades" after its god ruler, is where the souls of dead mortals are sent to face the afterlife.

Charon: A psychopomp ferryman who carries mortal souls across the River Styx where they will face Cerberus before gaining entry to the Underworld.

Cerberus: Monstrous three-headed watchdog of the Underworld who grants entry to mortal souls where they can never leave. Cerberus devours anyone who tries to escape.

<u>Regions of the Underworld</u>

Generally, there are three regions in the Underworld: Tartarus for the worst souls, Asphodel Fields for good souls and Elysium for the best souls. In addition, there are rivers of fire, fields of mourning, the Great Marsh and five rivers, including the Styx.

Lethe: One of the five rivers of the Underworld where souls can drink its waters to be reincarnated and return to the mortal world. It is the domain of the goddess Lethe.

Styx: One of five rivers of the Underworld. Along with the River Acheron, it carries souls to the Underworld. It is the domain of the goddess Styx.

<u>Kingdom of Van Lang</u>

The Kingdom: Filled with many gods and goddesses, much like Olympus. There are four symbols of the kingdom: the Turtle, Dragon, Unicorn, and Phoenix.

Ong Troi: King of the gods known as the God of Heaven. He is the counterpart to Zeus.

Than Vien: The mountain god, one of the four immortals.

Than Giong: Giant Boy, one of four immortals.

Chu Dong Tu: Marsh Boy, one of the four immortals.

Lieu Hanh: Princess, "Mother God" and one of the four immortals.

Tao Quan: The Kitchen God.

Ong Dia: The Land Spirit.

Trac Trung and Nhi Trung: The Trung Sisters. They were heroines who fought bravely in many wars of Van Lang. Both died in battle and became spirits worshipped by the mortals of Van Lang, after which they became deities of the Kingdom.

Table of Contents

PROLOGUE

That spring, the slopes of Mount Olympus were resplendent–what we Greeks call *perilanpros*–with pastels of hyacinths, poppies, orchids, and peonies. The mingling of fragrances was intoxicating. Once again, I would be wending my way toward the summit through familiar meadows and over perilous ridgelines. All the while rehearsing in my mind and, at one point, to an audience of ravens and magpies what I should say to the ruler of the universe.

"Oh, great Zeus…" The magpies chattered their disapproval. "Most powerful Zeus, All-Father of the universe."

The raven leader clacked his large black beak, signaling modest approval, so I added, "Supreme ruler of the gods," to which my audience flapped its collective approval. Gaining an increased level of confidence, I continued my upward journey.

Before I proceed with the remainder of my story, I best start at the beginning. I am Alagon, a Greek storyteller, traveler and trickster. Because of my 'talents', the Olympian gods and goddesses rely on me as a messenger between their palaces on Olympus and the Underworld. Of course, it helps that my mother, Dimitria, was a mortal of great beauty who lived in Litochoro, a village known as the City of the Gods, in the foothills below Mount Olympus. On a spring day much like today, Zeus appeared to her in the sanctuary of Leda in the form of a swan, just as he had done with Leda, the daughter of King Thestius of Aetolia, a union that produced Damon, Castor and Helen. The short of it is that Zeus is my father, which makes me a hemitheoi, a demigod like Achilles and Hercules. Like them, I have been granted certain supernatural powers, but I am (not yet) a hero of Olympus.

Perhaps the greatest advantage for me is the ability to travel freely from the mortal world to the Kingdom of Hades, the Underworld. My mother and the mortal father who raised me are there in Elysium, along with many of my mortal friends who have taken the journey down the River Styx. On one of my visits there, I heard rumors of a "lost portal" leading to an unknown world called Van Lang. My father took me to a remote area of the Elysian Fields and showed me what looked like a fortress being guarded by soldiers called green and blacks, carrying strange weapons. I gathered as much information as I could before meeting with Hades and his wife, Persephone. They informed me of other strange happenings throughout the Kingdom. It became clear that I should return to Olympus and warn Zeus about a disturbance in the Underworld.

As I approached the gleaming white palace of Zeus and Hera, Mount Olympus was shrouded in clouds. Lower to the ground, there was a fine mist that clung to the alabaster columns of the Temple of the Immortals, sparkling like the jewels on a maharaja's scimitar. As I walked the path leading to Hera's Garden, I entered the sacred grove of olive and almond trees dedicated to the goddess Athena. The cuckoos and peacocks were as noisy as ever. Reaching the gate to the garden, the perfume of orange, lemon and peach blossoms awakened my senses to thoughts of why I was there. I paused to savor a pomegranate. As Hera approached the gate, I was sure she could see the worry on my face and the steel-gray look in my eyes. What if the warning message I am about to deliver to Zeus is too late? Could the strange events in the Underworld truly be a threat to Olympus and the immortals?

My mortal persona took hold when Hera's glowing presence, the aura that surrounds this queen of the cosmos, penetrated my thoughts. Dropping the pomegranate from my hand, I reached for her outstretched hand and kissed it lightly. She took my hand, leading me through the garden to meet my Olympian father. Here began my story, a tale of a hidden portal and a quest to save Olympus and the Underworld.

PART I

Disturbance in the Underworld

Chapter 1
Children of Zeus:
The Gathering at Isthmia

My briefing of Zeus was tension-filled. There I was, informing the ruler of the cosmos that he and the immortals might be under threat from the Underworld. It didn't take long to get the customary reaction. The walls of the palace began to tremble, and thunderbolts cracked through the air. I steadied myself and tried to continue, "Father, I met with Hades and Persephone."

Like thunder, Zeus' voice boomed out, "I know my brother and his wife will defend the Underworld, but the rumors of a lost portal may be the greater threat. This I cannot tolerate." He rose from his throne and began to stroke his long, white beard. His eyes began to glow.

I felt a wave of cosmic energy pass through my body. The All-Father placed his hands on my shoulders. "Alagon, I have granted you special powers to help thwart whatever dangers might lurk in my brother's kingdom." He handed me a small piece of parchment on which was written six names.

I was instructed to locate those on the list and tell them to make their way to Isthmia, a village in the Peloponnese. His final words still ring in my ears after all this time.

"Guide them to my brother Poseidon, and quickly." This was a command punctuated by a raised hand clutching a bolt of lightning.

Hera walked with me to the garden gate. Neither her eyes nor her face revealed any evidence of concern. She spoke to me in a whisper, "If you are to succeed, you must use every one of the powers your father has granted to you." She smiled and retreated into the mist of the garden.

Picking up my half-eaten pomegranate, I thought about Hera's advice–use your powers, but how? Suddenly, an eagle flew from the garden and perched in an olive tree to my front. I turned and looked back toward the palace. I raised my arms, and they instantly became the wings of an eagle. In two days', time, I had flown to Athens, Thessaloniki, the islands of Corfu and Mykonos, where I located the six individuals on the list I had been given by Zeus. I found that I could use my mortal voice to relay the command from Zeus for them to proceed to the Temple of Poseidon. At that point, it became clear how I would use my transformative powers.

Over time, I would transform into various birds, snakes, and animals as I followed the progress of the quest that Zeus had set in motion. Whether in mortal or transformative form, I witnessed or heard about all of the events detailed in the story that I am telling here for the first time.

ʖ   ʖ   ʖ   ʖ   ʖ

They convened at Isthmia, a pantheon of gods and demi-gods: Ares, Athena, and Hermes, alongside mortals Damon, Castor, and Pollux, all summoned by the mighty Zeus himself. The mist of the Mediterranean nearly obscured the Temple of Poseidon as they entered the grand concourse and approached the throne where Poseidon was waiting. His voice resounded off the thick granite walls of the temple, "Children of Zeus, come near and hear the message of he who is father to us all. He commands you to heed his call, as it is for a great purpose. Ares, as the most battle-tested since the days of chaos, you have been chosen to lead the others on a quest to the Underworld."

Ares bowed down on one knee. "I am in your service in the name of our great father, Zeus. What would you have me do?"

"The demi-god Adecius is leading a revolt in the Underworld, which poses a threat to the Olympians. Now you must go to Delphi, where the Oracle will prepare you for your journey."

Without a word, Ares turned and exited the temple. The others followed. They set out immediately on foot for the nearby city of Corinth, from which they planned to sail to Delphi. As they prepared to embark for Delphi, trumpets began to sound from a nearby hillside. A loud voice boomed down upon the harbor,

"Ares, this is Adecius. We know of your quest and are prepared for battle with you and your salmagundi assembly of so-called warrior-gods and put this to rest here and now."

Ares stood on the deck of his ship and replied, "In due course, Adecius, another place and another time, when the full might of Olympus shall come down upon you." He raised his sword and commanded, "Cast off!"

Warm winds filled the sails and their small galleon edged forward. With the sun rising to their backs, 'the Six', as they now called themselves, maneuvered their craft out into the Gulf of Corinth. Adecius' trumpets pierced the morning air as Adecius raged on,

"Ares, turnabout now and save yourselves. This is my last warning. The path to Delphi will lead only to your destruction."

The air fell silent as they sailed on. Ares stood on the bow. Even a god, he mused, could sense trepidation at a meeting with the Oracle. Their northerly course took them past Archeologikos Choros and the ancient city of Philippi, replete with temples to Zeus and his wife Hera, coliseums built by the Romans, and the battlefields of a long-ago uprising against the Olympians. The sails billowed with the warm onshore breeze as Athena called to Ares, "When will we reach Delphi?" He turned and took her hand as she joined him in the bow. "I judge by tomorrow night."

Athena, wise in her understanding, knows her brother Ares not just as a ruthless warrior and fierce protector of Zeus but also perceives the underlying tension that always simmers within him. Ares turned to face her, and her suspicions were confirmed. His azure eyes and slightly furrowed brow spoke volumes.

"What are your thoughts, Ares? What do you know of Adecius?"

"I was at Olympus when Perseus and Andromeda were to be wed. Adecius was a commander in the army that Phineus raised to stop the wedding so that he could have Andromeda. It was at a time when Perseus possessed the head of Medusa."

Athena took a deep breath and looked out over the moonlit bay. "I know that part of the story. Hera told me that Perseus held Medusa's head in front of the army, and all were turned to stone. What happened to Adecius?"

"Adecius had taken a dozen soldiers on a flanking maneuver to surprise the wedding party from the rear. When he and his troops witnessed the fate of their fellow warriors, they retreated over the mountains to the Gulf of Macedonia. There were numerous rumors as to where they went, but no one seemed to know for certain."

"Poseidon said Adecius is now in the Underworld. What do you think he's up to?"

"I suppose that's what the Oracle will tell us. Whatever it is, we've been commanded by Zeus to stop it.

As always, doing the bidding of our father is a dangerous proposition. But you know me, Athena, I prefer to meet danger head-on. You're the strategist, not me. As always, I will trust your judgment. The only thing we can do now is to sleep as if surrounded by the clouds of Mount Olympus, from which we can draw strength for what lies beyond." She brushed her hand across his long, dark curls and kissed his cheek. With her departure, Ares turned his gaze to the heavens.

The remainder of their journey was uneventful until they reached the shores of Itea. As they disembarked, trumpets sounded once again. On a ridge above the harbor, the silhouette of Adecius and his minions could be seen. A large fire burned in their midst. Their chants and incantations could be heard. Ares gathered his companions close to him as if to prepare for combat. The sound of the trumpets faded and the thundering voice of Adecius echoed in every direction.

"Ares, I have warned you. Do not walk the treacherous path that Zeus has set for you. Your powers will never match the might of my sword nor the hammer blows of my army. Retreat now, and you will be saved."

Ares drew his sword and thrust it toward the ridgeline. "Show yourself, Adecius and we can decide this moment whose powers will prevail."

With that, the silhouette of Adecius could be seen rising to a great height. He, too, wielded a sword. Its great length began to glow white hot as it seemed to touch the very sky above. As Adecius' words echoed forth, his voice possessed such power that it began to tremble the very earth beneath Ares and his unwavering allies. Instinctively bracing themselves, they prepared for an imminent assault. Amidst this tension, shouts erupted from among the Six, a chorus of readiness and defiance.

Castor answered, "Ares, we stand ready."

"We will not falter nor retreat!" Pollux yelled in agreement.

Cheers rose among them as Adecius began to rage, saying, "Ares, it was you who said that Corinth was not the time and not the place. It is unworthy of you to challenge me now with the time and place of your choosing. I have shown you but a small measure of my strength and powers. Should you ignore my warnings and persist with the vengeful quest that Zeus has thrust upon you, you and I will meet in my domain, and all the powers of the Underworld shall rain down upon you. Even Zeus will be powerless to save you."

With those words, the trembling of the earth ceased. All that had been visible on the ridgeline, Adecius, his soldiers and the blazing fire, faded into the darkness of the sky. All was silent until Hermes drew near to Ares. His words were strong but measured.

"Ares." He turned to the others. "All of you. There is no truth in what Adecius has said. I fail to believe that Zeus will not protect us or that this pretender, Adecius, has more power than the Olympians who have empowered us to watch over the world and the Underworld. As Pollux has said, we shall not falter. We must triumph over these evil forces. Athena, am I not right?"

She embraced Ares and the others, each in turn. She pounded her fist on the breastplate of her armor. "Hear me, brothers. We have fought many battles without fear and always in the name of our father Zeus and mother Hera. We will triumph. Failing to do so, we will be but dust in the cosmos and the epoch of the Olympians will fall into darkness."

Shouts and cheers arose from all as swords were drawn and shields clattered against their golden armor. Ares dropped to one knee. The others followed in turn. Ares spoke in his most solemn tone, "We are now one. We enter this quest without fear and without reservation. The mighty hand of Zeus is our true armor, and our mother Hera shall be our sword. This we pledge." They rose with fire in their eyes. The air was filled with tension and anticipation. Ares pointed to the spot where Adecius had been seen and heard. "We must secure that high ground before we advance further."

Ares unleashed a war cry that was known to strike fear into the hearts of his enemies. His shrieks could even be heard above the din of battle. This was a signal to the others to form an attack line. Athena's face revealed her excitement at the thought of an engagement with their now-known enemy. She directed the others to form a line and move forward. They began navigating their way up the slope–a steep hill covered with fig and lemon trees, oyster plants, hyacinth and pungent herbs, which lent a surreal character to their advancing march.

Their pace slowed as they reached the crest of the hill. Nothing remained of Adecius or his troops except for a large circle of scorched earth where Adecius must have stood. Castor bent down and grabbed a handful of the still-warm earth and held it close to his nose. As he thrust it down, he angrily proclaimed to the others, "This is the smell of the enemy of Zeus. The smell of the Underworld." There were shouts and raised swords in agreement with Castor's words.

Ares pointed his spear in the direction of Mount Parnassus. He spoke in a reassuring tone, "Let us follow the scent of this pretender as we would follow a wolf to its lair. We shall do just that, but for now, the trail to the wolf's lair runs through Delphi." They followed the ridgeline until it intersected with a trail leading back to the pathway to Delphi.

Chapter 2
The March to Delphi

A day's march to the east lay Delphi on the slopes of Mount Parnassus. This was the domain of Apollo, among the most revered of all the gods–god of archery, music and dance, and healing. Foremost, he is the god of truth and prophetic deity of the Delphic Oracle, Pythia. It is in his temple that she resides and communicates with mortals on behalf of Apollo. Nearby is the Omphalos of Delphi, a stone called the 'navel of the world'. It marks the spot on Mount Parnassus where Zeus created the world. It is protected in the Temple of Apollo. There, the Oracle sits upon a gilded tripod in the lower chamber of the Temple.

Those entering the chamber are immediately aware of the strange vapors emanating around the Oracle. It is said that these vapors can alternately cause her to enter a trance-like state or, under the divine possession of Apollo, become frenzied and unintelligible. Across the millennia, the Oracle has received thousands of supplicants from kings and warriors like Alexander the Great and scholars and sages such as Sophocles. Yet many more were common folk–farmers, merchants and assorted public leaders.

All of this was on the minds of Ares and his troops as they proceeded across the valley leading to Mount Parnassus and the Oracle. They remained on guard against Adecius and his soldiers, knowing the travails of ancient quests: Perseus defeating Medusa, Achilles and Paris at Troy, Jason and the Golden Fleece. These are stories they know well and revere. Not knowing the true nature of their quest is not a cause for fear or speculation. All that matters is that Zeus is guiding their path.

As darkness approached, a light could be seen in the center of a clearing just ahead. They approached cautiously as Ares quietly issued commands.

"Athena, stay by me. Castor, you and Pollux approach through those trees on the right but stop short of the clearing until Athena gives a signal. Damon and Hermes, conceal yourselves behind that rock on the left and wait for my command. Athena and I will approach from the center."

Without further communication, each of them took up their positions. Ares signaled Athena to come closer. "Athena, what do you make of this?"

"I would say it's a trap. For what reason, I can't say. Or, some trickery of the nymphs, or perhaps Hermes' old friend Autolycus. Whichever, caution is warranted."

She signaled the others to be on alert and at the ready as she and Ares moved cautiously to the opening of the clearing. Still no movement or signs of danger. Athena motioned for the others to close in on the center, where a fire continued to blaze.

Hermes was the first to enter the clearing. As he did so, the flames died, and in their place stood a tall, bedraggled human, a traveler and thief well known to Hermes. "Yes, it's me, Alagon."

"Hermes, my dear friend," I began. "I have come with good news but also a warning. Please beckon the others to join us and hear my words."

Hermes signaled the others by raising his sword high above his head until it began to glow with a golden aura. Cautiously, the others entered the circle and surrounded me, yet not in a threatening manner. Hermes stretched out his arms and addressed them.

"Come closer and you shall meet this wise traveler, a master thief who has many times needed my protection. In repayment, he brings me news from Olympus and the Underworld. What say you this time, Alagon?"

"With the help of Zeus, I have been to the Elysian Fields and visited my father Ephesis. It was during that visit that I heard of Adecius' plot to seize a lost portal, kill Hades and Persephone and wrest control of the Underworld."

Ares moved closer. "What is this about a lost portal? Surely Zeus would know of any such path to the Underworld?"

"Not so, Ares. That is why I am here. I can only tell you that a human-caused disturbance in the ancient region of Van Lang has revealed an entrance to the portal through which Adecius and his soldiers are disrupting the order of the Underworld. Zeus commands that they be stopped, and the secrets of the portal be conveyed to the Olympians. Such is the purpose of your quest."

Castor put his arm on the shoulder of Pollux and raised his sword. "Brother, if there is danger of war, then

Zeus will use our powers to protect the Underworld and the sanctity of Olympus."

Damon placed his sword across his shiny gold breastplate and vowed, "And with the powers that Zeus has placed upon me, I will surround each of you with the protection afforded by the sacrifice of my life, as Zeus shall command."

"There will be time for heroism and sacrifice, but for now, you must make haste to Delphi and heed the words of the Oracle. Although Adecius is said to be engaged in battle at the portal, there is no guarantee that he will not use his trickery to keep you from completing this most crucial beginning of your quest."

Ares raised his right arm with a closed fist. "I shall be my father's right arm in battle and in every challenge that lays ahead."

"And I shall be his left arm to destroy his enemies and convey them to Tartarus," Athena added. "Where they shall dwell among the worst of transgressors and be banished from the Underworld for eternity."

"As my sister Athena and I are joined as one," Ares responded, "so it will be for us all. Now let us hurry to Delphi and kneel before the Oracle of Apollo and receive the word of Zeus."

There was shouting and the echoing sounds of swords beating upon armor breastplates.

Ares and Athena, stepping forward with purpose, led the group out of the clearing, setting their course towards Delphi. Castor and Pollux, ever in sync, fell into step behind them, followed closely by Damon and Hermes. In their eyes sparked a glow of anticipation, and their jaws were set firm with unyielding resolve.

As they departed, I shouted after them, "May good fortune follow you all. The fate of Olympus is in your hands."

Chapter 3
Approach to Parnassus: Attack of the Pygmaioi

I was right; there were no guarantees of a safe passage to Delphi. As the slopes of Mount Parnassus came into view, there was great shaking and shifting of the ground beneath them. A wide crack in the earth opened to their front. They were startled to see hundreds of pygmaioi emerge–the tiny pygmies that once tried to kill Hercules. One who appeared to be their leader commanded the hordes to form ranks that blocked the singular path to Delphi.

These were well-armed soldiers wearing armor and helmets and carrying shields, spears, and clubs. Although they stood two feet tall, they were known to be fierce fighters who could overwhelm their enemies with their sheer numbers. The soldiers stood fast as their leader approached the defenders of Zeus. Behind him was an entourage of two dozen servants carrying a wooden stand. Several feet from where Ares and Athena stood, the platform was raised, revealing ladder-like steps on one side. The diminutive leader slowly climbed to the top and stood on the platform. He began to speak. Athena and Ares were puzzled but quickly realized that it would be impossible to communicate if they did not draw closer to the platform. They approached the platform and knelt.

"Who are you and why are you here?" Ares inquired.

"I am Voltera, king of the pygmaioi. I speak for Adecius."

"Adecius, why would…"

"You were twice warned. Abandon your quest or face certain death. As you can see, we have many hundreds of soldiers, and we can summon thousands more if you persist with this fool's errand. I shall withdraw and await your decision … but mark my words. You have only as long as it takes for the first rays of the sun to pass below Mount Parnassus."

Voltera climbed down from the platform. His minions retrieved the platform and followed his march back to the assembled warriors. There was a roar of approval from the soldiers as Voltera strutted back and forth. With a wave of his arms, there was silence. The Lilliputian army stood at rest.

Pollux gestured toward Mount Parnassus. "By my measure, we have just minutes to decide our course. I say we draw swords and kill them where they stand. Brother Castor and I stand ready."

"Ares." Damon approached. "You and Athena are the wisest in these matters, but this challenge by the pygmaioi is a threat to Zeus' power. They have been dispatched by Adecius, who, we are told, is at the heart of this threat and the purpose behind our quest."

Ares drew closer to Damon and said, "Athena and I agree, Damon. I sense we all agree. So, let us prepare for battle and call the bluff of this imperious rogue Voltera."

Although his words were meant for Damon alone, his decision spread quickly through the group, and everyone responded with loud cheering and a rattling of their swords.

Hermes signaled for quiet, and the noise faded as he spoke, "Hear me out, my stalwart friends. I have been acquainted with these small creatures ever since their attack on Hercules while he slept. When he awoke, they were swarming over him. With his strength, he gathered them up, rolled them in a lion skin and carried them to Eurystheus.

"We can defeat them in a similar fashion. We should wade into their ranks and push them back toward the earthen crevice from which they came. We can then form a solid line to their front and press them backward into the opening. Those that set upon our bodies should be gathered up and tossed into the depths."

"Pray tell Hermes," Ares laughs lightheartedly, "am I not the god of war and so with fair Athena? Yet you have set the fire of Hercules upon us with your plan. And so it shall be."

Once again, Pollux thrust his arm toward Mount Parnassus. "The time is upon us. Let us punish these puny devils and be on our way."

With more shouting and the clammer of swords and shields, they formed a line standing an arm's length apart, Ares and Athena at the center. Pollux and Castor to their right, Damon and Hermes to their left. It would take but four strides to reach the ranks of soldiers to their front. Moving suddenly and aggressively toward their enemy would provide an element of surprise and, hopefully, disorder.

Athena raised her sword and swiftly thrust it downward. "Hail mighty Olympus." With that, the sons and daughters of Zeus moved apace to confront King Voltera and his forces. Once there, the battle plan formulated by Hermes was put into action. The six defenders of Olympus locked arms and began pushing the pygmaioi backward. Those in the back rank began tumbling into the crevice, some catching themselves on the edge and attempting to pull themselves back to the surface. These were futile efforts as more and more soldiers cascaded over the edge, taking others with them. Because of the sheer numbers of the combatants, many were able to set upon the bodies of the Six "giants" by standing on one another's shoulders. Thus, they were able to thrust their diminutive spears into the calves and thighs of the warrior-gods before being plucked up and tossed into the depths.

Without warning, the earth trembled again, more violently this time. Behind Ares and his group of valiant companions, a fissure tore through the ground, a gaping rupture that threatened their path. An almost deafening roar emanated from within the opening as thousands more pygmaioi poured out of the earth and joined the fray. They attacked the warrior-gods from all sides with spears, clubs and arrows. They formed ladders with their bodies tall enough to reach the warriors' shoulders to begin attacking their heads and eyes. The warriors had to break ranks in order to deal with the onslaught, as Castor went down onto one knee.

Pollux turned to help when a pygmaioi soldier thrust a tiny spear into his neck. He had to shout to be heard above the din, "Athena, can you help Castor? I have to deal with these little climbers."

"I'll try Pollux, but I'm surrounded! I think we should try to pull back, but we'll need a way around that crevice behind us. Damon, can you see a way around on your side?"

"Nothing here, only armed attackers in every direction. I'm afraid we're trapped. Our only choice is to stand and fight."

"You're right, Damon," Ares shouted above the din, "but we must make sure that at least one of us gets to Delphi to send a message to Zeus! Hermes, you're the fastest and you are the herald who can speak to the Olympians. All of you hear me. We must concentrate our efforts on the left side so that Hermes can slip through. On my order, summon all your strength and charge to the left to create an opening. Help Hermes free himself from those little beasties. Hermes, no matter how small the gap, you must race through. Only a few strides and you will have a clear path to Mount Parnassus. Get ready. When I raise my sword, fight your way toward Hermes."

Before Ares could give the signal, the sky grew dark and there was a cacophony of flapping wings, rattling bugle calls and hissing–the unmistakable sounds of cranes–the mortal enemies of the pygmaioi. The soldiers ceased their attack. On order from Voltera, his forces regrouped and assumed a defensive posture in preparation for an attack from above.

The warrior-gods now stood in the vacant space between the two gaps in the earth. As the opposing forces stood still and silent, three cranes descended to the space between the Six and Voltera. The flapping of their wings created a large dust cloud. As the dust was settling, the crane in the middle turned about three times and was transformed into a beautiful woman dressed in silk and gold. A large medallion hung from her neck.

"Athena." She clutched the medallion as she spoke, "I'm sure you recognize me. You should tell your fellow travelers who I am and why you alone can recount how my beauty became my undoing."

"You are Gerana, once queen of the pygmaioi."

The warrior-gods gazed from one to the other, both puzzled and concerned, in view of their current predicament of being surrounded by the forces of Voltera. Gerana took notice.

"You need not worry. I have been sent here along with my two guardians by Hera herself to help with your quest." She placed one hand on each of the cranes that accompanied her, and they were instantly transformed into tutelar spirits, the personal guardians of Hera. They stood twice as tall as any among the Six. Their build was that of Hercules or Achilles. They did not move or speak.

Athena bristled at Gerana's words. "This is a trick. When you were worshipped by the pygmaioi as their goddess queen, you pronounced that you were more beautiful than any of the Olympians–Aphrodite, Demeter,

Semele, and Hera. It was Hera who metamorphized you into a crane.”

“That is true, but you also know that my transformation made me a leader among the cranes, the sworn enemy of the pygmaioi.”

She raised her arms and looked toward the sky. Hundreds of cranes were massed and bugling their readiness to obey Gerana. “Do you still think this is a trick, Athena? Then come closer and gaze into this medallion.” She held the medallion out as Athena stepped forward and peered into a large stone in the center, where she saw the image of her mother, Hera. Athena smiled broadly when she recognized the polos on her mother’s head. Hera’s matronly countenance reassured Athena that Hera and Zeus were watching over the Six.

Hera spoke and her voice projected across the battlefield, “Ares, Athena, warrior-gods, you have been chosen by my husband Zeus to pursue a quest against Adecius and the forces disturbing the Underworld. I have sent Gerana in her earthly form to protect you against the pygmaioi. If they resist, they will perish at the mercy of

Gerana's legions of cranes. All this you can trust in the name of Zeus."

Athena nodded and rejoined her fellow warriors. She took a knee and placed her sword across her breastplate. The others followed, to indicate their allegiance to Hera and accept the truth of what she had said. Gerana and her guardians turned and approached Voltera and his assembled forces. In a firm and chilling voice, Gerana spoke, "By the force and command of Zeus, you are ordered to halt your attack and return to the depth from which you came. You are further commanded to cease your connection with Adecius and his traitorous forces. Failing to heed the commands of Zeus will prove fatal."

In a scene that bordered on the comical, Voltera's minions shuffled forward, awkwardly carrying his ladder platform. With deliberate slowness, Voltera climbed the ladder and positioned himself atop the platform, now standing face-to-face with Gerana.

"Gerana, I see you have been set free to return to your subjects. We welcome you." He turned to face his soldiers and stretched his arms out in celebration. They responded with shouts and cheers. Voltera turned about to face Gerana.

"Now, my queen, let us dispense with these progenies of Zeus." The din of cheering and stomping from pygmaioi forces grew to a pitch. Gerana leaned down to be face to face with Voltera–and it was an ugly face, at that. It could well be the face of one who had been turned to stone by Medusa. Steep crevices lined his cheeks and along his beak-like nose. His eyes were amber with flecks of gold.

"Voltera, you have heard my warning. Now stand down or suffer the consequences."

Voltera banged his spear twice on the platform, signaling his soldiers to advance. Immediately, Gerana's two giant guardians stepped forward and began using their feet to push the pygmaioi back, row upon row. The guardians reached down and began scooping up the diminutive combatants a dozen or more at a time and tossing them into the depths of the crevice. Despite their efforts, the rows of soldiers continued to press forward. During the struggle, Voltera was trapped on his platform, trying to rally his men.

Gerana stood upright and stepped back from the fray. She grasped the medallion and raised it toward the sky. A brilliant beam of light was projected into the sky, illuminating a sedge of cranes stretching as far as Mount Parnassus. They began circling and formed a funnel aimed at the ground below. When they reached the battle line, the massive birds tore into the ranks of Voltera's army. Wave after wave of diving cranes laid waste to hundreds of soldiers. Hundreds more were swept into the fissures from which they had emerged. The slaughter was unabated until Voltera sensed his defeat. He raised his spear in both hands above his head in a sign of capitulation.

"We accept the commands of Zeus. We will depart and have no further contact with Adecius or his soldiers." His voice trembled as he pleaded, "But, my queen, I beg you to depart with us."

With those words, there was silence across the battlefield. Once again, Gerana held the medallion in her hands. As before, a brilliant beam of light was projected into the sky. This time, the light spread across the sky, much like a blazing sunrise, a sign that the sedge of cranes should return to the sky. As they flew upwards, the pygmaioi soldiers began returning to their subterranean kingdom.

Gerana again spoke to Voltera, "Voltera, you were there when Hera set my fate, a fate that was of my own doing, my hubris. My return to the queen I was once is but a short reprieve. I have performed my duty as commanded by Zeus. Having done so, you and I will once again be enemies. We shall meet again on some distant battlefield. Leave now, before you never get the opportunity."

Voltera turned abruptly and summoned his servants. He left his platform and walked to the edge of the original crevice, where his servants assisted him with his departure. Gerana and her guards turned and faced the 'Six'.

She removed the medallion from her neck and placed it on the neck of Athena. "This now belongs to you. It is a gift from Hera." Athena nodded in recognition of her mother's love and the protection she was offering to the Six. Hera's image was no longer visible, so Athena gently rubbed her fingers across the polished surface of the medallion. "You must wear it throughout your quest. The rest of you must protect it at all costs. Now, I must take my leave. Good luck to you all."

There was a bright flash of light. Gerana and her guardians were transformed to their avian form to rejoin the triumphant multitude above. And then they were gone. These were the birds of omen, the avengers of Ibycus at Corinth. Ares looked to the sky and repeated the words of that famed poet of Greece,

"Take up my cause, dear cranes, since no voice, but yours answers to my cry."

Chapter 4
Pythia and the Temple of Apollo:
The Oracle Speaks

A radiant sun lit up the columns of the temple as the Six reached the top of Mount Parnassus–the Temple of Apollo at Delphi. Beneath the temple floor was the Cella, , the small chamber where two oracular priests gathered in support of the Oracle. Below that was the Adytum, a secret room where the Oracle received supplicants known as consultants, "those who seek counsel." Consulting the Oracle was a Greek tradition for a thousand years. They could be farmers, merchants, travelers, and poets such as Ovid, Plato, Homer–even Ibycus, who implored cranes to take up his cause. Regardless of their status, those seeking counsel were bound by the same Oracular procedures, all of which centered on the Oracle.

Throughout the ages, the mantle of oracle had been borne by many: from those born into wealth to humble peasants, from the vibrant youth to the wise and elderly. Each, in their own time, had served as the voice of prophecy. All were citizens of Delphi, though perhaps the most famous of these was Pythia. She was known to speak utterances and prophecies when under divine possession by Apollo, son of Zeus. Apollo is the oracular god who became the deity of the Delphic Oracle. The first temple dedicated to Apollo was built at Delphi and it was there where the Oracle of Delphi resided. This was the temple where the Six arrived, as instructed by Poseidon at Isthmia. They were greeted at the entrance by two 'officiants,' priests of Apollo. They were in charge of the temple and its various chambers in service to the Oracle.

One of the priests stepped forward. "I am Tarellus, and this is Artimeous. Welcome to the temple of Apollo. All of Delphi welcomes you. By the grace of Hera, you have survived the treacherous acts of Adecius. Through your bravery and the help of Gerana, the pygmaioi will remain in their ant-like state beneath the earth." It was obvious that the priests knew of events surrounding the battle with the pygmaioi and the intercession of Hera. Tarellus continued, "The pygmaioi have been the scourge of Olympus and the mortal world, causing mayhem wherever they appear. We can only hope that through the defeat of Voltera and his hordes, they will remain below. Come, we shall eat and drink while we await the summons of Pythia."

As a herald of the gods, Hermes had been selected as a spokesman for the supplicants. "We humbly accept your kind offer, but we arrive at a time of urgency. Can we see Pythia without delay?"

"Great gods and children of Zeus," Artimeous replied, "you are in the divine presence of Apollo. He will speak to you through the oracle. You must accede to the practices within his temple. Do not concern yourself with time. The Olympians will guide your progress. Now let us enjoy the gifts that Apollo has spread before us."

They sat on the stone floor around a low wooden table filled with golden platters of goat meat, cheeses, fruits, dates, and pitchers of wine and nectars. This was a welcome repast that would revive their strength after the strenuous battle of just a few hours earlier. Nevertheless, their minds were on the impending meeting with the Oracle and the continuation of their quest. Tarellus and Artimeous watched in silence as the warriors bantered about the day's exploits.

Ares raised a golden goblet of wine to propose a toast. "A toast to Hera for our deliverance on this day."

There were cheers and the clanking of goblets.

Athena was next. "And to Gerana, whose fate became intertwined with ours in the heat of the battle."

Caster followed her. "And, to her mighty crane army."

Cheers and laughter persisted as the feasting continued, and shortly thereafter, Artimeous left the table, returning with branches of laurel and a pitcher of water. "Friends," he told them. "It is time to prepare for your meeting with the Oracle. These laurel leaves and this holy water from the Cassotis Spring is sacred to Apollo. He bids us to treat your wounds of battle and cleanse your bodies before you enter the cella chamber. Please continue with your food and drink as Tarellus and I pass among you."

Each of the warriors had many pricks to their legs and arms from pygmaioi spears and arrows, as well as a wound to the neck suffered by Castor. Laurel leaves were laid upon each wound to stanch their sting while the two priests cleansed their bodies with the sacred spring water. This anointing would ensure that the supplicants would be purified of all private faults. When finished, the priests led the Six along a corridor with a glowing light at the far end. They entered a large portico. Its walls were lined with statuary honoring the Twelve Olympians–the greatest and most powerful in the pantheon of the Olympians. Zeus and Hera were represented there, of course, along with Apollo, Dionysus, and Aphrodite. Three of the six warriors of the quest were among them: Athena, Ares and Hermes. Each statue was crowned with a wreath of fresh laurel. At their feet were small gifts and treasures left by supplicants hoping to see the Oracle. There was a large cauldron in the center of the room, which, in addition to its brightness, gave off a pleasing smell of scented oils and herbs.

There was a doorway in the wall behind the cauldron, where the priests halted the group. Tarellus drew them close together. "We are about to enter the Cella. Once there, Artimeous will instruct you on the procedures to follow before your audience with the Oracle. Please follow me."

A winding staircase led to a chamber devoid of everything but six white and gold robes laid in a circle upon the floor. Tarellus assisted the Six with putting them on while Artimeous collected their swords and shields. "We are honored by your presence. We know of your quest. But only the Oracle can convey the guidance of Zeus on your perilous mission. Before we enter the Adytum, please take these laurel branches as a symbol of the journey you have made."

Just before they went inside, Artimeous added, "And be aware that the Oracle is thoroughly aware of why you are here. She will tell you all that Zeus and Apollo dee you to know. Now, please follow us."

Then, the priests led them downstairs to the Adytum, a much smaller chamber where the Oracle received supplicants. As they entered, the Six could almost feel the presence of Apollo. At the far end of the chamber, Pythia sat in a cauldron at the top of a golden tripod. She was draped in a scarf of purple. The supplicants surveyed the room and took in the smell of the vapors rising from a cleft in the floor below the cauldron. These vapors were said to be the 'breath of the soul'. Whatever their properties, there were numerous testimonials as to their effect on the Oracle.

They also felt they were in the presence of Zeus. Here, they could see the Omphalos, watched over by two golden eagles, signifying the center of the earth. Their attention was drawn back to the cauldron and the Oracle. Pythia removed her scarf, revealing a plain white dress and a laurel wreath upon her head. She was an old woman, but traces of her former beauty could be seen on her face. Her black eyes were focused on the Six warrior-gods standing before her. Minutes passed before she began to move her head at strange angles and flail her arms.

All the while, she was moaning and babbling incomprehensible words–the kind of gibberish she was noted for when under the spirit of Apollo. Suddenly, she bolted straight up with arms at her side as she began to speak,

"Oh, great Apollo, son of Zeus, these warrior-gods need your guidance and the succor of all Olympus. Possess me and I will speak." She began to twist about, her face contorted, her eyes glowing, and she called forth to Apollo, "Your wisdom is in me. I will use your strength to guide this sacred quest." Directing her attention to the Six, she spoke these words,

"Travel now to Lerna and enter the domain of Hades and Persephone. Go swiftly to Elysian Fields. Time is your enemy. The waters of Lethe will sustain you. A guide will lead you through the lost portal where your quest will be at risk."

Once again, she entered a trancelike state and began uttering cryptic words and phrases:

It's plain, it's plain

Fields of fire, base of fire

Giant green cranes

Rivers become spokes of the wheel

Dragons spit fire from above

Portals for rats

A road from north to south

These are the signs of the lost portal

Adecius awaits you there

It is there where your strength will be tested

Pythia grew silent and returned the purple scarf to her head. The priests signaled that the consultation was over. Before they departed, Hermes stepped forward. Removing his golden armor breastplate and laying it beneath the oracle's cauldron, he spoke carefully, "We take our leave with gratitude for your prophecies. Please accept this golden armor as a symbol of faith in you and your deity, Apollo. We accept this quest in service to Zeus and our brothers and sisters of Olympus."

Afterward, when he rejoined the other warriors, they all followed Tarellus and Artimeous to the Cella and from there to the temple chamber before halting at the burning cauldron, where they had first entered. There, the priests offered a blessing and bid the group farewell. Finally, Ares and Athena led the way as they followed the long hallway that led to the temple entrance. Shielding their eyes as the glowing sun of Mount Parnassus greeted them, without speaking, they turned in the direction of Lerna. The quest had begun.

Chapter 5
Lerna: Portal to the Underworld

In their audience with Poseidon, the Six had learned the disturbance in the Underworld was the reason for their quest. The Oracle confirmed the existence of a "lost portal" to the Underworld, which for the Six, was interesting and puzzling at the same time. Since my story centers on the discovery of an unknown portal, it seems prudent to inform the reader concerning the existence of three "known" portals to the Underworld. Taenarus, south of the Peloponnese (Cape Matapan), is the site of a cavern through which Hercules dragged Cerberus, the multi-headed dog, to the Underworld. Cerberus guards the gates to the Underworld to prevent the dead from leaving. I have been there many times and visited my friend Charon. Lake Avernus lies within a vast volcanic crater in Cumae, Italy. Its sulfurous vapors identify it as an entrance to the Underworld, as described by Virgil in the Aeneid. Its name means "birdless" since birds flying over the lake would fall dead, according to local legend.

Lastly, there is Alcyonian Lake at Lerna, the destination of the Six. This "bottomless" lake provides an entrance to the Underworld, only for the gods and heroes of Olympus. One of those was Hercules, who, along with his nephew Iolaus, discovered the lair of the nine-headed snake monster, Hydra. Hercules attacked Hydra and with Iolaus' help, cut off its heads, the ninth of which was the only mortal head. Hercules buried that head at the side of the road to Lerna, then dipped his arrows in the venomous blood of the corpse.

By the early hours of the next morning, the Six had successfully journeyed to Itea, marking another stride in their ongoing quest. Their boat was still tied to the small wooden landing in the harbor where they had left it. Ares gathered them on deck. "Damon, I see you've found our supplies. Pass around some food and wine while we discuss our plans for getting to Lerna. First, we will retrace our voyage to Corinth," he explained. "We must remain on alert, even though we are told that Adecius is occupied somewhere in the Underworld. Athena lay out the plan you and I worked out on the way here."

Athena rolled out a parchment on which she had sketched the route they would take upon entering the Underworld at Lerna. The group gathered around as she detailed the plan.

Before they could begin, though, Hermes pointed to the map and joined in, "Here are the caves of Lerna, and here is the location of the Lerna portal. You should recall that Circe led Odysseus to this portal while I was with her on her home island of Aeaea. If we follow the path of Odysseus, it will lead to the Grove of Persephone at the entrance to the Underworld."

Without pausing to answer him, though, Athena continued outlining the plan, "The path will lead us to the crossing of the River Styx, here, and from there across the Asphodel Fields on the way to the Elysian Fields. Beyond there, we hope to locate the lost portal."

Pollux expressed concern, "I remember that Pythia said we will have a guide to lead us to the portal, but what about getting past the fires of Phlegethon and across the Styx?"

His brother Castor echoed those concerns, "If time is our enemy, we can't afford any delays."

Ares stepped forward. "I share your concerns, but we need to trust that Hermes' knowledge of the Underworld will get us through safely. I'm sure there are more issues to resolve. For now, we need to depart for Corinth and spend this night preparing for our march to Lerna."

A resounding cheer rang out as the Six took their assigned positions on the boat and prepared to cast off. There was a good tailwind blowing, which would allow them to reach Corinth the following day. The "crew" settled in for another night crossing.

𝕺　𝕺　𝕺　𝕺　𝕺

The Underworld is a complex realm where individuals go upon death after their psyche or essence is separated from the corpse. Commonly known as Hades after its patron god, it is a realm for the dead only, with very few exceptions–Odysseus being one. Souls entering the portal at Lerna are greeted by Hades and his wife Persephone at a grove of black poplar trees and sterile willows. There, souls are destined to be sent to one of four regions. Tartarus, for the worst transgressors; Elysian Fields for the most excellent; Fields of Mourning for those hurt by love, and the Asphodel Meadows for most ordinary people. As souls make their way to the center of the Underworld, they must cross the River Styx, one of five rivers leading to the 'infernal regions.' The Styx is the river of hatred and unbearable oaths, which circles the Underworld seven times.

Crossing the Styx involves paying Charon, the boatman, with coins on the eyes or under the tongue of those seeking passage. Charon then ferries each soul across the river, where they will be greeted by Cerberus, the three-headed dog guarding the entrance. All are allowed to enter, but none may leave. From there, individuals are 'sentenced' to a specific region–mostly to the Asphodel Meadows, more or less, the neutral zone. However, the Six warrior-gods are not mortals. Their passage through the Underworld would be different. But "different how?" was the question before them as they sailed back to Corinth. Normally, the gods would have free and safe passage, particularly with a mandate from Zeus, as in this instance. However, after the encounters with Adecius, the battle with the pygmaioi, and the cryptic warnings from the Oracle, the journey of the Six might be anything but normal.

As before, Athena went to the bow of their small galleon to take over navigation from Ares. Torches were lit to brighten their path while the crew settled into their stations around the deck. Damon took the watch at the stern and called out, "Nothing follows."

In response, the others tended to the sails as Ares went below to work on the 'battle plan.' In case there could be a battle. He spread out fresh parchment on a large wooden table and began his task by assessing the strengths and weaknesses of the Six. They had been selected by Zeus himself, presumably because of the powers and skills they each possessed. He began to make notes on the parchment, listing his own attributes–good and bad. As the Olympian god of war, he was fierce to the point of being ruthless. Among the other Olympian gods, perhaps even to his sister Athena, his passion for war was seen as bloodlust, punctuated by a shriek so loud it could be heard above the din of any battle. Yet, his bravery was well known. He was considered the patron deity of warriors. If there was a battle ahead, Zeus could not have chosen a more formidable combat leader.

Surely, Zeus was aware that not all battles were won by brute force alone. It was said that his daughter Athena was born fully armed to assume the role of Goddess of War. She possessed great wisdom as the patron deity of scholars and poets. She adopted an intellectual approach to war and was considered the most capable military strategist of all the Olympians–the singular patron of the military. Her participation in the quest to find the lost portal could serve as a leavening force to her brother's fierce disposition.

Ares' next notations were regarding the twin brothers Castor and Pollux. Their exploits were known throughout the Olympian pantheon. When they were quite young, their sister Helen, later to be considered the cause of the Trojan War, was kidnapped by Theseus and Pirithous and carried off to Sparta. The twins pursued them and rescued their sister to great acclaim. Later, they sailed with the Argonauts expedition and rescued Orpheus from a great storm when stars appeared over their heads. Castor is known for his prowess with horses and Pollux as a boxer and athlete. Their skills and tenacity, as displayed in the battle with the pygmaioi, would be valuable assets for the impending quest.

Next, Ares considered Damon, the trusted and loyal friend of Pythias. Ancient stories tell how Damon had been accused of plotting against Dionysus, the tyrant of Syracuse. Damon was allowed to go home to put his affairs 'in order'. Pythias volunteered to be a hostage in case Damon did not return. When Damon returned, Dionysus was so taken with the strength of their friendship that they were both set free. Throughout the Olympian pantheon, their story is a symbol of trust, loyalty and true friendship. To Ares, this translates to a dedicated spirit, a warrior prepared to defend and protect his fellow warriors to the last measure. No doubt that, given command in battle, Damon would lead by example.

Ares knew that Hermes would play a number of key roles in their quest. Like Castor and Pollux, Hermes was a superior athlete. His winged sandals and gold helmet made him the fastest god among the Olympians, which supported his role as messenger to the gods, but he also possessed a much broader range of skills. He is the patron deity of commerce and science–and 'eloquence', making him the ultimate diplomat. Then there are his skills at trickery and theft. Ares was sure that Hermes would be critical to the entry into the Underworld. Of all the gods, Hermes was said to "get along" with Charon, the ferryman at the River Styx who was designated as a psychopomp, one tasked with carrying the souls of the mortals to the shores of the Underworld.

Albeit the Six are gods, not mortals, there was no way to know what disruptions were taking place in the Underworld, nor whether their combined skills and powers would ensure the success of their quest.

As Ares pondered what he had written, Athena came below with food and wine. "Making progress?"

"I've just finished my analysis of our group to see how prepared we are to enter the Underworld and pursue our quest."

"Your conclusions?"

"Zeus has done us great justice. We have what must be the most formidable compliment of skills and leadership ever assembled on behalf of the Olympians. Our father trusts us to turn back any challenges to his power and the cosmic sovereignty of the Olympians."

"And don't forget." Athena clutched the medallion around her neck. "We can count on support from Olympus along the way."

Ares stood and walked toward Athena. "Certainly, from Hera," he told her. "But I'm not sure what we can count on once we enter the Underworld. I was just about to inventory the weapons and supplies we have for our quest. Want to help?"

"Sure. Where do we start?"

Ares returned to his parchment while Athena went to a small storage area at the stern. She called out each of its contents as Ares marked them down. The Six did not come unprepared. Not only had Athena been born fully armed, but she also had several unique "magical" weapons befitting the Goddess of War. Her protective power comes from the Aegis, a shield borrowed from Zeus, upon which is a gorgon, the head of Medusa, given to her by Perseus after he killed the snake-haired monstress.

The semblance of Medusa symbolizes the petrifying fear that enemies would experience when looking upon it. Her golden helmet symbolizes the fact that wisdom and strategy are the best tools for overcoming your enemies, though, for insurance, she also wields a lance dipped in the blood of Medusa and an impenetrable breastplate, both of gold.

Ares continued his notations as Athena produced the remaining items from the storeroom: Hermes' winged sandals, golden helmet and Caduceus, his magical staff with twisted snakes and wings at the top. Its power can force gods or mortals to fall into deep sleep, though Ares preferred to fight with his spear, as did several of the others. There were bows and arrows, several of gold, and one with magical powers, breastplates, armor, protective animal skins, brass shields, a great assortment of swords and knives, and one very unique gift from the Olympians, a cape of invisibility, the Helmet of Hades, sometimes worn by Athena and Hermes when encountering supernatural entities.

This arsenal of mortal and magical implements of war would normally carry the warrior-gods through any battle. In this instance, however, the unknown challenges they might face in the Underworld and the mysterious prophecies of Pythia had to be considered. Ares knew all too well that the wisdom and strategic reasoning of his sister Athena would see them through whatever lay ahead.

Up on the main deck, the remainder of the crew had gathered under torchlight, where they were drinking wine and speculating on the true nature of their quest. At the center of their discussions were the words and prophecies of the Oracle. All agreed that her words were mysterious. Moreover, they seemed to be divided into two parts, the first pertaining to the Underworld, the domain of Hades and Persephone, the Elysian Fields and the waters of Lethe, while the second part was the most puzzling, as reiterated by Damon, "Fields of fire, giant green cranes, portals for rats?

These don't sound like anything we know about in the Underworld, yet she repeats, 'it's plain, plain.'"

Suddenly enough, Pollux interrupts, "It doesn't seem plain to me, but as we know, the Oracle mostly speaks in riddles."

In seeming agreement, Damon continues, "That's true, but what good is a prophecy that we don't understand?"

Hermes had been adjusting the sails to take advantage of a strong night breeze and listening closely to the discussions. "I'm most interested in her admonition that time is our enemy," he said. "It makes me believe that things in the Underworld are going badly, that we must somehow prevent them from getting worse, and do it quickly."

In response to these perceived frictions, Castor pours wine all around. "One thing we do know..." he warned gently, "Is that Pythia identified Adecius as our enemy and somehow, he's using the lost portal to go in and out of the Underworld."

"That's right." Ares came back on deck, joining the group. "Find the portal and we find Adecius."

Once again, their night voyage was calm. Orion, Taurus, Pegasus, Virgo, and Andromeda were visible overhead–warm breezes would carry them back across the Gulf of Corinth. Once they arrived in Corinth, there would be no time to waste. If Adecius or his minions were waiting for them, everything would depend on the element of surprise.

Corinth was shimmering in the bright afternoon sun as the crew eased their small galleon into the harbor. There were no signs of Adecius or his minions as they began to disembark. Nevertheless, they remained on high alert as each warrior prepared for the march to Lerna. Breastplates were strapped on. Weapons were distributed. The sun glinted off gold shields and helmets as they took up swords, knives, and spears. Hermes donned his winged shoes and helmet and slung the magic bow and gold arrows across his back. Athena carried the Helmet of Hades and the Aegis. In due course, they were fully outfitted and ready to proceed. It was time to implement the plan that Athena had laid out during their voyage.

Hermes was the fastest runner among them, in all of Greece, for that matter. His mission was to run to Lerna to determine if the route was safe. If all went well, he was to fire a single gold arrow into the sky. A second gold arrow would follow in the event there was trouble along the way. Barring any problems, he would proceed to the cave at Lerna and locate the portal to the Underworld.

The others gathered around him and wished him luck as he sped away. Ares motioned for the group to move up to a small clearing at the head of the path to Lerna. "It won't take Hermes long to get to Lerna," he assured them, "so let's be ready to move out. Athena, give us one more briefing on the next steps."

"Sure. Assuming we see the one arrow signal from Hermes, we proceed to Lerna at all due speed. Ares will take the lead. Pollux and I will be behind him on the right, Castor and Damon on the left, creating an arrowhead formation. We will take signals from Ares in the event of trouble. You each have food and wine for the journey. Water will be available from local streams. In the event we get separated, make your way to the high ground above the harbor. I will use my helmet of invisibility to investigate potential threats and then join you there. Are we ready?"

General shouting ensued as they raised their weapons and pointed them toward Lerna. They continued to search the sky in the direction of Lerna. Castor was the first to see it: a golden arrow glowing like a torch above Lerna. Time seemed to stand still as they waited to see if there would be a second arrow. None appeared. They quickly assembled in formation. Ares unleashed his thunderous war cry, resonating with ferocious intensity, as they hastened their pace to rendezvous with Hermes at the gateway to the Kingdom of Hades.

Chapter 6
Battle with the Colchian Dragon:
Enter the Spartoi

Although the warrior-gods were focused on their mission and the need to proceed with alacrity, they couldn't help but notice the beauty around them. Cypress and pine, juniper, myrtle, and oleander were resplendent in the hills surrounding their march. They could hear wild boars grunting and snorting as they rooted for food among the juniper and laurel hedges. Jackals were calling out to their mates, some of which could be seen on the ridgeline above. Athena offered a word of caution to the group, "Be on guard. Any of these creatures could be Adecius or his minions set to attack." Among the sounds, herons and storks competed for attention, and to the delight of Athena, there were owls calling out to the travelers. This was the ultimate domain of the Olympians: a peaceful order of both gods and mortals. Soon, their reverie was broken by a gold arrow soaring in the sky overhead.

Ares raised his golden spear to signal the group to halt. As the brilliance of the golden arrow faded, the group grew closer. "Until we know Hermes' intent for firing a second arrow," Ares warned, "we need to conceal ourselves in the trees and shrubs." Quickly, then, he signaled to his left and right, and everyone took cover. They scanned the terrain around them for any signs of trouble. Not long after, Hermes appeared and called to them.

"Assemble here," he whispered fiercely. "I have news."

Without hesitation, they joined Hermes, eager to hear his message. Before they could, though, Ares slapped Hermes' shoulder. "Good to see you are safe. What have you learned?"

"I found the cave leading to the portal. As I entered, I saw that the entrance to the portal is guarded by a giant dragon being attended by six soldiers."

"Soldiers of Adecius?"

"It's difficult to say. I had to keep my distance from that nasty beast. I was able to survey the cave and particularly the surroundings of the portal. Athena, we will need a plan of attack if we hope to gain access to the portal."

Athena paused and then addressed the group. "It would seem the immediate threat lies in the cave. Hermes, did you see or hear anything of concern between here and the cave?"

"None."

"Then let us proceed with haste to the cave. Once there, I will use my helmet to become invisible to the dragon and its attendants."

Ares and the others nodded in agreement. Without delay, they fell in behind Hermes, who would lead them to the cave. The march to the cave was uneventful. Once there, Athena tested her helmet. By placing her hands on the sides of the helmet, a veil of mist was created, through which she could not be seen. Ares and his comrades took firm control of the cave entrance, establishing a secure position. Athena, with a measured stride, advanced toward the portal situated at the farthest end.

Suddenly, there was a disturbance within the cave–growling and hissing, apparently by the dragon and agitated voices of the soldiers Hermes reported seeing. Athena reappeared at the entrance. "Something very strange is happening here," she told everyone as they gathered around. "The guardian at the portal is none other than the Colchian Dragon, and those are not Adecius' soldiers, at least as we saw them on our way to Delphi. These are six Spartoi!"

If what Athena observed is accurate, some part of the Olympian world has been turned on its head. Starting with Ares' connection to the Colchian Dragon. It was in the sacred grove of Ares that Jason and the Argonauts found the Golden Fleece guarded by two "Drakons". One of the dragons was slain, while the other was said to be put to sleep by the magic of the witch Medea. The teeth of the slain dragon were harvested by King Aeetes, who commanded Jason to sow them in the sacred Field of Ares. The seeded teeth produced a tribe of warlike men, Spartoi, who sprang fully grown from the earth. Over time, the Spartoi engaged in fierce battles with mortals and the gods but were eventually defeated and disappeared from the Olympic world.

How, then, could these artifacts of a past epoque be present at Lerna? To the Six warrior-gods, it was simple. That's the way things work in the Olympian cosmos. Castor and Pollux were with the Argonauts as they pursued the Golden Fleece. Ares held sway over the sacred grove, where the dragons provided protection along with the Spartoi. Whether directly involved or not, every one of the Six knew the appearance of the Colchian Dragon and the Spartoi was a bad omen. However, there was little time to ponder the meaning. The warrior-gods needed to gain access to the portal without delay.

Ares and Athena huddled to discuss an attack plan. Thanks to the inventory and analysis they had done on the voyage back to Corinth, it didn't take long to fashion a plan. Ares called the group together to review the plan and make any final adjustments before they launched. To set the tone, Ares turned toward the entrance to the cave and let loose his signature war cry. The sound reverberated on the walls of the cave, leaving no doubt that those inside knew who would be leading the attack, as he turned around to address his impromptu "army".

"This calls for full armor," he began. "Make sure you have all you need. We will attack in three stages in rapid succession. Athena and Hermes will go first and peel off to the left. Pollux and Castor go next to the right and hold when you are about halfway to the portal. Damon and I will hold at the entrance until we see how things develop. Athena, fill us in on the rest."

"Here is the entrance to the portal." She used her spear to sketch the attack plan in the dust. "The dragon is positioned in the center, about here. The six Spartoi are divided, three on each side, totally blocking the entrance. They have armor, shields, and two-pronged pikes. As we know, they are fierce fighters and extremely good with their weapons."

"Hermes and I will focus on the three on the left. I trust that showing them the Aegis will startle and confuse them. Hermes will move forward with the Caduceus and project its power toward the dragon to force it to sleep."

Hermes interrupted, "That may only work for a short time," then he explains carefully, "so the rest of you will need to act quickly."

Athena nodded. "Pollux and Castor," she continued, "you will go to the right and hold here. There's a small grotto to provide you with cover. From there, you can place arrows on the dragon's neck and engage the Spartoi as needed. No surprise, Ares prefers a frontal assault. If the rest of us are successful, he and Damon will put anything, or anyone left standing, to the sword."

Ares exhorted them to action, "Sister, brothers, we will fulfill our sacred duty to Zeus and Olympus and celebrate our entry into the portal by drinking the blood of the Colchian Dragon." Once again, Ares unleashed his piercing battle cry, signaling the commencement of the Six's assault.

Athena was the master of combat strategy. Logically, she took the lead in this instance, with a great deal of confidence in a successful outcome. Yet, she must have been the first strategist to verbalize the axiom in her words. "Everyone has a great strategy until the first spear is thrown," she swore. It seemed that truer words could never have described their current engagement. No sooner had she and Hermes entered the cave when three of the Spartoi warriors rushed toward them with flaming torches that temporarily blinded the gods, preventing them from deploying the Aegis and Caduceus. In addition, the enemy soldiers were swinging strange disc-like weapons over their heads that made a screeching sound like the giant owls of Trikala. The whirling discs began throwing off scores of small darts, some of which stuck in the Aegis. Still others plinked off the warrior-gods' breastplates.

They stood their ground and Hermes called out to Ares and the others, "Attack their left flank. Aim for their weapons. Athena and I will move to the right to distract their attention."

"Pollux and Castor are in position and ready to fire," Ares called back. "Hold at a safe position." He pointed his spear in the direction of Pollux and Castor and gave the signal to fire. One after another, golden arrows flew toward the enemy with great accuracy. In short order, their spinning weapons were wrenched from their hands. The two archers shifted their aim. Their arrows began penetrating the Spartois' protective animal skins. As they turned to fend off the incoming arrows, Athena and Hermes unleashed a furious attack on the enemy's rear, Athena with her poisonous spear and Hermes with the tip of the Caduceus.

The guardian dragon was intently observing the combat to its front. The three enemy soldiers now lay dead or dying, which caused the Colchian to bellow and roar and swing its head and long neck from side to side. The ground shook as it slowly moved toward Athena and Hermes. Its menacing forked tongue projected in their direction amidst constant hissing. With three of the Spartoi soldiers neutralized Pollux and Castor turned their attention to the remaining three. Two of them were wounded by the time the brothers had exhausted their supply of arrows.

"Pollux and Castor!" Ares began shouting orders. "Move in with your swords and destroy the enemy soldiers. Athena, you and Hermes move closer to the dragon to keep its attention on your movements. Hermes, try the Caduceus once more. Damon and I will head straight for the dragon's neck. At my call–now!"

It was over in a matter of minutes. Apparently, the Caduceus had begun to work. The dragon became ponderous with his steps, and his head began to droop. Pollux and Castor moved in for the kill while dispatching the remaining enemy soldiers. When Ares issued another battle yell, the dragon briefly turned its head toward the charging God of War and his capable guardian, Damon. The Colchian's long neck remained exposed as Ares and Damon thrust their spears deep into the exposed area. Athena and Hermes struck from the left. Scales on both sides of the monster's neck turned blood red as the behemoth dropped to the ground with a thud that shook the entire cave.

Finally, the Six had prevailed–and felt certain, moreover, that Zeus and all of Olympus would be proud.

With the final coup de grâce, blood was spilling from the beast's neck. One at a time, the warrior-gods passed by and filled a wine goblet with the blood. Ares raised his vessel and the others followed. "We have been tested once again and each of you evidenced your skill and bravery, but it is as a team that we succeeded. All hail Zeus and all hail Olympus." With cheers and shouts, they banged their cups in unison and drank up.

Chapter 7
The Goddess Styx:
Journey to the Kingdom of Hades

Five rivers cross throughout the Underworld–Cocytus, Phlegethon, Acheron, Lethe, and Styx. Each of them has their unique characteristics and purposes. Cocytus is the river of lamentation and wailing, while Phlegethon is the river of fire. Both flow into Acheron, the river of pain. Styx is known as the river of hatred. Lethe is the river of forgetfulness or oblivion, where "good" souls spend eternal life. Drinking water from the Lethe can offer reincarnation to the dead. All five converge into a great marsh at the center of the Underworld. It is there that the ferryman Charon rows souls to the River Styx for entry into the Underworld. For the most deserving souls, the journey will end in the Elysian Fields, the paradise where heroes granted immortality by the gods are sent. As per Pythia's guidance, the Six embarked on a journey to Elysium, the sacred realm, in hopes of finding the lost portal.

Hermes would lead the group, now the "Omada", the team, as Ares had pronounced them, through the Lerna portal. He knew they would exit into Phlegethon, the land of fire. From there, they would try to follow the Cocytus River to the Great Marsh, where they could contact Charon. As they exited the portal and stepped into the Underworld, a blast of heat halted their progress. They were standing on the edge of Phlegethon, the land of fire. There was nothing between them and the Styx but a raging inferno through which there was no discernable path forward. To their right was the River Cocytus, with the most turbulent waters of any in the Underworld. One look at the river of fire and there was no wondering why it was the river of wailing. Athena was the first to comment, "We might be gods, but even we can't conquer these hellfires. Hermes, what are our options?"

"I've never entered through the Lerna portal in the past. I entered through the Grove of Persephone, which provides a clear path to the Great Marsh. We'll have to see if we can work our way in that direction, even though it will double the distance we need to travel."

Ares surveyed the situation and broke his silence. "Lead on Hermes. We must reach the Styx by any means possible."

Hermes chose a path parallel to the Phlegethon River but at a safe distance from the river's blazing fire. Once again, the group formed into an arrowhead formation and remained on high alert. As their journey had so far proved, there could be trouble at any turn ahead.

They soon entered a small grove of trees with a cool stream flowing through. It was a good time to rest and regain their strength after the vicious fighting at the entrance to the portal. Soon, all were asleep. In what seemed like just a few minutes, they began to stir. A haziness stood in the air, disorienting Castor and driving him toward what had been the edge of the grove. He began shouting to the others, "This is not where we stopped to rest!"

"Peering through the haze, I can see a great body of water. Come see and at the shore are masses of what must be the unburied souls of the Underworld."

The others hurriedly joined Castor. Collectively, they were trying to discern where they were and how they had gotten there. The discussions were suddenly interrupted by a flash of light and the appearance of a shadowy figure in black robes carrying a bident, the two-pronged pitchfork carried by Hades. The Six knew immediately that this was not Hades; it was Styx, goddess of the River Styx. Ares spoke in a low voice, "This could be good, or this could be bad."

Styx was a nymph, one of the three thousand daughters of the Titans Oceanus and Tethys, who had become prominent during the Titanomachy, known as the "Clash of the Titans", when she was the first to rush to the aid of Zeus. As a reward, Zeus gave her name to the binding oath taken by the gods, swearing "by the River Styx" to tell all truth. As such, Styx became the deity in control of the River Styx, the connection to the Underworld for all souls. Curiously, the Styx River was known to have miraculous powers that could make anyone who bathed in its waters invulnerable, as when Achilles' mother dipped him in the Styx during his childhood. He became invulnerable, except for his heel, by which his mother had held him. He died during the Trojan War after being struck by an arrow in that heel.

Yet, the River Styx was commonly known through mythology as the "River of Hate". It was also referred to as stygian, a place of foreboding darkness and gloominess. Since all four of the other rivers flowed into the Styx, and hence the Great Marsh, it cast that dark and gloomy pall over the entire Underworld. Styx was seen as a strong and assertive goddess, both feared and respected, so it was hard to say whether Zeus might have done her a great favor by giving her dominion over the river of punishment.

"Great warriors. Brothers and sister, children of Zeus. I welcome you to my domain."

She lowered the bident and bowed graciously to the Six. "Your arrival was foretold to me. I am here at the request of Persephone to aid in the search for the lost portal. Do not be alarmed that through my magical powers, you have been transported here to the shore of this sacred river. While you slept, the fires of the Phlegethon were turned back, and it was Charon himself that ferried you here."

Stepping forward, Athena bowed to the goddess. "We are honored by your presence. It is good to hear that you have been summoned by our father. What now would you have us do?"

"Charon will ferry you across the river. When you reach the far shore, you are to traverse the Asphodel Fields and proceed to the Palace of Hades. Persephone will greet you at the gate. There, you will feast and rest before continuing your search for the lost portal. Hermes, you are the most familiar with Charon. Please lead the others down this path to board the ferry."

Hermes nodded, holding his sword across his breastplate in tribute. "We are most gratified by your presence. We pledge to you, all the deities of the Underworld and Olympus, we shall not fail."

At that, the Six crossed their swords with cheers of "All hail Styx. All hail Hades. All hail Zeus," and Hermes led them away–though suddenly, the goddess was gone. As promised, the path led directly to the ferry landing site.

There, standing in the middle of his ferry, was Charon. He raised his arm and called out to Hermes. "Hermes, my friend. It is too long since we have been together. I am here to help you with your quest. Please come aboard." He strode to the front of the barge to welcome the Six on board. Alerted by Styx, he knew who his special passengers would be.

Hermes boarded first, again placing his sword across his breastplate. "Charon, we are grateful for your help."

There was a short silence as they plowed ahead. Charon broke the silence. "That which is important to Zeus is important to us all. I will speed you on your way."

The barge made creaking sounds, almost like moaning, as the waters of the Styx slapped against its sides. There was a steamy haze coming off the river, blocking any view of where they might be heading. An acrid smell wafted in from the direction of the Phlegethon. Several torches on the barge provided the only visible light. When all were on board, Charon took up his place at two large oars at the center of his craft. He made groaning sounds as he pulled on the oars, and the barge moved forward at a smooth and steady pace.

The Six peered into the darkness ahead. Ares finally broke the strained silence. "Charon, it's an honor to be summoned to Hades' palace, but I trust that will not delay our progress. Pythia advised us that 'Time is our enemy'. We will need to…"

"Don't worry, young gods, we will speed your progress to the portal, but you will need the help and wisdom of Hades and Persephone. Cerberus is expecting you, but it's not what you think. He will present no danger. The Goddess

Styx has offered him a special cake that causes him to sleep–that will be the case when we reach the far shore."

Athena smiled broadly. "Just when we were beginning to have so much fun, the dog goes to sleep." Light laughter rippled through the group, though none expressed disappointment at the revelation. Upon reaching the distant shore, they found Cerberus in a slumber, yet the serpentine heads atop his three necks writhed and hissed in an ominous manner.

Charon announced their arrival. "Don't worry about them; they have no power when Cerberus is sleeping. Now, you may depart without delay. The unburied souls that I bring over must transverse the Asphodel Fields in that direction until they reach the Vale of Mourning. You young warrior-gods must follow this path. It is a direct route to the Palace of Hades. It also bypasses the Plain of Judgement. In the name of Zeus, may your quest be a successful one."

As they stepped from the barge, Hermes came forward and spoke to Charon, "My friend, we are grateful for your assistance and that of the Goddess Styx. We shall inform Hades and Persephone of your valued service."

Chapter 8
The Palace of Hades and Persephone: Alagon Reveals the Source of the Disturbance

Assuming they were under the protection of Styx and Hades, the Six had proceeded briskly and without incident. There, in the middle of the Asphodel Fields, was a vast plain of green "poa," a meadow grass, and orchids like the plains of Pelion near Mount Olympus. They all wondered if this was the plain prophesized by Pythia. In the center of Hades' domain was a gleaming multi-towered palace. As instructed by Styx, the Omada approached the gate where Persephone was waiting to greet them.

"Hades and I welcome you as you continue your quest. My mother has guided you here. Now, Hades and I will offer you brief comfort and a chance to regain your strength. The next part of the journey will be the most difficult."

Athena stepped forward, still grasping the medallion given to her after the battle with the pygmaioi. When she reached Persephone, she took her hand and kissed it. "We come with the blessings of Hera and our father Zeus. We are anxious to be on our way, but we are grateful for your hospitality."

The Six surrounded Persephone, kissing her hand and embracing her. Touching the medallion, she looked at each of the Six with an understanding gaze and glowing eyes. "All praise to you for accepting this quest. Hades and I will do all in our power to aid you." She led them through the gate and under an archway that led to an open courtyard. At the far end, Hades was sitting upon a large throne befitting the God of the Underworld. There were two large stone benches in front of the throne where the visitors were seated after bowing appropriately to their host. Hades spoke formally, "We are aware of the challenges you have faced thus far and of those you are yet to face. We have important information that you will need to locate the lost portal. But first, you will bathe in healing waters which have been brought from the Lethe, and then you will join Persephone and me for a hearty feast."

Guided down a lengthy corridor, the group emerged into a luxurious garden. Bursting with vibrant hues, the garden boasted an array of colorful plants and trees, their fragrances intermingling hints of lilac, honeysuckle, lavender, and lemon balm filling the air.

Terraces reached upward and at the top was an alabaster pavilion with golden statues of Zeus and Hera and all of the Titans, gods and goddesses of Olympus. Each of the terraces contained a steaming pond of water where the Six were invited to bathe and refresh with oils and perfumes. They were given long, white robes, much like those they had worn at Delphi, and led up winding stairs to the pavilion.

As Hades had promised, laid before them was a feast of every imaginable delicacy of fruits, oranges, pomegranates, melons, dates, grapes and more. Golden plates of meats, fowl and fish, all surrounded by pots of honey, nuts of every variety, and bowls of the most fragrant of spices. Large vessels of wine were on a table, along with melogian, a powerful drink of boiled honey and herbs. Hades sat at the head of a long marble table, with Persephone seated at the other end. The warrior-gods sat three on each side. There were gold plates and goblets at each place, with gold trays of food arrayed from one end of the table to the other. Soon, all were eating, drinking, and bantering among themselves.

As they passed around trays of sumptuous fruits and pots of honey, their goblets were filled with melogian. Toasts were offered to Hades and Persephone. As they finished, a bell rang three times, and Hades stood up and offered a toast to the Six, recognizing their willingness to pursue the quest Zeus had requested of them. As he spoke, his mood became somber, lowering his voice until it rang somewhat muted. "Tomorrow," he said softly, "you will resume your quest. We know there are many challenges ahead, so you must be always on guard. You are aware that certain disruptions are taking place within the Underworld. Adecius is but one part of the troubles. Our purpose tonight is to provide you with the details, as far as we know them."

Hades paused briefly as a familiar traveler approached the king and bowed appropriately. "You have all met Alagon on your march to Delphi. He is much more than a traveler, a poet and a trickster." I smiled broadly, and muted laughter passed among the Six, stifling itself, as Hades continued, "He is a direct representative of my brother Zeus, a messenger from Olympus to my kingdom." He gestured toward Persephone. "And not least, he is a brother of my beautiful wife. His status allows him to easily move between here and the world above. Thus, he is able to visit his father, Ephesis, in the Elysian Fields. I've asked him to provide you with an enimerosi of what he has found."

I stepped forward. Using my talents as an actor and magician, I turned about and bowed deeply. Upon standing, an owl appeared on my right shoulder and a golden dove on my left. The Six reacted with laughter and applause. With a clap of my hands, the sacred birds disappeared.

"Hello again, my friends and greetings from Zeus. I have just returned from Olympus, where I provided the great father and other Olympians with the information I will impart to you now. Not long ago, I was visiting with my father in Elysium. He confided to me his concerns that the order of the Elysian Fields had been disturbed. To prove his point, he took me to the region said to be the location of the mystical Eridanus River. There, I saw what can only be described as a fortress. It is guarded by a collection of gods, mortals and monstrosities. Their leader is none other than Adecius, whom you have 'met' on more than one occasion."

Hades interrupted, "And which is he, Alagon, a god, a mortal or a monstrosity?"

"As far as I can tell, he may be a bit of all three."

As the briefing continued, I revealed for the Six the source of the recent disturbances: Cronus, the God of Time, King of Elysium. As my audience knew well, Cronus was one of the twelve original Titans born to Uranus (heaven) and Gaea (earth). These were the pre-Olympian gods that ruled the cosmos after Cronus killed his father, Uranus. These earlier gods were subsequently challenged by the Olympians in a ten-year war called the Titanomachy. The Olympians, led by Cronus's son, Zeus, won the war and imprisoned the Titans in Tartarus, the Dungeon of Torment, in the Underworld. However, things were more complicated when it came to the fate of Cronus. After all, he is the father of all those who participated in his overthrow as ruler of the Cosmos. Not least, he is also the father of Zeus' wife Hera. Yet, even as a son of Zeus, I have never dared to ask why he chose to release Cronus from Tartarus and grant him the Kingdom of Elysium.

The Elysian Fields (Elysium) is where the most favored mortals and "heroes" were conveyed by the gods. It is a paradise of immortality where those chosen by the gods, 'the righteous and heroic', could lead a blessed and happy life to pursue whatever employment they had enjoyed in life.

If Cronus was responsible for the disturbances in the Underworld, it would be a monumental betrayal of Zeus and his own progeny. I was certain that betrayal was well underway. The "fortress" I had seen in Elysium had been built by forced labor with materials not before seen in the Underworld. It was unclear where the labor and materials had come from. My father told me that no one in the Elysian Fields could account for the strange activity occurring in their paradise. Ares interrupted, "What?" he asked, "about the portal? You told us before Adecius had located a 'lost portal,' something to do with a connection to the mortal world?"

I attempted to conceal my sense of disappointment. "Sadly, right now, I don't know much more than I told you when we last met. The portal is said to connect to Van Lang, an ancient region inhabited by mortals. Let me say I've not been to or seen the portal. All the information I have comes from my father and those around him. They have observed warriors with green and black skins carrying 'lightning sticks' engaging in battle with the forces of Adecius. It is presumed that these clashes are taking place at the entrance to the portal, but that has not been confirmed. The suspicion is that Adecius' warriors and some enemy forces are using the portal to travel between Elysium and Van Lang. Their purposes are unknown."

Hades stood up from his throne, signaling the end of my briefing. "My fellow Olympians," he addressed the Six, "the fate of the Underworld and perhaps Olympus rests with you. Zeus has chosen well, and it is with his blessing that Persephone and I bid you farewell as you continue your quest. Alagon will show you to the sleeping chambers and he will see you on your way in the morning."

I led them along a lush garden path to what looked like a minor temple. Alagon explained that it is the residence of Styx when she visits her daughter Persephone. It contains a number of sleeping chambers and a large bathing pool surrounded by chairs and couches, flowers, and small fires emitting vapors of oils and incense. Golden pitchers of wine sat on several tables. I filled goblets with wine and passed them to the Six with an invitation to be seated. I rolled out a large parchment and laid it on a table in front of the guests. It contained a map of the Elysian Fields and surrounding features of the Underworld.

"This map shows the route you should take when you leave here in the morning. Unfortunately, I need to return to

Olympus, otherwise, I would go with you." Referring to the map, I pointed out the locations of the fortress, the suspected location of the portal, and the area where the green and black warriors were seen. Also shown was the Lethe River. Because of its proximity to where the activities of Adecius' forces were taking place, I thought there might be a connection. Finally, I identified the area where the Six could rendezvous with Heleron, a noble warrior, in order to get an update on the situation in Elysium. "Now, you must rest and prepare for your journey. I wish you luck and hope to see you sometime in the future." I toasted them with a goblet of wine and departed.

Hermes was the first to speak. "Astounding," he said. "Cronus building a fortress in Elysium, Adecius doing battle with green and black warriors, a portal to a place called Van Lang. Ares, what do you make of all this?"

"I sense this situation is more far-reaching than we suspected. If I'm right, the threat is not confined to the Underworld. All of Olympus is at risk. Athena?"

"I agree. I recall the words of Pythia that 'Time is your enemy'. We thought she meant we should pursue our quest with all due speed. I now believe she meant that

Cronus–Cronus is our enemy. Cronus has betrayed Zeus and the Olympians, but why?"

Damon offered his view. "Alagon confirmed the threat posed by Cronus and Adecius, but I don't think we will be able to answer Athena's question of why until we find the portal and confront Adecius."

Ares stood and raised his goblet of wine. "I think we can all agree with Damon. For now, let us rest and prepare ourselves for battle. Check your weapons and food supplies. I understand that a bell will ring when it's time for our departure. At that point, let's meet back here. As usual, Athena will brief us on the order of march."

She reacted to her new assignment, "Oh, then I had better get to work."

With that, Athena departed for her sleeping chamber. The rest of the troupe disbanded and headed to their sleeping quarters as well. A small oil lamp was burning in Athena's room as she entered and began to inventory her weapons and equipment. When she was finished, she sat down and began to fashion a plan for reaching the Elysian Fields and locating the lost portal. The smell of sweet perfume wafting into the chamber drew her attention to the doorway.

There stood Persephone. "Athena," she whispered, "I came to give you my personal blessings as you prepare to leave us and to tell you my mother Demeter will be watching over you from Olympus." Then she took Athena's hand and kissed it tenderly. "My dear Athena, please be careful. Zeus and Hera anticipate your return to Olympus." Persephone departed and Athena returned to her thoughts about the quest and the importance of, as she saw it, preserving the order of the Cosmos. Before long, she became drowsy and fell asleep.

Chapter 9
Elysium, Heleron and the Legion of Aeneas

The Six arrived at the Elysian Fields without incident. Immediately upon arrival, they were stunned to find themselves surrounded by the heroes and happy souls of Elysium, who escorted them to the Garden of Aeneas. Heleron, among others, was there to greet them. He wore a robe of purple and gold, signifying his status as a hero of Olympus and dipped a golden sword in salute to these honored deities. "Welcome to the domain of Cronus," he beckoned. "I am here to serve you in any way you might require. Please join me at my grotto for some food and wine."

Ares spoke for the group, "We come with greetings from Persephone."

"Ah, yes, our most beautiful queen."

"She told Athena where we could find you and said you could lead us to the lost portal."

"Indeed, I can, but first, there is a great deal of information you need to know before we depart. Sit. Eat. Drink. And I shall tell you all that I know. But first, Athena, I would be honored if you would sit by me."

"It will be my honor, Heleron."

Heleron began his enimerosi by describing the situation with Cronus and Adecius. Rumors about a lost portal began circulating within the Elysian Fields about the same time that Cronus commanded that a temple be built to honor the god Adecius. No one in Elysium had ever heard of this 'god', so Heleron and his friends began to investigate. They first visited the temple and discovered it was actually a fortress surrounded by guards of unknown origin, as well as creatures never before seen in Elysium. Both Cronus and Adecius were regularly seen entering the fortress, but Heleron and his companions could not get close enough to determine what was going on inside.

While keeping a watchful eye on the fortress and its occupants, Heleron was able to follow several of the guards marching toward the Lethe River. Before they reached the river, a large tower appeared through the mist. At that moment, Heleron's gaze fell upon the entrance to the portal.

A sight unfolded before him–peculiar warriors wielding weapons that spat fire, an unexpected encounter in the vicinity of the mystical gateway.

When Heleron finished his briefing, the Six had a myriad of questions. Hermes spoke first, "What about the Lethe?" he demanded. "Was there any activity at the river?"

"None that I could see," the ancient one responded. "The guards followed a path directly to the tower."

"But these 'guards'," Athena asked breathlessly. "What did they look like? How did they act?"

"They are extremely tall, maybe half again taller than all of us. They have black armor covering all parts of their bodies and long spears with golden tips that appear to glow. They carry shields of the same gold. As they marched in line, there was loud grunting and stamping of feet. Clearly enough, these are ferocious beast-like warriors, not to be messed with."

A veil of shock seemed to pass over Athena's face. An unusual effect for the Goddess of War. The muscles in her jaw tightened and both fists were clenched as her intensity rose. "Heleron, you have described what we know are the Spartoi. We just battled with them at Lerna!"

"This is strange," Pollux admitted, joining in. "For a long time, it had been certain that the Spartoi had fought among themselves, and none had survived. Now, they appeared at Lerna, where we killed them all, and more are here in Elysium. Ares, Athena, what do you make of this?"

"Here's another mystery that Pythia prophesized," Ares answered, "but I'm not sure we know the true meaning of all her words at this point. Yet, as Athena has said, it is now certain the Oracle's admonition that time is our enemy refers to Cronus. We just need to find out why. Let's hope our journey to the portal will lead to the answers we need. Heleron, anything we should know before you lead us in the direction of the portal?"

"Yes. The actions of Cronus and the appearance of Adecius are worrisome to the heroes and warriors of Elysium. It is not yet clear how we might help you in your quest, but like you, we must all heed the words of Zeus that the Underworld and perhaps Olympus itself are threatened. Therefore, we have formed the Legion of Aeneas, a fighting force that will be at your disposal should the need arise. In the meantime, I suggest we begin our journey immediately to determine just what you may be faced with."

Thereafter, their march was unimpeded. As they emerged from a fragrant grove of trees and flowers, a bright light could be seen in the distance. Heleron halted their march. "There it is. That light is from the entrance to the portal. I suspect that it is true that the source of the light is from the mortal world above–the place you have said Pythia called Van Lang." Pointing in the direction of the light, he said, "In that direction, you will find a large tower, which I observed at one point."

Hermes stepped forward. "Yes, Heleron, Pythia knew that you would guide us here, and I'm sure she knows of the dangers we face. Now, we must forge on. Ares, I would like to take Damon with me to approach the portal and gather the information we need for our passage through the portal."

"Good idea. While you are gone, the rest of us will explore the surrounding areas, including the Lethe River. Signal us with one golden arrow if you need help. Otherwise, return here and we will set our plans. Heleron, we thank you once again for your help. Please return to Elysium and tell your forces that we will most likely need their help.”

“Thank you, good friends, for pursuing the quest that our father Zeus has entrusted to you. In the name of Hades and Persephone, I take my leave.”

Chapter 10
The Reconnaissance and Return to Hades' Palace

At the departure of Heleron, Hermes and Damon sped away toward the light from the portal. Athena and Castor moved off in the direction of the tower, while Ares and Pollux proceeded in the direction of the Lethe. If their reconnaissance efforts went well, they would all rendezvous back at the departure point, prepared to strike out for the portal.

Hermes and Damon were able to conceal themselves in trees and tall grass as they approached the portal entrance. Suddenly, several Spartoi appeared and greeted someone exiting the portal. It was Adecius, and to the astonishment of Hermes and Damon, he was accompanied by none other than Cronus. There was great activity surrounding their arrival. Soon, they were followed by green and black warriors and Spartoi guards exiting the portal. They did not carry shields or swords but rather what must be the "firesticks" that the Six had been warned about. If what they'd heard was true, their own weapons and armor would be no match against these new warriors and their strange tools. Several Spartoi, with mysterious green boxes strapped to their backs, traversed the scene. From these enigmatic containers emanated voices and loud screeching, adding an eerie dimension to the unfolding spectacle.

In strange harmony with all this varied discord around them, Cronus and Adecius were talking in an agitated manner. Periodically, Adecius would bow deeply in supplication to his master god, and after a while, Cronus broke off the conversation and began striding in the direction of Elysium on a path that led to the trees and grass where Hermes and Damon had secreted themselves. Adecius followed behind Cronus.

Suddenly, a deep voice boomed across the fields. It was the voice of Cronus. "Adecius, come close and hear the words of your god and master." From there, the two spoke in low tones, though loud enough for Hermes and Damon to hear, "Adecius, you are my right arm. Together, we are building an army such as Olympus has never seen. And, with you as my commander of the legions, I will control the lost portal and establish New Elysium in the world of the mortals. But this time, you have failed me."

"How so, my god?"

"Just now, we have visited what you have described as fortifications. I saw them as piles of mud with strange entanglements on top. One small legion, as I have seen at Thessaly and Salamina, could overpower the occupants within and put them to the sword and spear."

"My master , you must know that we have discovered new weapons that no one in the Underworld or Olympus can defeat. On your next visit through the portal, I shall demonstrate the power of these weapons, such as the firesticks we now have, which are called 'guns.'"

"I shall be pleased to see it and trust your word that all is as it should be. Now, I must return to my palace while you hasten to my temple and continue the planning and preparation for the battles to come."

"You are my god and my master . I shall not fail you."

With that, Adecius and the Spartoi guards proceeded quickly toward Elysium as Cronus entered a nearby grotto. Hermes and Damon followed him at a distance, watching as he knelt near a large cypress tree at the center of the grotto.

"Hear me, Zeus," he began calling out to the heavens. "I have sworn to avenge your cruelty toward me. Now, I will prove to you that I should reign over Olympus, the Underworld, and all the mortal universe… I will build this new Elysium and mount an army that will storm the Underworld, banish Hades and Persephone to Tartarus, and take my place as ruler of the Underworld. From there, I will command the forces of New Elysium and use the power of time to cast you out of Olympus. This I swear."

He stood and began to rub needles of the tree between his fingers, whereupon the pleasing aromas of citrus and spice began to fill the grotto. Satisfied with all that he had spoken, Cronus departed the grotto in the direction of his Elysian palace.

Before long, the Six reconnected at the starting point of their explorations. Indeed, Hermes and Damon would have the most consequential story to tell, but first, they would hear from the others, starting with Athena and Castor. There was excited banter and gesturing among the group when Athena commanded their attention, "Let us begin. Castor, tell the others what we have learned."

"Athena and I followed a winding path to an area of tall grass close to the tower. From there we could see that the tower is a tall wooden structure with a covered platform on top. There are spirals of thorny vines all around. Ladders of wood lead to the top, much like we saw when we encountered the king of the pygmaioi."

"I hope we won't see that ugly face again." Ares injected to a chorus of laughter.

The laughter broke off as Castor continued, "Two Spartoi guards occupy the platform. One of them has a green box on his back. There is a long black tube on a tripod. Next to it is a box with a large mirror. We were not close enough to hear what the guards were saying. They appeared to be talking to the voices coming from the green box. With that, we slipped back through the grass and returned here. "Did I miss anything, Athena?"

"Just that their attention was always on the entrance to the portal where they could see everyone coming or going. Ares, what did you and Pollux find?"

"We made our way to the banks of the Lethe, where we could observe the souls on the other side. Many were lined up at a point where they could drink the water. From there, they would enter a large meadow surrounded by tall trees and shrubs. All were embracing, talking, and singing. It was a happy scene for everyone. We saw additional movement further along the banks, so Pollux traveled in that direction to investigate."

"Yes. Not far up the river, I could see numbers of green and black soldiers crossing the river in the direction of the portal. There were others being carried from the portal area to the river. They appeared to be dead. Here and there, I could see groups of the green and blacks, as well as Spartoi, forming into small legions and marching toward the portal."

"The soldiers wore green armor and carried strange weapons." Ares completed his report. "Some with firesticks, others with long tubes, both green and black, and golden belts crisscrossed over their chests. All carried large green packs on their backs and some with those green boxes that made noises we could not understand. It must be the same as Athena and Castor encountered. As for the soldiers, they were chanting together with unintelligible words."

Every revelation echoed through the group, leaving them astounded. Conversations swelled, growing louder and more fervent as speculation blossomed, attempting to decipher the profound meaning behind the extraordinary sights they had witnessed.

"This is the work of Cronus, a warping of time, or trickery, not to be believed," shouted Pollux.

"This all appeared real to me," responded Ares, "Although I was not able to touch anything to see if the images were trickery as you suggest, Pollux."

Athena interrupted their speculations. "Wait," she said in a calming voice. "I have my own suspicions about what we are seeing. First, Let's hear from Hermes."

Hermes got their attention. "Listen now to what Damon and I have seen and heard." He recounted their observations at the portal and the appearance of Adecius and Cronus as they exited from the mortal world above. The other members of the group shook their heads in disbelief. It was true then that Cronus and Adecius were at the heart of the disturbance in the Underworld. This explained the building of the fortress in Elysium, the attempts by Adecius to prevent the Six from pursuing their quest, and the presence of the Spartoi guards.

Yet there were greater revelations when Damon recounted the words that Cronus had spoken to Adecius and those that he'd uttered back in the grotto.

"We can now see Cronus' grand plan. Somehow, he is assembling a great army with weapons and armor that must be from the mortal world. These will be so powerful that neither the forces of the Underworld nor Olympus can resist. Heleron is right to be forming the Legion of Aeneas, but it will take much more than that to counter the pernicious plans of Cronus."

A brief silence fell over the Six. They were laying down their weapons and removing their armor in preparation for a meal. Eventually, Ares let out one of his near-deafening war cries and beat his chest wildly, "Ahhhaggoow… Now we know the true nature of our quest. Our father Zeus has entrusted us with saving the future of the Underworld and Olympus."

In unison, the Six began to chant, "All hail Zeus. All hail Hades. All hail Olympus."

The Six returned to Hades' palace and had a short meeting with Hades and Persephone to tell them what they had seen and heard on their journey to and from the portal. However, the real purpose of returning to Elysium was to meet with Heleron and several leaders of the Legion of Aeneas to begin planning the next phase of their quest. They met in the small temple on the hillside where Hades and Persephone had hosted their welcoming meal. Once again, there would be plenty of food and wine to go around, but the warrior-gods were anxious to get underway with their planning efforts.

Heleron introduced the two members of his command as Arcelium, a former legion commander from the Trojan Wars, and Tanaurus, protector of Athens. They were briefed on what the Six had discovered at and near the portal. They, too, were amazed that Cronus had appeared with Adecius, but they resolved to defend the Underworld and Olympus at all costs. The Six were effusive in their praise of the men before them and all who would join with the Legion of Aeneas.

Then Athena stepped forward. She was wearing her golden helmet and carrying the Aegis to signal both her wisdom and her strength. The golden lance with the blood of Medusa was likewise at her side, and her eyes seemed to burn with fierceness and beauty as she addressed her assembled gods and warriors. "As Ares has said," she began, "now is the true beginning of our quest. We must enter the portal and face whatever lies on the other side. Based on what we learned through our reconnaissance, Ares and I have agreed on the strategy for getting through the portal. We will move in silence and avoid contact with the guards and warriors of Adecius. Should we encounter any of them, they must be destroyed, and their bodies hidden to avoid detection by others."

"It is most important," Ares broke in, "that Adecius and Cronus do not know we entered the mortal world, what Pythia called Van Lang. When we get there, we must find ways to maintain our secrecy."

Athena continued her description of the strategy for getting to the other side of the portal. Each of the Six would focus on their special powers and weapons. Damon would take the lead, wearing the Helmet of Hades. This would provide him with the power of invisibility in the event he detected enemy soldiers at his front. Athena and Hermes would follow at a distance. Athena would carry the Aegis to frighten and freeze the enemy, should they appear. Hermes could support their efforts by deploying his Caduceus to cause attackers to fall asleep.

Ares, they agreed, would be third in line, flanked by Pollux and Castor. Each would be heavily armed with swords and spears. Pollux would also carry a bow and a quiver of magical arrows that, when fired, could blind and freeze the enemy. Ares would use his sword to destroy any enemy that could survive the gauntlet created by the advancing warrior-gods. Bodies of those killed would be dragged away to any spaces available nearby. All of this was the contingency plan. Ares and Athena repeated the primary objective–get through the portal without engagement and without being detected.

Heleron's two commanders volunteered to go ahead of the Six and create a diversion near the entrance to the portal by posing as reincarnated souls from across the Lethe. If anything went wrong, or if conditions at the portal had changed, Arcelium and Tanaurus would rendezvous with the Six at the gathering place between the tower and the Lethe.

Satisfied that Athena had laid out a solid strategy and encouraged by the support of Heleron's commanders, Ares offered these final words, "In the morning, we shall fulfill our destiny and honor Zeus and all the gods and goddesses of Olympus. Before we depart, let us have a feast, drink our wine and rest in peaceful slumber."

Chapter 11

Cronus, Adecius and the Dog Soldiers

Early the next morning, the Six reached the gathering place. Arcelium was there to meet them. "Friends, there is strange news to report," he explained the situation at the portal. "Tanaurus and I walked along the banks of the Lethe until we reached the point where Pollux described the presence of the green and blacks and Spartoi. Looking across the river, we saw the same happy scenes of souls drinking the waters and then rejoicing and singing. But there was no other activity–no green and blacks, no Spartoi, no bodies being carried from the direction of the portal, just the sounds of the celebrants across the river."

"That can't be true," Pollux interrupted. "I know what I saw and Ares could see the activity from his position."

Before anyone else could answer, though, Ares joined in, "That's right, I saw the warriors moving back and forth from the river. That's why I sent Pollux forward to observe them. Why would…"

"There is more important news," Arcelium interrupted. "Since there was no one about, Tanaurus and I moved to a point where we could observe the entrance to the portal. We could not see any activity at or near the portal, and the tower so closely observed by Athena and Castor is no longer there."

There was a buzz then among the group as they turned to look for the tower that before could be seen off in the distance. Nothing there.

"What do you make of this, Arcelium?" Hermes asked. "Has someone cast a spell over us? We are very clear as to what we observed yesterday."

"I do not know, but I can say that these are strange phenomena never before seen in the Underworld. Here comes Tanaurus. He ventured to the portal entrance, let's hear what he has to report."

Tanaurus reached the gathering point, somewhat out of breath. He faced the group and began to speak, "Sister and brothers, as Arcelium has undoubtedly told you, we saw no trace of the green and blacks or Spartoi, nor was there any observed activity at the entrance to the portal. So, I proceeded cautiously in that direction, though there was nothing within sight or hearing that would reveal that the area had ever been used by Adecius or his soldiers."

Again, a buzz of comments and consternation spread throughout the group. This was indeed compelling and vexatious news, though before they could make much of it, Tanaurus continued, "I was able to enter the portal." Then said, "unimpeded. Already, I could see that I could do so and walk for some distance. It was empty. All was still and quiet. I then made my way here to report what I have seen."

"But what of the tower?" Athena inquired. "Were there any remnants of the wood and sharp vines we saw or the strange weapons?"

"None. Nor were there any signs that the grass and soil of that area had ever been disturbed."

There was silence as Ares began to pace, though he didn't get far before swinging around to face the group. "Whether this is magic or trickery," he swore, "we must forge onward, face what may. We must also get to the bottom of these strange happenings."

It didn't take much for the Six to conclude that Cronus was at the center of the "strange happenings". This was bolstered by Pythia's prophecy that time would be their enemy. Who but the god of time could cause a disturbance to the entire Underworld and perhaps to the mortal world on the far end of the portal? To learn more about the situation, Tanaurus and Arcelium were instructed to return to Elysium and report the developments they had witnessed to Heleron. It had become imperative that the operations of both Cronus and Adecius should be infiltrated and that the findings of those efforts be reported to the Six as soon as possible. The Six would proceed to enter the portal, and if all went well, Hermes would be dispatched to return to Elysium to confer with Heleron and his commanders. If Hermes did not appear in two days' time, Heleron would assemble his legions and march to the portal. As the two commanders departed, the Six formed into the marching order prescribed by Athena and set off for the portal.

They had secured their armor and weapons to avoid any rattling or clanking as they marched. To avoid detection, they marched in silence and communicated with established hand signals. Before long, they had reached the entrance to the portal, where all appeared just as it had been described by Tanaurus. There were no guards or warriors. Indeed, the area where the tower had stood was undisturbed. The surroundings were calm and peaceful, though nonetheless, the group halted in utmost caution as Damon entered the portal.

A few moments later, he returned. "The portal is dark," he reported. "However, there is a dim light off in the distance, which I assume is coming from the portal exit. All is clear as far as I can see. As I went further toward the light, the air was increasingly hot and misty, similar to what we experienced at Corinth and Delphi. The silence is palpable and somewhat eerie."

Ares nodded, giving an immediate order. "Let us proceed with haste," he determined, "being always on the alert."

So, without further comment, the Six fell into formation and stepped off into the unknown. As Damon had reported, the further they marched, the heat and mist increased, at some point uncomfortably so. Naturally, the light from the presumed portal exit grew brighter as they continued at a steady pace. It would not be long before they would reach the exit and make their way into the mortal world above.

Without warning, the entire portal was bathed in light, temporarily blinding the Six. When they recovered, they could see that light was coming from glowing balls hanging along both sides of the portal. Members of the group spun around in all directions, trying to comprehend what they were seeing. Along both sides of the portal, there were long trenches and box-like holes in the ground, scattered in every direction.

Athena observed. "These look like preparations for a great battle. Not for us, since we are only Six. Then for whom?"

There was no time to ponder the question, though, as strange noises could be heard coming from the direction of the exit. As it grew louder, groups of advancing soldiers could be seen faintly through the mist. Without hesitation, Ares commanded, "Disperse. Damon, Athena and Hermes to the right. Pollux and Castor with me on the left. Take cover and maintain silence. Avoid contact unless directly threatened. Watch for my signals when possible."

Each moved to their positions as directed, some in the trenches, others in the square holes. All had their eyes on the shadowy figures approaching their location. The waiting seemed intolerable, but in due course, the identity of those approaching was known. It was the green and blacks, and they were marching four rows across and perhaps twenty ranks deep. Strange black weapons, perhaps "firesticks," were slung over their shoulders.

"One, two, three, four, left, right, left. Your left, your left, your left right left."

One of the leaders called out, "Who are we?"

The soldiers responded in unison, "Dog Soldiers, Sir!"

"Who are we?"

"Dog Soldiers, Sir!"

"I can't hear you!"

A near-deafening roar came from within the ranks, "*Mighty* Dog Soldiers, Sir!"

The Six sequestered themselves deep within their earthen positions as the marching soldiers began passing by without noticing their presence. They marched on and took up another chant. Another leader called out, "Who is our leader?"

They responded, "Adecius. Adecius."

"And who is our god?"

"Cronus. Cronus," they responded collectively.

After each reply, the soldiers stamped their feet loudly as they marched on. Eventually, the sound of their chants grew faint as they disappeared into the mist. When they were out of sight, Ares signaled for the group to gather at his location. He addressed them in a low tone, "Do any of you have an idea of what we just witnessed?"

They shook their heads no, but Pollux spoke quietly, "I was able to get a close look at some of those soldiers when they passed by. They are not Spartoi... I also saw their shoulder ornaments. They are a green circle and in the center is an image of Cerberus. That must be why they chanted Dog Soldiers and mighty Dog Soldiers."

Ares raised his hand to ask for silence. "I'm sure we all noticed things that could be valuable to our assessment of what we are confronting," he conjectured. "Let's take time to hear about your observations, but we need to move forward while the path ahead appears to be clear."

After a brief huddle, they learned that the Dog Soldiers all wore the same green and black clothing and black boots. The breastplates were thick, also green, and more like a vest in style. Various objects were attached to their vests and around their waists– some the size of small pomegranates, knives in leather sheaths, and pouches containing small green jugs. They wore round helmets covered with green and brown cloth, looking like the leaves of the forest. Like the guards and soldiers at the tower, many carried "fire sticks," none of which were on fire, while others had small tubes slung across their backs. They were uniformly clean-shaven, and each had a small piece of metal on a chain around his neck.

As mysterious and possibly threatening as this information was, the group had to speed ahead in hopes of reaching the exit without further incidents. They resumed their march using the prior formation. Only this time, Damon was to move further ahead of the group using the helmet of invisibility to avoid being seen by oncoming soldiers or guards. He could then warn the others to take cover as before.

Back in Elysium, Heleron and his two commanders were meeting with Hades and Persephone at their palace. They were explaining what had taken place at the portal and the request from Ares to infiltrate the operations of Cronus and Adecius. In that regard, there was good news. Members of the legion had taken it on their own to begin spying on the activities of Adecius at the fortress. Also, a highly placed servant in Cronus' palace was reporting on activities there. In anticipation of Hermes' return to Elysium, the legion commanders quickly gathered the information that these "infiltrators" had provided.

"As to the fortress, it is now being guarded by Spartoi and all approaches have been blocked," Heleron elaborated further, "those who happen upon any of the guards are taken prisoner. Two of those captured are members of the Legion. One of those was Pantarus, who managed to escape. Through him we know that there were no green and blacks within the fortress, but many of their weapons are being stored there for future use, we presume. Through stealth and at great risk, Pantarus returned to the fortress to gather more information. He crept to a room from which he could hear the voices of several guards or soldiers.

They were briefing 'Commander Adecius'. Our spy could not hear much of what they said. Yet it was clear they were discussing a battleplan…"

"Were there any further details?" Hades interrupted.

"Our young soldier was brave enough to approach the entrance to the room. From there, he was able to view a large map on the wall, which may reveal the masterplan…"

"Do go on, Heleron, but with urgency, please."

"As you say. The map shows the mortal world above the portal, with an area marked as FSB Cronus. Our commanders are trying to determine the meaning. On the far left of the map is Olympus with the words, 'Operation Chimera.'"

"Harkening back to that monster of old. What could it mean?" Persephone added.

"We believe it foretells an attack on Olympus. And, according to the map, the thrust of that attack will come from here–from Elysium." Heleron paused and motioned for someone to enter. It was a beautiful young female. "This is Cerenia, a trusted servant of Cronus. She is also the wife of

Galecion, a member of our legion. She can best tell what she has heard and observed."

She bowed as she approached Hades and Persephone. "It is a great honor to be in your presence."

Persephone seeks to calm her. "Dear child, it is you who honor us by the risk you are taking to come before us. Please tell us what you know."

"I am a servant in the palace of Cronus. I am required to be always at his side. I must see to his every need–bring food and wine, play the lyre and recite poetry, calming him with fragrances and oils, and soothing him to sleep. Because of my duties, I generally see and hear all that happens in the palace, all of which seems ominous. Cronus discovered what he calls the 'lost portal', which leads to the mortal world called Van Lang. He commanded Adecius to build a fortress here in Elysium and another in the mortal world and to prepare for great battles in the Underworld and Olympus."

Heleron interrupts, "Tell them about what he calls time distortion."

"Yes, he and Adecius have many times discussed how to use Cronus' powers of time to hide what they are doing."

"In what way?" Hades inquires.

"I believe this explains why the Six warrior-gods saw the tower," Heleron responds, "and the Spartoi guides and the green and blacks at the portal entrance, and yet my commanders saw no evidence of their presence."

"I heard Adecius say that operations at the portal are going well," Cerenia continues. "More new soldiers are entering Van Lang each day, and their training for Operation Chimera is on schedule. I don't know what it means, but Cronus has the same map that was seen in the fortress, and he constantly refers to it as the master battle plan."

Hades raised his hands to signal that he had heard enough, "Thank you, Cerenia. As Persephone has said, you are a brave young woman. Heleron, you have presented a warning to the Underworld and Olympus that action must be taken swiftly if we are to avoid a catastrophe. You have become the apotheosis of leadership here in Elysium. You shall henceforth be a divine presence at my side to command our forces against this evil plot of Cronus."

"Thank you, my gracious god, for your faith in me. I shall not disappoint."

"Now, tell me your plans."

As requested by Ares, Heleron and his commanders had prepared the Legion of Aeneas, now 1,000 strong, to march to the portal. There was still time for Hermes to return from the portal with news of the warrior-gods' progress. As agreed, if Hermes failed to return in a reasonable time, the legion would march straight away with some 200 chariots and a full complement of customary weapons. One hundred legion soldiers would remain behind to monitor activities at the fortress and to secure Hades' palace.

Before departing the palace to return to the legion, he heard this from Persephone. "I have been granted freedom to return to Olympus to see my mother Demeter and convey to her and Zeus the news you have just propounded. While I am gone, Hera will be watching over the Six. You are to pass this word to Athena as soon as you next meet."

The Six resumed their march toward the portal exit. As suddenly as they had appeared, the lights went out. By that time, the light from the exit was sufficient to guide their progress and to warn them of any activity ahead. Damon was still wearing the helmet of invisibility when he returned to speak with the others. After removing the helmet, he signaled to the group to gather at his location.

"I have been to the end of the portal," he told them. "Seeing no danger, I took a few steps into the mortal world, and I must say it is very much like Elysium–rivers flowing in many directions, tall grass and meadows … very serene."

"And you saw no danger, no green and blacks?" Castor inquired.

"None," he answered. "It seems safe for us to proceed in a cautious manner. I will take the lead again and remain invisible while approaching the nearest river. If I discern that the path forward is clear, I shall remove the helmet and signal you to come forward."

Ares and Athena concurred with Damon's plan, so Damon donned the helmet and proceeded to the portal exit. Thereafter, the others followed but halted their march at the exit to wait for the signal that it was safe to join Damon at the river. They could see the river in the distance, and it was, as Damon had described, beautiful and serene. Shortly, Damon removed the helmet and became visible to the group. He gave the signal to move forward. They joined Damon and began to survey all that was before them. The Six had now entered Van Lang.

PART II

THE KINGDOM OF ONG TROI, GOD OF HEAVEN

Chapter 12

Van Lang: The Ancient Realm of Gods and Goddesses

The parallels between Greece and Van Lang are many, but they particularly merge around 600 BC. In Greece, the city-states of Athens, Sparta, Corinth, and Thebes were flourishing as maritime and mercantile powers. Van Lang was divided into various regions controlled by successive dynasties and kings. However, unlike the Greek experience, ninety percent of the population of Van Lang lived in agricultural villages, which produced a prolific growth of rice and other plants–making them part of the Maritime Jade Road. Greece expanded its reach by establishing several overseas colonies, which fueled a high level of economic development in commerce and manufacturing. Both civilizations produced skilled sailors, fishermen, and superior warriors. Socially, there was a shared belief in religious deities, enjoyment of music and poetry, and a desire to live in harmony with nature.

A lesser-known aspect of Van Lang's culture was a fully formed mythology similar in character to that of Greece and Olympus. The counterpart to Zeus is Ong Troi, the God of Heaven. Son Tink is the Mountain God; Thig Tink is the Water God. There are four elements or symbols of the mythological world: the turtle, dragon, unicorn, and phoenix. The principal immortals of a structured hierarchy are Than Giong, the Giant Boy, the Mountain God Son Thanh, Chu Dong Tu or Marsh Boy, and the Princess God, Lieu Hanh.

The many gods and goddesses of Van Lang lived in their own realms, much like Olympus. They communicated with mortals and acted as benevolent spirits who were venerated throughout the Kingdom of Ong Troi. Like the Greek experience, mortals, such as courageous men and women, heroes of battle, and those performing great deeds in honor of the gods, could become spirits. They were revered as protectors against evil spirits and other manifestations–fairies, dragons, poisonous snakes they called crocodiles, and creatures of the surrounding seas. There was magic, trickery, powerful weapons like the 'magic crossbow,' genies from heaven, kitchen gods, and tattooed people. There was even a "Land of Bliss," not unlike the Elysian Fields.

In this context, it appeared that one mythological world was about to be joined to another through the discovery of the lost portal. Would there be another clash of the Titans or a joining? What role was Cronus playing in determining the outcome? And why was Adecius building an army that seemed to have its roots in the Underworld and its branches in Van Lang? Determining the answers to these questions, among others, was at the heart of the quest that Zeus had set in motion. Having traversed the tunnel and entered Van Lang, the Six were now faced with finding those answers.

𝕺   𝕺   𝕺   𝕺   𝕺

As the Six surveyed the river to their front and its lush surroundings, there was a sudden eruption from the earth behind them. There was a thunderous noise and shock waves hit their bodies. The ground shook as large clumps of earth and grass flew high into the air, along with steaming hot pieces of steel. The warrior-gods stood entranced by what they were seeing and feeling beneath their feet. Suddenly, there were several more "eruptions" with the same impacts as the first. Only this time, much of the earth and molten metal was projected toward the Six. They all flinched but stood their ground as the debris began to rain down. In the face of the perilous situation, each warrior-god swiftly reacted, brandishing shields, spears, and swords to skillfully deflect the oncoming onslaught.

Ares shouted above the din, "We must retreat." Pointing to the open area to their right, he guided them, "Move quickly, that way!"

They began to make their way through the tall, thick grass to a clearing, which, at least at that point, seemed safe. "Spread out and take a low profile," Athena shouted, "in case there are more eruptions. Ares, you and I should…" But as she turned in the direction from which they had come, Ares was not there, nor was he anywhere within their "safe" zone. Alarmed, she called out, "Ares, we're over here."

No response.

"Ares, can you hear me?"

Still no answer.

"Has anyone seen Ares?" she shouted to the others, their responses were uniformly negative. Castor was the closest to her, so she motioned to him. "Castor, come with me to find Ares. He may be hurt, so let us move quickly."

They retraced the steps they had taken from the site of the eruptions. As they made their way through the tall grass, there was a rustling sound ahead. Undoubtedly, Ares was making his way toward them.

"Ares," Castor called out, "we're over here."

There was silence until a strange figure parted the grass in front of them and began shouting in a gruff voice. "What the hell's goin' on over here? Don't you people recognize incoming when you see it? I swear to Christ they're not teaching you people shit at Benning or Bragg, wherever the hell you came from–and you'd better stop yelling for this 'Ares' shitbird unless you want to invite Charlie over here…" He paused in mid-sentence as if he had just taken notice of those he was barking at.

"What the fuck is this? Pardon me, Ma'am, but I don't think the troops are up to a USO show right now. You best get on back to Dong Tam before the real shit begins to fly!"

Athena and Castor were astounded by what they were seeing and hearing. The person speaking to them was green and black. They could see immediately that these were not the colors of his skin but from his strange clothing. He carried a small weapon like the firesticks the Dog Soldiers had carried. There were various items strapped around his waist and he wore an armor breastplate of green and black material. Most curious of all was that he had a small white cylinder hanging from his mouth that produced puffs of white smoke.

Athena asserted herself by brandishing her sword and pointing it at the throat of the green and black. "Who are you? Answer me before I run you through and put your head on a pike." The green and black staggered backward.

"Listen, little girl, I'm impressed with your performance of Joan of Arc, but we're about to be overrun by a main force regiment if we don't beat it outta' here … Perez! Perez, get your ass over here."

Castor lowered his spear and edged closer to the strange intruder. Before he could speak, the tall grass parted and another green and black appeared. His clothes and accouterments were the same as the first intruder, except that this "Perez" carried a green box on his back like those seen and heard at the portal. Once through the grass, he stopped short and surveyed the bizarre scene. His lips were moving, but there was no sound coming out. He cleared his throat. "A-a-ahem, S-s-sarge, this doesn't look so good."

"Perez, you are the master of understatement–you'd better radio the captain and tell him to get the entire team over here, now!"

Perez grasped the handset to his radio and contacted the team leader, Captain Galanis. "Orion 6. This is Orion one-six Romeo, over."

"This is Orion 6, over."

"Orion 6, one-six requests that you proceed to our location. This is an alpha-level urgent message."

"Roger, tell one-six we're on the way, ETA seven or eight minutes. Orion 6, out."

Orion one-six is Master Sergeant (MSG) Bobby Travis, the senior non-commissioned officer of the 43^{d} Special Forces A-Team. Specialist Perez is his radio telephone operator (RTO). The A-Team is led by Captain Antonio "Tony" Galanis (Orion 6). Since there appears to be a standoff between Athena and Travis, the hope is that Captain Galanis and the other A-Team members will be able to resolve the situation. While they were waiting, Athena and Castor relaxed their threatening postures and tried to engage with the potential enemy. Athena broke the silence, asking Travis, "Have you been sent here by Cronus?"

"No, I've been sent here by LBJ."

"Is that one of your gods?"

"No, our 'god' is named Westmoreland."

Both Travis and Perez laughed and let go with an obviously rehearsed condescension, "Shiiiit."

Castor followed with a serious query. "Have you come through the portal?"

Travis didn't understand the question but was determined to stall for time until the rest of the team arrived. "I don't know about any portal," he answered, "but whatever that is, we flew in here a week ago from Dong Tam Base."

Athena was taken aback. "You *flew* here? Where are your wings?"

Once again, both Travis and Perez let go with a laugh. Perez pointed to a badge on his uniform. "These are our wings–Airborne, Ma'am!"

Travis raised a hand. "Okay, Perez, I don't think they know anything about jump school."

"I am Athena, daughter of Zeus," she interrupted. "You will stand aside or face the wrath of the Olympians." She motioned to Castor. "Come, we must continue our search for Ares." Then they started off in the direction of where Ares was last seen.

After taking a few steps into the tall grass, Athena came face to face with Captain Galanis. There was a brief pause, and they looked each other up and down. Galanis got a rather wry smile on his face as he surveyed the Goddess of War. The sunglasses he was wearing helped to blunt the effects of the sun glimmering from her golden breastplate. For Athena's part, she was staring at the name tag on his uniform as she mouthed, "Galanis, Galanis."

Galanis raised his glasses, "Yes, Ma'am."

Her attention was drawn to his eyes. They were a striking azure in color, with the intensity of a true warrior.

Finally, she broke the silence, "You are Greek! Have you been sent from Zeus?

The captain reacted, somewhat irritated, "Sergeant Travis!"

Travis made his way through the grass and responded, "Yes, Sir?"

"Bobby, what the hell is going on here?"

"My question exactly when I bumped into this traveling circus. I thought they were with the USO. But what the hell would they be doing out here? Then they pointed their weapons at me. Believe me, they're not props. The woman seems to be in charge. She held her sword to my throat and asked if I was sent by Cronus, whoever that is. Then she shouted that she is the daughter of Zeus, so I'd better watch out."

"Anything else?"

Sergeant Perez appeared through the grass. "She said she was the Goddess of War and asked if we had come through the porthole . She must think we're in the Navy."

Travis looked at his RTO. "Perez, she said portal, not porthole, sometimes, Peres! Captain, any idea what this all means?"

"I guess I should say it's all Greek to me, but this might be more serious than we think," he addressed Athena. "If you're Athena, why are you here in Vietnam–in the middle of a firefight?"

"We know nothing of this 'Vietnam.' This place we know to be Van Lang, and we have come here to save our Underworld and to protect Olympus from Cronus and Adecius. But now we must find Ares so we can continue our quest."

Travis interjects, "See, Captain Galanis, this is some kinda' joke, we need to…"

"We need to get the hell out of here," Galanis interrupted, "and take them with us. We can sort out the details once we're back at base camp." Almost simultaneously, there was weapons fire close by and Perez's radio came to life with a frantic message.

"Orion 6, this is 5. We're taking incoming fire." More shots could be heard in the background. Orion 5 is

Warrant Officer Tom Fredericks, the assistant detachment commander (ADC). "We better di di mau," he continued. "The bad guys have spotted us, and they're headed this way."

Galanis broke in. "Tommy," he began, "this is 6. Move the team to my location and we'll head out together."

"Roger ... ah, we have another situation here."

"Go ahead."

"We found a guy over here dressed up like Hercules or somebody–he's KIA. Should we leave him here?"

Castor lunges at Galanis and grabs the radio handset, screaming into the earpiece, "That is not Hercules, that is Ares, the God of War… our leader! What is this K–I–A?"

Galanis snatched the handset back. He pointed at Castor and motioned to his right. "Get over there and stay there." The radio crackled again.

"Six, this is 5. What should we do with this guy? Over."

"This is 6, hold on for now, out." Galanis turned and faced Athena, "Look, miss…"

"I am Athena!"

"Okay, look, *Athena*, my men have found your friend."

She pushes past Galanis and starts toward the direction of the gunfire. "Castor, we must go."

With a head nod from Galanis, Sergeant Travis moved to block their path and commanded, "Halt right there!" Gods or not, they knew they should comply. Once again, Galanis focused his attention on Athena.

"Listen, sounds like my men have found your friend, 'Ares,' and I'm sorry, but he's dead. KIA, killed in action."

"That cannot be true; it's just Cronus' trickery."

"There is one way to prove it." He grabs the handset. "Tommy, this is 6. Bring the team to my location and bring the KIA with you."

"Wilco, 6. Orion 5, out!"

More gunfire and small explosions, probably from enemy grenades, could be heard getting closer to the team's location. The order to move out had come at just the right time. Ten minutes had passed when the A-Team could be heard crashing through the tall grass. They broke through to find their team leadership group standing in the small clearing, along with two others dressed in the same manner. Some would say gladiators from a B movie. This was far from a movie. The last two team members to enter the clearing were carrying the bloodied body of Ares.

Both Athena and Castor bowed their heads in disbelief. Slowly, they approached the body of their fallen leader. Athena touched the face of her brother with a feeling of profound sorrow, but that moment was short-lived. The A-Team knew that enemy forces were stalking them. It was imperative they leave the danger zone where they had congregated before it became a killing zone. Galanis was consulting his compass and map. He got the attention of the group. "Listen up, we need to follow the river for about three kilometers and then head west past the old village, and from there, back to base camp. Let's move out–this way."

"No." Athena turned and rushed toward Galanis. "We must go that way to rejoin the others!"

"Others?" Galanis turned to Athena and took hold of her arm. "What others?"

"Our team. We are the Six, sent here by Zeus. We must continue our quest. Ares must be revived so we can continue."

"I've had enough of this nonsense. Now get in line and move out!"

"Captain, the choice is not yours to make." With that said, Athena spun around and raised the Aegis. With her arm outstretched, she raked the shield across the line of A-Team troops. All were immediately frozen in fear as they looked at the writhing head of Medusa. She turned back to an astonished Captain Galanis. "This is the Aegis, given to me by my father, Zeus. It helped to defeat our enemies, as Apollo defeated the Achaeans to save Hector. Do you still think that we are a traveling circus, or should I show the full power of the Aegis?"

"No, a further demonstration will not be necessary, but I need you to bring my men out of their trance before we follow you to your team's location. I hope we can sort all this out when we get there."

"Good. When I lower the Aegis, your men will be back to normal. Have them follow Castor and me quickly!"

The horrified soldiers awoke from their 'trance' and Galanis motioned to them. "Let's move out. We need to follow those two, ah, two people. I'll explain later." They moved out smartly as Athena and Castor ran ahead. They were all on a path to link up with the rest of the Six when mortar rounds began to rain down on the clearing they had left only moments before. Sergeant Travis was behind the captain as they picked up the pace. Travis shouted above the din of the explosions to their rear, "Jesus Christ, Captain, I think we're running into a trap, thanks to those actor weirdos."

Galanis shouted over his shoulder, "They're not actors, Bobby. Take my word for it."

Chapter 13
De Oppresso Liber

As time went on, I spent countless hours in conversations with Galanis and the Six, trying to understand the strange phenomena I was seeing and hearing. In my role as a messenger to Zeus, I attempted to assure the Olympians that things were going well on the far side of the portal. As a storyteller, I absorbed all that I could about the A-Team.

The primary fighting force of the Green Berets is the Operational Detachment Alpha (ODA), or A-Team. The 43^{d} ODA racing behind Athena and Castor has the standard A-Team composition of 12 members–Detachment Commander and Assistant Commander (ADC), along with Non-Commissioned Officers (NCOs) specialized in operations, weapons, communications, medical response, and engineering. In addition to their specialties, all team members are Airborne and Ranger qualified and speak at least two languages other than English. They are proficient in the use of more than sixty friendly and enemy weapon systems and combat vehicles. All of this supports their primary capability to conduct independent, sustained combat operations against hostile forces anywhere on the globe. In this case, that means South Vietnam.

The Base Camp that Captain Galanis referred to is a term the team uses loosely. It is much more a camp than a base (in military terms). It consists of camouflaged foxholes and firing positions surrounding an improvised bunker of bamboo and mud, which serves as a command post (CP). There is nothing permanent about it since the team moves regularly, destroying their existing camp on the way out.

The importance of the team returning to base camp at this point was two-fold. First, it would put distance between them and the oncoming enemy force, which could be anywhere between a platoon of 20-30 soldiers to a regiment of 300. Second, once at their base camp, Captain Galanis and his senior team members could contact Headquarters Command in Dong Tam with an intelligence update and targeting information. It's not something easily done on the run. Certainly not while dealing with the inexplicable presence of those claiming to be from the Underworld.

As Athena and Castor sped onward, it would have been easy enough for the team to drop Ares' body along the way, peel off into the tall grass and head for the river as Galanis had intended, but Galanis' instincts told him something bigger and perhaps more ominous than this encounter with the Six could be in the offing. His choice was to follow Athena and Castor to see the 'others' for himself. With the talent and firepower of his team and his leadership, he was sure they could handle any situation.

As Athena and Castor neared the clearing where the others were waiting, she announced their arrival, "Hermes, it's Athena and Castor; do not be alarmed!"

"Come ahead," Hermes responded. "By the grace of Zeus, we are all reunited."

Quickly, she and Castor broke into the clearing and were immediately surrounded by Hermes, Pollux, and Damon, with enthusiastic greetings all around.

Pollux was the first to notice the absence of Ares. "Athena, where is Ares? Is he behind you?"

"Yes, Pollux, he is behind us. Oh, great father Zeus, let it not be true." She began to wail. "He is dead. My brother is dead. All of Olympus must grieve for him."

The others stumbled back as if struck by an invisible force. Hermes took hold of Athena. "Tell us, Athena, tell what has happened." She stood silently with fists clenched. Hermes turned to Castor.

"Where is he? You left him behind?"

Before Castor could respond, Galanis and Tom Fredricks, the ADC, appeared at the edge of the clearing. Damon raised his spear as Hermes drew his sword. They edged toward the green and blacks. Athena stretched out her arm to halt their progress. "No. I have brought them here. They found Ares and brought him to us. I can explain, but we must hurry. There are more explosions and noises of firesticks nearby."

She led the others forward and introduced Captain Galanis, "This is Orion 6, Captain Galanis, he is Greek."

"This is Tom Fredricks," Galanis interjected, "my assistant commander. He was in charge of the soldiers that found your friend, Ares."

"Where is he now?"

"A short way back on the path. We had to make sure it was safe to bring the entire team here. I assume you understand." He turned to Fredricks. "Get on the horn and tell Bobby to get everybody up here, now!"

A few minutes passed, and the team members began to cautiously filter into the clearing, weapons at the ready. They mingled with the warrior-gods and looked them up and down in disbelief. Sergeant Travis wasted no time in bringing them back to reality. "Alright, goddam it, you know what to do, or have you suddenly forgotten how to set up a security perimeter? Rob," he said, referring to Sergeant First Class Robert Salinas, the assistant ops sergeant, "let's get spread out and make sure you have adequate fields of fire. Maintain radio silence unless you see some bad guys. Perez, stay here with your radio. I'm sure we'll need it before long."

"Roger."

As the team members deployed to their designated positions, the Senior Medical Sergeant, Master Sergeant George Santini arrived, along with Engineering Sergeant Mason "Brick" Osbourne. They were carrying the body of Ares. The warrior-gods gathered around. They laid down their weapons and formed a circle around their fallen leader.

As they each took a knee and bowed their heads, Galanis directed his men to place the body at the center of the clearing. Once there, he asked Santini for a report.

"Well, Sir, it seems like these 'people' got caught in the same mortar attack as we did, except they didn't have a clue as to what was happening. Bobby told everyone to disperse and take cover. Brick and I jumped into the grass and nearly landed on top of this guy." Santini explained that he examined Ares and determined he was deceased. His wounds indicated he had been struck in the neck by flying shrapnel and bled to death from a punctured jugular vein, probably within minutes. Galanis and Santini agreed there was nothing left to do but to bury Ares and get the hell out of the area before whoever was tracking them discovered their location, one completely unsuitable for defending.

The warrior-gods were standing in a huddle and talking loudly to one another when Galanis approached to speak with Athena. "Listen, miss, ah, Athena, we're in a tight situation here. Enemy soldiers are on our trail and closing in. We cannot stay here much longer. There's just enough time to bury your friend."

"No," she reacted with astonishment. "We will not bury Ares. He is to be returned!"

"He what–returned where?"

"Returned to us, here. Now we must hurry. Reviving him may take some time."

Galanis had no idea what she was talking about. Before he could question her further, she raised the Aegis and swept it across the clearing. Galanis and the others behind him were frozen in place. It was time for Athena and her team to act. Castor came forward and handed Athena a small vessel, usually containing wine. In this instance, it was filled with water, which Castor had collected from the Lethe River before the Six entered the portal. He could not have guessed how important his serendipitous action would become.

None of the warrior-gods were sure that the powers of the Lethe would operate outside of the Underworld. In addition, they were concerned about the effects that the water would have on Ares. Lethe is the "river of forgetfulness". Mortal souls who drink the waters must forget their earthly lives before they can be reincarnated into a new life. If Ares was given Lethe water, would he remember his life as the god of war and the son of Zeus? There was no time to ponder those issues further.

Athena took the vessel from Castor and walked to her brother in repose at the center of the clearing, and the others followed. She knelt beside Ares, gently parted his lips and began to pour drops of the sacred water into his mouth. There was no immediate reaction, so she increased the flow of water. She was reticent to use all of the precious liquid in the event another need would arise, but, at this moment, the fate of Ares was all that mattered.

Suddenly, there was movement in Ares' hands. He seemed to be reaching toward his neck, perhaps feeling the pain of his wound, even though there was no longer any sign of his injury. Athena looked up at the others gathered around. Could this be a sign that Ares' memory was intact? As Ares began to slowly raise himself up, small arms fire could be heard nearby, followed by four or five explosions. Instantly, Perez's radio squawked to life. It was Bobby Travis, "Six, this is Bobby, over!"

The crackling of gunfire nearby drowned out his urgent message. There was no reply. "Six, we need to pull back and get the hell outta here before we get overrun." There was continued silence. "Captain, we're blowing claymores and pulling back to your location, out."

All this activity was disturbing to the warrior-gods. So much so that Athena sprang up and passed the Aegis in front of Galanis, Fredricks and Perez. Their trances were broken, and they were briefly confused about what had happened. Athena ran to the recovering group. "Galanis, Galanis, there is trouble!"

Just then, there was a series of extremely loud explosions, followed by another tense transmission from Sergeant Travis. There were strange voices yelling in the background. "Six, we're pulling back. There are bad guys all around. You'd better double-time outta there. The rest of us will cover the rear and catch up when we can.".

"This is 6, Roger."

Chapter 14
Joining Forces:
Firefight in The Plain of Reeds

It was too late. Several enemy soldiers appeared at the edge of the clearing behind Galanis and Fredricks. Without hesitation, the warrior-gods let fly with their arrows and spears and charged at the intruders with swords drawn. They moved so rapidly that the enemy had no time to even raise their weapons, much less fire them. Galanis, Fredricks and Perez assumed an attack stance and pointed their weapons at the enemy troops. But there was no need. All four of the enemy lay on the ground, dead or dying. Athena used her venom-tipped spear to ensure that none would survive.

Perez reacted to the carnage, "Jesus Christ, what the fuck just happened?" There was no time to even contemplate an answer before Sergeant Travis and the remaining members of the team came running into the circle at full speed. Several were turning and firing their weapons to the rear.

Travis was shouting, "Let's go! Let's go! Move it." When all were inside the clearing, there was a series of explosions around the perimeter.

Galanis ran over to Sergeant Travis. "Bobby, whatta we got?"

"Just a minute, Sir. Rob, spread your guys out over there. Gage, have your folks cover that side." Then, turning to Galanis, he continued, "Okay, Sir. We're probably facing a company-size unit of the PAL (People's Army of Liberation) 148th Division. They have obviously zeroed in on us. We were able to set up a line of claymores to block their advance. That should give us time to hold them while you beat it out of here."

"Okay, Bobby, just don't outstay your welcome. When you break it off, use the loop route back to the river and rally with us at the Tan Lai Cemetery."

"Roger. We could use some more grenades, Captain."

"Right." He turned to Fredricks and handed him two grenades. "Tom, take these and whatever you and Perez can spare and distribute them along the line. Hurry up, we gotta run."

Unfortunately, time was not on their side. Travis' radio blared out a stark message. "Bobby, this is Brick. Guess who's coming to dinner? Over."

"Brick, what the…" The rest of his transmission was drowned out by loud, continuous small-arms fire interspersed with the explosion of grenades. Most alarming was that a serious number of rounds were cracking and popping over the heads of those standing in the clearing. The A-Team was now in a full-blown firefight–a fight for its life.

The radio cracked again. This time, it was Staff Sergeant Stacey Diggs, the medical sergeant. It was clear that he was in the middle of the action. "Six, this is Diggs, Hoppy's been hit." He was referring to Sergeant First Class Dennis Hopkins, Senior Engineer. "Brick and I need to get him outta here right quick. Over."

Galanis grabbed the handset from Perez's radio. "Roger, we'll do our best to cover you."

Before anyone could react to the call for help, Perez shouted, "Captain, look out!" Enemy troops were closing in on the clearing. Travis and Santini fired two long bursts at the intruders, and they fell to the ground, yet to no avail. More of the enemy began to appear from the tall grass surrounding the clearing. They were pushing several A-Team members into the clearing at gunpoint. It was clear that they were all about to become POWs or worse.

In the din and fog of battle, no one had the time nor the inclination to pay attention to Athena and the warrior-gods. They had sequestered themselves at the far end of the clearing, where they could hear and observe all that was taking place. They were ready to protect themselves, but they were now linked to these green and blacks. So, it seemed they would sink or swim together. As the fate of the A-Team grew dimmer by the minute, Athena huddled her team and developed a plan to intercede before it was too late. That would require the use of every weapon, tactic and mystical power they could bring to bear.

They might also have the element of surprise in their favor. Neither the A-Team nor the enemy could suspect what was going to happen next. As soon as the entire A-Team, including the wounded Sergeant Hopkins, were herded into the center of the clearing, a piercing sound permeated the clearing–a sound so loud that both the enemy and their captives were temporarily frozen in place. It was the war cry of Ares, literally back from the dead. The Six burst out of their sheltering spot with Ares in the lead, wielding his sword and spear. His eyes burned black as he set upon the enemy soldiers with grisly vengeance.

Blood flew in every direction as severed heads rolled about the clearing. Ares' actions were so swift that the enemy had no time to even cry out. Meanwhile, Athena and Hermes acted with the same alacrity as Ares. Hermes ran to the path where more enemy troops were filing in. He raised the Caduceus and ran down the line of twenty or more attackers. Each of them fell by the wayside, not dead but asleep, to be dealt with later.

Once again, Athena deployed the Aegis as she swept through the opposite side of the clearing from Ares. A dozen enemy soldiers were frozen in place, only this time she used her golden-tipped spear to eliminate them one by one. As she labored away, Castor was busy circulating among the enemy soldiers who were directly holding Galanis and his team at gunpoint. They couldn't know what Castor was up to since he was wearing Hades Helmet of Invisibility. They only knew that some "force" was relieving them of their firearms.

In their confusion, they were twisting around and swatting in the air, hoping to confront their attackers.

Speaking of the element of surprise, these troops were admittedly shocked when scores of arrows began piercing their bodies. Pollux and Damon were systematically killing the attackers. When they all lay dead on the ground, the A-Team let loose with volleys of automatic rifle fire. The Six joined the fray once again, slashing and spearing enemy troops as they entered from various directions. Ares let out a war cry as he wreaked havoc on the enemy, including cutting off the hands and arms of those who tried to raise their weapons. The combined efforts of the two teams of "friendlies" were successful in ending the carnage. A strange silence enveloped the clearing as the smoke and dust of battle permeated the clearing, along with the smell of blood.

The green and blacks began to mingle with the warrior-gods as congratulatory backslapping and handshaking broke out. It didn't take long for Galanis and the other team members to notice that one of those "mingling" was Ares, back from the grave. There were startled looks all around as the adrenalin rush of close-quarter combat began to fade. The A-Team needed some answers and quickly. However, they weren't going to stay around waiting for more visitors. "Listen up!" Galanis stepped forward. "Everyone gather over here."

The A-Team was still pumped, so there were hoorahs and high fives as they closed around the CO. Galanis signaled for their silence, then looked across the clearing where the Six were having their own celebration. Galanis waved them over. "Athena," he called, "can you and your team join us?"

"Of course, Galanis. You are now our brothers."

The Six joined the team and paid their respects by crossing their swords over their golden breastplates as Galanis continued, "First, is anybody hurt or wounded, Bobby?"

"Yes, Sir. You know about Hoppy. He took a round in his leg. It's still lodged in his upper thigh, but Doc stopped the bleeding and patched the wound."

Sergeant Santini spoke up, "He'll be able to limp back to camp. I can dig the slug out when we get there."

"Sergeant Taylor has a nasty cut from a bayonet," Sergeant Travis continued, "Taylor, you Okay?"

"Shit, Sarge, I've had worse cuts from a barfight in Fayetteville."

"Anyone else?"

There were no responses.

"Well, Sir," he went on. "We were goddam lucky to get outta this with our asses intact."

Galanis approached Athena, placing his hand on her shoulder. "Well, I speak for us all," he said. "Without these Six, the outcome would have been very different."

Athena motioned to Ares to come forward. "This is my brother and the leader of our quest, Ares, the God of War."

The two leaders shook hands, and Ares spoke up, "Captain, greetings from our father Zeus, and you have my personal gratitude. Without your assistance, the outcome for me would surely have been different."

Galanis smiled broadly. "I appreciate that, Ares. Now, we need to wrap this up and hightail it to our base camp. Both teams have questions to be answered. That will have to wait. Until then, Bobby.”

“Yes, Sir.”

“I need two 'volunteers' to do a quick recon of the enemy position so we can notify Dong Tam.”

“Roger, Sir, Gage, you and Kit just volunteered.”

Galanis addressed the two 'volunteers', “I want you to get as close as you can to their command group but not too close,” Galanis addressed them. “Get in, get out. We need to move out of here in thirty minutes. Okay, you two, move it on out…”

“Galanis,” Ares interrupted. “I think we can help… show him Athena.”

“We have a way to secretly spy on the enemy.” She held out Hades Helmet. “Let me show you its power.” Then she placed the helmet on Pollux's head, and he instantly disappeared.

“What the fuck?” Kit Rogers blurted out.

Sergeant Travis gave him the look. "Cool it, Rogers! Excuse me, Ma'am, but what does it mean?"

"It means one of you can become invisible and walk right into this 'command group' of the enemy and not be detected. Would you like to use it?"

"I'll answer that," Galanis broke in, "Yes. I don't care how or why it works. Let's get this done. Gage, you're our best language specialist for eavesdropping. You okay with a little magic to help out?"

"Damn right, Sir!"

Pollux removed the helmet from his head and placed it on Gage's head. Heard but not seen, Gage departed, "See y'all on the flipside."

It worked. Gage returned to the clearing with time to spare. He reported on all he had heard, *and* he managed to produce a map that he'd snatched up from right under their noses. Galanis had heard enough. Leaving out the participation of the Six, he reported the firefight, including a body count of thirty enemy troops, to their headquarters in Dong Tam. Based on the information and map acquired by Sergeant Gage, Galanis also reported the disposition and strength of the enemy units and their coordinate locations. Luckily, there were several helicopter gunships close by, patrolling the river. They were diverted by Headquarters to begin an attack on the enemy units identified by Galanis. Rob Salinas popped a green smoke grenade to identify the clearing as the location of friendlies. Within a few minutes, two Cobra gunships and a UH-1 (Huey) command and control ship rolled in over the clearing. Once past the clearing, the gunships began firing rockets and twenty-millimeter cannons at the enemy positions.

The Six stood awestruck in the middle of the clearing. This was the prophecy of Pythia: giant green cranes in the sky. They raised their swords and spears to the sky in defiance. Ares let out his now familiar war cry, "This is a challenge to our quest. We must find a way to destroy them!"

Tom Fredricks overheard Ares' words and rushed over. "No, no, those are ours, 'friendlies.' They carry weapons to kill our enemies. I guess you could say they're *our* 'magic powers.' Nothing for you to fear."

Galanis interrupted the discussion, loud enough for all to hear over the noise of exploding rockets and cannon fire, "Okay, let's head out. We need to get back to the base before dark. Bobby, you lead the way. Let's move at a fast pace but observe normal security procedures. Ares, have your folks mix in with ours and just follow what they do. Sound okay? I mean, is that acceptable?"

Ares was quick to respond, "Roger."

Hermes approached Ares then, and they had a short conversation. Thereafter, Hermes turned to address Captain Galanis, "Sir, Captain, I must return to the Elysian Fields. Ares and Athena can explain the urgency. All of you can go on, and I will join you as soon as possible. I bid you a temporary farewell and look forward to rejoining the team." Then he sped away, without pause, in the direction of the portal.

As the team departed the battlefield, Ares and Athena joined up with Galanis and his ADC. Athena spoke first, "Galanis, you must understand. We do not know who the enemy is that we fought today, but there is a much more pernicious enemy at work here in Van Lang."

Ares added, "As you have reported to headquarters, what you call Dong Tam? We must inform Hades and those in the Elysian Fields what has happened here."

"But what about Hermes?" Galanis interrupted. "He could be killed, and you wouldn't be able to 'revive' him, and how will he find us if he returns, and I mean *if.*"

As they pushed on toward the A-Team base camp, Ares and Athena revealed to Galanis and Fredricks the details of what was taking place in the Underworld–the threats by Cronus and Adecius to use the portal to establish a New Elysium in Van Lang, the construction of the temple fortress, the buildup of weapons and forces, the Dog Soldiers, and the rest. Lastly, they spoke of Heleron and the Legion of Aeneas, who were waiting on word from the Six about a potential battle at the portal or in Van Lang. Icing on the cake for Galanis and his ADC was the revelation by Athena that not only would Hermes be protected by wearing the Helmet of Hades, but she had given him the medallion given to her by Hera. *That*, she knew, was how he would find the base camp when he returned from Elysium. Galanis and Fredricks could only shrug and press on toward the base camp.

Chapter 15
A Single Fighting Force:
"Dig, Goddam It, Dig."

After returning to the A-Team base camp, Galanis conducted the usual debrief with his team and the remaining members of the Six. It was time to sort out the details that everyone wanted to hear. They all gathered in a large bunker where the A-Team secretly stored its food, supplies and ammunition. Before beginning, Galanis tried to explain to the Six that the bunker is booby-trapped when the team is gone. If triggered by unwanted intruders, they and the contents of the bunker would go up in a mushroom cloud of napalm. The Six looked puzzled as they looked from one to another and then back to Galanis with blank stares. Galanis grimaced and fumbled for the words, "Explosion, ah, ah, fire. Shit, you don't understand what I'm saying."

With Galanis' cursory knowledge of the Greek language, he was sure "booby trap" was not easily translated into ancient Greek. However, he did know *pagida* meant trap, as when his grandmother set out *mouse pagidas*. "Pagida, big pagida, fire!" More blank stares from the student audience. "Bobby, help!" Bobby Travis tried his luck by moving his hands and shouting boom, like an explosion. Finally, Sergeant Taylor drew a picture of a volcano in the dirt, with flames coming from the top. The Six listened intently without much reaction, so Sergeant Travis showed them the barrels of napalm and the fuses used to set them off.

"Pagida, pagida," Ares repeated in a low voice, but it was Pollux who got the correct answer to the charade puzzle. "Ah, eruption pagida, eruption pagida!"

At that, there was laughter all around. Easily enough, the point had been made that the Six should not try to enter bunkers, friendly or enemy, on their own. The more important point of the exchange was the recognition of a serious communication problem. If somehow this teaming relationship needed to continue, hand gestures and drawings in the dirt wouldn't work.

Over the next several days, the two team "partners" conducted a variety of briefings aimed at answering the question, "Where do we go from here?" Since the Six were the "visiting team," they were asked to go first. Ares and Athena took turns explaining the backgrounds of each warrior-god and why they had been sent on their quest to

Van Lang by Zeus. They talked of their encounters with Adecius, and their battles with the pygmaioi, the Colchian dragon and the Spartoi. Eventually, their focus turned to the disturbances within the Underworld and the lost portal. Much of what they described made sense to the members of the A-Team in terms of their high school-level knowledge of Greek mythology. However, nothing of what they said could explain how it was possible for them to be in the mortal world in the middle of a war. Nor could they provide much useful information about what Cronus and Adecius were up to, other than what Ares and Castor had overheard Cronus vowing in his grotto pontifications.

One by one, the warrior-gods told of their specific encounters and observations, including the green and black "Dog Soldiers" and the weapons they carried. All familiar, of course, to the A-Team. Then they described the green boxes carried by some of the Dog Soldiers. PRC-25 radios carried by Perez and other team members. Castor described the tower platform with the sharp vines, black tube, and large glass mirror–a guard tower with barbed wire, heavy machine gun and spotlight. Athena drew a map of Elysium showing Hades' palace and Cronus' temple fortress. She marked the location of the Lethe River, the entrance to the portal, the trenches and holes dug along the portal pathway and the glowing balls (US Army light strings) that lit up the entire portal.

She concluded her briefing by discussing the significance of the Lethe River and the role it had played in bringing Ares back to life. That was more than enough information for the team to absorb in one day. So, they broke for an evening meal. Tomorrow, it would be the home team's turn.

In the meantime, Sergeant Travis and his troops continued their ongoing indoctrination of the new team members. There was an introduction to C-rations, the use of the P-38 can opener, and how to open a beer. They were taught to use Halazone tablets to purify river water and to take daily malaria pills, although no one knew if warrior-gods could get malaria. Best of all, they learned to chow down like any GI on beanies and weenies, spaghetti and tomato sauce, pork slices with gravy and white bread in a can. They even liked the ham and lima beans, which GIs routinely threw away. There was only one remaining important detail: the art of flavoring every meal with Tabasco Sauce.

Early the next morning, Galanis huddled with his team in preparation for their briefing of the Six, having made his command decision. "However strange these recent events have been," he began, "we're going to have to play this hand through to see where it leads. No doubt that none of us would be standing here right now or maybe not even be alive without the help of the Six."

Sergeant Travis interrupted, "Sir, I can speak for the entire team. Just tell us what you expect of us, and we'll get it done."

There were nods of agreement all around, and ADC Fredricks joined in, "Without any doubt, Sir!"

"We need to form a single fighting force," Galanis continued, "to do away with any thoughts of 'them and us.' I will lay out our approach at this morning's briefing and ask for concurrence from the Six. If they agree, you will all go into full training mode, just as if you were dealing with new recruits back at Bragg. Any questions?" Hearing none, the team headed for the bunker to begin their briefing of the Six.

Galanis began by providing his "recruits" with a brief history of the Vietnam War as a backdrop to explaining why the 43[d] Special Forces A-Team was there. He asked each of the A-Team members to identify themselves, provide a brief bio and define the roles they play as an A-Team member. The ADC then took them through the training and experience required to become combat ready.

Galanis then wrapped it all together. "We have a mission here in Vietnam. Van Lang, as it was called in ancient times. You Six are here on a quest, the mission given to you by Zeus. If we are to accomplish those missions, we must join together, as I have told my team, to create a single fighting force. That requires trust and a leap of faith on both our parts. Ares, would you agree?"

"Yes, Captain. Our meeting with you and your team was not by chance. It was foretold by the Oracle of Delphi; therefore, we must all work and fight together in faith and trust, as you have proclaimed."

"Agreed. Therefore, starting now, we will begin to teach each other the skills we will need to work and fight together. Sergeant Travis, get 'em organized."

Sergeant Travis' face lit up with a broad grin and an anticipatory sparkle in his eyes. "Roger that, Sir. Alright, fall in." This was the cue to form ranks in front of Sergeant Travis, in this case, three ranks of five troops each, minus Hermes. In short order, the NCOs demonstrated how to form ranks, how to stand at attention, and how to stand at ease. Travis barked out instructions for the first training exercise–guard duty. The A-Team's standard practice was to set up two listening posts (LPs), a one-man hidden position at least two hundred yards outside the base camp, to do what it implies: listen and inform the team of any enemy activity. Three perimeter guards would occupy camouflaged foxholes about fifty meters from the Command Post (CP). Guards and LPs would be rotated every four hours to maintain "fresh" eyes and ears to the front. For training purposes, albeit in a "live" combat mode, each A-Team guard would be paired with a warrior-god.

The night passed without incident, and the entire team assembled outside the CP for morning chow. The warrior-gods were swapping stories about their experiences of the night before, and the A-Team joined in. They all allowed that the main difficulty was maintaining what the NCOs called noise and light discipline–what with shiny gold breastplates, rattling swords, and clanking spears! But the lessons had been learned, the first of many.

Into the midst of this shared comradery walked Hermes back from Elysium. Several A-Team members jumped to their feet with weapons at the ready before they recognized the winged god. Galanis stepped out of the CP to see what was going on. He was relieved to see that Hermes had returned. Galanis offered his hand. "Hermes, looks like Athena was right that Hera's medallion could lead you back."

"True Captain, Sir, and I come with important and startling news from Elysium."

"You're here just in time for the morning briefing. We're anxious to hear what you have learned, but first, your teammates can introduce you to C-rations. You can catch up on the ins and outs of formations and guard duty later."

There was resounding laughter from all. Hermes was puzzled until Damon, Pollux and others coached him on what they had learned. Sergeant Travis was gratified, or just plain proud, that his recruits were getting with the program. After breakfast chow, the teams filed into the bunker for the morning briefing. Galanis asked Hermes to proceed with his briefing.

"Thank you, Captain, Sir…"

"Hermes," Galanis interrupted, "you can call me 'Captain' or 'Sir'. No need for both."

"Yes, Captain. I went to the portal straightaway. I did not encounter enemy soldiers or Dog Soldiers. The portal was full of light, as we had experienced before. When I got to the Underworld, there was great activity. Again, as we had observed, the tower was there, Spartoi were there with Dog Soldiers, and souls were passing in and out of Lethe. I did not stop but raced directly to the Elysian Fields, where I met with Heleron and his commanders."

"Any signs of Cronus or Adecius?" Castor interrupted.

"None. According to Heleron, Cronus and Adecius spend all their time at the temple fortress working on their battle plan. Heleron receives daily reports on their activities from spies and servants."

Hermes went on to recount the information Hades and Persephone had received from Cerenia and me. He then turned to the "grand plan" as seen on the maps at the fortress and Cronus' palace. Heleron's commanders, Arcelium and

Tanaurus, interviewed those who had seen the map, details from which they were able to prepare several copies. Hermes had brought one of those copies with him.

"I suppose the issue is what to do about the Legion of Aeneas. I told Heleron and his commanders about what we encountered since entering Van Lang, including the ah, ah, 'problem' with Ares, and they agreed to pass the information to Hades and Persephone. In the end, I told Heleron to hold tight until we can further understand the situation here in Van Lang."

Chapter 16
Operation Golden Arrow

Before training could begin, the Six would need weapons and ammunition, clothing, boots, packs, and standard combat supplies of water, first aid kits and the like–logistics in English, or *epimeliteia* in Greek. SFC Hopkins had recovered from his leg wound, suffering through the enduring jibes of troops calling him "hop along." Now, he was back to just plain "Hoppy". He and Sergeant Perez were in charge of the logistics plan for the upcoming "Operation Golden Arrow," as ADC Fredricks had named the joint training exercise. As Hoppy allowed to Perez, "What the hell, Manny, even a latrine detail needs to be an 'Operation'. Let's just show how we do it here in the 'boogie-down delta.'" They boarded a Huey on the way to Dong Tam. Two days later, their requests for logistics support were approved, and Operation Golden Arrow was underway.

Hopkins and Perez walked down the ramp of a CH-47 "Chinook" helicopter as pallets of weapons, supplies and combat gear were being rolled off by the chopper crew. It was a choreographed exercise that took no more than ten minutes. The Chinook was too big of a target to stay on the ground for long. Before the ramp went up, Rob Salinas and Weapons Specialist Vince Taylor went on board. Their mission was to locate a site for a new base camp. As the prop wash of the helicopter dissipated and the dust cleared, the team members gathered around the pallets and began to inventory what they had received.

The resupply served two purposes. First, ammunition, claymores, and grenades expended during the firefight needed to be replaced. Second, and just as importantly, the Six needed to be fully outfitted for the training that was to begin the next morning. So, additional rations were added, along with fresh water and two luxury items, cigarettes and one case of beer. The beer and some mess hall food from Dong Tam were for a small celebration the A-Team had planned as the last meal at the present base camp. However, there was much work to be done before any "partying" could begin.

The Six stripped off their armor and accouterments. In short order, they were green and black, armed with M-16s. They balked somewhat at having to wear wool socks and jungle boots, but they strutted and stomped about the camp to confirm their new status. Castor offered a brief testimonial, "We are now A-Team!" Then, all six let out a series of hooahs. Their enthusiasm was short-lived. The recruit training that Captain Galanis spoke of was about to begin.

Sergeant Travis had assigned one member of the A-Team to each of the Six as training "partners." They would be more like drill sergeants. Bobby Travis would be the "Top" sergeant orchestrating a full range of recruit training: marching drills, weapons, first aid, patrolling, radio communications, fighting, ambush techniques, compass navigation, etc. However, to get started, as with all recruits, the Six needed to be taught the ins and outs of discipline: the so-called "Army way." Later, they would learn the Special Forces way.

There were six jumbled piles of rations, ammunition, clothing, and gear laid out near the command bunker. Sergeant Osbourne had created a display set of gear as a training aid. With the Six and their partners gathered around, he issued curt instructions on how to pack a rucksack and in what order. He continued with the use of the "pistol" belt, i.e., where to place ammo pouches, first aid packs and canteens. When he was finished, Brick stood before them as a combat-ready trooper and barked out an order, "A-Team, take command of your recruits and get 'em squared away.

You have 10 minutes." He checked his watch, and all hell (or Tartarus) broke loose.

There followed a typical scene straight out of an Army training film. The drill sergeants got in the faces of their recruits, with expletives and spit flying in every direction. "Top" was on the scene, and he bellowed out to the group, "What the fuck are you slackers waiting for?"

The drill sergeants held up rucksacks to the trainees and Brick reminded them sharply, "You have nine minutes."

The Six began flailing away at their gear, creating clouds of dust, as cans of C-rations rolled away along with bottles of malaria pills and halazone tablets. That was the least of it. The drill sergeants harangued them mercilessly as the frustrated warrior-gods put on twisted pistol belts with ammo pouches and canteens upside down. When Sergeant Osbourne called time, the Six were covered in sweat and dust and gulping air, more confused than ever. Perhaps the greatest part of consternation was the concept of 'ten minutes.' They didn't have watches, nor would they know how to use them if they did. "Jesus Christ," Top chimed in again. "What a collection of sad sacks. Do you think Zeus would be proud of that performance?"

After being coached by the drill sergeants, through more swearing and more spit, the Six shouted in unison, "No, Top!" As a 'reward,' they were instructed in the art of the push-up and required to repeat "No, Top" with the completion of twenty repetitions.

After more than two hours of ten-minute drills, the Six had mastered their first period of instruction. There were six neatly packed rucksacks lined up and six recruits standing tall in proper uniforms and gear. It was a long, hot day for the recruits: M-16 operation and target practice, use of claymore mines, hand grenades and C-4 explosives, all live fire, not like basic training hand holding. Then there were more mundane tasks, like the use of the M1-A1 Entrenching tool, 1 Each, Collapsible, which is Army-speak for "shovel."

Each recruit had to dig a regulation foxhole, replete with camouflage and stakes marking fields of fire. The drill instructors (DI's) showed no mercy. As Kit Carson put it, "Suck it up. You're not back in Olympus eating grapes, drinking wine, and getting it on with your sister, or Rosie, the slave girl. Dig, goddam it, dig!"

While the recruits continued their training throughout the day, Galanis reviewed the map Hermes had brought from Elysium. He noted there were various symbols for what appeared to be an order of battle, i.e., the names and strengths of military units, some in Van Lang, others in Elysium and Olympus. With luck, the team could use the map to locate Adecius and FSB (Fire Support Base) Cronus. There were also arrows leading in and out of the portal, access to the Lethe, and pathways to Cronus' temple fortress and Hades' palace. To the A-Team commander, this appeared to be a straightforward battle plan, but he would have to rely on Ares and Athena to interpret other words and symbols.

The CP radio came alive, then "Six, this is Salinas," a voice fizzled through the airwaves. "We found a secure location for the new base camp and have started prep work for your arrival. I've sent the encrypted coordinates to Orion 5, over."

"Roger got 'em. We're taking off before first light tomorrow and should be at your location in two days, over."

"Roger, we'll stay in touch, out."

The recruits were hustled into the bunker by their respective drill sergeants. Sergeant Travis had taken charge of setting up the celebration. In his view, the first full day of training had gone well. The troops deserved a short break before facing the ass-busting phase of training that Travis had in store for the next two days. The meal was steak and potatoes, green beans, and coleslaw. Perez deserved the credit for sweet-talking the cook back at Dong Tam into class A rations. There was iced tea, coffee, and pound cake to round out the banquet.

Sergeant Gage handed everyone a carton of cigarettes, which they could smoke or trade. He then produced his Zippo lighter and demonstrated its use to the Six. When the flame flicked on, the warrior-gods were startled, while their instructors laughed and lit up their own lighters. Just another way of "messing" with recruits. However, the Six may have had the last laugh when they each took out a cigarette and asked Sergeant Gage for a light. As they puffed away, the A-Team had no clue that the Greeks had been smoking various plants and herbs for some two thousand years. Bobby Travis laughed heartily and spoke for the group, "Well, I guess that's one on us."

Finally, each person received one warm beer. Top offered a toast, "To our new recruits. They took whatever we could dish out without a single complaint. You just might be good enough to wear the green beret if I can keep your sorry asses alive long enough. Salute!" Everyone joined in.

The Six responded, "Chin, Chin." Then it was Galanis' turn.

The instructors were not about to let their recruits get one up on them with the cigarette gag and Sergeant Diggs had the perfect solution. He had a small cassette player at the ready. As Galanis stepped forward to address the group, the voice of Arthur Brown reverberated throughout the bunker, "I am the God of Hellfire, and I bring you fire," which was followed by Brown's maniacal and menacing laughter. The Six grabbed their M-16s and jumped to their feet as the music stopped. A cacophony of laughter and hoots ensued. Sergeant Diggs turned to Sergeant Travis, "Well, Top, I'd say that's one on them."

Galanis intervened, "Sergeant Diggs, I guess we're all glad there weren't any rounds in those weapons."

Diggs slaps his forehead. "Oh, shit!" He paused. "Just kidding, Sir."

Galanis continued, "Ares, Athena, you have a team to be proud of–and we are proud to join with you. However, I must warn you that the next two days will test all of us to the max. In addition to your training, there will be danger all about. But, before we get outta here tomorrow, there's a lot of work to be done."

On cue, ADC Fredricks stepped forward, "Listen up! You A-Team members know the drill, but it never hurts to go through the checklist." Addressing the Six, he went on, "For you newbies, pay attention, 'cause I'm only gonna say this once." Pollux raised his hand, as the recruits had been instructed to do to gain recognition. "Yes, Pollux?"

"Sir, what is this 'newbies.' Have we done something wrong?"

There were chuckles among the A-Team. Fredricks smiled broadly and replied, "No, it's just another word for recruit and it's a lot nicer than some of the things you've already been called today." Fredricks proceeded with his checklist. All rucksacks were to be double-checked and ready to go in the morning. Any items that could not be carried or noted as unserviceable were to be dumped into the foxholes surrounding the camp. C-4 explosive charges were to be set in each. Trash, outdated code books, maps and other paperwork needed to be collected and placed in the center of the bunker. The Six were instructed to separate the special weapons they planned to carry with them–the Caduceus, Hades Helmet, magic spears and arrows, and, of course, the Aegis. A-Team members would be assisting them with burying their armor plates, shields, swords, and other gear in camouflaged pits, the coordinates of which were recorded to allow for future recovery.

After those tasks were completed, it was time to set up the security posts, as the night before, and post the guards. Even with guard rotations, there wouldn't be much thought of sleep as the hours until their departure ticked by.

Chapter 17
The March to Base Camp Zeus

An hour before daylight, the word was circulated for all LPs and guards to pull back to the CP, making sure no trash or loose items were left behind. By then, there was just enough time for some canned peaches or toasted bread with cheese spread–and always, coffee, and hot chocolate. Galanis and Sergeant Travis came out of the CP with the last of their morning coffee. Travis issued the command call to "saddle up." The Six were confused since there were no horses anywhere to be seen, another teaching point for the recruits. When it was confirmed that they were departing, Ares let out his war cry. In response, Kit Carson yelled over, "Goddam it recruit, don't do that! One of these days, you're gonna stampede a fucking heard of water buffalo right over our asses."

Ares was a bit chastened, not a usual circumstance for the God of War. He looked to the sky as if seeking supplication from Zeus. With a look of sincerity, he turned to Sergeant Carson. "Sorry, Sergeant Kit."

Travis piped in, "Alright, girls, enough of the pattycakes. Let's get moving."

As Galanis and his ADC led them out of the base camp, explosions from the bunker and foxholes roared in the background. Detonation of the napalm in the bunker was enough to shake the earth like a small earthquake aftershock. Training of the Six took hold immediately. The A-Team instructed them on flank security, rear security, and the standing requirement for noise discipline. Galanis had mapped out their route and used his compass to keep them on course. As they proceeded, the recruits were being schooled in the use of their compasses. They viewed these as tiny sundials, but, of course, the sun had nothing to do with it. Periodically, Galanis would call a halt, at which time LPs were sent out to the flank and rear to ensure the team was not being followed. If nothing was seen or heard, Sergeant Travis would get on the radio net, "Hold your positions for fifteen mikes. Smoke 'em if you got 'em." This is Army speak for *We're taking a fifteen-minute break, so you can light up if you want,"* which was a lesson that the Six did not need repeated. Instead, they joined their instructors, dragging on their cigarettes while observing their surroundings with weapons at the ready.

The recruits were fast getting the picture of Van Lang. They were tracking through the Plain of Reeds, what the locals called "the black swamp," a large floodplain some 2,500 square miles in size. It is part of a massive wetland and drainage system forming the Mekong River Delta. To the troops, it was simply head-high grass, water, mud, and more water. They weren't marching to their new base camp; they were slogging. Then there was the heat, humidity, mosquitos, and leeches to contend with while wondering what was behind that next thick patch of grass. While they were on break, Salinas checked in from Base Camp Zeus, "Six, this is Salinas, over."

"This is Six, over."

"SITREP follows."

SITREP is a situation report. They are issued regularly between separated units and on up to headquarters to ensure that operations are proceeding as normal or to report enemy activity. In this instance, Sergeant Salinas notified Galanis that preparations at Base Camp Zeus were proceeding apace, including the arrival of the first supply mission from Dong Tam. He concluded his report, "One last thing, the supply mission pilots reported seeing a squad-size unit of bad guys close to your route of march. Vince sent the encrypted coordinates to the ADC, over."

"Roger, we'll be on the alert. Gotta get going. 6, out."

ADC Fredricks had selected a location where they would remain overnight. It would take at least two hours to get there, which would give them time to set up their night defensive position (NDP). Along the way, Sergeant Santini, who was paired with Damon on the right flank of their formation, called Sergeant Travis to report on the sighting of what appeared to be abandoned enemy bunkers. The team halted while Travis went to check it out. Once there, he called for the remaining warrior-gods to come to his location. Travis and Santini then gave the recruits instructions on how to clear and search abandoned bunkers, whether enemy or friendly, followed by the use of hand grenades to destroy them.

As they prepared to return to the main body, Castor approached Travis. "Top, before I made my explosion, I found this in the bunker." It was a silver necklace in the style of a military "dog tag," only with strange markings and symbols. Athena quickly identified it as the necklaces worn by the Dog Soldiers they had seen marching into the portal.

Ares interpreted the markings, mentioning, "This is the mark of Cronus, and this one must be of Adecius." He turned the tag over. "Here is the image of Cerberus. Below is the name Zanatar."

"That must be the name of a Dog Soldier," Hermes shouted. "They are here!"

As Galanis and his team pondered the surprising finding, they continued their march to the overnight location. They needed time to set up a solid defensive position and to prepare for any potential threat or threats. What Galanis did not know was whether the enemy sighted by the chopper pilots were locals or forces of Adecius. He also had to ponder whether his newbie recruits were at all prepared for night combat operations. Suddenly, he was recalling his first command as an Infantry lieutenant when he led a squad of what Travis would call "cherries" on a night ambush. Twenty minutes after setting up a standard V-shaped ambush, three of his troops were dead. Albeit that was a training exercise but one that he had never forgotten. The current situation was startlingly different. It was a live fire!

His thoughts were interrupted by the sound of entrenching tools carving out fighting positions and the chatter of instructors "encouraging" their recruits to dig deeper or wider.

Always handy with a phrase, Diggs intoned, "Get your shit together, troops, or you're gonna die in Vietnam!"

As darkness approached, a more somber tone took over, particularly when the ADC announced that a six-man (person) ambush patrol was to be sent out one hour after dark. This was quite routine for the A-Team, but this time, they were joined by warrior-gods, facing the unknowns of Dog Soldiers and underworld bad guys. None of that really mattered. It was time to lock and load and head downrange.

The ambush detail would include four A-Team members and two recruits. There was a bit of consternation evident when Athena was selected as one of the recruits, the other being Hermes. Kit Carson reacted to the news in a sidebar with ADC Fredricks, "Sir, you know the military rules don't allow females to participate in combat operations. Do you think it's a good idea to pick Athena for an ambush patrol?"

Fredricks glanced over to the area where members of the patrol were in final preparations for their mission. He turned back to Kit, answering, "Sarge, you must've noticed by now that in this situation, there *are* no rules. Besides, from what I've seen, Athena could take on three of us and never break a sweat. Now that I think of it, I doubt if gods and goddesses sweat."

Kit couldn't help but laugh. "Yeah, I get it, but this is the strangest trip I've ever been on, and I don't even do drugs."

It was Fredricks' turn to laugh, but their repartee was interrupted by Gage's call to saddle up. As Senior Weapons Sergeant, Gage was the designated patrol leader. He had finished his final inspection of the troops. Kit Carson returned to the group and Gage gave his final briefing to the patrol, "Kit, you're partnered with Athena. Osbourne, you take Hermes. Remember, this is a live mission, but it's also another training opportunity for our recruits. Athena and Hermes, stay close to your partners and don't take unnecessary chances."

The warrior-gods responded with a resounding, "Yes, Sergeant." Gage continued. "As we discussed earlier, this will be an L-shaped ambush. You all know your positions and assignments. Once we're set up, maintain silence and noise discipline until I blow the first claymore. Any questions before we take off?"

But there were none. "Okay," he concluded. "Lock and load and follow me."

The ambush site was about two kilometers from the NDP at a location where two narrow paths crossed. Sergeant Gage took the lead, using his compass to guide their progress through tall grass and swampy meadows. He was followed closely by Athena and Hermes. The others provided flank and rear security. Gage halted the group several times while he checked his compass readings, using those occasions to allow Athena and Hermes to observe and learn. As they approached the ambush site, Gage signaled for everyone to take up their positions. Osbourne, Diggs, and Hermes formed the long leg of the L, Athena and Kit formed the short leg, with Gage at the apex. This provided a killing zone of interlocking fire aimed at the crossing of the paths. Claymore mines were set up at the crossing point, one of which would be used by Sergeant Gage to initiate the ambush. Nothing left to do but wait and listen.

It was nearly dawn when the sound of shuffling feet could be heard approaching the crossing. Along the ambush lines, muscles tensed, and all eyes were focused on the killing zone to their front. They continued to watch as five shadowy figures entered the crossing. They halted their march and began talking amongst themselves. When Gage was certain there were no others joining the group, he squeezed his clacker, the small triggering device that sends an electric pulse down the wire connected to the claymore. Seconds later, a flash of light enveloped the crossing, followed by a cacophony of noise from the explosion and gunfire from every A-Team position hidden in the tall grass.

A few more tension-filled seconds passed. Then, claymores along the trails were detonated to ensure that others who might be following behind the group in the crossing would be neutralized. This all happened in less than two minutes. As prearranged, there was a ceasefire after the secondary explosions on the trails. The killing zone fell silent as smoke and the smell of cordite permeated the scene. Members of the patrol listened intently, but all remained quiet. Gage signaled to Athena and Kit to move up and check the killing zone for results. When they arrived at the crossing, they signaled to the others that the site was secure. The others left their positions and began securing the trails on either side of the crossing. It was time to mop up and head back to the NDP.

When the area was secured, the team gathered at the crossing to assess the results of the ambush. There were body parts, weapons and gear strewn in every direction, but not enough to identify who the presumed bad guys were.

Diggs was the first to hear a low moaning coming from the tall grass on the far side of the crossing. He alerted the others and approached the area. "Sergeant Gage," he beckoned, "check this out." Gage and several others joined Diggs, where they discovered a wounded soldier. The soldier was conscious and attempting to get up. Diggs spoke to him, "Hold on. Keep still. You're going to be okay. Sergeant Gage, I don't know who this guy is, but he is one lucky son-of-a-bitch to have survived the blast of a claymore."

Gage leaned down for a closer look. "I've seen this before. He was probably standing at a distance where the concussion of the blast blew him all the way over here. What d'ya think? Can we take him with us?"

"I think so. Let me sit him up and I'll check his vitals. Hermes, give me a hand."

It wasn't until the wounded soldier was sitting up that his identity became clear. Hermes jumped to his feet. "Fuck, Sarge. He's a Dog Soldier."

Chapter 18
The Cronus Factor

Less than two weeks had passed since the Six had walked out of the portal and into Van Lang. The A-Team and their recruits had been working continuously to create that "single fighting force" that Galanis and Ares had agreed to form. At the same time, Adecius and his Dog Soldiers were hard at work claiming territory in the name of Cronus, the precursor to building *New Elysium*. The fortress of mud, vines and grass that Cronus had chastised Adecius about was now nearly completed. On his next visit, Cronus would see a modern-day fortress with gun towers, barbed wire and spotlights, with a small bustling "village" inside the perimeter. Hundreds of slaves were pressed into service to ensure completion before Cronus arrived to inspect Fire Support Base Cronus. Even in its unfinished state, FSB Cronus was a secure base from which to launch the first phase of Operation Chimera, gaining control of the Plain of Reeds and establishing New Elysium.

Adecius was right to want to please Cronus. He and Cronus struck a bargain that would ultimately make Adecius the King and ruler of New Elysium and the entirety of Van

Lang. None of that would be possible without the magic and might of Cronus.

Ꙩ   Ꙩ   Ꙩ   Ꙩ   Ꙩ

As a boy, I would sit at the feet of my father, Zeus, as he told wonderous stories of gods, goddesses, monsters, and most intriguing of all, the Titanomachy. "It all began," he would say, "with the birth of my grandfather Ouranos (Uranus)." He recounted that Ouranos was the *protogenos*, the primordial god of the sky. His consort, Gaea was the earth, the mountains, the sea. Together, they were the personification of heaven. Their union produced the twelve Titans, including Oceanus, Hyperion, Rhea, and the rest. The most important of these was Cronus. It was Cronus who acted on his mother's desire to seek vengeance on Ouranos. When Cronus killed Ouranos, he caused the separation of heaven and earth and became the undisputed ruler of the Titans and the world. Thus, had begun the Titanomachy, a ten-year war between the Titans and the Olympians, led by Zeus and his brothers Poseidon and Hades.

Cronus was no ordinary god. He possessed amazing strength, fifty times that of mortals and twice that of the Olympians. His powers were myriad, starting with chronokinesis, the ability to disrupt the flow of time and travel anywhere through time and take those of his choosing along. He exercised control over the earth through terrain manipulation, earthquakes, and transmutation of rocks and minerals. For good measure, he had telescopic vision, super leaping ability, and, some believed, he could take flight.

Of course, Cronus never used those powers to create peace and order on earth or in the cosmos. He became a destructive and all-devouring force destined to rule over heaven and earth unchallenged. It was not to be. He was betrayed by his hubris and his two greatest weaknesses, uncontrolled violence, and jealousy of his own children.

It was said that Gaia helped Zeus and his siblings to oppose Cronus and the Titans. That possibility notwithstanding, Zeus was able to release his uncles, the Cyclopes, and the hecatoncheires that were born to Uranus and Gaia and whom Uranus had imprisoned below the earth. The hecatoncheires, known as the "hundred-handed", were gigantic beasts with fifty heads and one hundred arms, each of great strength. With their help and Zeus' use of his powerful thunderbolts, the Titans, including Cronus, were banished to Tartarus.

It is unclear to mere mortals or even demigods like me why Zeus eventually released the Titans from Tartarus, particularly his father, Cronus. Even more peculiar, Cronus was granted rule of the Elysian Fields, a place of peace and tranquility for the best and bravest of mortal souls. Perhaps the only reasonable explanation is that Cronus is the god of time, and the Elysian Fields are outside the existence of time. Regardless, being the "king" of the Elysian Fields is a far better option than spending eternity in the abyss of pain, but that's no consolation when you were deposed from being the ruler of the Cosmos by your children. Cronus could never forgive Zeus and the Olympians for his humiliation.

It became clear to me and those in the Underworld that the discovery of the lost portal presented an opportunity for Cronus to right the wrong that had been done to him. Adecius was a rebel like Cronus and hungry for power in his own right. It was a partnership literally forged in hell, with the destruction of Olympus at its heart. Cronus would use all his powers to create New Elysium, while Adecius developed the strategy–the "grand plan"–to lead a mighty military force equipped with "magical" weapons into the heart of the Underworld and from there to Olympus.

◊   ◊   ◊   ◊   ◊

After the discovery of the lost portal, Cronus didn't waste any time in putting his plan into action. He summoned Adecius to his palace, "Come in, Adecius. It is good to see you."

"Thank you, my god. How can I serve you?"

"As you have told me, this Van Lang is ideal for my plan to establish a new Elysium in the mortal world."

"It is that."

Cronus described his foray into Van Lang and his discovery of an ancient race known as the tattooed people. While there, he met Hung Vuong, ruler of the Kingdom of Van Lang, who told him that many villagers tattooed their bodies to ward off sea monsters they called crocodiles, dragons and evil spirits. Hung Vuong did not know that the Greeks viewed tattoos as a sign of "otherness," a stigma reserved for slaves, criminals, and captives. Before departing back through time, accompanied by hundreds of tattooed "slaves," Cronus learned all he could about Van Lang, the Kingdom of Ong Troi, the god of heaven, the immortals of his "cosmos," and its many deities.

After briefing Adecius on what he had seen and heard, Cronus returned to the subject of New Elysium, "My travel through time provided me with a vision of our new world, one without Zeus and his sycophantic gods of Olympus. In Van Lang, there is a great swamp with five rivers and large meadows of grass, as in the Elysian Fields. There are heroes and warrior-gods, magic dragons, and other beasts. There are mortals who build temples for their deities and worship them every day. Yet, this is untouched by the cosmos I once ruled and that is now 'ruled' by Zeus."

Adecius was spellbound by Cronus' resounding voice, and he could feel the tension growing in his massive limbs. His eyes began glowing red as he waited for his god and master to continue. There was a deadening silence as Cronus summoned Cerenia. She entered through a small doorway. "Yes, my god. How may I serve you?"

"Bring us wine and prepare a table where Adecius and I can continue our discussions."

"Yes, my god."

When she left, Cronus looked toward Adecius. "To begin, we must also establish a fortress. Let's call it a temple.

Here in the Elysian Fields, I have used my power of time travel to find a workforce of slaves to help you in this effort."

Adecius smiled broadly. With his leadership and cunning and Cronus' powers, New Elysium would become a reality, and the Olympians would be vanquished. As a reward, Adecius would assert his right to become a true god, more powerful than all other gods of the new cosmos, save for Cronus himself.

Chapter 19
Surprise, Kill and Vanish

The ambush patrol arrived at the NDP about an hour after sunup. They had their Dog Soldier prisoner in tow. Diggs had patched up his minor wounds and his hands were tied behind his back. Athena and Hermes had taken charge of him on the march back to the NDP to see what information they might glean for debriefing Galanis and the rest of the team. They could see by his silver ID tag that his name was Portellis and he identified himself as a member of the Cerberus Legion of Dog Soldiers, a fact confirmed by his shoulder patch. His unit was based at FSB Cronus, along with a mixture of other units, slave workers, Adecius, and his command group.

Bobby Travis had seen to it that hot coffee and warmed C-rations were available for members of the patrol. As they chowed down and smoked cigarettes, Gage, Athena, and Hermes conducted a debrief of their mission. Naturally, all eyes were focused on the prisoner as Gage described the success of the ambush. He pointed out the participation of Athena and Hermes, including the fact that she and Hermes were responsible for blowing the claymores along the trails, another sign of their A-Team acculturation. The other warrior-gods did high-fives with the returning heroes. The debriefing continued as Athena and Hermes explained what they had learned from the prisoner Portellis.

When they were finished, Galanis addressed the group. "First things first, Sergeant Travis, you and Hermes take the prisoner over there and see if you can get more information about his unit, and particularly about FSB Cronus."

"Roger." He paused to look around. "Hermes, will you escort our guest to the interrogation suite?"

"Right on, Top!"

"Hermes, you've been spending too much time around Sergeant Diggs."

Galanis continues, "Athena, I need you here so we can discuss our strategy going forward,"

"Yes, Sir."

"The ADC and I have been over our options and here's what we have. We can report what's been happening here since the Six came through the portal to the commander at Dong Tam, or go alone and do what we can to stop Cronus and Adecius' plans for establishing New Elysium in Vietnam."

ADC Fredricks added his analysis, "If we report this to Dong Tam, the commander and staff will flip out. I can just imagine everybody from Westmoreland on up to President Nixon himself getting involved, not to mention the CIA, Congress, and the United Nations."

Sergeant Diggs chimes in, "Yeah, it would be like one of those 'Godzilla Attacks Tokyo' movies."

Galanis thought how surreal it was to be commanding a unit with six icons of the mythology he studied in school. As he looked around the campsite, it all seemed so natural—Castor leaning against some sandbags, cleaning his weapon and smoking a cigarette, Bobby Travis and Perez joking with Pollux about "losing his cherry" as a real A-Team fighter. Nothing seemed out of sync with reality. He drained the hot coffee from his ersatz coffee mug made from a C-ration can and took up the analysis again, "If we decide to go it alone, we can't hit Adecius and the Dog Soldiers head-on. We'll have to go to ground and use our combined skills to disrupt Adecius' operations until we can entice him onto a battlefield of our choosing, at the time of our choosing."

"Captain Galanis," Ares interrupted, "can you tell us more about this 'disruption'? How can it be done?"

In Galanis' mind, the die had been cast. He and Ares would lead the most unique and perhaps the most powerful fighting force ever assembled against Cronus, the former Godhead of the Greek Cosmos, and his army of mysterious Dog Soldiers. His strategy was based on a little-known tactic used in the Second World War by a group called Jedburghs. These were soldiers formed into three-man teams that went behind enemy lines to disrupt Nazi operations in Europe as a prelude to the Allied invasion of Normandy. Their method, "Surprise, Kill and Vanish."

Galanis brought his attention to the warrior-gods. "I know the Six don't know anything about our big war," he admitted, "but I know from my study of the Greek wars that many of the same strategies and tactics were used."

"Sure," Pollux interrupted, "but what about Jason and the Argonauts?"

"And the Trojan Horse?" Damon suggested.

"Exactly," Galanis continued. "For our purposes, the force in waiting is the Legion of Aeneas back in Elysium. If we do our best at disruption, there will come a time when we can deploy the Legion. Hermes, I will need you to return to Elysium and organize all the troops you can gather. I assume you can use that 'magic' helmet to go to and from Elysium."

Hermes' excitement was palpable. "When do I leave?"

"We'll get to that, but first, there's a lot of planning to do. When we get to FSB Zeus, Athena, the ADC, and I will prepare the Ops Plan for phase two of Golden Arrow. That's it for now. Let's pack up and police the area. We'll move out at 0900–Sergeant Travis!"

"Yo."

"Finish your interrogation and get ready to move. I'll expect your report when we get to the new base."

"Roger that, Sir."

In short order, the team was trekking through the grass and swamps of the Plain of Reeds. The A-Team and the Six were now one team and ready for action.

Chapter 20
The Opposing Force

On Hermes' last visit to Elysium, Heleron had raised an army of 1,000 soldiers. Somehow, they would have to be equipped and trained before they could engage with the Dog Soldiers. There was no way to know the size of the force that Adecius was assembling. However, it was clear his troops were well-trained and equipped with weapons and gear that belonged to the US Army. Regardless of the readiness, or lack thereof, of the two armies, they were headed for a set-piece battle in the Plain of Reeds.

ø ø ø ø ø

As Galanis and his team were on their way to the site of their new base camp, Adecius was welcoming Cronus to the newly completed base he had commissioned in the name of his god-master, Cronus. Adecius was beaming with pride, confident that Cronus would be pleased. As they walked through the massive front gates of the camp, Adecius spread his arms out.

"This, my god, is Fire Support Base Cronus–all glory to you, my master."

Even Cronus had to be impressed with what he saw before him. There was a large training field in the center of the compound. On one side stood a formation of 300 fully equipped Dog Soldiers. Adecius commanded them to attention and present arms as a salute to Cronus. As they snapped their M-16 rifles forward, the camp resonated with repeated shouts of, "All hail Cronus." Cronus dipped his head to the troops in recognition of their salute. Adecius raised his hand and the soldiers returned to the position of attention.

On the other side of the field stood 300 tattooed slaves, uniformly dressed in the bright traditional clothing of Van Lang villagers. Adecius again raised his hand. The slave captives bowed deeply and chanted, "Toàn thé kēu Cronus– *All hail Cronus.*" On command, the soldiers marched forward and passed by Cronus for inspection. Adecius pointed out the "magic" weapons and equipment the soldiers were carrying, all of which were acquired through stealth raids on warehouses at Dong Tam and various stockpiles, aided by the powers of Cronus.

Once the soldiers had all passed by, Adecius escorted Cronus out through the main gate to a newly completed firing range. Six Dog Soldiers stood in firing positions with M-16 rifles. Downrange were six targets, each representing one of the six warrior-gods. Adecius snapped a small red flag into the air and hundreds of rounds began piercing the targets. When the flag was lowered, the firing ceased, and a second group of soldiers started to approach the target area. Cronus was somewhat startled when commands began blaring from several tactical radios. In a mock attack, soldiers began throwing grenades, setting off mines, and raking the targets with machine gun fire. With a signal from their leader, the troops let out a war cry and charged the targets with fixed bayonets.

As smoke and dust settled over the scene, Cronus started to clap his hands as his voice boomed out, "New Elysium is ours, and now, Zeus and the Olympians will feel my wrath." He turned to Adecius. "I will leave you now, but the final test of our power belongs to me."

Just as soon as he spoke, his eyes glazed over, and he stood still as if in a trance. Clouds began to billow up from the ground surrounding the base camp. "Adecius, I have promised to use my powers to defeat Zeus. These clouds will protect this place from intruders. Now, build your army and let us do battle.”

Adecius slapped his fist to his chest in salute to his god and master. “All hail Cronus, all hail New Elysium. Death to Zeus and the Olympians.”

Cronus put his fist to his chest and uttered the words that would become a touchstone of Adecius’ rise to power, “All hail Adecius!” With that, Cronus departed in the direction of the portal.

Chapter 21
Qui Audet Adipiscitur:
"Who Dares Wins"

One week after the ambush and the capture of the Dog Soldier Portellis, FSB Zeus was fully operational. The "Jedburghs" were organized and trained, and the teams were prepared to deploy the following day. Galanis called a team meeting. Already, he could sense the tension and excitement in the air. There were "hurrahs" all around as he got their attention. "Okay," he began, "settle down. You'll be getting into the action soon enough. Sergeant Travis, the ADC and I are all very proud of the work you've done."

More shouts from the troops as he continued,

"Now, we have just about reached our goal of becoming the single fighting force Ares and I envisioned. But, before we can claim success, there is one last piece of business to attend to. Tom, Ares, please step forward."

As the ADC and Ares took their places to the left and right of Galanis, Sergeant Travis began barking out

205

commands to the group, "Attention! You five recruits form a single rank in front of the commanders."

The five warrior-gods complied as Sergeant Travis moved forward, "Sir, the candidates are assembled."

There was an exchange of salutes. Travis handed a small box to the ADC and returned to the group. Galanis began to announce the purpose of the assembly, "Attention to orders, 43^{d} Special Forces A-Team, Plain of Reeds, Republic of Vietnam, the following individuals are hereby promoted as indicated below. Further, having completed the requisite training and tactical experience as required by AS 600-8-22, are officially granted status as members of the A-Team elite force commanded by the undersigned. Pursuant to the status granted hereunder, the same individuals are hereby authorized to wear the Green Beret. Presented to each on this 24th day of August 1968. Signed Antonio Galanis, Captain, Commanding."

As the names were called, the new "graduates" stepped forward and received their rank insignia, shoulder patches, and berets. Galanis read on:

"Lieutenant Ares,
Warrant Officer Athena,

Sergeant First Class Hermes,

Sergeant Pollux,

Sergeant Castor,

Sergeant Damon."

Cheers erupted from the entire elite force team. Cigars were passed out, and Bobby Travis hauled out a bottle of scotch for the traditional toast, "De Oppresso Liber."

𝕺　𝕺　𝕺　𝕺　𝕺

After a few hours of interrogating their Dog Soldier POW, the team had learned what Cronus and Adecius were up to in Van Lang and the Underworld: the construction of FSB Cronus, the "tattooed people" slaves, theft of Army weapons and equipment, and the daily influx of Dog Soldier recruits coming through the portal. There were additional, very startling revelations. The "recruits" were coming from Lethe and the Styx with Cerberus' cooperation. Further, they learned that all those recruits, at least 1,000 of them, were being trained by US military personnel, which Cronus had brought to the base camp through his ability to create a discontinuity in time, what we call time travel. Portellis was unsure how many of these trainers were at the base camp, but he revealed they were confined in a secure area guarded by Spartoi soldiers. Galanis and Ares were convinced they had sufficient information to launch the next phase of Operation Golden Arrow. Time was of the essence if there was any hope of stopping the buildup of an overwhelming force at FSB Cronus. Fulfilling that objective was now in the hands of eighteen Green Berets.

The ADC announced the team assignments, "Listen up, we have six three-man, ahem–there I go again. I mean three-*person* teams. Assignments are as follows. For now, Bobby, you and Sergeant Damon will remain here at basecamp with me as the operational control group. Our call sign will be Zeus Control."

He further explained, "Captain Galanis will lead team Apollo with SFC Hermes and Perez. They will proceed to the portal. Once there, Hermes will use Hades Helmet to return to Elysium. Galanis and Perez will monitor activity in and out of the portal and, hopefully, track arriving Dog Soldier recruits to the location of FSB Cronus.

"WO Athena will lead Taylor and Gage. Your call sign is Selene. Your mission is to return to the ambush site with Portellis in tow and have him retrace his unit's route to the trail crossing.

"Lieutenant Ares has team Hercules with Hoppy and Kit. You need to recon along the river, then back to the firefight area... you know, the area where Bobby discovered the USO team wandering through the grass."

There was a chorus of laughter, all except Sergeant Travis. "Shit, I guess you guys will never give up on that!"

Thanks to Sergeant Diggs, the Six had learned about the USO and had been "coached" into pulling a gag on Sergeant Travis. When Travis was done growling, the Six locked arms and began a kick dance reminiscent of the Rockettes. Everyone but Travis was howling. Travis folded his arms and looked on, eventually unable to avoid laughing at the antics.

The ADC signaled it was time to get back to business. "Okay, where was I–yeah, here we are, Salinas. You get team Perseus with our resident comedian Diggs and Sergeant Castor. You need to visit our old base campsite to see if anyone has been around since we left. Hold there for further assignment.

"Finally, we have team Artemus. Santini, you're with Sergeant Pollux and Osbourne. We're expecting a resupply from Dong Tam at 1400. You guys hitch a ride back to Dong Tam, recon the area and find out if anyone knows about the theft of weapons and gear the POW told us about.

"You all have copies of the Ops Plan and your individual mission plans… read, memorize, and burn them. Synchronize your watches and confirm your radio frequencies with Sergeant Travis. We kick off at 0500 tomorrow, so get some chow and sack out early. Once you're on the move, you'll have to get by as best as you can."

"Athena," he asked, "you have a message for the team?"

She moved to face the team and clutched the medallion hanging from her neck. "The message is from our Queen Hera."

There was a bright flash of light, causing the group to shield their eyes, followed by the appearance of Hera in the medallion. She said, "On behalf of Zeus and all Olympians, we wish you success in your quest. We send our sincere appreciation to those of you who have joined in this most important mission. I leave you with the motto of our ancient legions and raiders like you… 'Qui Audet Adipiscitur.'"

Who Dares Wins

PART III

The War Within a War

Chapter 22
The Breach of FSB Cronus:
POWs Recovered

The more I followed the actions and adventures of the A-Team (including the Six), the more I learned about the "art of war." Take, for example, what ADC Fredericks called intelligence gathering. His opinion was that virtually every battle ever fought throughout history relied on intelligence gathering for battle planning. These efforts commonly relied on spies, informants, captured enemies, and local inhabitants to create a picture of troop dispositions, fortifications, terrain features, barriers, armaments, and enemy strength. Successful armies and their commanders could solve the puzzle of who and what they were facing.

Fredericks explained, "Special Forces A-Teams are steeped in the art and science of military intelligence. Ranging around in small groups and oftentimes behind enemy lines, they become the eyes and ears for collecting intelligence. That information is reported to intelligence officers and commanders for analysis and incorporation into operational plans for engaging the enemy. This is the objective of the Jedburgh teams we dispatched from FSB Zeus."

His words were helpful, but it became clear that I was not suited for military service.

ADC Fredericks, Travis, and Damon were the designated command and control group. The command post bunker back at FSB Zeus contained multiple radios with encryption devices, maps, code books, and intelligence collection forms for compiling reports as they filtered in from the teams in the field. Although FSB Zeus was isolated and well camouflaged, the team had placed listening devices, claymores, and booby traps around the perimeter.

Fredericks addressed his team, "Alright, let's review where we are. We should start to receive SITREPs from the teams later today. Bobby, you need to log all incoming reports and get Damon pooped up on what to do so that you can switch off every four hours. I'll man the radio on the Dong Tam frequency to call in mission requests…"

Damon broke in, "Sir, will you tell them about our combined teams? I mean, about the Six?"

"No. All mission radio traffic will be handled by A-Team members… I mean 'original' A-Team members."

"Yeah, Damon," Sergeant Travis elaborated, "our guys can call in artillery and gunships just like normal … so many troops in the open, or bad guys dug in along a tree line. No one will know or care whether those are Dog Soldiers, Spartoi or whatever, if we call in a body count. The more the merrier."

Fredricks continued, "I'll take the logs and SITREPs and compile them into a prelim intelligence assessment for the CO. Needless to say, let's stay tight on security and make sure you are using two-way encryption for all communications. Any questions?"

Travis and Damon responded in unison, "No, Sir."

The first SITREP came in around 1800. It was from Team Artemus. Santini reported, "SITREP follows: arrived Dong Tam, contacted Quartermaster, confirmed some warehouses raided, gear and weapons missing. The hot topic here, no one else is talking. Contacting friends at aviation for support of our ops. Out."

This was part of the cover story that Galanis and the ADC concocted to get the gear and weapons needed to outfit the Legion of Aeneas and others when they arrived in Van Lang. Santini, and his team were preparing phony requisition orders for some 2,000 sets of gear and a similar number of weapons, ammunition, and supplies. The purpose of the requisitions was listed as "Top-Secret." The source was shown as the CIA. In other words, this was to be a "no questions asked" operation. The implication was that the CIA was once again creating a secret army for purposes unknown. Santini presented the requisitions to the Quartermaster and the Aviation Brigade commander. The ruse worked. Santini and his team began inventorying the material they were about to purloin. When finished, Team Artemus would stand by for further orders.

Over the next several days, messages were received from the other teams:

Team Hercules: Searched firefight location. No enemy activity noted. Moving to join Team Apollo.

Team Perseus: Spotted several Dog Soldiers at the old base camp. Halted the team and waited for dark.

Neutralized four enemy, Jedburgh style. Seized documents and maps. Holding this location.

There were other enemy encounters. Hermes was about to enter the portal wearing Hades Helmet on his way to Elysium when a platoon-size unit of Dog Soldiers and Sportai exited the portal in formation. Hermes sped back to Galanis' location and reported the sighting. Galanis and Perez followed Hermes to the portal entrance. Hermes went on his way to Elysium, while Galanis called in an artillery fire mission and, and he and Perez watched as the enemy unit was decimated. The result was a body count of thirty-eight reported to Headquarters Dong Tam.

Shortly after, Ares and Team Hercules joined Galanis and Perez. Galanis directed them to follow the path the enemy troops were using and exert all efforts to find FSB Cronus. Galanis planned to recon an area to the south to find a staging area for the anticipated arrival of the Legion troops.

Suddenly, there was big news involving the special weapons carried by Athena and Ares. Athena and Team Selene had Portellis guide them from the ambush site where he was captured to a large clearing that appeared to be a Dog Soldier supply depot. According to Portellis, this is where weapons, gear, and ammunition stolen from Dong Tam warehouses was being stockpiled before being moved to FSB Cronus. Transport to FSB Cronus was provided by a couple hundred tattooed slaves, controlled by Spartoi guards. Portellis also described the path used to travel to FSB Cronus.

With that information, Athena was ready to make a move. Taylor and Gage moved to the edge of the clearing and began making noise to attract the attention of the enemy troops. As the Dog Soldiers scrambled to investigate the disturbance, Athena appeared brandishing the Aegis. The approaching soldiers were instantly frozen in stone. Athena sent a SITREP to the ADC explaining the situation. She and Fredericks agreed that the stone soldiers should be hidden in the surrounding grass and swamps. Then, Team Selene was to follow the path being used by the slave porters, assuming it would lead them to FSB Cronus.

Ares and his team were already at FSB Cronus, sequestered in the tall grass and shrubs about half a kilometer away. They were waiting for darkness to put their plan into action. Sergeant Rogers had scouted the perimeter and located a potential entry point on the compound's north side opposite the main gate. He saw two guards posted at the doorway to a small building. If they could be eliminated, the team could find their target, the ammunition storage area described to them by the prisoner Portellis. Just after sunset, Sergeant Rogers led the others to the entry point.

Sergeant Hopkins used his wire cutters to gain entrance to the compound. The area where they entered was dark, except for a small amount of light coming from the building where the two guards stood. Fortunately, Ares had brought the Caduceus along for just such an occasion. He stepped into the light, facing the guards. They were Spartoi dressed in US Army uniforms and carrying AR-15 rifles. Before they could react, Ares passed the Caduceus before the guards. They fell asleep and dropped to the ground.

Before moving on, the team decided to investigate the contents of the building. Hopkins and Rodgers cautiously opened the door while Ares stood by with the Caduceus. They were shocked to see three "soldiers" seated around a table playing poker! The team members immediately knew that these were the individuals captured by Adecius. Hopkins signaled the group to remain quiet. He approached them and spoke in hushed tones, "We are with a Special Forces A-Team operating in this area. We heard that you had been captured and brought here. No time to explain all this.

We're on a hit-and-run raid. Remain here. We'll be back and take you with us. Be ready to move out on the run."

A lanky Army captain stood up and whispered to Hopkins, "Sergeant, we're happy you're here." His voice cracked. "But you should know this is a strange place. The people here are some sort of aliens."

"We are very familiar with what is going on here," Hopkins replied in an excited tone, "We'll explain everything once we get you safely out of here."

Chapter 23
SFC Hermes Reporting, Sir!

I was at Hades' palace when Hermes returned from Van Lang. He was beaming with excitement as he shook my hand and slapped me hard on the back as if we were two reunited soldiers. "Alagon, I have a SITREP, ah, important news, from the other side of the portal. I must meet with Hades immediately."

It was only then that I took note of his appearance. He wore the uniform of the green and blacks and the same heavy black boots. His face was streaked with charcoal and on his head was a strange green cap with a badge of two gold crossed arrows.

I almost spit out my reaction. "What is this, Hermes? Have you joined the green and blacks? What is the news that you bring?" Hermes laughed and removed his cap, which he explained was a "beret." He called the marks on his face "camouflage." As we talked further, he disabused me of any thought that he had joined with the green and blacks. In my startled condition, I knew we needed to seek an audience with Hades. As we walked through the lush pathways of

221

Persephone's Garden, I could sense that Hermes had changed. He walked with a swagger and a bearing of confidence even beyond that of an immortal. My curiosity peeked when we entered the great hall. Hermes gave a puzzling greeting to the palace guards with something he called a "high five."

We proceeded to the far end of the great hall where Hades and Persephone were seated. Persephone was the first to see us approaching. She was smiling broadly as she stood with open arms. "Hermes, dear one, come close." He went to her, and she placed her hands on his face. "Hades and I have been worried for your safety. We have been hearing horrible tales of war and destruction in this place called Van Lang."

"Do not worry," Hermes responded. "I am here with good news." Persephone took a step back and nodded in a sign of respect. Hermes took two side steps, placing himself in front of Hades. Hades' face showed amusement and puzzlement as Hermes came to attention and saluted, "Sir, Sergeant First Class Hermes reports."

Hades abruptly stood and looked sternly at Hermes. "What in the name of Zeus?" Before he could say anything further, the great god, ruler of the Underworld, burst into laughter that nearly shook the pillars of the palace. Regaining his composure, so to speak, Hades stepped down from his throne and approached Hermes. He looked Hermes up and down, felt the fabric of his uniform and looked intently at his beret. Hermes could not hold back a broad smile as he conjured thoughts of Hades in the role of Master Sergeant Travis. Instead, Hades put his arm across Hermes' shoulder.

"I'm sure you can explain this strange behavior," Persephone opined, "I trust this is not some spell cast upon you?"

Hades raised his hand. "Come, my dear, and you, Alagon, let us adjourn to the garden where we can eat and drink while Hermes tells his tale." As Hermes spoke, we were all spellbound. Imagine the King and Queen of the Underworld sitting motionless as if struck by the power of the Caduceus, hanging on every word of "sergeant" Hermes. The astonishing facts poured out: a description of the Plain of Reeds, lush as the meadows of Elysium, explosions from the earth and sky, the death and revival of Ares, encounter with the A-Team and subsequent battle with an enemy force, ambush of the green and black soldiers of Adecius' army, and the formation of the single fighting force commanded by Captain Galanis. Hades gasped as he interrupted Hermes' strange tale, "If what you say is true, there has never been a more fantastic or dangerous quest in the history of Olympus."

Persephone reached over from her throne and touched Hades' arm. A mixture of puzzlement and concern overtook her countenance. "Dear husband, we must use all the powers of your kingdom to stop this treachery. Zeus should never have freed Cronus from Tartarus!"

Hades took a long draught of wine and wiped his lips. His tone was almost guttural, "I agree with you, Persephone. Hermes, what do you propose?"

"Sir, ah, excuse me, most cherished Uncle, I am here not only to convey greetings and wishes from Captain Galanis and the entire A-Team, but to present the details of our teams' operations plan."

Slowly stroking his beard and looking puzzled, Hades inquired, "What does it mean?"

"It's what we call a battle plan, like the Trojan attack on Troy. Before I present the details, I must request that Heleron and his Legion commanders be present."

"As you wish. Alagon, please summon Heleron and his commanders, and quickly."

As I departed for the Elysian Fields, I heard a bemused Persephone ask, "Hermes, why do you continue to stand so stiffly? You are an Olympian, not a servant." As I hurried along, I could not hear his response. Later, I learned that Hermes' indoctrination as a Green Beret was complete. He had been standing at attention, waiting for the command of "at ease."

☂   ☂   ☂   ☂   ☂

I love the smell of chamomile. That smell permeated Persephone's Garden as I escorted Heleron and his commanders into the great hall. I noted that Hermes was no longer at attention, I surmised at the insistence of Persephone. We quietly approached the rulers of the Underworld. Heleron was in the lead, with Tanaurus and Arcelium following two paces behind. In perfect unison, they dropped to one knee and crossed their breastplates with golden swords. With military precision, they rose and assumed a position of attention. Heleron's deep voice echoed throughout the magnificent chamber and into the garden, "Glory to our gods. We are at your service."

Hades' face brightened as his fingers ran through his beard. With a regal nod, all those present could relax as he spoke in measured tones, "Persephone and I beg your indulgence as we hear from this, this transformed immortal. Hermes, please proceed."

As Hermes stepped forward, Heleron and his commanders could observe him for the first time. Although trying to maintain their military bearing, the three had a look of shock on their faces, which quickly changed to fierce anger. Arcelium took a step toward Hermes and drew his sword. Hades abruptly raised his hand and Arcelium returned to his former position. To my amazement, Persephone put a hand to her mouth to muffle her laughter. "My faithful warriors," she said after regaining her composure, "you are no more surprised than Hades and I were when we first saw this, ah, what you call," Now she was puzzled and looked to me. "Alagon?"

"A green and black," I responded.

"Ah, yes, a green and black, but let's hear from Hermes what or who he really is."

"I bring you all greetings from Captain Galanis, Commander of the A-Team." His face and body language exuded pride when he announced, "A fighting force of which I am now a member, along with the others sent there by Zeus." He held up his headgear (as Sergeant Travis called it). "We are Green Berets!"

That was the beginning of Hermes "SITREP," which lasted long into the night. Trays of sumptuous foods and pitchers of wine and honey drinks were passed around. There was never a moment when the eyes and ears of the audience were not captivated by what they were hearing. I hastily grabbed my writing kit and began to scribe these notes:

- Time was drawing near for the Legion of Aeneas to travel through the portal to Van Lang.

- The A-Team was preparing a campsite where the Legionnaires would be equipped and trained as part of "Operation Golden Chariot," the plan to defeat Adecius' Legion of Cronus and expel Cronus from Van Lang.

–   Hermes was to remain in Elysium to work on specific plans for the troop movement with Heleron and his commanders. This would include familiarizing the Legionnaires and their leaders with the weapons and devices Hermes had brought with him.

–   There was a lengthy discussion regarding additional resources that could be provided from the Underworld, including any mystical powers that could be used to counter those of Adecius and Cronus.

–   Hermes had brought the cloak of invisibility with him. This was necessary for Heleron and his two commanders to travel undetected to and from Van Lang. Their first trip through the portal would be to accompany Hermes to a meeting with Captain Galanis and the A-Team.

As morning broke, servants appeared with the most delightful repast of meats, roasted fowl, fruits, sweets, and most exotic, peacock eggs, lightly poached, and garnished with the petals of saffron crocus. I was beginning to feel that being a son of Zeus and a nephew of Hades had its rewards.

Hermes raised his goblet of wine and pronounced a toast, *"Stin Heia Mas."*

All those present responded, "To our health." Putting down his goblet, Hermes' face abruptly took on a stern, if not worrisome, look.

Both Hades and Persephone reacted to Hermes' sudden change in demeanor by looking intently in his direction. "What have you to say?" Hades demanded.

Hermes assumed a military stance as if reporting to a commanding general. "My King and Queen, I must depart now." Gesturing toward Heleron and his commanders, he continued, "These brave soldiers and I have much work to do, work that is the best hope for stopping Cronus' sinister assault on your kingdom."

"Dear Hermes," Persephone interrupted, "we have every faith that you and the others will prevail in the quest that our father Zeus has set upon you."

Hermes relaxed. "Surely, I do not mean to alarm you, but I must leave you with this message sent to you from Captain Galanis and Lieutenant Ares." Taking a folded paper from his shirt pocket, he read the following:

"Greetings from Fire Support Base Zeus. We are joined as one force in the fight against Cronus to save your kingdom. With your help and that of Heleron and his faithful Legionnaires, we will be ready for battle. Yet, you must know that our position is tenuous. The number of Dog Soldiers coming through the portal is increasing daily. There have been more raids on supply depots, resulting in a massive stockpiling of arms and ammunition at FSB Cronus.

"Perhaps most worrying is Cronus' attempts to seek support from the King of Van Lang and possibly arrange the intercession of the God, Ong Troi. His tactic is to convince them that the Olympians, with the aid of invading mortals, want to destroy Van Lang and its people. If we are to be successful on the battlefield, we need your help in two ways:

1. Stopping the flow of 'recruits' from the Underworld to FSB Cronus and other locations in Van Lang (Vietnam).

2. Make every effort to contact the Kingdom of Van Lang and, if possible, with Ong Troi, the God of Heaven and counterpart to the All-Father Zeus.

"As Hermes has informed you, since the Six and the A-Team's first encounter, we have formed a single fighting force dedicated to preserving the existence of Vietnam, the Underworld, and Olympus, confident that *Who Dares Wins!*

"Yours respectfully, Antonio Galanis, Commander, Captain, A-Team (Augmented) and Ares, Son of Zeus and Hera, First Lieutenant, A-Team (Augmented)."

As Hermes finished reading the message, Hades and Persephone, still seated on their thrones, reached over and clasped hands. Looking at one another, their faces revealed a mixture of love and concern. Silently, Persephone rose and took several anemone flowers from a vase next to her throne. Even now, I can recall the image, her heavenly countenance, the flowing white silk of her gown and the gleaming gold crown upon her head. The pink and purple of the anemones were a beautiful contrast to her white gown. In my mind, she will always remain frozen in that moment. Our group stood spellbound as the Queen approached Hermes with outstretched arms. Handing the flowers to Hermes, she softly said, "My Prince, you go with our blessings." Hades nodded his head in concert with her words.

Hermes clutched the flowers to his breast. Breaking from his military stance, he bowed deeply and caught his breath. "I repeat the pledge we have made to Zeus, 'We shall not fail!'" He came to attention and saluted the royal couple. Heleron and his commanders saluted with their swords. Hermes turned and led us out through the garden on our way to the Elysian Fields and our appointment with the assembled leaders and soldiers of the Legion of Aeneas.

Chapter 24
Operation Golden Chariot

Things were coming together in the Plain of Reeds. It was time for the Jedburgh teams to return to FSB Zeus. ADC Fredericks' team logged the incoming SITREPs and added the information to their intelligence assessment. In addition, they continued to monitor local radio networks, including Dong Tam, FSB Cleopatra, forty kilometers to the south, and several Vietnamese "enemy" units. The ADC issued a coded broadcast message for the recall, "Dionysus has returned, I say again, Dionysus has returned."

By early the next morning, the A-Team, minus Hermes, was back at FSB Zeus and chowing down on C-rats and LRRPs. Members of the Six indulged in their newfound habit of smoking Winston cigarettes. They soon gathered in the CP, where the Jedburgh teams were swapping stories of their exploits. Each of them was trying to lay claim to being the baddest asses around. As Sergeant Travis would say, "Some things never change."

Perhaps I should add, "Even after 5,000 years!"

They worked while they talked. Weapons and gear were cleaned, ammunition replenished, LRRP rations and cigarettes were restocked in individual rucksacks. Sergeant Travis' coffee was a big hit, spiked with a modest amount of brandy from his private stock. From a distance, Galanis looked on with a sense of satisfaction–the satisfaction that commanders get when they realize their soldiers are ready for the battle to come. He knew they would follow him without hesitation. More importantly, he thought every one of them would risk their lives to save the lives of their fellow Green Berets.

Fredericks interrupted the commander's thoughts with a slap on the back and the offer of a cigarette and coffee. Galanis accepted them both. His face and eyes brightened as he turned to his ADC. "What do you think, Tom?"

"I think you guys did a helluva job out there. Can you believe how the Six, the 'former' Six, has performed? I never even had a class this good back at Bragg."

"Yeah, it's easy to forget where they came from. We've come a long way." He chuckled. "Since Bobby bumped into the 'USO troupe' wandering through the grass."

Fredericks laughed heartily. "Oh yeah."

Galanis shifted gears. "By the way, how did the debrief go with the three POWs?"

"They're still somewhat in shock and mystified, trying to figure out what the hell happened. Yet, the info they've provided so far about FSB Cronus and Adecius' organization is a real gold mine. Travis and Sergent Damon are getting it all down as part of our intelligence analysis."

After a last drag on his cigarette, Galanis stamped the butt out on the ground. "Good. So, what should we do with them? Have they asked to return to their units?"

"That's not clear yet. We'll need a day or two."

"Right. How about if, for now, we get them introduced to the team? You take the lead."

"Roger."

What Sergeant Travis calls "jaw jacking" continued apace while Galanis and Fredericks strategized. WO Athena was holding forth on the prowess of Team Selene, verbally sparing with Kit Carson. I thought I heard a giggle. Who ever heard of a Goddess of War giggling? Or smoking! That's when I realized the situation was even more twisted than anything an old trickster like me could conjure.

"Kit, you know we were the best team out there, right? Gage?"

Sergeant Gage was busy brushing his teeth. "Uh ah."

Athena looked to Sergeant Taylor. "Vince?"

"Hell yes, who else located a shitload of weapons and ammunition–enough, I might add, to support a brigade-size unit. Oh, and our fearless leader, Athena, just took out a platoon of bad guys with one wave of that watcha call it."

Amid general laughter, Sergeant Hopkins broke in, "Aegis, it's the Aegis, doofus. So, while you guys were playing patty cake with a bunch of Dog Soldiers recruits, our team just happened to break into the enemy base and blow up a humongous stockpile of weapons and ammunition, probably twice as big as that puny pile you found."

This was a typical taunting among comrades, greeted by a chorus of "ooohs," as Hopkins pressed on, "And left through the backdoor, with three POWs in tow." A stream of hoots and whistles followed. Just then, Galanis and Fredericks entered the fray. Galanis shouted above the din, "Listen up!" The chatter and laughter died out, allowing their leader to continue with a laugh, "I don't think the BS can be piled any higher, so let's get to work. Tom, you're up."

"Roger. First, I want to thank all of you for the incredible work you accomplished over the past two weeks. Thanks to you, our intelligence assessment is nearly complete, but I want to meet individually with the team leaders to see what else should be added. Sergeant Travis is handing out copies of what we have so far for your review."

Galanis reappeared. He was escorting the three POWs. After recognizing their bravery and determination, he asked the three to introduce themselves. The entire A-Team stood up and saluted. Loud cheers ensued as a tall Army captain stepped forward. His fatigue uniform had several tears and was stained with mud and sweat. Several dark splotches appeared to be blood. He wore a black beret with a distinctive yellow and black Ranger tab. His voice was scratchy. "I, I'm Captain Gordon Kellogg, Commander, LRRP Detachment Zebra. This is my team," he said, motioning toward the other two. "Lieutenant Nguyen Tran, biet dong quân, RVN Rangers." Tran wore the customary "tiger" camouflage fatigues and a maroon beret with a badge ironically containing a winged arrow in a wreath. You could sense his steel-hard resolve as he snapped to attention and saluted the team.

A stillness settled over the scene as Captain Kellogg identified the third member of his team as US Air Force Technical Sergeant Justin Alexander, a forward air controller (FAC). Another cheer went up. Sergeant Salinas came forward and offered each of their "guests" a cigarette. Pollux jumped in, flipping open his lighter, pronouncing with pride, "Zippo." Laughter ensued as smoke encircled the three LRRPs. After a few drags on his cigarette, the captain cleared his throat. "Ahh, unfortunately, we lost our other team member, Warrant Officer John Savage, our senior radiotelephone operator."

Looking at the ADC, he said, "Tom, I'll give you all the details when we talk, but I suppose you'll know more about this than we do. He just disappeared. I mean before our eyes!"

Ares blurted out, "Fucking Adecius! Ah, sorry, Sir."

Galanis said, "We'll hear much more about this and what went on at FSB Cronus as soon as Captain Kellogg and his team get some chow and a chance to rest."

The A-Team went back to their chores as their chatter resumed, only the topic had changed to concerns about what the LRRP team had gone through and about the missing team member, John Savage. As Fredricks escorted Kellogg and his team to the command bunker, much of what everyone wanted to know would be revealed.

Chapter 25
"My Life as a Water Buffalo"

After Hermes, Heleron and his two commanders left the meeting at Hades' palace, Hades and Persephone reviewed the message sent from Galanis and Ares. They were focused on the request made for support from the Underworld. Hades was showing his anger, almost stammering his words. "We must act!" he growled, throwing his goblet of wine to the floor. It shot across the marble floor all the way into the garden.

"You are right," Persephone said, attempting to calm her husband. It worked. Persephone handed him a fresh goblet of wine and they continued to talk.

I was gazing into my third or fourth goblet of wine, listening to the gods of the Underworld discuss a threat to their existence. "Alagon!" There it was again, that booming voice that could shake the pillars of the Parthenon.

Jumping to my feet. "Yes, my God," I responded.

Hades continued, "Persephone has prevailed in her thinking. She and I will take measures to secure the Underworld while you journey to this mysterious Van Lang."

"Yes," offered Persephone, "you will be an envoy from Olympus to the Kingdom, first to see if Cronus has made inroads there."

Hades added, "Second, determine if it is possible to contact Ong Troi, the one referred to as the God of Heaven."

I protested, "Are you sure you want me to do this? How can I …"

There it was, that look I knew so well, a snarl befitting Cerberus, eyes burning like liquid gold, and clenched teeth, meaning he was done speaking. Nothing left for me but to bow graciously, groveling if you will, and take my leave. I went straight away to the Elysian Fields. I contacted Hermes and Heleron and informed them of my instructions from Hades and Persephone. Hermes reminded me that he, Heleron and the two Legion commanders were preparing to go to Van Lang for operations planning with the A-Team. I decided to go with them. After that, I would be on my own. So, I thought, *what use is a trickster if he can't use his special powers to get through the portal and into Van Lang?*

Hermes approached me with the Legionnaires at his side. I could see a sense of concern on his face. "Alagon, we are ready to depart. I believe the invisibility cloak will cover the four of us, but perhaps not five."

"I thought of that Hermes, and I have a solution." As the group started to move out, I turned several times around and landed flat on the ground as a large serpent. Hermes reached down and placed me over his shoulders. I had no sense of time or distance. I confess, I slept most of the way and awoke in the bright sunshine of Van Lang.

ය   ය   ය   ය   ය

Once in Van Lang, I needed a disguise. Thanks once more to powers given to me by Zeus, I transformed myself to look like one of the local cattle grazing nearby. Hermes laughed when he told me later, "They're called water buffalo." Almost immediately, I discovered that I was hungry and began to sample the reeds and water plants that abounded in every direction. With a much enhanced sense of smell, I detected the sweet smell of honey orchids and the familiar aroma of star anise. Even as a water buffalo, that smell of anise sparked memories of drinking ouzo with my friends in a taverna back home in Plaka.

I began lapping the cool waters at my feet while swatting away at an assortment of flies and mosquitoes (*kouvoútti* in my native Greek language) with my whiplike tail. Suddenly, a familiar smell wafted into my rather large nostrils. It was the smell of burning wood mixed with roasting animal flesh. I was hoping that it was from a creature other than a water buffalo! This was no time for musing. I set off in the direction of the smoke. It was then that I realized that in choosing my transformation, I neglected to account for the soup-like mud that rose as high as my underbelly as my legs were sucked downward.

Eventually, I found a dry path to walk on, which led to a large pond filled with thousands of plants that I recognized as lotus blossoms. Just then, the smells of smoke and cooking meat grew even stronger. I stopped to sample the tender shoots of some rice plants as cacophonous sounds of bells, gongs and drums startled me. I could see a vast village before me when I raised my head. A red and gold gateway led to a large open court surrounded by poinciana and tamarind trees. My acute sense of smell propelled me forward until I reached the gate. I could see scores of people dressed in colorful silks and wearing sandals with fine gold ornaments. There were marketplace stalls along the outer edges of the square. The proprietors were hawking fruits and vegetables such as I have never seen. There were roasted geese and other fowl dressed and hanging in rows. In addition to the roasting meat I had smelled from afar, large pots of broth, rice, and vegetables exuded the most exotic aromas. My nostrils tingled with delight.

Coming out of my culinary reverie, my attention was drawn to a group of old men smoking long-stemmed pipes emitting the odor of opio (opium). They were playing a board game that reminded me of Senet, a game I had once played in Egypt. It was time for me to revert to my mortal state, so I wandered down a path that skirted the outer wall of the village. I briefly encountered several villagers bound for the market, I presumed. I entered the water at the side of the path and began grazing, all the while swatting those damnable insects with my tail. When the path lacked passersby, I reared up on my hind legs, turned about and reappeared as Alagon of Olympus. I went straight away to the village gate and into the marketplace. This caused an immediate commotion among the villagers, most likely because of my clothing and footwear; white linen tunic, cloak (chiton and himation), and leather sandals. I also wore a purple sash with a gold brooch presented to me by Hera.

I need not belabor the excitement and agitation that ensued. It is worthy only to say that I was surrounded by no fewer than a dozen curious men, bowing and chanting in a language unknown to me. I was escorted beyond the square and marketplace to a large ornate structure in the fashion of many palaces seen in Rome, Egypt, and elsewhere. I was ushered through large wooden doors some five meters high, inlaid with gold and ivory. Two priest-like men, or perhaps guards, took me in hand and led me down a long corridor decorated with skins of tigers and leopards, the tusks of elephants, and mounted heads of beasts I had never encountered, not in Ethiopia, India, Persia, or myriads of places where I had wandered. There were golden weapons, brightly colored vases, and accouterments too numerous to set down here.

Another set of doors was flung open to reveal a large, ornate room worthy of any Roman emperor or pharaoh of Egypt. At the farthest end of the room was a gold and bejeweled throne occupied by Hung Vuong, the King of Van Lang, the very personage I had come to see.

I was summoned to approach the King. Walking slowly forward, I recognized the smell of coriander and mint, along with strange flowers, trees and plants wafting into the great hall from an adjoining garden of great size and beauty. I was about two meters from the throne when King Vuong held up his hand with the palm facing me. I stopped and there was silence for several moments, which gave me time to observe his eminence more closely. His skin was darkened by the sun. Black piercing yet welcoming eyes. A long white beard went down to his waist. There were several purplish scars on the exposed parts of his arms, which I surmised were from past battles. His face took on a mysterious look as he spoke in a voice that echoed throughout the chamber, "Who are you and why have you entered my kingdom?"

"I am Alagon, and I have come from a faraway place called Olympus. I bring greetings from my god, ah, King, Zeus."

"What do you want? Answer truthfully, or I will have your head prominently displayed in the village square."

"One of the Olympian gods, Cronus, is said to have…"

"Cronus!" he bellowed and abruptly jumped up from his throne. The redness of his face almost matched the red of his royal robes. His eyes were of a fierceness I had only seen in Hercules when he slew the Nemean Lion. "If you are here for Cronus," he shouted, "You will certainly lose your head. He came into my kingdom acting as a friend and then through some evil trickery, he took away hundreds of my people."

"As I said, I am here on behalf of Zeus," I pleaded.

His anger rose even higher as he smashed an ornate vase on the floor and sped toward me with bulging eyes and a frothing mouth. "Tell me where my people have gone, or I will kill you myself," he shouted as his tirade continued.

It is well to remember that I am a practiced trickster and a famous actor in the Theater of Dionysus in Athens. I quickly took the sash from my waist, "Here," I said, handing it to him. "If you find that I am lying, you may strangle me as you wish."

A broad smile appeared on his face, followed by the most raucous laughter. With outstretched arms, he turned halfway about and commanded, "Come, sit. Let me hear more about this Zooz and why you have come to Van Lang."

We talked at length. Trays of colorful fruits and nuts, most of which I did not recognize, were set before us. Then, bowls of a fragrant soup called phở were offered, followed by roasted pig, spiced duck, and chicken feet in a sauce that I found most pleasing. To drink, there was rice wine and a heady liquor made from the roots of ginger plants. The royal garden was a palate of white, pink and yellow blossoms. The King called them jasmine, hibiscus and bougainvillea. These flowers and others filled the night air with an almost hypnotic aura.

I did my best to describe to the King, 5,000 years of Greek history, encompassing the defeat of the Titans, the advent of Zeus' reign as ruler of the world and cosmos, as we had known it until now, and the Underworld ruled by Hades and Persephone. Then, I focused on Cronus and his attempt to establish New Elysium in the Plain of Reeds. There was another burst of anger. "I must find this devil Cronus," the King intoned, "I have the forces to crush him, sacred warriors and militias, cavalry with elephants and horses. My riverine boats," meaning his navy, "can search every branch and river of the Mekong until he is found."

I tried as best I could to iterate the powers and "magic" of Cronus. He listened intently as we sipped tea flavored with lotus flowers, without the narcotic effects experienced by the lotus-eaters of Greek history. The pensive look on the King's brow made me wonder if my storytelling prowess had failed me for the first time, at least in my view. Although distressed, his movements were delicate. Holding the rim of the teacup with both hands and inhaling the fragrance in his nostrils, offering me sweets on a stunning plate of deep blue and white with the figure of a serpent or dragon in the center.

Closely examining the sash I had given him, he stood up in a regal manner. Holding my sash in his outstretched hands, he said earnestly, "Alagon, I believe what you have said, and I trust you. It is not for me to aid your cause. It is for our Father in Heaven, Ong Troi. Go now and tell Zooz these matters are in the hands of *our* god of heaven and earth. He will send a sign to all who have invaded his domain, and then there shall be justice."

We said our farewells as he walked with me through his magnificent garden and out into the brilliant sunlight of the palace square. As I made my way through the market stalls, with smells of spices and incense, I paused to watch the women filling their baskets with speckled fish, bananas, sweet potatoes, and melons. As I have seen in India, their children ran helter-skelter under banyan and breadfruit trees while their dogs lazed in the sun. When I reached the village gate, its red and gold ornamentations were ablaze with the setting sun. I turned for a last look at this strange yet familiar scene. I thought of the sun setting behind the Acropolis and my family in Plaka, close to the Theater of Dionysus. I am briefly overtaken by a longing to strut upon that stage, to hear the echoing applause of my beloved Athenians. My thoughts are like acanthus leaves driven by winter winds across the hills of the Agora. I was startled by the thought that a storyteller must resist the temptation of becoming the story.

Circling the path along the rice pond I had come from, I sensed it was time for another transformation. There were large birds, giant ibis, circling overhead as if looking for their accommodations for the night. I was among them all at once, floating in the hot, pulsating air from below. At the last glint of the crimson sunset, I sailed away for the Plain of Reeds.

Chapter 26
Camp Savage:
The Arrival of Heleron, Tanaurus and Arcelium

It seems there was a tradition in the Vietnam War of naming fire support bases and camps for fallen heroes. As the planning of Operation Golden Chariot progressed, there was a consensus among A-Team members to designate their base camp, "Camp Savage," as a tribute to Warrant Officer John Savage, the soldier who disappeared from FSB Cronus. Captains Galanis and Kellogg concurred. When Hermes and the three Legion commanders joined the others already at the new camp site, there was a large sign over the entry gate reading "Camp Savage, Home of the Legion of Aeneas."

Galanis and Ares greeted the visitors. As they entered the camp, Galanis commanded "present arms." The entire A-Team, which now included the three former POWs, saluted, followed by a loud cheer of *O tholmón miká* (Who Dares Wins!). The Legionnaires were briefly stunned. With a nod from Heleron, all three returned the salute by placing their swords across their breastplates. The team members broke ranks and surrounded the Legionnaire commanders, offering handshakes and greetings. With a signal from Sergeant Travis, the entire entourage moved toward a large tent sequestered in a nearby tree line. He had arranged for a modest repast of wine, cheese, cold cuts and fresh fruit. No one ever knew how Travis seemed to pull food, booze, and cigarettes *apo kapélo* (out of a hat).

The tent also served as a forward tactical operations center (TOC) where the planning for Operation Golden Chariot would commence in earnest. The Legion commanders were escorted to their places at a long table. There, they found uniforms, boots, combat gear and M-16s to facilitate their transition as members of the operational command structure. After offering formal greetings and welcoming remarks, Galanis made introductions all around. When he finished, Commander Heleron spoke for the first time, "Captain Galanis, Captain Key-log,"

Hermes politely interrupted the honored visitor, "Kel-log, Sir."

"Ah, Kel-log indeed," Heleron pressed on. "You and your team have received the highest praise from our King Hades and unbounded gratitude from our All-Father, Zeus."

He motioned to his commanders. "Commander Tanaurus and Commander Arcelium." They snapped to attention as Heleron continued, "are at your service." If it is possible to evidence a stern countenance and smile simultaneously, Heleron had mastered the technique. "As for me," he continued, "I pledge to you, all of you." He raised his cup of wine, swept his arm in a motion that recognized the team members seated around the table, and went on, "One thousand five hundred soldiers of the Legion of Aeneas will join you in the fight against Cronus and his devil-god Adecius. Under your leadership, we will prevail."

Once again, the Legionnaires were startled and perplexed as team members raised their cups to a raucous round of hooahs, the loudest of which came from the Six.

σ σ σ σ σ

It was time to get down to business. The ADC and Sergeant Travis rose from the table and approached three large boards set upon easels at the far end of the TOC. One contained a large color map of the Plain of Reeds. The other two held briefing charts regarding the operations plan and coordination points. As the briefing team was getting situated, Lieutenant Ares seemed to be replacing Sergeant

Diggs as the team's jokester. "Sergeant Hermes, isn't it time to introduce our visitors to their right to 'smoke' if they've got 'em?" Heleron and his commanders looked at one another, confused at the chorus of laughter that had broken out.

Hermes assumed his best drill sergeant persona as he replied, "Roger, Sir. Sergeant Damon, I believe you should do the honors." Continuing the joke, Damon jumped to his feet, passed a cigarette to each of the Legionnaires, and, as he was wont to do, snapped open the cover to his Zippo lighter and produced the familiar blue and yellow flame.

The Legionnaires recoiled at the sight as all of the team members lit their own cigarettes, exhaled and, in unison, let go with the standard "Shiiiit!"

Their fun ended abruptly. "Alright, knock off the grab-ass," the ADC barked as he gave the team his best Sergeant Travis look. "I'm sure our visitors are duly impressed with your professionalism." Dead silence. "Oh, by the way, Ares, you and Damon have just laughed your way into pulling LP duty for the next two nights."

Sergeant Travis chimed in, "Shiiiit." Immediately, all heads turned toward the briefing team, with eyes fixed straight ahead. This was a testament to another Army tradition. Never even look at those getting zapped with "the duty," or you might be next

Later, when Heleron and his commanders returned to Elysium, I learned about the substance of the briefing that took place that day at Camp Savage.

- The map identified the important geographic locations within the Plain of Reeds relative to operations planning. FSB Zeus, Camp Savage, FSB Cronus, the portal entrance, Dong Tam Base, etc.

- Camp Savage stood out, outlined in bold black lines with the label "Camp Savage. Top-Secret," emphasizing its covert nature to safeguard the true purpose of the operation. (More details on this will follow.)

- One chart depicted the command structure of Operation Golden Chariot. The Legion forces were to be divided into two "Regiments," a unit designation going back hundreds of years in the military systems of mortal kingdoms and republics.

Warrant Officer Athena would command *Pegasus Paraskinia (Wings of Pegasus)*. The *Elysian Sciritae* (Elite Corps) would be under the command of Captain Kellogg. Lieutenant Ares would command the *Dýnami Sfyiou* (Hammer Force) as the Legion reserve.

- Captain Galanis would be the Supreme Legion Commander, with Heleron as his deputy, along with selected team members as Legion staff.

- An advanced element of 300 legionnaires was to be hand-picked by Heleron and his commanders for a special assignment, 150 to each of the two regiments.

- Ares and Galanis would collaborate on assigning A-Team members to the regiments and command group.

- Operation Golden Chariot was scheduled to commence as soon as Camp Savage was fully operational. At the completion of the formal briefing, the participants were assigned to three- or four-member working groups to develop various portions of the operations plan. The usual details were worked out for logistics and supply, operational security, communications, intelligence gathering, and command and control. The results of those efforts were turned over to the ADC for inclusion in the Ops Plan. Yet, three over-arching issues remained. These would be addressed in the final hours of the briefing –*after* chow.

☙ ☙ ☙ ☙ ☙

During the usual "sumptuous" meal of C-rations, LRRP meals, coffee and pound cake, the visitors regaled the A-Team with stories of battles and heroes of Greek wars from millennia gone by. Heleron was delighted with his beanies and weanies in tomato sauce. Arcelium thoroughly enjoyed his chicken with rice LRRP until, as the team members looked on in anticipation, he emptied a quarter-bottle of Tabasco into the cooking pouch. The Six were cringing, some even turning away, recalling their introduction to the fiery sauce. Perez buzzed to the others, "Reminds me of those Saturday cartoons where hot peppers caused flames to come out of the big bad wolf's mouth and black smoke to billow out of his ears." However, in good Spartan fashion, the commander said not a word as sweat formed on his forehead and rolled down his crimson cheeks.

Coming to his rescue, Heleron swallowed the last of his Falstaff beer and surveyed those seated around the table, "Friends," he said emphatically. "My commanders and I want to assure you that the soldiers we are prepared to bring here to Camp Savage are the bravest sons ever produced by Greece. Those, like Meledon, who killed 300 in a single day of battle in the Peloponnese."

"And my good friend Vestia," Tanaurus interjected, "a hero of Thermopylae."

"And many others," Heleron continued, as he accepted a cigarette and light from Rob Salinas, "from Marathon, Salamis, Troy and on. Hermes, you know all of this."

"Indeed, but as you have heard here today, none of us, including these, ah, *us* Green Berets, has ever faced a battle as we must now fight."

The ADC stood, "Well said, Hermes. As I am about to explain, we have several issues to resolve before we can move ahead." Sergeant Travis placed another briefing board on an easel at the front. All eyes were directly focused on that chart as if the team were preparing for a night bombing run over Dresden.

☙ ☙ ☙ ☙ ☙

The issues that Tom Fredericks referred to were these:

1. How to build out Camp Savage by procuring tents, uniforms, weapons, combat gear, aviation assets, radios, food, water, and sundries for more than 1,500 combat troops? And how to ensure the secrecy and security of an extended combat operation?

2. Can Hades, Persephone and those of the Underworld facilitate the movement of the Legion from the Elysian Fields through the portal and into Vietnam without detection or delay?

3. Will the combined powers of Olympus and the Underworld prove effective in neutralizing the special abilities of Cronus and Adecius, preventing a potential defeat of the Legion on the battlefield?

When the briefings at Camp Savage ended, Heleron and his commanders needed to return to Elysium and begin preparations for getting the Legion to Camp Savage. Ares and Galanis were there to see them off at the gate where they had entered. Hermes stood ready to escort them through the portal under the invisibility cloak. Galanis marveled at what he was seeing; four souls, five, counting Ares, who stood beside him, had been plucked out of mythology and landed, of all places, in the AO of the 43^d Special Forces A-Team, his A-Team, in what they believed to be Van Lang, the ancient mythical world of Vietnam. This scene could have been any departure of comrades off on a dangerous assignment, but they all knew it wasn't that.

Ares spoke on behalf of the other team members. "We wish you a safe journey. We look forward to your return. Until then, please accept these gifts, compliments of Master Sergeant Travis." Each commander received a carton of cigarettes, a Zippo lighter, C-ration chocolates (referred to as "John Wayne bars" by the troops), and a small bottle of ouzo. As every A-Team member knew, "Don't ask where it came from."

"Here are your copies of the draft Ops Plan," Galanis said as he handed one to each commander. "I'm relying on you to complete the sections related to the resources and capabilities of your Legion. Hermes, here is a copy for you to present to Hades. Be sure to note any comments or questions he might have for us."

"Roger, Sir."

As a blood-red sunset spread across the Plain of Reeds, the tall grass, and even the waters of the Mekong, seemed to catch fire. Heleron's face took on a look of gritty determination as he noted somewhat wistfully motioning toward the setting sun. "This is a sign from the Gods. *I Moira Tous Einai Sta, Chéria* Mas."

Hermes translated, "Their fate is in our hands."

There were handshakes and bearhugs all around. Galanis and Ares looked on as the burning sun dropped below the horizon, and the heroes of Elysium disappeared into the darkness. With a single thought dominating his mind, Galanis addressed Ares in his most authoritative command voice, "Lieutenant, we need to get to work."

Chapter 27
The Ruse

It was another blistering hot and humid day across Vietnam as a Huey helicopter carrying three "VIPs" landed at Ton Son Nhut Air Base near Saigon. A military sedan took the mysterious passengers to a hotel in the city near the American embassy. Upon registering, the group leader identified himself as Arthur Jensen, an American businessman and contractor with USARV (US Army Vietnam), traveling with two business associates. They were all wearing military fatigues sans rank, insignia, and identification.

Once in their suite, the guests quickly relaxed, feasting on food and drink befitting their VIP status: lobster tails and tiger prawns steamed in Dom Perignon and Jack Daniels on the rocks. Mr. Jensen called their "business meeting" to order. "Gentlemen, let's review our plans for this afternoon's meeting." Those words were so officious that one of the associates, Mr. O'Neil, nearly choked on his drink. Mr. Clark, the third group member, simply smiled and took another bite of lobster dripping with butter.

The meeting they were discussing was scheduled to take place at the embassy that afternoon. Participants would include a top-level member of the Ambassadorial staff, senior Army and Air Force officers, and a civilian advisor to General William Westmoreland, Commander, Military Assistance Command Vietnam (MAC-V), the top military commander of the Vietnam War. The purpose of the meeting was classified as Top-Secret.

The three "Misters" moved to a sitting room with several large windows that offered a sweeping view of downtown Saigon. Thousands of mopeds, Honda scooters and cyclos were jammed together, competing for entry into several large roundabouts. Just across the square from the hotel stood Notre Dame Cathedral, a monument to six decades of French imperialism dating back to the 1880s. Sipping strong black coffee from a porcelain cup, Mr. Jensen pondered the question of how this current occupation by the US military would end. He finished his coffee, lit a cigarette, and turned to the two associates, "Time to suit up!"

Mr. O'Neil went to a large closet at one end of the room and slid the doors open to reveal three sets of clothing and accouterments. Thirty minutes later, they stepped out of the hotel into the choking, humid air on Dong Khoi Street.

Messrs. Jensen and O'Neil were identically dressed in black suits, white shirts, red ties, and highly polished Italian shoes. Mr. Clark was wearing a tropical tan suit, blue shirt, a Madras tie, leather-weave loafers, and a classic Stetson fedora. All three wore Ray-Ban Aviator sunglasses. Jensen and O'Neil carried identical black leather courier bags, minus the handcuffs.

As the group approached the embassy on Thong Nhut Boulevard, Mr. Clark took a table at an outdoor café and ordered a doppio espresso. Jensen and O'Neil continued on until they reached the main gate to the Norodom Compound. Looking through the iron gates they could see the embassy and the great seal above the door: *United States of America Embassy.* They presented their credentials to the Marine guards at the gate and waited. With their credentials verified and courier bags inspected, they were issued badges marked "Top-Secret, Escort Only." Several minutes later, their escort arrived at the gate, an attractive young woman in a navy blue Pierre Cardin business suit, Mikimoto Pearls and red pumps. "Mr. Jensen, Mr. O'Neil, I am Sara Davenport. Welcome to the embassy. I will be your escort while you are within the compound area. Please follow me."

I don't presume to understand what occurred in the embassy meeting or the nuances of diplomacy. Therefore, I can only recount what I was told by the three businessmen a short time after the event. They gathered in a secure conference room on the fourth floor of the embassy. Each of the participants introduced themselves, shook hands and took their seats. A military steward served coffee, tea, and finger cakes. A Deputy Ambassador opened the meeting. "Good afternoon, my name is Thad Wilson. On behalf of the Ambassador, welcome to the US Embassy, Vietnam." As he spoke, the muffled sounds of outgoing artillery could be heard in the distance, likely from Long Binh Army Base, some 20 miles from where they were sitting. No one in the room took note, as the Deputy Ambassador continued, "This meeting has been called at the behest of the Secretary of Defense. His instructions were to meet with Messrs. Jensen and O'Neil, at which time..."

There was a knock at the door. Mr. Clark had arrived late. "I'm very sorry to be late, not my style, believe me, but when the General commands your presence for a briefing– well, you all know the picture. Sorry, Mr. Wilson, please continue."

"Thank you. As I was saying, our two visitors are here from DC, Langly to be exact, to brief us on a Top-Secret mission. Mr. Jensen."

Jensen stood up as Mr. O'Neil retrieved two stacks of documents from the courier bags and began passing copies out to the participants. "Greetings from the Director." If they hadn't guessed before, the participants knew immediately that Jensen and O'Neil were agents of the Central Intelligence Agency (CIA). To relax his audience, Jensen loosened his tie and paused to light a cigarette. His demeanor was that of a no-bullshit operator as he moved to the head of the Titanic-sized conference table. Commencing with the briefing, he said, "Mr. O'Neil is passing out maps and documents related to a 'Company Operation' (a euphemism for the CIA) in Long An Province. As you will see in the handouts, you are directed to provide any and all support in furtherance of this operation."

The audience was listening intently, perhaps with the trepidation that comes with orders from the Secretary of Defense and Director of the CIA. The steward brought in cold drinks with several plates of cheese and fruit. A grizzled old Army Colonel sat at the far end of the table, chewing on a Cuban cigar, and snorting occasionally. Mr. Jensen continued, "Gentlemen, please open the map that Mr. O'Neil has provided, and I will walk you through the basics of our operations plan."

There was another knock on the door, and Ms. Davenport entered. The Deputy Ambassador appeared to be annoyed at the intrusion until Ms. Davenport announced, "Excuse me, Thad, there's a phone call for Mr. Jensen; it's the Secretary." Jensen reacted quickly, "Oh good, can we put him on the speakerphone?" Ms. Davenport acknowledged the request and stepped away. The call came through, and a voice crackled from 9,000 miles away.

"Hello, Art, are you there?"

"Yes, Mr. Secretary."

"Excellent, who do we have?"

"Deputy Ambassador Wilson, Army and Air Force senior staff, Mr. Clark from MAC-V and my partner, Mr. O'Neil."

"Hey, Ronnie," referring to Mr. Clark, "How the hell are you? Is Bill Westmoreland keeping you on your toes?"

Clark leaned closer to the speakerphone. "Mr. Secretary, I'm sure you know the answer to that."

The Secretary laughed, "Well, I know you're up to the task, or I wouldn't have sent you there. Look, I must get over to the White House in a few minutes, so I'll make this brief. The Director and I have informed the President of the critical nature of this operation, ah, Art, help me out."

"Operation Golden Chariot, Sir."

"Right. I simply want to say that there can't be any slack or pusillanimous pussyfooting, as a certain Vice President is wont to say, when it comes to this operation. Am I clear?"

The participants offered the only response possible, "Yes, Sir."

The call ended, and Mr. Jensen continued his briefing. The operations map depicted a large swath of terrain on the eastern edge of the Plain of Reeds. It was labeled Camp Savage-Notional Training Camp. However, the purpose of that training was "classified." This was a no-questions-asked mission. The Army was tasked with providing uniforms, weapons, combat gear, and materiel "necessary to sustain a fighting force of up to 2,000 soldiers for an indefinite period of operations. The Army and Air Force would jointly provide transportation and logistical support on an "on call" basis. Both would provide tactical air support upon request. In addition, the Army would respond to artillery fire mission requests from identified commanders.

In his summation, Jensen revealed that preparations for Operation Golden Chariot had been ongoing for several months. "The 43$^\text{d}$ Special Forces A-Team, augmented with certain classified elements, is in position at Camp Savage, as shown on your maps. They will have control of all phases of the operation, as directed by Captain Antonio Galanis, the Detachment Commander. The packets you received from Mr. O'Neil contain unit rosters, call signs, encrypted communications frequencies, and coordinate locations of friendly units, as well as potential enemy targets. On-station Air Force assets will be controlled by the Forward Air Controller identified in the unit roster, along with tactical frequencies for air-to-ground operations."

The briefing ended with a period of questions and answers of little note since Jensen invoked his best company-speak, "That remains classified. I'm not at liberty to discuss those issues. I'll get back to you on that. That's above my pay grade."

With that, the meeting whimpered to a close with handshaking and back slapping. The three "businessmen" heading back to their suite at the Continental Hotel on Dong Khoi Street were the only participants smiling on the way out the door.

𝕺   𝕺   𝕺   𝕺   𝕺

As the three entered the room, the full cast of characters involved in the ruse were present, offering cheers and toasts to the returning heroes. Each of the three principals had played their parts to perfection–proof of which was that Captain Galanis and the team back at Camp Savage were already receiving contact and coordination messages from Army and Air Force staff, various transportation and logistical commands, and Dong Tam Headquarters. Sergeant Perez had also intercepted an encrypted Top-Secret message from Air Force Command declaring Camp Savage a no-fly zone. All on the hush, hush, as they say.

ADC Tom Fredericks related to me how it all came together, "We needed a way to get the vast amount of equipment and materiel to support Operation Golden Chariot, and to ensure the security and secrecy of Camp Savage. After a full day of brainstorming, it was Sergeant Castor who brought up the Trojan Horse tactic that allowed the Greek army to capture Troy. Meaning, couldn't the A-Team use trickery to get what it needed? Captain Galanis picked up on the idea. It's what the military calls a ruse–making the enemy believe what you want them to believe and accept it as the truth."

Special Forces A-Teams are steeped in methods of deception and PsyOps (Psychological Operations). Their motto is "Persuade, Change, Influence." The case here was, whom do you want to persuade, change, or influence? All agreed it would have to be at the highest levels of the military and the government agencies responsible for operations in Vietnam. Rob Salinas had once worked in communications in the Langley Virginia headquarters of the Central Intelligence Agency (CIA). What other agency could mount clandestine operations on a grand scale without even informing the Department of Defense? Those at the "company" relished the idea of setting up rebel armies and private militias to protect American interests. The CIA offered the perfect cover. Department of Defense (DOD), through its Secretary, wielded absolute control over the military assets in Vietnam, subject only to the directions of the President. Supporting the CIA with a clandestine operation like Golden Chariot was not likely to land on the President's desk. That meant including the Secretary of Defense in the ruse. Sergeant Perez thought he knew a way. He could set up a communications link to DOD, which could be plugged into the comms network in Saigon. Making it appear that directions were coming directly from the Secretary.

Then there was the final piece. What was the one place where CIA operatives could bring Langley, DOD, and MAC-V together for a Top-Secret meeting? Galanis had the answer, the US Embassy in Saigon. A place where he was often summoned to provide intelligence summaries to higher commands. In particular, operations with a focus on the "hearts and minds" program, which DOD described as "winning the loyalties of the local population through emotional or intellectual appeals to gain strategic military advantages in a war setting." Sounded like something straight out of the Clausewitz playbook that Galanis learned at West Point, but that's a subject for another time. The embassy in Saigon would be the *élément central* of the ruse.

With his experience at Langley, Rob Salinas was selected to be Mr. Jensen. Tanned, square-jawed, with steel blue eyes, Damon became Mr. O'Neil, a true company man. Kit Carson had some amount of acting experience, so he was tagged as Mr. Clark. Sergeant Travis was the "Artful Dodger," sending Gage, Taylor and Osbourne into the streets and back alleys of Saigon to procure fake IDs, wardrobes, counterfeit "Top-Secret" documents, and the "businessman" setup at the Continental Hotel.

At 1400 hours that afternoon, Travis gave them the thumbs up to proceed to the embassy. Perez was on standby to place the call from DOD, with Sergeant Diggs playing the well-rehearsed role of the Secretary. By 1630, the three principal players had returned to the hotel, where, thanks to Stacey Diggs, they were greeted by the sound of Sergeant Barry Sadler blaring out the *Ballad of The Green Berets*, declaring them as "America's best." It was clear that the ruse had worked, but everyone knew the biggest challenges lay ahead.

Chapter 28
Time to Circle the Wagons

Support for Operation Golden Chariot soon began to resemble the Berlin Airlift. Tons of materials were arriving by the hour. Every team member, regardless of rank, was tasked with creating a training camp comparable to any at Forts Bragg or Benning. And it had to be done in days, not months. Perforated steel plating (PSP) had been laid down to create a runway suitable for Air Force C-130 cargo planes and Army transport helicopters. Crates of uniforms and combat gear, along with pallets of small arms ammunition, claymores, hand grenades and banded wooden boxes of M-16s and assorted other weapons, were rolled down the ramps of C-130s and stacked at the sides of the runway.

More sorties arrived with tents, cots and bedding, others with food, water, and mess-type equipment. The buildup was so rapid that it kept at least four members of the team busy day and night recording what had been received and where it was located on the ever-sprawling site. Fortunately, or perhaps unfortunately, the nature of the operation dictated that there would be no paperwork or bureaucracy to deal with. That sometimes left team members drinking from a firehose as they tried to inventory what they had received.

The next problem was manpower. "Top, how the hell are we gonna get this shit in place before the Legion arrives?" Sergeant Salinas opined to Bobby Travis. "Even the 'gods' are worn out!"

"Never fear, Rob; I've seen what the CIA can do when it's driving the train. The CO is back at Dong Tam right now, expecting to get the train moving at high speed in our direction."

Sergeant Pollux came into the TOC, where Travis and Santini were busy reviewing inventory sheets turned in from the night before. "Goddam, Top! There are three more C-130 sorties inbound in the next thirty minutes. We're already asshole deep with this stuff. Where do you want us to put whatever it is that shows up this time?" Pollux halted his diatribe, lit a cigarette, and stood there waiting for an answer. Both Travis and Santini did double-takes as they looked at one another, and then at Pollux, and then back at each other.

For a minute, it looked as if Master Sergeant Bobby Travis would be at a loss for words for the first time in his twenty-six years of military service. But he recovered as he turned to Salinas, "Rob, help me with this. Is that the little pissant recruit we had to wean off his momma's tit if he were ever gonna wear a green beret?"

"One and the same, Top."

"And we've turned him into a kick-ass troop that even John Wayne would be proud of?"

"I like to think that's due to my superior training skills."

All the while, Pollux stood nervously in front of two leaders he had come to trust and admire, wondering whether their observations were good or bad. His concerns were quickly dispelled when Travis let out with an extended belly laugh, hardly able to get his words out, "Pollux, I can't believe it. You are a bona fide fuckin', as the Marines say, 'salty troop'."

Pollux shuffled his feet and grimaced. "Is that good, Top?"

"That's more than good," Travis responded. "It means you deserve to wear that green beret. Pappy Zeus is gonna be real proud of you when you return to Olympus."

Pollux's face exuded his sense of pride. Without warning, he snapped to attention. "Thank you, Top, Sergeant Santini," he said as he dropped his salute, "but I don't want to return to Olympus. I want to stay here with the A-Team, as does my brother Castor. As you have said, we are STRAC Green Berets"–another sign of his total acculturation referring to an oft-use mantra: Super Trained Ready Around the Clock.

Pollux's jaw tightened, and his fists were clenched as if he was ready for hand-to-hand combat with Adecius himself. "We will never give up our Green Berets," he said in a raised voice and then caught himself, "Sorry, Top, but that is how we feel!"

Travis nearly swallowed the stub of his cigar as he leaned forward in his chair. "Jesus Christ, did I hear you right? You don't want to leave here?" Before Pollux could summon a reply, Travis continued, "And, by *we*, you mean you and Castor?" He stuttered to get the words out.

Pollux extinguished his cigarette in a C-ration can ashtray. His prior demeanor returned, "Ah, ah…I think there are others."

Travis stood up and positioned himself face-to-face with Pollux. "Now listen to me, soldier," Travis bellowed out in his best DI voice, with spit flying from his mouth with each word, "You'd better get those thoughts out of your head right now." Pollux was once again standing at attention with sweat pouring out from underneath his prized green beret. Travis caught his breath and continued, "If I hear of this again, I'll have Hermes wrap you in that magic blanket of his…"

Santini was enjoying the entire show and decided to join in. "Cloak," he said through his broad smile. Travis spun around and quizzed Santini, "What?"

"Cloak, Top. It's a cloak, not a blanket."

"Cloak, schmoke. This troop will find himself back in Hades polishing Legionnaire breastplates and pouring wine for the troops before the tide goes out in the Mekong."

"I don't think we can do that," Santini said with some trepidation. No need to get on Top's shitlist, but he needed to make the point, "Remember, they're on a 'quest,' and they brought along some very special weapons and much mojo!"

Travis returned to his desk, relit his cigar and began tapping his fingers on a stack of inventory reports. A minute went by, then two. Santini started squirming in his chair. "Well, Top," he said in a muted voice, "Whaddaya want to do?"

Still tapping his fingers with his gaze fixed on Pollux, Travis responded matter of factly, "We'll have to take this up with the CO and the ADC."

Sweat dripped off Pollux's chin and cascaded onto his boots after getting the Travis "look." Travis pounded one hand on his desk loud enough to make Pollux and Santini jump. Again, using the voice that could curdle the blood of any new recruit, the Top Sergeant shouted at Pollux, "As for you, get your raggedy ass out of my sight and don't say another word about this *to anyone*. Understand?"

"Yes, Top," Pollux answered while executing an about-face and bolting out of the TOC at a trot. Sergeant Travis just shook his head, puffed on his cigar, and went back to reviewing the inventory reports.

ɞ   ɞ   ɞ   ɞ   ɞ

The CIA speeding train hit Camp Savage just two hours after the colloquy with Travis, Santini and Pollux in the TOC. Suddenly, the sky above the camp was filled with Pythias' prophesized "giant green cranes." Six CH-47 "Chinook" helicopters were inbound. One by one, they slowed to a final approach and touched down with the elegance of the flamingos I loved to watch at the Agora marshes. My mother knew them well. I recall her instructions to me as I labored over my studies. "Alagon," she would say, "the Ancients have taught us to reflect on the symbolism of the flamingo, which includes beauty, balance, potential and romance." To those needing assistance in war, the Chinooks possess a certain kind of beauty, balance, yes, potential undoubtedly, romance, I'm not so sure.

Galanis was in the lead bird, as they were called, and he radioed to the ADC. "Tom, get every swinging dick out to the runway and take charge of the offloading. Otherwise, we're gonna have a clusterfuck of the first order!"

Fredricks laughed into his handset and responded, "What's new?" Fredricks ran to the TOC. "Top, get everyone out to the airstrip ASAP. We've got six inbound

Chinooks, and the CO is riding shotgun!" The ADC's words were like throwing red meat to a starving lion. Travis couldn't get out of the TOC fast enough, stopping only to retrieve the green beret that catapulted off his head as he raced to the airfield. "Perez, get your ass over here." Travis kept bellowing until Perez caught up to him halfway to the landing strip.

Out of breath, Perez coughed out, "What's up, Top?"

"Get on the horn and get every swingin' Richard down to the strip, and I mean double time."

Perez complied, and soon, team members came racing from every direction. Perez's radio squawked to life. It was Galanis. "This is 6, let me speak to Bobby."

Later, Sergeant Perez described to me what happened next. "Chinooks, we call them 'shithooks,' are very large helicopters that carry up to fifty-five troops or ten tons of cargo. The six that landed at Camp Savage that day brought 200 combat engineers along with the tools, equipment, fuel, and materiel to construct a fully operational training center to house, feed and train up to 2,000 officers and men. The mission was to get the work completed in 48 hours."

I thought that was impossible, but Sergeant Hopkins, our Senior Engineering Sergeant, clued me in. His father was with the Seabees in World War II. "That's what we call the 'Big War,' Alagon." And Hoppy heard hundreds of stories from his dad and those that were there in the Pacific about building 10,000-foot runways in a single day, docks and beachheads out of solid rock, and barracks compounds over filled-in swamps. Okay, I got the history lesson, but I still had to see if a full-blown training camp could appear in two days' time.

Well, it happened! Hoppy and Brick Osbourne, the two seasoned engineers, took charge of the work even before the last chopper was unloaded. At their direction, scores of young, muscled, and tanned engineers set upon the mountain of boxes, pallets, and containers lining the airfield. A hundred 20-man tents were swiftly rolled out, with 10-man crews promptly initiating their assembly in a spacious rectangular area at the camp's far edge. Following the tents, administrative tents, mess tents, and two substantial Quonset huts (metal buildings) were put into place for storing weapons, ammunition, and supplies.

Floodlights were erected, powered by huge growling generators, so that work could continue around the clock. By sundown of the second day, the entire A-Team was lined up at the airstrip, saluting the departure of the tired and sweaty miracle workers riding the birds back into the sky. Nothing left but the ribbon cutting for the new city they had created. Still, there was more work to be done.

The following morning, six more Chinooks landed and disgorged an Army Engineers Construction Company, a platoon of Signal Corps technicians, eighteen tons of timbers, cables, winches, tower components, generators, and a medium-weight rough terrain construction crane.

Before sunup the next day, a 125-foot wooden tower with cables, pulleys and winches was standing 100 yards from the training compound like an ersatz version of the Eiffel Tower. On the other side of the billeting area next to the TOC and storage buildings, the Signal guys had erected a 60-foot communications tower topped with satellite dishes and Top-Secret communications devices connected to banks of radios, two-way encryption radios, message intercept processors, and two 25-channel switchboards. For good measure, radar scanners at the mid-level of the tower provided radar tracking through two (classified) radar scopes in the comm center below.

Team members got a crash course in operating the various system components, after which the techs were heading over to the airfield to catch their ride home. Not before pointing to the seven boxes of specs and manuals in one corner of the tent and wishing us good luck with whatever it was that we were up to.

Chapter 29
Hades Takes Charge:
Chaos Reigns in the Underworld

After saying farewell to King Hung Vuong and the exotic environs of Van Lang and joining a congregation of ibis bound for the Plain of Reeds, I landed at the entrance to the portal for my journey back to Elysium. I suppose I should say my "flight" back to Elysium since I took the form of an ordinary bat. Unnoticed, I landed in a large almond tree in Persephone's Garden. I suppose I was distracted by the wonderful jasmine and lily smells and transformed back to my demi-god form while still among the branches. The snapping of my perch and the fall to the garden floor caught the attention of those in the palace. Before I knew what was happening, I was being dragged, and I mean roughly, into the presence of Hades. He raised a hand to my captors as the signal that they should desist from further attacks on my person. Sipping from his customary goblet of wine, "So, Alagon, you have returned," he growled.

I said nothing. It was my first opportunity to scrutinize those who had accosted me. I struggled for words.

"But, Uncle, brother of Zeus, these, these are the Furies!" It was impossible to curtail my astonishment. "What are the Erinyes doing here?" I had never seen them before in all my comings and goings to the Underworld. My good friend Homer wrote of them in his immortal Greek poem, *The Iliad*, as "the Erinyes, that under the earth take vengeance on men, whosoever hath sworn a false oath."

They are much more than that. These three goddesses took a human form but with the wings of a dragon or demon. They are merciless in seeking revenge and retribution for any crimes against persons or the "natural order." Hades sensed my trepidation, if not fear, of those three creatures that towered over me. "Alagon, much has changed since you were last here," the King said in a calm, steady voice, "I have summoned these goddesses and many others to heed my call for ridding my kingdom of the foul and evil threat of Cronus and Adecius." Now, the tone and tempo of his speech changed as he flailed his arms to and fro, "I have opened the gates of Tartarus and brought forth the Cyclopes and Hecatoncheires. The demon *Eurynomus* is now among us. Charon and Cerberus are again under my control." Stepping away from his throne and flinging his cloak to the floor, he strode into the garden. I followed.

As his anger reached a fever pitch, I was compelled to inquire, "I don't understand why Cheron and Cerberus would *not* be under your control, and…"

My inquiry was halted by the most menacing voice I had ever heard Hades conjure. "Cronus, Alagon, Cronus! He has disrupted the very fabric of the Underworld with his treachery. Even Styx and Lethe were coerced by threats of kidnapping and torture!" He tore a blood-red peony from its stem and crushed it between his gnarled hands. He began tugging on his beard so fiercely I thought he might uproot the entire growth from his majestic chin!

"Then, there are reports from Heleron, through his spies and informants," Hades continued, "that a cult has been growing within the Elysian Fields, called the Circle of Cronus!" His eyes burned red as he turned about and reentered the palace. A servant greeted him there with a cold towel and a large chalice of fermented nectar. I gathered that this frothing and flailing about had been going on for some time.

I had to find Persephone. She will calm him and inject some sense into his ranting. Just then, I remembered that Persephone had been granted permission to return to

Olympus to see her mother, Demeter, and carry the news from the Underworld. Hades nearly collapsed onto his throne with the cold towel covering his head. "It is done, Alagon," he said as he bolted upright and threw off the towel.

I grabbed a goblet of wine from a side table, quaffed it down, and reached for another. I approached the throne and placed one hand on his shoulder. "What can this mean?" I begged for an answer. "Are we to lose the Underworld to Cronus?" There was no answer, just a familiar gesture of his hand, signaling that he was to be left alone. I walked out to the garden that Persephone had so masterfully created and wished she were there in this hour of doom. I sat by the garden wall, demoralized and adrift, as I drank my wine.

𖤣   𖤣   𖤣   𖤣   𖤣

After returning from Camp Savage, Heleron and his commanders established a command center in the fashion of the TOC where they had been briefed by the A-Team. The command group was beginning to implement their portion of the Golden Chariot ops plan. They filled in the organizational chart as Stratigos (General) Galanis had directed. Tanaurus was assigned as the *Tagmatarkhis* (Executive Officer) of the Pegasus Regiment under Warrant

Officer Athena. Arcelium would have the same role for the Sciritae Regiment commanded by Captain Kellogg.

Each Regiment consisted of three *Lochoi* (Companies) with 250 *Hoplites* (soldiers) each, commanded by the best and bravest *Lochagos* (Captain). Interestingly, the commanders found this "modernized" scheme to be much like the *Taxis* armies they had fought with in many battles divided into smaller lochoi. In this instance, each Regiment would field 600 of the best soldiers ever to take to the battlefield.

With the organizational structure set, the first task was for each company commander to select 50 of their strongest and most seasoned soldiers to form what the ops plan designated as the advance party of 300 STRAC troops. Once assembled, they would be led by Hermes, Tanaurus and Arcelium through the portal and on to Camp Savage. Until that time, each soldier would receive instructions and rudimentary training, as outlined in the draft ops plan. Breastplates, shields, helmets, pikes and other weapons would not be needed. Swords could be carried by officers and leaders. Officers and soldiers were to carry a goatskin (what my Spanish friends call a botta) of water and one day's rations of their choice. Commanders were to issue each soldier one gold coin with the image of Zeus.

Since the three Legion commanders had returned from Van Lang in Army uniforms, along with M-16s and field gear, they were able to demonstrate the new clothing and equipment each Legionnaire would be issued at Camp Savage. Of course, Hermes was a trained and anointed Green Beret. He was able to lead the troops in some of the same drills the Six had gone through, particularly how to do pushups. He would leave the other elements of recruit indoctrination to Sergeant Travis and the A-Team DIs.

σ σ σ σ σ

As I slowly recovered from the shock of Hades' utterances, I began walking to the Elysian Fields and the encampment of the Legion of Aeneas, not knowing that Hermes and the Legion commanders had already returned from Van Lang. When I arrived to find a command center abuzz with activity, I located Hermes. I grasped him in a bear hug and kissed him on both cheeks. My fervent hope was that he could calm my fears and explain the dire circumstances Hades had conveyed to me. As I looked into the perfect Hellenic features of his face, I pleaded, "Dear brother, tell me what has happened in my absence."

He sensed my agitated condition and grasped my hand. "Alagon, what is it that troubles you so?"

"Surely it can't be true," I said as Hermes squeezed my hand in his to quell my shaking. I rambled on, "These beasts in the palace, kidnappings, torture, Charon and Cerberus threatened. Hades himself said, 'It is done.' We have lost the Underworld to Cronus. Your mission to Van Lang will mean death to you all!"

Hermes looked perplexed but sympathetic as he put his arm on my shoulder. "So, Hades didn't tell you what really happened?"

Now, I was perplexed. "Yes, as I have just told you. I, I heard him…"

As he stepped back to look directly into my face, Hermes halted my bleating pronouncements and, of all things, began to laugh loudly. Catching his breath, he said, "Alagon, you have misunderstood. Come, sit and pour some wine, and I will tell you what has happened."

Over more than a few goblets of wine, Hermes recounted the machinations that had taken place throughout Hades' kingdom after the King had received the news from

Van Lang delivered by SFC Hermes. Hades had paid particular attention to the request from Galanis and Ares that the Elysian Fields and the portal be secure to get the Legion of Aeneas to Camp Savage without delay or disruption. In a somewhat unprecedented move, Hades accompanied his wife on her journey to the Grove of Persephone, through which she would enter the mortal world and travel to Olympus.

Having seen her off, the King turned his attention to Cheron and Cerberus at the crossing of the River Styx. In that dark and dank corner of his Underworld kingdom, Hades was able to retrace the steps he had taken when he first entered the mystical realm of his kingdom. Once at the river, he could discern the demon-like face of Cheron emerging from the mist and acrid air that clung to the river like the caldera of Santorini. Cheron halted his barge, having returned from his delivery of freed souls to Cerberus on the far side.

Cheron knew why Hades had left his palace to travel to the far reaches of his kingdom. With a little prodding from his master, Cheron revealed the depth and perniciousness of what, up to that point, was perceived only as a "disturbance in the Underworld." It began when Cronus appeared at the river and threatened to throw Cheron and Cerberus into the depths of Tartarus for eternity if they did not carry out his orders and those of Adecius. The two guardians of the gateway to the Underworld had little doubt that Cronus could and would carry through with his threats.

What Cronus and Adecius had devised was a simple plan of stealing souls being delivered to Cerberus and taking them to the Asphodel Fields, thus avoiding the Plain of Judgement. All souls crossing the Styx would be evaluated by three judges, Minos, Aeacus and Rhadamanthus, based on their actions in life. The best went to the Elysian Fields, the worst to Tartarus, and most (the average) went to the Asphodel Fields to live out their eternal afterlife. By thwarting the judgment process, so to speak, Adecius and his cohorts took thousands of newly arrived souls directly to Elysium and from there to the Lethe River. Once there, they were "processed" as recruits for Adecius' army. They became Dog Soldiers, so named since Cerberus was instrumental to the success of the scheme. I had to interrupt the telling of the story. "But, Hermes, how does this account for the words and actions of Hades that I just witnessed? I thought he had gone mad!"

He replied, "Alagon, I know you are a great storyteller, but on occasion, you need to pause and let others tell the story in their own way." Surprisingly, this was a lesson I learned for the first time. He might as well have said, "Alagon, you are a great actor, but quit upstaging me." I poured more wine and said not another word as Hermes told the rest of the story.

Hades was not going mad; he was merely exhausted. After hearing the words of Cheron, he knew that his kingdom must be cleared of the pestilence that Cronus had set in motion. That's when he opened the Gates of Tartarus and summoned forth the horrible creatures from within. All manners of chaos ensued. Fire began spewing from below. The Styx and all the great rivers of his kingdom overflowed. Monsters and demons sought out all that could be implicated in Cronus' foul scheme and devoured them. Others were captured and thrown into the depths of Tartarus. The goddesses Styx and Lethe were freed from the dungeons where Adecius had imprisoned them. It was carnage run amok, orchestrated throughout by Hades. The Furies were always at his side to impose vengeance and retribution on the guilty and innocent alike.

👁   👁   👁   👁   👁

When the debauchery ended, Hades had accomplished the cleansing of his kingdom. From the Asphodel Fields to the palace grounds, not a single collaborator could be found. Cronus' Temple cum Fortress had been overrun, and its occupants stripped of their flesh by the Euonymus. Members of the Cult of Cronus were captured and eviscerated by the hecatoncheires. All of this happened until the Styx ran red with the blood of the conspirators. Finally, there was the matter of the portal.

The green and blacks and their Spartoi masters at Lethe and the portal entrance were eliminated by the Cyclopes and demons from Tartarus. What was left of their flesh and bones was thrown into the Styx. With its heavy machine gun, radios, and spotlights, which Cronus had once tried to conceal, the tower was seized by Heleron's troops and served as an observation post. Other Legionnaires armed with seized M-16s were dispatched to the Van Lang end of the portal to intercept any Dog Soldiers trying to enter. Barring any magic or tricks from Cronus, access to the portal was for friendlies only.

Hermes' face lit up with the glowing light of an Olympian. "So, you see, Alagon." I sat there, entranced by what he was saying. "When Hades said, 'it is done,' he meant the destruction of Cronus' henchmen and minions in his kingdom was complete."

"Then," I quizzed, "this means Cronus' and Adecius' access to souls from the Underworld to become Dog Soldiers is ended?"

Hermes' smile nearly blinded me as he responded, "Roger that!"

Chapter 30

Welcome to Camp Savage:
The Buildup Begins

With the portal secured, the advanced party of 300 elite troops departed Elysium. After humbly taking my leave from Hades, thankfully, the Furies were no longer hovering about; I decided to join the Legionnaires bound for Camp Savage. Hermes led the way, accompanied by Tanaurus. We arrived without incident, although I discovered that the flies and mosquitoes that pestered me as a water buffalo, tortured me, to be more precise, loved to torture mortal beings just the same. As the lead elements of our "party" sighted the camp gate with its sign declaring the camp to be their own, a cacophony of cheers, chants and foot stomping ensued. The A-Team was assembled at the gate. Ares fairly drowned out the entire 300 with his piercing battle cry. The rest of the A-Team followed with the now traditional chorus of hooahs. At that point, being a demi-god had no meaning. I was awestruck. My heart was pounding, and tears welled up in my eyes as I realized the final stage of the quest of the Six was about to begin.

SFC Hermes introduced me to his Green Beret comrades as I proceeded down the length of a receiving line worthy of a visitation by Alexander the Great himself. I was happy to reconnect with the Six and thoroughly impressed with Captain Galanis and his team. I believe Hermes could have forewarned me, but I suppose my reputation as a trickster preceded me. Sergeant Damon was the last in line. He placed what I learned was a cigarette in my mouth and lit it with something called a Zippo! There was laughter from the entire team as I fumbled with a smoldering tobacco stick. At some point, I vowed to show him what trickery was all about. However, I should report that I enjoyed what they called a Winston and was honored to receive my very own Zippo, which took me several days to master.

I was escorted to the TOC, where I learned about every aspect of the training the 300 would undergo, as well as the overall battle plan. I have set forth all of this below, relying upon maps, ops plans and other documents that ensure the story's accuracy as related herein.

჻ ჻ ჻ ჻ ჻

The camp had been divided into two large training areas. One on either side of the runway. The area furthest from the TOC and "Tent City," as it was called, belonged to Athena and her Wings of Pegasus Regiment. This was the area where Army engineers had constructed the tall tower with its cables and pulleys. For what purpose I could not divine. I was further perplexed by the large sign at the entrance, upon which was painted what looked like a large, white crocus, upside down, with strings or ropes attached, surrounded by eagle wings. An image of Pegasus was emblazoned below, with the words, **Death From Above**. I spoke briefly with Athena, and she encouraged me to return to the area later that day when training was to get underway.

Next, I visited with Captain Kellogg, whom I had met briefly in the receiving line. We spoke at some length as the 150 Legionnaires assigned to his Regiment were being organized into rows and shouted at by several members of the A-Team. "Alagon, welcome to our regimental training complex," he said as he shook my hand with the grip of Hercules. "You're welcome to observe our training, but as you can see, we're just getting organized."

As he spoke, I noticed a large painted sign similar to that at the other training area. This one had a white background on which was painted a curved symbol, much like a rainbow, only black, with the word RANGER

inscribed in yellow. Words below the symbol professed
Rangers Lead the Way. I was sure to learn more about what
it meant, but in the meantime, Captain Kellogg evidenced a
sense of pride as he showed me around the complex.

"Generally, this is state of the art," he said as we
walked through an "obstacle course." "This is our firing
range for training with these," he continued as he held out
the weapon he was carrying. Pointing to the far side of the
training area, "and those tents are for classroom training on
tactics, reconnaissance, communications." He stopped
abruptly. "I'm sorry, Alagon, I've just been giving you my
best Fort Benning Ranger School VIP tour, and you probably
don't know what the hell I'm talking about." He was correct,
but I noted the preparations being made to strike at Cronus
and his army of stolen souls and vicious mercenaries.

As I returned to the TOC, a gigantic gray beast
appeared in the sky and several more. They were coming
straight at me. I presumed they planned to devour me. One
by one, they touched the ground and rolled down the metal
plates of the runway. A-Team members bolted out of their
tents and raced toward the roaring and smoking behemoths
with what I thought was an intention to attack and kill them.
Castor was one of those running by. He stopped to reassure

me that these were friendly "birds" delivering supplies. Nonetheless, I did a fast trot back to the safety of the TOC.

𝕺   𝕺   𝕺   𝕺   𝕺

That evening, I attended a Commander's Briefing along with the Legion commanders and officers of the 300. There were maps and charts all about. The ADC stepped to the front and quieted the group. "Good evening, I'm Warrant Officer Tom Fredricks, Assistant Detachment Commander. You're probably wondering why I called you all here tonight." There was light laughter and murmuring as Fredricks continued, "Especially those of you who came all the way from Elysium just to be here with our team–we're the ones with the funny green hats." The group roared with laughter. As an accomplished actor, I must say I couldn't have done a better job of warming up the audience. Then, it was time to get to work as Fredricks unveiled one of the charts on an easel at the front. "This is…" He was using a pointer to focus attention on the chart, which read Operation Golden Chariot, D-43, "the most important information to know right now. It means we have just over one month to D-Day, the day we will strike at Adecius and his Dog Soldiers." All of the Legionnaires stood, cheering and stomping their feet. A clear sign that they were ready for battle.

As they sat down, Fredricks summoned the two regimental leaders, Athena, and Kellogg, to come forward. Athena had a large green sack strapped to her back and a pot-like helmet fixed tightly on her head. Kellogg was accompanied by Lieutenant Tran, the hardcore RVN Ranger. Both wore full-face camouflage, tiger fatigues, soft Ranger-style patrol caps and black jungle boots. They carried an assortment of weapons and gear–assault rifles, compasses, night scopes, one 40mm grenade launcher, first aid packs, and hand grenades. Both wore .45 caliber pistols as sidearms. All of the weapons and gear were taped or wrapped with cloth to eliminate reflection and noise.

Fredricks continued his presentation. "My three demonstrators represent the purpose for bringing you and your men here before the main body arrives at Camp Savage." The three props, we might call them, came to attention and playfully saluted the ADC. "You will undergo specialized training, very difficult training, I might add," he announced as his facial expression and demeanor became that of the meanest Tactical Officer of the Fort Benning Ranger Course. "Those of you assigned to Pegasus Paraskinia, commanded by Warrant Officer Athena and assisted by her Executive Officer Tanaurus, will become *Strike Force Alpha (Airborne)*."

Athena turned ninety degrees so that her large backpack was facing the ADC. Fredricks tugged on a cord hanging from the pack, and what I later learned was a white silk T-10 standard Army parachute billowed out of the pack and landed at his feet. Athena dropped the pack and turned to face the audience. It was an electric moment. What could be more powerful than the Goddess of War and Green Beret Officer Athena assuming such a command position? Even in full combat dress, her magnificent beauty was still on display. She reached down, took hold of a corner of the chute, and held it up to the now spellbound group. "This, gentlemen, is *Death From Above*." Members of the A-Team stood, saluted and shouted in unison, "Airborne, Sir!"

Not to be outdone, Captain Kellogg stepped forward. "Thank you, Warrant Officer Athena, very impressive." The standard round of hooahs ensued. "But" he continued, "Everyone knows that," his voice boomed out, "Rangers lead the way!" Once again, the A-Team stood en masse and shouted, "Rangers lead the way, Sir!" Without warning, Lieutenant Tran approached Kellogg from behind and executed what the Army calls a "rear takedown and strangle" move. Others call it a chokehold, a silent form of killing your enemy. Kellogg was on his back on the ground. Tran lay on his stomach with his forearm across Kellogg's throat. With his hands locked together, Tran began to apply pressure, which, if continued, would crush the enemy's windpipe. Kellogg began clapping his hands, which in training is a signal for the attacker to release his grip.

The combatants stoop up. "Soldiers of the Elysian Sciritae," Tran said, "This is just one lethal way to neutralize your enemy, the Dog Soldiers." He was interrupted as the Sciritae Legionnaires stood, chanting, "Ranger! Ranger! Ranger!" and stomped their feet.

Tran restored order and continued, "You will learn many more as part of Strike Force Bravo." Chaos erupted once again.

All went silent as Captain Galanis came forward. After Athena and Kellogg had spoken, it was easy for the "newbies' to recognize that Galanis was wearing parachute "jump wings" on his chest and a Ranger "tab" on his left sleeve. Signaling, I suppose, that he would have no favorites in the unit competition that seemed to have spontaneously broken out. "Fellow warriors," he began, "friends, let me add my gratitude to you as leaders and sons of Zeus for participating in what we in Special Forces call 'hell week'– the worst week of training our instructors could dream up. I must warn you; you are all about to experience a 'hell month.' Unfortunately, that is all the time we have to prepare for the coming battle." The silence was palpable, as many shook their heads in acceptance of the challenge. Others stiffened their backs and flexed their contoured muscles in an apparent rush of adrenaline.

Galanis motioned to Ares, who was standing at the far end of the tent. "Lieutenant Ares, come on up here." As Ares proceeded to the front, Galanis said, "Not long ago, knowing the dangers we both faced from Cronus and his army, Ares and I agreed to form a single fighting force as Green Berets. Now, you all have joined forces with us to defend the Underworld and Olympus."

There was loud cheering as Ares began to speak," Brothers of Zeus, defenders of Olympus and the Underworld, I ask only these things. Will you attack our enemies without mercy, as you know I have done as your God of War many times? Will you spill their blood into the five rivers of the Mekong? And may we Six, sent here by the All-Father, have the privilege of leading you back to the Elysian Fields, once again, as the heroes of Greece?" One at a time, each Legionnaire rose, came stiffly to attention, made a fist and placed it over his heart, meaning *I pledge my heart and my life to this just cause*. There weren't going to be any quitters in this crowd.

ʘ   ʘ   ʘ   ʘ   ʘ

Strike team training was to begin the following morning. Galanis and Ares met after the Commander's Briefing to determine A-Team assignments. Several hours later, Sergeant Travis posted the assignment list in the TOC. The oldest member of the team at age 43, Top had seen it all before, as a 17-year-old Private in the Korean War, and just three years before his A-Team assignment to Vietnam, he deployed to someplace called the Dominican Republic as a paratrooper with the 82[d] Airborne Division. I learned all of this while sitting in the TOC smoking cigarettes (yes, I got the habit) and drinking coffee while Bobby—he insisted I call him Bobby or Top—told war stories worthy of the Iliad. I sensed the current period of anticipation of the coming battle made him nervous as a chariot horse at Thermopylae. Proving my point, he growled like the wild boar of Calydon, "Perez." No response. "Perez, goddammit, get in here, fuckin' now." Perez nearly stumbled as he shot through the entrance to the TOC.

"Here, Top."

"Where the hell have you been?"

"Outside."

"I know that smartass. Can't you hear me calling you?"

"Yes, ah, I did hear you, Top, but I, ah…"

"Ah, what?"

"I was taking a dump!"

After Perez had left, Bobby explained what Perez was doing, a quite interesting euphemism. So, old Top continued addressing Perez, "Okay, dufus. I just posted the A-Team assignments. Get on the horn and tell those sorry-ass excuses for Green Berets to get over here and check the list–if any of 'em can read."

The assignments were these:

- Galanis, Heleron, Fredricks, Travis and Perez were assigned to the Command group.

- Sergeant Alexander, the Air Force FAC, temporary assignment to the Command group pending field assignment.

- Gage, Diggs, Osbourne, and Pollux were assigned to the Elysian Sciritae Regiment.

- Taylor, Santini, Hopkins and Castor were assigned to the Pegasus Paraskinia Regiment.

- Salinas and Rogers were temporarily assigned to Task Force Alpha as Master Parachutist Instructors.

- Ares, Hermes and Damon were assigned to the Command Reserve.

Ares told me that these assignments were meant to achieve a balance between the two regiments. Each would have a weapons sergeant, a medical sergeant, an engineering sergeant, and a member of the Six as liaison to the Legionnaires' commanders.

ʘ　　ʘ　　ʘ　　ʘ　　ʘ

Tom Fredricks was in the TOC until well after midnight. He was puzzling over several maps and planning documents. The Operations Center was staffed 24/7, so Kit Rogers replaced Sergeants Travis and Perez for radio watch and SFC Salinas as Officer of the Day (OD). I could listen in on what was going on, radio chatter and SITREPs being called in. In between naps, I learned that there were other night duties being performed by team members. As Sergeant Santini explained, "Camp Savage is well hidden. Even if Adecius' forces can spot the airlift and resupply missions, they can easily be disregarded as 'local activity,' if you know what I mean?"

"Sorry, Sergeant Santini."

He interrupted. "Rob, you can call me Rob."

"Okay, Rob, what does it mean, 'local activity?'"

"You mean no one has told you? There's a shooting war going on here in Vietnam between two opposing armies, North and South. From what Athena has told us, it's a lot like the Titanomachy between Cronus and the Olympians."

More puzzled than ever, I inquired, "Then why are you here? Why is the A-Team here?"

"Alagon," he replied with a wry smile, "You'll have to stay around here several more years to get an answer to that."

We returned to his original discussion of Camp Savage and Operational Security. It was still necessary for team members to set up listening posts at night and send out five-man patrols to protect against surprise attacks. The ADC wandered over to the coffeepot, which also operated 24/7 and then joined in on the discussion, "Rob, that's part of what I've been fretting over. We haven't seen or heard anything from Adecius, or his Dog Soldiers since Team Artimus raided their base camp."

Santini handed me another cup of coffee, drew one for himself and then replied to Fredricks comments, "I agree that's a big problem, Tom. What's your plan?"

"I've already talked this over with the CO and Captain Kellogg. I want Lieutenant Tran to organize a long-range patrol to get as much poop on the bad guys as possible before I finalize the intel annex to the ops plan."

I sat up abruptly in my chair, spilling my coffee. I was thinking, first, *it's taking a dump, now it's poop*. And I thought this was some sort of advanced civilization! Fortunately, the ADC set me straight. It means getting inside information. Maybe like my visit with King Hung Vuong in Van Lang. Seems like Fredricks was way ahead of me on that. "I've heard much about that, Alagon, and I think we can use your talents." My mouth suddenly got very dry, as if I were about to go on stage at the Theatre of Dionysus in front of an audience of 25,000. With a somewhat devious smile on his face, Fredricks continued, "Well, we'll leave that up to Lieutenant Tran." He paused as if pondering his next words and lit a cigarette. "I also think we should use the former Dog Soldier. What's his name?"

Santini looked shocked. "Portellis. Do you think he's a genuine chieu hoi?" Without my asking, the ADC explained it means "open arms" when an enemy soldier surrenders and then switches sides. Fredricks sat on a corner of his desk. "I asked Top the same question, and he's okay with it. That's good enough for me," he said in between yawns, "I gotta' get some sleep. We can continue this in the morning."

Santini stood up. "Roger, Sir. Good night." I bid them both a good night and left the TOC, heading for my assigned tent. The moon was full, casting shadows of the tents in Tent City and the Legionnaire guards walking the perimeter. A cooling breeze began blowing across the airfield. Looking toward the airborne training area, I saw Athena and Galanis silhouetted in the moonlight, standing by the jump tower. I was too tired to join them and went off to bed.

Chapter 31
Tran's Raiders: Reconnaissance in Force

I was constantly hearing strange military terms being discussed, which I would need to ask a team member to explain. ADC Fredricks got his wish to send a long-range patrol to FSB Cronus to get an update on what the enemy forces were doing or not doing. This he called a *Reconnaissance in Force*, which the US Army describes as a "deliberate combat operation designed to discover or test the enemy's strength, dispositions and reactions or to obtain other information." Rather than head-on engagement with the enemy, a series of probings are initiated in the enemy's area of operations (AO). Also, as the ADC had requested, Lieutenant Tran would constitute and lead the reconnaissance force. Dubbed *Tran's Raiders*, the force needed to be able to move rapidly and silently. Keys to their success were stealth and surprise, which Lieutenant Tran characterized as, "Get in and get out before the enemy knows you are there."

After completion of the recon mission, members of the force immediately resumed their duties with strike force training. Therefore, it was difficult for me to get information on what had taken place. But I did manage later to get a copy of Lieutenant Tran's After-Action Report:

There were two targets of our reconnaissance: the portal and FSB Cronus. It was most important to learn how Cronus and Adecius reacted to the so-called cleansing of the Underworld and, particularly, the seizure of the portal by Legionnaire forces.

With respect to FSB Cronus and its surroundings, we had planned multiple probings of their perimeter, starting with the elimination or capture of soldiers manning listening posts or observation posts. This would be followed by an infiltration of the base itself.

To accomplish the operation, I personally selected nine personnel for the mission, making a total force of ten, four of which had previously been inside FSB Cronus, myself, Sergeants Hopkins and

Carson and the former Dog Soldier Portellis. Hermes and Castor were the best choices for reconnoitering the portal. Weapons Sergeant Taylor was tasked with assessing the enemy weapons capabilities. Medical Sergeant Diggs would be needed if we suffered any casualties. Finally, I chose Legion commanders Tanaurus and Arcelium. It was a risky move to involve two senior commanders in such a dangerous mission, but Captain Galanis and both commanders agreed they were our most valuable asset for evaluating the disposition of enemy forces, weapons placement and command structure relative to the mindset of the opposing "general" Adecius.

Having spent years traveling in and out of the Plain of Reeds, I could map out our route of march–four kilometers from Camp Savage to the Bassac River, twenty kilometers upriver on sampans to our point of departure (PD). Hermes and Castor would follow a five-kilometer trail to the portal entrance while the rest of us trekked overland (using the term loosely in the Mekong Delta) to reach FSB Cronus.

It was dusk when we arrived at the PD. Hermes and Castor departed with instructions to meet the other team members at prearranged coordinates within four hours. If, for any reason, there was trouble or a need to abort the mission, I would fire a single red flare, and the entire force would rendezvous at the departure point.

I led the remainder of the force to a small clearing a kilometer from FSB Cronus. We could see lights and hear noise from time to time. There would be no problem with finding the objective. We dispersed into the tall grass surrounding the clearing and waited for the arrival of Hermes and Castor.

When Hermes and Castor arrived, they quickly reported that there had initially been a clash between Dog Soldiers and the Legionnaire guards at the portal, but all was currently quiet and under control. That seemed to indicate that Adecius and the leaders of his army had abandoned the idea of trying to reenter the Underworld. They now found themselves isolated in Van Lang.

There were only four hours left before sunrise. It was time to get in and get out. The reconnaissance began with three probes of the perimeter, looking for a point of entry. Amazingly, there were no LPs or OPs set up, meaning security was lax, or should I say non-existent. We soon discovered that a gate had been built on the far side of the compound to provide access to their firing range and training area outside the perimeter. Sergeant Hopkins cut through the fence next to the gate. One or two at a time, we stepped through the wire and began to spread out, acting as if we belonged there. We allotted one hour for observation and intelligence gathering. Those of us who had been inside the compound previously were able to guide the others, particularly the Legion commanders, on where to go without drawing attention.

Portellis was by far the most inconspicuous member of the force. He blended in as if he had never left. He later reported that there were so many new recruits and soldiers in the compound that he could walk freely throughout the base. The remaining members went about their individual tasks, counting the number of living quarters, ammunition stockpiles, heavy weapons, etc. At my request, Hermes donned Hades Helmet and used his invisibility to get an accurate headcount of Dog Soldiers, Spartoi, and tattooed slaves. Hopkins and I followed the perimeter fence around the area where I and others were held as prisoners. The building was empty and unguarded. As we were leaving the area, a group of Dog Soldiers and Spartoi passed by, grunted, and walked on, assuming we must be new recruits. The fact that they were seriously intoxicated might have helped.

Having synchronized our watches, everyone knew when it was time to rendezvous at the gate where we had entered.

We gathered just outside the perimeter fence, and I took a headcount. All accounted for except Portellis. No one had seen him since we had entered the compound. His absence was concerning, but in accordance with my instructions, we would only wait 10 minutes for stragglers. The purplish glow on the horizon signaled that sunup was minutes away. We waited. Still no Portellis. I gave the signal to saddle up, and we set off for our original point of departure. When we arrived there, I thought we might see Portellis waiting for us, thinking he misunderstood the plan and my instructions. For security reasons, we kept moving until we reached the bank of the Bassac River where we had left our sampans.

At that point, we were far enough away from FSB Cronus to break for morning chow. More importantly, we needed to conduct an immediate debrief of what we had seen and heard while our collective memories were still fresh. I took out a checklist I had prepared and began taking notes.

1. Portal–Secured by Legionnaires from Elysian Fields. Hermes and Castor interviewed the guards. All Dog Soldier attempts to access the portal had ceased. All parties are ready for the departure of the Legion of Aeneas for Camp Savage.

2. Security–Hopkins, Carson, and Diggs all reported no security or activity outside the perimeter. No boobytraps or detection devices. Guards posted in watch towers, mostly sleeping. Gates lightly secured. The headquarters building is heavily secured.

3. Infrastructure–Hopkins and Carson reported size of the compound has more than doubled since Team Artemus had rescued POWs. Troop housing, mess facilities and training areas greatly expanded. Perimeter security consists of 12-foot sandbag walls, topped with 6 feet of barbed/razor wire. No firing ports or gun emplacements were noted.

4. Weapons and Ammunition–Taylor counted more than 10 ammunition/weapons

stockpiles. Estimates 4,000 to 5,000 small arms.
Only 300 heavy machine guns are visible. Two
large buildings could hold several million rounds
of small arms ammo, plus grenades, etc. Unable
to access.

5. Military Assessment–Tanaurus and
Arcelium needed more time to compare notes, as
it were, but agreed that what they observed was
familiar. Loose command structure (no one
seemed to be in charge), the buildup of troop
strength versus other important resources, and a
general siege mentality. All would seem to rest on
the invincibility of Cronus. Hermes concurred
with their report by adding his estimate of troop
strength, which by his measure had grown to
more than 5,000 troops, including more than
1,000 Spartoi. Very concerning news.

We stowed our gear in the sampans
and were about to board when the sound of
someone or something crashing through tall
grass to our rear caused everyone to hit the
deck and assume a ready position. The grass
parted, and there was Portellis, out of breath
and dragging an unconscious Spartoi soldier
behind him. We needed to find out what the

hell had happened, but no time for a debrief. We scurried into our boats and headed downriver. The Spartoi prisoner was secured with ropes and placed in a boat with Hopkins and Taylor. Our next stop was Camp Savage.

Chapter 32
Athena Et Galanis

As the scribe of this story, I need to reveal all that I know took place. I refer now to that moonlit night when I observed Athena and Galanis standing by the jump tower. I had forgotten the moment until sometime later when Athena walked into my tent and confided in me.

"This is a modified jump tower," Galanis was briefing Athena on how airborne training would proceed. This was important information to absorb since she would be the first to receive the training. Galanis reinforced the concept that she needed to *lead by example.* "Standard jump towers are more than twice as high," he said as he walked to the base of the tower and pointed to the various pulleys and cables that would be used to hoist the trainees and their parachutes to the top.

"Can you show me?" Athena asked. Evidencing her excitement, Galanis agreed. He took a harness from a nearby bin, helped Athena put it on, and tightened the straps.

"This cable system will pull you to the top. When the chute reaches the release," he was pointing, "up there, you'll begin the descent, landing over here. This is where you will execute a PLF."

"PL what?"

"Sorry. PLF stands for parachute landing fall, the move you execute as your feet make contact with the ground."

"Why would you want to fall? I can jump a great distance, like from a high garden wall and land on my feet."

"Maybe because you are a goddess."

"No, now I am a Green Beret!"

"Still, I'd better show you how it's done." This was spoken as he climbed onto a four-foot-high platform in the middle of the training area. "Like this," he shouted to Athena as he stepped off the platform. He hit the ground below, ankles and knees tight together, bending his knees as a shock absorber and then rolling to the right as his body hit the ground.

"Now, I will PLF," she said as she scrambled onto the platform.

Galanis was standing below, suddenly immersed in the radiance of her face and the aura of the moon behind her. He recovered and intoned, "Okay, I'm sure you're a quick study, even for a Green Beret."

She jumped using the technique Galanis had shown her. But she failed to rotate her body quickly enough and hit the ground with an audible thud. She was stunned more than hurt. Galanis offered her a hand up. As she took his hand, something like an electric shock, although altogether pleasant, passed through his body. Athena appeared to float up from the ground. They were not touching, yet it seemed to Galanis that they were embracing. She touched his face and faintly whispered, "Galanis, you are a god of Olympus."

As she looked into his azure eyes, Galanis' thoughts were spinning out of control. As if in a dream, he was walking through the Temple of Athena atop the Acropolis with the flickering lights of Athens below. Next, he was at Hadrian's Gate, surrounded by nymphs and fairies of great beauty. They were rubbing him with fragrant oils and stroking his long blond hair. They escorted him to a palace where he was offered wine and pomegranate seeds. There was thunder and lightning as Zeus appeared before him. He bowed and kissed Galanis' hand but spoke not a word.

Athena dropped her hands from his face, and they kissed. Not the kiss of lovers but a kiss that made them one. Still in silence, they began walking toward Tent City with their hands clasped tightly together. As they approached the runway, its metal plating was ablaze with the light of the sacred full moon. Athena stopped and tried to explain what had happened. "You recall when we first met?"

Galanis nodded. "How could either of us forget?"

"You walked out of the tall grass," I said, "Galanis, you are Greek."

"And so I am."

"In that instant, I knew that you are a son of Olympus. You are a god like me. You have but one name, like all the gods and goddesses. You are Galanis. You deliver us from harm and ruin."

Galanis tried to gently explain, "Athena, we have no idea why our two worlds have collided. It's certainly true that I am Greek, but I was born to two wonderful Greek parents in Chicago, Illinois. Not that you would know where that is."

"Let me interrupt," Athena said with a look of solemnity Galanis had never seen before, "You're A-Team has joined forces with six gods in a quest to save the Underworld and Olympus. You trained us and awarded us Green Berets. You and my brother Ares have molded us into a single fighting force. And yet, you believe being born in Chicago means you can't be a son of Olympus."

They walked on and would soon part for the night. As they reached Athena's tent, she uttered the most provocative words that Galanis would ever hear. "You must accept that you are my brother, my lover and my commander." Neither of them knew that Hang Nga, the Van Lang goddess of the moon, was watching them. The moon streaked across the sky like a giant meteor and disappeared into the darkness of the night sky. Somehow, Athena and Galanis knew at once that this was a message from Ong Troi, the God of Heaven. Something about their coming together had awakened the gods of Van Lang. Was this a welcome or a warning?

Chapter 33
Crunch Time

In just five days after the embassy meeting in Saigon, Camp Savage was up and running. The 300 elites from the Legion were outfitted with uniforms, weapons and combat gear, and the Legion commanders were briefed and ready for action. That left just 40 days to prepare for a combat assault unlike any other. The ADC, Kellogg and Athena worked non-stop until the details were hashed out.

Strike teams Alpha and Bravo would have three weeks for their specialized airborne and ranger skills training. One week after training commenced, the main body of the Legion would arrive at Camp Savage for outfitting and indoctrination as part of their three-week intensive training period. Thanks to Sergeant Travis and his DIs, each of the three training units would have its own hell week. Physical training, marching and drill, harassment, sleep deprivation, and more physical training. In the first week of airborne training, trainees would be taught to execute PLFs and become familiar with the standard Army T-10 parachute and how to pack them. The second week would focus on the jump tower. Standard training incorporates the use of a 34-foot tower and occasionally a 250-foot tower. The 100-foot tower at Camp Savage was more than adequate to meet the training requirements. A mock door trainer is used to simulate the mass exiting of aircraft. There are other skills to be learned—how to steer your chute, recover from being dragged on the drop zone from high winds, and use of the reserve chute. The third week is jump week. The ADC arranged for the use of C-130s and Chinook helicopters in hopes of getting all 150 students airborne qualified.

The Ranger Strike Force had their hell week with grueling PT, endless hours on the obstacle courses, marching, and drilling. Captain Kellogg had not forgotten those weeks he spent in the piney woods and swamps of Georgia and Florida, nor the pride he felt when he was one of the forty percent of students to graduate and earn that coveted Ranger tab. He and Lieutenant Tran, who probably became an RVN Ranger under worse conditions, had no trouble pushing their trainees to the limit. The tall grass, mud and swamps of the Plain of Reeds offered a perfect setting for forced marches without food or water, long-range patrolling and navigation, and always more physical training. As the two leaders observed the results of hell week, they were optimistic that there wouldn't be a sixty percent dropout rate among their seasoned warriors.

$$\circ \quad \circ \quad \circ \quad \circ \quad \circ$$

Once the two training cycles got underway, the ops team turned its attention to the anticipated arrival of Heleron and his Legionnaires. Despite the rigors of airborne and ranger training, bodies were needed to process the incoming troops. After normal training hours, fifty strike force soldiers were detailed in the processing effort. Sergeant Travis had designed a smaller version of what the Army called a reception station. Essentially an assembly line with a series of stations where the recruits stripped off their clothing and sandals, picked up uniforms, boots, helmets, field gear, first aid packs and two C-ration meals. At the end of the line, there were six dressing stations. The still naked troops were inspected for strength, health and attitude, i.e., were they gung-ho, as defined by Sergeant Travis. As the Six had once done, they deposited their new gear in a pile on the ground and were instructed to don their clothing and gear in a manner displayed by the strike force soldiers standing at each dressing station. Other troops were there to assist the recruits as needed. It was somewhat chaotic, even without harassment and hazing by the cadre. The point was to get the

Legionnaires through the gauntlet and move them out in platoon-sized units to their living quarters in Tent City. On average, each troop made it through the line in less than thirty minutes.

𝕠   𝕠   𝕠   𝕠   𝕠

Command and staff briefings were held daily in the TOC between 0600 and 0700 hours. At the end of each week, Regimental commanders, and leaders down to the company level attended mandatory "round robin" meetings where each commander would present the results of that week's training, provide a readiness report, and identify problems encountered, if any. The first of these meetings occurred at the end of hell week for strike forces Alpha and Bravo.

Galanis opened the meeting. "Good morning everyone." All responded, "Good morning, Sir!" He continued, "I'll start by saying you all are doing a helluva job pulling this extraordinary team together. I have been visiting all the training areas, and I'm just in awe of the way your trainees are responding. Athena, Captain Kellog, make sure to pass that on to your troops. The rest of your commanders are to be commended for the discipline and morale you have instilled throughout the ranks. Thank you."

He paused and glanced at the status reports laid out in front of him, then continued, "Top, I'd like to hear from you first."

Sergeant Travis was at the far end of the table nonchalantly puffing on his cigar but snapped to with his response, "Roger, Sir. Camp operations are proceeding smoothly. Daily resupply from Ton San Nuet continues on schedule. Pilots report some rough spots on the runway. I've worked with commanders to establish a repair and maintenance crew. All volunteers, of course." There was general laughter around the table since they all knew Top employed the "hey you" duty roster. Looking at his notes, Travis continued, "Of course, the big news is yesterday's arrival of the main body of the Legion at around 1400 hours. Processing began immediately and should be wrapping up later this morning, thanks to the strike force crews that worked through the night."

Fredricks interrupted, "I hear you had a little surprise concerning the headcount."

Travis leaned back in his chair with his hands clasped behind his neck, took a long puff on his cigar and let out the ubiquitous "Shiiiit," followed by general laughter. Most of those around the table already knew what Fredricks was alluding to. Travis sat up in his chair. "Yes Sir," Top responded as he nodded toward the Legion Commander, "seems that Commander Heleron rustled up 300 of his own volunteers to replace the Strike Force troops, so we now have a total Legion force of 1,800." Heleron smiled broadly and nodded back to Travis.

Galanis laughed along with the others and shook his head as if to say, "Bobby, you're a gem." Each commander was asked to report their unit status. This generally consisted of "All present for training, performance satisfactory, no problems noted." There was a slight deviation when it was time for Captain Kellogg's report.

"Rangers lead the way, Sir!" he began and then reported, "All present for training, performance satisfactory. Rangers do not report any problems; they fix them. No dropouts so far." A chorus of groans ensued from the Strike Force Alpha leaders and members of the A-Team.

"Uhump." Heleron cleared his throat to get Galanis' attention. "Stratigos Galanis," meaning general in the hierarchy of the Greek military. Galanis turned and faced Heleron. "Sir, as someone has recently suggested to me, you can call me Galanis."

"Fine, Heleron agreed, "then it will be Galanis. May I comment on Captain Kellogg's report?"

"By all means."

"Captain Kellogg,"

In his best command voice, Kellogg boomed out, "Yes, Sir!"

Heleron continued with a wry expression on his face, "Since my first visit to Camp Savage and my contacts with you, I am convinced your 'Rangers' are an elite force with the highest standards of training. But might I suggest that there will be no need for your future report to address what you referred to as 'dropouts.' I assure you there won't be any."

"Sir, from what I've seen so far," Kellogg said, "I believe you are correct." Athena and her Airborne leaders let go with a few hoots and some high fives. Galanis called for the group to settle down, but he obviously was enjoying the antics.

"Thank you, commanders," Galanis said, while trying to keep a straight face. "Okay, let's get back to business."

𝓞   𝓞   𝓞   𝓞   𝓞

To those preparing for Operation Golden Chariot, time seemed to be evaporating. Jump tower week had come and gone. In Captain Kellogg's review, Rangers continued to lead the way. Some would say *right into the swamp.* Despite the joking and the healthy competition of the two strike forces, continuous progress was being made. Surprisingly, the Legion's main force training was the most problematic. The Legionnaires needed to learn and master skills in three weeks, which an Army training company at Bragg or Benning would learn in eight weeks. For the Legionnaires, that meant long days and long nights. However, there were several factors working in their favor. To a man, these were hardened soldiers at the peak of physical strength. I know because I have lived among them in the Elysian Fields, and for many, I have witnessed their prowess in battle. They could march day and night for a thousand kilometers, followed by days of unremitting combat. I've seen them pierced through with arrows and lances yet fight on until their enemies were vanquished. If

335

necessary, they could stand motionless for hours in the broiling sun of the desert. Perhaps best of all, they were disciplined, able to follow the orders of their leaders and carry them out with precision. Heleron's admonition to Captain Kellog also applied to these troops. "There won't be any dropouts."

If there were any doubts or concerns about the results of training (I'm not sure why there would be), they were dispelled at the end of the training cycles when Galanis held his weekly review. They were now at D-16 Galanis called on Athena first. In a tongue-in-cheek mockery of Captain Kellogg, she saluted and shouted, "Airborne, Sir! Strike Force Alpha reports we are now 'Death From Above'." There was loud cheering and clapping, and congratulations were offered all around.

Galanis broke in, "I attended the school graduation yesterday, and I would say, ah, Athena, it's your story; I'll let you tell it. But first, please come forward." Every eye was on her as she strode forward, a true vision of strength and beauty, from her green beret down to her bloused jump boots.

"Warrant Officer Athena reports," she said crisply while rendering another salute to the commander.

Galanis smiled broadly. "Stand at ease." Then, addressing the group and taking a pair of jump wings from his pocket, he grew serious in his tone, "Athena, it is an honor for me to announce that you are Strike Force Alpha paratrooper number one and are hereby authorized to wear these jump wings as a symbol of your remarkable achievements."

The entire A-Team and leaders of Strike Force Alpha stood and saluted with a resounding chorus of "Airborne, Sir!" Galanis pinned the wings to her uniform and saluted. They shook hands, and Athena returned to her place at the table.

Sergeant Gage spoke up, "I think everyone should know that Athena made three jumps, two from a C-130 and one from a Chinook." More applause followed. Athena was anxious to change topics. She reported that all 150 Strike Force trainees completed airborne qualification and would receive their wings from Sergeants Salinas and Rogers, who were the principal instructors/jumpmasters, in a ceremony at the training site. All were invited to attend.

Captain Kellogg was the next to report, "Like Athena, I am justly proud as is Lieutenant Tran of Strike Force Bravo. Commander Heleron was right; we didn't have a single dropout." Heleron nodded and smiled. "We began with the reconnaissance in force of FSB Cronus and then swung immediately into hell week," Kellogg continued, "Every one of our troops exceeded expectations. There was no letting up despite the terrain, weather, leeches, and mega-mosquitoes. Our training team—stand up guys, Taylor, Santini, Hopkins, and Lieutenant Tran, consider the soldiers of Strike Force Bravo to be Ranger qualified."

Now, the Rangers tried to outdo their Airborne counterparts. They all dropped to the ground and began doing pushups, shouting with each repetition, "Bravo Rangers, Sir! Bravo Rangers, Sir! Bravo Rangers, Sir!"

When they were done, Lieutenant Tran offered these words, "Athena, gentlemen. You are here in Vietnam, known to you and my ancestors as Van Lang. It is the place of my birth, the motherland for which I have been fighting my whole life. Our war between the North and South continues to be devastating. But now it seems we have a cosmic threat. I say this because I believe in Ong Troi, as you believe in Zeus. Their powers are far beyond our comprehension. We must put our faith in them and in ourselves to end the scourge of Cronus and Adecius. Our strike forces will be the fangs of the Tiger that will pierce our enemy's line of defenses." In view of the seriousness of his remarks, the response around the table was muted.

The last up was Ares. He was tasked with organizing the command reserve of 600 Legionnaires, dubbed the Hammer Force. The ADC explained it to me this way, "It is a unit or units held back from the main battle unless or until they are called forward to help in the fight. Such forces may replace units with high casualty rates or plug a gap between friendly units. Our military history is replete with examples of reserve forces saving the day. The overall commander, like Captain Galanis, can commit the reserves with input from his field commanders." Knowing that, I listened intently to what Ares had to say.

"Sergeant Travis and his DIs, how well I remember them, have done a blow-up job of…"

Top was laughing so hard he almost choked on his cigar when he called out to Ares, "Jesus Christ, Lieutenant, you might be in for some remedial training." Ares squinted and took on a sheepish look, not knowing what might be coming next. Travis was using his cigar as a stubby pointer aimed at Ares in jest. "Look, son, if you're going to praise someone for doing a good job, at least get it right! I think you meant 'bang up' job, not blow up."

"Yes, Top, bang-up!"

Galanis stepped in and said, "Ares, are you going to let him pull your chain like that?"

Ares hesitated. "No, Sir! Sergeant Travis, Atten-shun!" Top snapped to. Ares paused ten seconds and wadded back in, "Sergeant Travis."

"Yes. Sir?"

"I believe you have accepted my praise on behalf of your team."

"That is correct, Sir."

"Then as you were," meaning Travis should be seated.

As usual, it was back to business after these bouts of comedy and repartee. Ares and his two commanders, Hermes and Damon, had completed their coordination with the Regimental commanders as to which soldiers would be assigned to the Command Reserve of 600 troops. They would be moved to a separate staging area to begin the final runup to combat operations as the Hammer Force Regiment.

For the next three days, all 1,800 officers and men would receive instruction in advanced fighting techniques: laying down a base of fire to allow adjoining units to advance, leapfrogging one unit forward at a time when coming under enemy fire, use of the bayonet, wire and bunker breaching techniques; command and control including hand signals, use of PRC-25 radios and network protocols; first aid and processing of casualties; collection and handling of POWs; escape and evasion for those that might be captured, and basic survival skills if lost or separated from their units. These are the same skills and techniques taught to all US Army Infantry soldiers over the course of weeks. Here again, discipline, experience, high morale, and 18-hour training days made the difference. Walking among the troops, Galanis and his leaders could almost feel the adrenalin building in the ranks. Galanis turned to his ADC with a tightened jaw and piercing eyes. "Tom, you're up next."

Chapter 34
Battle Plan

Tom Fredricks had been compiling intelligence reports since the very first days at FSB Zeus when the Jedburgh teams were dispatched to recon the entire area of operations from Dong Tam to FSB Cronus. Hermes and Heleron provided valuable information on the Legion of Aeneas and their network of spies. Most recently, the results of Tran's Raiders' reconnaissance in force provided the in-depth information he needed to complete the Intelligence Annex to the Operations Plan. Each of the Raiders had been debriefed and confirmed the findings in Lieutenant Tran's after-action report. They also provided maps and sketches from memory of various layouts in and around FSB Cronus. Most crucial of all was the input of the chieu hoi, Portellis and the captured Spartoi, Elian.

When inside the base, Portellis wandered into an unguarded command center. He had sufficient time to examine maps and documents, responding to the ADC's request that the Raiders look for battle plans and any signs that Adecius was aware of the existence of Camp Savage.

When interviewed, Portellis reported, "I could see on several maps that the base had grown quite large since I was there last. Not just within the compound. Large areas surrounding the compound were labeled 'New Elysium'. I recognized the symbols on the map, which indicated those areas might contain soldiers or slaves. There was no way to confirm the possibility."

Fredricks asked, "What, if anything, did you find regarding the location of Camp Savage?"

Portellis responded, "One of the maps had circles drawn around the site where my patrol was ambushed, and another indicating the location of FSB Zeus. Ah, oh, there was a path marked on the map that leads from the base to the portal entrance."

"Any battle plans or tactical maps?" Fredricks asked as he continued the interview.

"Nothing specific," Portellis said while pondering the question. "No, from what I could tell, FSB Cronus is designed as a fortress, from which Adecius and his forces will defend their 'New Elysium'."

As the interview was concluding, Fredricks asked Portellis if there was anything to add. "Yes, Sir," Portellis said emphatically, "I wish everyone to know, the A-Team, that I was stolen from Lethe by Adecius and his Spartoi to become green and black. Over time I could see that Adecius is profoundly evil and the Spartoi are crazed killers. I wish to join the Legion to help crush these *kakos*, as we say, 'evil ones.'"

Before his interview with the Spartoi Elian, the ADC asked to meet with Ares. Fredricks was familiar with the slaying of the Colchian dragon and how the Spartoi, meaning "sown men," had sprung from the teeth of the dragon as fierce warriors. However, Ares was the only one of the Six who witnessed the events. The dragon and the garden that produced the Spartoi belonged to Ares.

Ares entered the TOC. "Sir, Lieutenant Ares is standing tall before *the man*." Ares tried to keep a straight face but to no avail. He let go with a half-laugh, half-screech but quickly recovered.

Fredricks was not so amused. "Dammit, Ares," he said in a huff. "Haven't Bobby Travis and I told you before?

Quit spending so much time around Sergeant Diggs and his peanut gallery?"

"Peanut gallery, Sir?" Ares asked in his befuddled state.

Fredricks pulled a chair out from the conference table and motioned to Ares. "Oh, forget it. Get over here and sit down. We have work to do."

Fredricks had prepared a list of questions he wanted answered by the Spartoi POW. He reviewed them with Ares. The plan was for the ADC to begin the interrogation with "softball" questioning and then have Ares enter and take over. Fredricks didn't need to explain "good cop–bad cop" since Ares was, and would always be, the bad cop. Ares left, and the Spartoi was brought in. He was well above six feet tall, with jet-black hair falling from under his blackened helmet. His large, jagged teeth overshadowed his facial features. His muscular build was such that he could stand up and kill his interrogator with one blow—a point not lost on Fredricks.

The prisoner was offered coffee, which he tasted and spit out, and a cigarette, which he chewed up and swallowed.

So much for the good cop routine. Fredricks began with the usual questions. What's your name? Where did you come from? What's your position with the Dog Soldiers? The prisoner said nothing. He was focused on biting at his claw-like fingernails and spitting the clippings onto the ADC's boots. As he looked up into the prisoner's face, Fredricks assumed the demeanor of a Regimental doctor and said, "You know, that's a filthy habit?" The prisoner grunted and put his hands down.

As prearranged, Ares strode into the TOC like a commanding general. His AR-15 was slung across his chest, and he was carrying the Caduceus. Both he and Fredricks were alarmed by what happened next. The prisoner let out what can only be described as a yelp, stood up and tried to bolt out of the TOC. Ares reacted by placing the Caduceus in the path of the prisoner, putting him to sleep. "What the hell was that?" Fredricks shouted to Ares.

Grabbing one of the Spartoi's arms, Ares said, "Give me a hand, and I'll explain." He and the ADC placed the dazed warrior back in his chair. Ares looked around the TOC until he located a coil of rope. He gave one end of it to Fredricks and said, "We'd better tie him to the chair before he comes out of it."

As they were securing the prisoner, Fredricks repeated his inquiry, "Ares, what the hell was that?" As he tied one end of the rope, he continued, "And why are we tying him up?"

As they sat down, each lit a cigarette, and Ares briefly told his tale. "I thought the name Elian sounded familiar, but I wasn't sure until I came into the TOC just now. He is one of the original Spartoi who sprang from my garden. You remember the story?"

Fredricks nodded. "Sure."

"No doubt he remembers me from that distant past, and knows of my powers as a son of Zeus. He simply wanted to escape. Trust me, there won't be any problems when he awakes—which will be any time now."

When the prisoner regained consciousness, he yelled and began struggling with the rope holding him to the chair. As a precaution, the ADC asked Sergeant Perez to stand by in the TOC in case there was trouble. And there wouldn't be any trouble once Ares began to speak. "Elian, you remember me?"

The Spartoi soldier had become docile. He nodded in the affirmative and replied, "Ares." Ares offered him water, which he gulped as Ares poured it into his open mouth. He stopped straining on the rope and began to answer Ares' questions.

Most of the information Elian provided was included in the ADC's Intelligence Annex to the ops plan, but it is worth summarizing here.

- Elian was one of the last of Adecius' soldiers to exit the portal in response to Hades' rampage. He confirmed that hundreds of souls from Asphodel and Lethe were forced to exit the portal into Van Lang before the portal was closed. They increased the size of Adecius' army to more than 5,000 soldiers, including the Spartoi and tattooed slaves.

- He was familiar with the areas outside the base that Portellis had identified. However, they were highly secretive camps that only Cronus and Adecius could enter.

- There was confusion among Cronus' command group as to what forces had ambushed Portellis' patrol and twice entered the base compound, including freeing the American POWs. There was a general assumption that these were carried out by US forces operating in the area.

- Other patrols had encountered local forces and done battle with them. Several green and blacks had been killed. Their bodies were carried back to the Lethe. They returned to the base after drinking the waters of the Lethe.

- Thanks to Cronus, the base and surrounding area remained shrouded in thick clouds and fog to avoid detection. Elian pointed out how and where Adecius' soldiers entered and exited the base in those conditions.

- Due to Adecius' defensive posture, patrolling had virtually ended once the supplies and equipment needed for the defense were obtained from Dong Tam and elsewhere. This led Elian to the same conclusion as Portellis. There was no evidence that Adecius and his command group were aware of Camp Savage or its operations.

❡   ❡   ❡   ❡   ❡

When Fredricks and Ares completed their debriefing and interrogations, only one critical piece of the intelligence assessment was missing: what of Ong Troi and the gods and goddesses of Van Lang? I had delivered the message to Hades and Persephone that I had received from King Hung Vuong during my time as a water buffalo. Communication with Ong Troi concerning Cronus and his New Elysium would need to come directly from Zeus. This was a stunning concern. Was it even possible for two cosmic godheads to communicate? What would happen if they clashed and disrupted the order of the universe? The more immediate concern for Galanis, particularly the Six, whose quest was at the heart of the conflict to come, was the potential that Ong Troi would join forces with Cronus to overtake the Olympians.

Those concerns were the subject of Galanis' weekly command meeting, at which time Athena announced that she had important news from Olympus. Persephone had arrived in Olympus and informed Zeus and Hera of all that was going on in the Underworld and Van Lang, as Hermes had reported. She also related what I had learned when I visited with the King of Van Lang. Zeus' reaction was immediate as Hera conveyed to the team at Camp Savage through the medallion that Athena carried at all times:

"Commander Galanis, Heleron and all of you brave Legionnaires. Zeus has asked me to convey the gratitude we have for all of you and, of course, the Six who have so valiantly pursued their quest. I need only say that my husband has left Olympus and now resides in his kingdom in the sky. He has commanded Helios, our god of the sun, to carry him across the universe to the Kingdom of Ong Troi. As you commence with the battle against my father, have faith that Zeus will join the battle with or without the aid of Ong Troi."

As the vision of Hera disappeared and the glow of the medallion faded, there was a deafening silence around the conference table. Heleron spoke in a somber tone, "We have our answer. We will survive or perish with the All-Father at our side."

ᗝ   ᗝ   ᗝ   ᗝ   ᗝ

When preparing for a major battle, commanders and their staffs would simply like to know *everything* before devising a battle plan. If that were possible, it wouldn't have taken Zeus and his brothers ten years to defeat Cronus in the Titanomachy. Tom Fredricks was a pragmatist. As he often said, "Comes a time when you have to go with what you've got." As he and his operations planning team began drafting the final intelligence assessment, they were surprised at the wealth of information they had obtained. Their challenge was to mold that information into a single document that the commanders could use during final preparations for deployment and aid them in the development of the final script, so to speak, as to how the deployment of their forces would/should unfold.

The gathered intelligence could also be plotted on maps–routes of ingress and egress, layouts of the base compound, general locations of the "secret" outlying compounds, key terrain, obstacles, and more. The commanders and staff would spend hours reviewing the maps and Tom Fredricks' final Intelligence Annex to the Operations Plan. I was privileged to attend several of the planning sessions and operations briefings. I retained copies of the intelligence assessment and ops plan. I have used these and other documents to inform the next part of my story. I begin with the Intelligence Annex.

ʘ　　ʘ　　ʘ　　ʘ　　ʘ

I first learned about the operations plan when I attended what the military called a "sand table" exercise. The title is self-explanatory. A large table is covered in sand in order to build a small-scale model of the battlefield for military planning or wargaming. Larger models can simply be set up on the ground. When I was a student, we called these an *abax*, which we used to study writing, geometry, and calculations. At Camp Savage, a large sand table model was constructed on the ground near the TOC. It represented the entire area between and including FSB Cronus and Camp Savage. Viewed from above, it was as if I were once again enjoying my flight with a congregation of ibis.

I beg the reader's indulgence. Seems I misplaced my copy of the ops plan which I most assuredly will locate. But, for now, I will refer to my memories of the day just before the battle. All the A-Team members and 18 of the unit commanders from Regimental to Company level, were assembled around the terrain model. Captain Galanis began,

"The operations planning team and I have developed a very solid ops plan. But it isn't final until we have your critique. So let's begin."

He wielded a long pointer, moving around the table like a Cyclops looking down upon a Greek village. Pointing to FSB Cronus and the surrounding area, he called out the important features, "Now, here is the base itself, and here are the two so-called secret facilities or compounds, about what, Tom, a kilometer away?"

The ADC responded, "Yes, Sir, according to our intelligence."

"Roger," Galanis said as he continued the briefing, "Over here is the Bassac River that Tran's Raiders used for their recon in force, and here is the access trail running from the portal to FSB Cronus." Portellis raised his hand. Galanis didn't appreciate the interruption but acknowledged him, "Yes, Portellis?"

"Captain, it may be important to show the trail from Dong Tam to FSB Cronus, ah, the one where I got my big headache." There was muted laughter among the A-Team members, recalling the ambush of the Dog Soldier patrol.

"Good," said Galanis, "show us." Portellis drew a line in the dirt extending from the area of the ambush to FSB Cronus.

Captain Kellogg spoke up, "Sir, I'll have a patrol scout that area tonight."

"Good idea," Captain Galanis said and moved on.

And so it went for the remainder of the day. Galanis and Fredricks alternately drew arrows pointing to various targets—small flags were placed at those locations, signifying the units responsible for attacking them. Participants in the briefing were encouraged to add information and to generally critique the plan. With a few minor details yet to be worked out, the plan was roundly approved by the leaders charged with its implementation and successful outcome.

*   *   *   *   *

By the time the ops plan was completed and distributed, it was D-10. That left three days for rehearsals and walkthroughs. The final two days would be devoted to checking and rechecking weapons and combat gear, verifying assignments and unit readiness, and eventually, a hot meal and a night's rest (if that were at all possible).

A large-scale model of FSB Cronus and its ancillary targets had been constructed for unit walkthroughs. The goal was to familiarize leaders and soldiers alike with the scope of the entire battlefield and where their unit targets were situated within a global context. Each unit, down to the company level, conducted its own sand table exercises, which identified the routes of ingress and egress to the target sites. The Rangers of Strike Force Bravo had confirmed the viability of using the trail identified by Portellis, which would allow a three-pronged attack plan, along with the Bassac River and the trail leading to the portal. Their mission was to test the strength of the enemy's defensive response with a reconnaissance by fire on three sides of the enemy base, *Objective Troy*. Based on the results of their recon, the main body units of the Elysian Sciritae Regiment would be called forward as directed by Captain Kellogg.

Athena's Strike Force Alpha was assigned a similar mission. Only their ingress would be from the air. Once again, I had to deal with several utterly strange terms to understand who was going where. I had previously learned that the giant gray birds that once attacked me at the airstrip were called HC-130 aircraft. I was shocked to be told that the "H" stands for Hercules. Oh, my God! *Death From Above* would be delivered by three of those flying beasts, each containing 50 paratroopers–called a "stick" since all 50 will jump from the same aircraft. All 150 would be delivered to the same target zone, not in a congregation, as with the ibis I flew with, but in *chalks*.

Three drop zones had been identified. One for each "secret" camp, *Objective Poseidon,* west of the main base, and *Objective Hera* to the east. The third stick of jumpers would use *Drop Zone Olympus,* one kilometer to the north of FSB Cronus, (*Objective Troy),* prepared to support the attacks on Poseidon and Hera, as needed. If all went well, the center force could be released to close in on the north side of the fire support base in concert with the Rangers' recon by fire. The plan was to create the perception that the base was under full-scale attack on all four sides.

Athena would be the first to jump, landing with the center stick to establish a mobile command post. As with Captain Kellogg and his regimental main force troops, Athena would exercise full control over when and how the main force of Pegasus Paraskinia would be deployed.

Mockups of the strike force objectives were set up with a view of how they might look from the air. Each stick commander grilled their troops to ensure they memorized the entire battlespace features. They did scramble drills using the airfield as simulated drop zones, with chutes deployed and stretched out behind them as if they had just landed. The instructors would blow a whistle and time how long it took each unit to unharness, gather chutes, packs, and weapons, and reach their assigned assembly points. Not surprisingly, the exercise, which was repeated several times, led to a serious point of competition among the units, peeling minutes off of each repetition. Shouts of "Airborne, Sir!" reverberated throughout the camp.

Ares had a uniquely different mission. In essence, he and his 600 troops would be on standby waiting for a call from Galanis. Not an enviable assignment for the Greek God of War, or a Green Beret lieutenant for that matter. To get things rolling, Ares asked Galanis and Fredricks to come to the Hammer Force team training area to explain the role of the Regiment to him, his leaders, and their troops.

When they arrived, Ares presented his concerns. "Captain, Warrant Officer Fredricks, I think you know that we, ah, the Greeks, the Legionnaires, we are aggressive fighters. We all want to enter the battle." The troops roared and stomped their feet as Ares let out his battle cry that left

Galanis and Fredricks covering their ears. Areas slapped his chest with a closed fist. "You see?"

"That's no different than Tom and I or Sergeant Travis. We're in charge of command and control, not up front with our M-16s and grenades. We all have our jobs. Operating as a team up forward or back at camp is what it takes to accomplish the mission."

Ares was listening, but his head was down as he kicked the dirt with the toe of his boot. His response was anything but enthusiastic, "Yes, Sir, I understand."

Galanis turned to his ADC. "Tom, you need to give these folks a quick tutorial on operating as the Command Reserve."

Fredricks moved forward where he could address the officers and men of the unit. "Roger, Sir," he explained, "The idea of reserve force units in combat is the same as employed by ancient Roman and Greek legions. Modern doctrine is based on two units forward and one back. In this case, Athena and Captain Kellog command the two forward-deployed units. Ares, you are in command of the reserve regiment—many times referred to as the quick reaction force.

You and your troops must be ready to move rapidly to assist forward-deployed forces that may be in trouble."

Damon raised his hand and, without acknowledgment from the ADC, blurted out, "You mean saving their ass?" There were roars of laughter from the troops.

Ares cut in, "Damon, how many times have I told you to quit spending so much time with Sergeant Diggs?"

This time, it was Fredricks and Galanis who were laughing. Fredricks recovered, "Okay, moving right along. Your other mission may be as a blocking force."

Galanis weighed in, "That's when the other regiments kick ass and send the enemy forces your way in a panic. Then you get to put them to the sword, as you might say." Naturally, Ares began to perk up. He turned to his troops and ran his open hand across his throat in a cutting motion, which elicited an even more uproarious response from the troops.

After the session with the troops, Galanis, Fredricks and Ares, along with all of the Hammer Force leaders, conducted a sand table exercise. It showed that Ares' regiment would move as a single force to Assembly Area Gold two hours after the departure of Strike Force Bravo. The Regiment would set up a temporary blocking force about four kilometers from Objective Troy when instructed. Once in place, they were to await further orders from Galanis.

Arrows on the sand table showed the direction of the march from the blocking position to Objectives Hera, Poseidon and Troy. The Hammer Force should be prepared to fast march to any of the objectives, depending on the developing situation on the battlefield. Fredricks briefed the group on what he called a "forward passage of lines." as he demonstrated on the sand table. "See, here is your established blocking position. When units of the other two regiments are called forward, you need to assist them in moving through your stationary position without delay."

One of the company commanders raised a hand and was recognized. "Sir, how will we know when they are coming, and what assistance should we provide?"

"Good questions," Fredricks replied. "First, each company should identify passage points and passage lanes within your sector." He scratched out several examples on the sand table as he continued, "Lieutenant Ares will receive a radio call from the approaching units. Each company will send guides rearward to make contact with the lead unit. The guide will brief them on the location of passage points and passage lanes. When the arriving units are ready to proceed, the guides will lead them through the blocking position."

The exercise was wrapping up as the sun began to set over the expanse of Camp Savage. Galanis and Fredricks both lit cigarettes and began their walk back to the TOC. They walked in silence as if each knew what the other was thinking. The breeze blowing across the runway carried the fragrant smells of bougainvillea and jacaranda, mixed with the aroma of chicken and steaks grilled for evening chow, and coffee brewing in the TOC. As the two leaders, indeed friends, entered the TOC, they briefly halted to take in the large posterboard on an easel by the coffeepot. It read in large print **D-4**.

Chapter 35
Mariscalcus:
Get Ready for The Big Dance

I can recall officers of the Roman Legions using the term 'mariscalcus' when putting their legionnaires in order before a battle. So, I was curious when I heard Sergeant Travis speak of "marshaling the troops". As a former Latin scholar with certain dialectic skills, I deduced that the two words mean the same—to methodically assemble or arrange a group, especially soldiers. I must say I am proud of finding the connection. Oh, forget that; my point is that D-2 was the start of a perfectly choreographed marshaling of the entire Legion of Aeneas. Since I had no official duties, I was free to walk about the camp and observe the process.

No matter which regiment, every Legionnaire, including officers, were required to lay out their weapons and gear. A-Team members passed throughout the ranks and checked every item—uniforms, helmets, boots, weapons, combat gear, water, rations, ammunition, and first-aid packs. No one was dismissed until they passed inspection and meticulously packed their gear. Packs were then laid out in rows in company formation, where they would remain until D-Day. One at a time, the companies were marched to one of a half-dozen firing ranges to test their weapons: M-16s, M-79 grenade launchers, M-60 machine guns, AR-15s and .45 caliber pistols. Once fired, they were cleaned, oiled and secured in the company areas. By the end of the day, troops were back in training mode, reviewing communication and first-aid procedures, circling the various sand tables to get a fix on their respective missions, and practicing hand-to-hand and bayonet skills. I was exhausted just watching them. They never seemed to tire. Their enthusiasm and morale were at a fevered pitch. I was starting (faintly) to wish I were going with them.

σ σ σ σ σ

The Strike Force Alpha paratroops followed the same routine as all the other units, but there was extra work to be done. Their M-10 parachutes were laid out on the runway. Sergeants Salinas and Rogers were on hand in their role as jumpmasters. With the assistance of Sergeants Gage, Diggs and Osbourne, members of the Pegasus Regiment, each chute was inspected along with its owner. If any defects were found in his chute, the trooper would be dispatched to draw a new one and have the inspection repeated.

Eventually, all parachutes were declared ready for repacking but there was one last detail to be attended to.

Warrant Officer Athena walked out of her CP near the jump tower and strode to the area where the chutes were laid out, fully opened. She was wearing her steel helmet with its chinstrap buckled; her jump boots were spit-shined, her fatigue trousers tucked in, paratrooper-style. Her prized jump wings adorned her breast pocket. I saw her then, and radiant does not begin to describe her countenance. She asked the A-Team cadre to have the troops assemble at her location. There was silence as she began to address her nearly mesmerized strike force. "In just a few hours, we jump!"

There was pandemonium in the ranks—shouts, screams, foot stomping and endless cheers of *"Airborne, Sir! Airborne, Sir! Airborne, Sir!"* Until she asked for quiet. Sergeant Diggs stepped forward with hands raised. "Listen up!"

Athena smiled, and I swear the sun overhead shone brighter, setting the airstrip aglow. "I will have more remarks for you before we depart on the sacred quest that Zeus has now set upon us all. For now, I have a challenge for you, STRAC paratroops of Strike Force Alpha." There were the usual hooahs, with a few right-ons, thanks to, yes, Sergeant Diggs.

Here was the nature of the challenge. Athena and her leaders had been discussing ways to elaborate on the theme of *Death From Above*. Someone in the group suggested that symbols could be painted on the parachutes. What better symbols than the fierce monstrosities, snakes and dragons of Greek mythological history? Enter Sergeant Travis, stage right. He and Diggs, the mortal trickster of this story, connived to get 200 gallons of paint of assorted colors (heavy on the red and black), helicoptered in from Dong Tam. I guess no one dared ask why you needed 200 gallons of paint for a Tent City. Nonetheless, Sergeant Diggs was grinning ear to ear as he unveiled six pallets of paint and announced to the troops, "Use it wisely, men, this shit cost Uncle Sam a thousand dollars a gallon." I don't believe anyone else present knew what he was talking about.

So, the challenge was on, at top speed. Troops scrambled to grab one or two gallons without regard to color and raced back to their chutes. There were only two problems. Most had no idea what they should paint or how to use just one or two colors. Maybe a black dragon with red eyes but no flames?

Sergent Hopkins stepped forward, waving his hands. "Listen up! Listen up!" Like good troops, they stopped in their tracks and looked toward their jumpmaster. "Now that I've got your attention, I'm disappointed in you all. You've been outta jump school for two weeks, and it seems you've already forgotten the core principle of your training. Can anybody tell me what that is?" There was silence. "Jesus Christ, Sergeant Rogers, do you believe this shit!"

The troops appeared to be frozen in place, many with buckets of paint in their hands. Finally, one trooper began to speak what sounded like "cawadado and taliate."

"Son, get the marbles outta your mouth and post your ass up here!" Hopkins said in his best DI voice.

What the trooper was trying to say was, "cooperate and graduate." The rest of the assemblage got the point. Many good artists within the ranks could help the others sketch out their monsters and demons. There were artisans who had once painted pottery or murals during their mortal lives. They worked out the color schemes and set the remaining troops to work in an assembly line fashion. Just several hours later, 150 painted chutes lay on the airfield, drying in the sun.

𝇏   𝇏   𝇏   𝇏   𝇏

I was curious as to how Ares and his troops were marshaling for D-Day, so I wandered over to their training area. The sand table exercise conducted by Galanis and Fredricks had been valuable for Ares and his leaders. When I arrived, I saw that the troops had been divided into three companies of 200 each. Sergeants Salinas and Rodgers had returned to the regiment after assisting Athena with the inspection of her regiment and the paratroopers. They were huddled with Ares and his company commanders, along with Damon.

Shortly, the commanders returned to their units and began shouting orders, "Left turn, march, right turn, march, come on line, take cover!" It looked like chaos to me. My immediate reaction was to thank the gods that I was an actor, not a director. I was able to corner Damon to ask if he knew what was going on. I had never seen him so excited. His face and body posture, the cut of his uniform, the slant of his beret, and a .45 pistol on his hip! Suddenly, I recalled rumors

I had heard about several of the Six wanting to stay with the A-Team after the battle was over but that was for another time.

"Damon, how are you," I inquired. "You've all been so busy I've missed seeing and talking with you."

He slapped me on my back with what seemed like the strength of Hercules. He came close to my face. "Alagon, how the hell are you?" he said as he reached into his pocket. "Wanna smoke?" I declined. Just then, I noticed that his beautiful, curled locks were gone, replaced by, in his words, "a real GI haircut." I bit my lip and carried on. I asked him to explain what was happening.

"It's not easy to move 600 men around when the balloon goes up." I blinked, thinking I must be talking to Sergeant Diggs. Damon continued, "Our regiment is expected to move out at H+2. That's two hours after the deployment of strike forces Alpha and Bravo. Each company has an assigned assembly area three to four kilometers from FSB Cronus. One to the west, east and center of Objective Troy. The units will hold there until instructed to move by the old man—ah, Captain Galanis."

"Move where?" I asked.

I could see my reflection in his "aviator" sunglasses as he responded, "One or more of the companies might be needed to assist a unit in trouble or maybe to chase down the bad guys trying to escape—you know, the Dog Soldiers!"

Okay, I'll skip over that part. As we watched, two companies left their rehearsal staging areas and began to form a single line facing forward with perhaps two meters between individual soldiers, stretching 800 meters from end to end. The third company formed a separate line to the rear of the front line. Essentially, the reserve of the command reserve. We were seeing what a regimental blocking force looked like, albeit in the open terrain of Camp Savage.

As I was preparing to head over to the TOC, we could see several troops from each company racing to the rear in our direction as a rehearsal of the passage through lines began. I gave a wave to Ares and the other leaders, observing what I then knew was not chaos but a disciplined military exercise in preparation for combat. Looking back as I slowly shuffled my way toward the ops center, there was Damon, looking every bit the STRAC Green Beret that he wanted to be, lighting a cigarette with his prized Zippo lighter.

ơ ơ ơ ơ ơ

When I entered the TOC, it was a beehive of activity. Various radios were squawking like geese at the market in the Agora. I was surprised to learn they were playing a game as I listened in. Eventually, Sergeant Perez clarified, "It's a *wargame*. We practice receiving and sending radio traffic using different scenarios. We must react to each situation as if it were live combat." This was their form of martialing. All radios were up and operational, frequencies checked and rechecked, encryption devices operational, batteries stacked at the ready and the howling monsters they called generators filled with a fluid that smelled like the emanations in the Oracle's Adytum back in Delphi.

By some means unknown to me, the equipment and supplies they were checking and testing as part of their wargame allowed the command group to talk to the regimental and company commanders involved in the battle. At one point, Sergeant Alexander, one of those who had been prisoners at FSB Cronus, showed me his equipment and explained (most of which I could understand), "Captain Galanis and his command group need to talk to the commanders in the field, and as you can hear, their communications come in hot and heavy." I had no doubt about that. During the short time I was listening in, there was simulated radio "traffic" from a unit under heavy fire, calls for medical help, a report that a company commander had been killed (KIA, as they called it), and requests for reinforcements. "My job," Alexander said as he continued, "is to talk with the support aircraft pilots, the *gubernators*." He used the Latin term that I knew as *helmsman*.

I started to inquire, "But, ah, how do you…" He laughed and interrupted, "Oh, I'm just showing off. I had three years of Latin in high school and college. I was going to be a lawyer, *advocatus*." We both laughed. "But then I joined the Air Force."

On D-Day, Alexander would be attached to Strike Force Bravo as part of Captain Kellogg's command group, as the Forward Air Controller (FAC). He would be controlling the airborne drops of Strike Force Alpha. If overhead conditions allowed (considering Cronus' manipulation of the weather conditions), Alexander would call for air strikes on designated targets. He might also be able to request artillery support from the batteries at Dong Tam.

ɤ   ɤ   ɤ   ɤ   ɤ

It had been an almost mind-numbing day of activity. I couldn't possibly understand how the commanders, the leaders and the troops could assimilate it all down to an incredible level of minutiae, knowing they were just one day away from what Sergeant Travis liked to call the "big dance". The command group grabbed cups of coffee and some day-old cinnamon buns. They chattered among themselves. Sergeant Travis relit the stub of his cigar. I surveyed the scene: Galanis, Fredricks, Travis, Hermes, and Perez. These were men whose names and the names of those they would direct in battle would be recorded in the history of the Universe.

Before leaving the TOC, I approached Captain Galanis. "Sir, you know of the special powers and abilities given to me by my father. If there is any way that I can help you or the Legion, ah, ah." I was beginning to stammer as if I were trying to recall my lines in the second act of Oedipus Rex.

Galanis looked up at me with an expression of kindness on his face and said, "Alagon, special powers or not, you are part of this organization, the Legion. As of now, since I am the 'supreme' commander of this outfit, you will officially be detailed to the Legion Command Group. Report here at 0600 hours for the commander's briefing."

I did the only thing that came to mind; I saluted, did an about-face, and left. Once outside the TOC, I let go with a hooah loud enough to flush a pandemonium of large parrots from the jacaranda trees on the far side of the airfield.

Chapter 36
Let the Games Begin

As directed, I reported to the TOC the next morning and prepared for the commander's briefing. The poster on the easel by the coffeepot read H-Hour, 0500, D-Day Tomorrow. The commanders and leaders took their places on rows of chairs facing the poster with its stark message. Coffee and donuts were passed around by two cooks from the mess hall. I heard a lot of nervous chatter, but mostly, there was joking and laughter, much like I would hear before going on stage. Captain Galanis entered the TOC with Heleron at his side. Sergeant Travis commanded, "On your feet!" Everyone stood at attention as the Senior Commanders strode past and took their place at the front, next to the D-Day poster. The "Supreme Commander" paused for a few seconds as he surveyed the assembled leaders of the Legion of Aeneas. In the front row were the Six, whose quest had now become the mission behind Operation Golden Chariot. Behind them, the 43$^\text{d}$ Special Forces A-Team sat shoulder to shoulder– "America's Best" according to the song Sergeant Diggs played incessantly. The Regimental Commanders and their deputies followed, and behind them, a row of nine Legionnaire Company Commanders.

Standing in the rear, I was sure I could feel the presence of my father Zeus. Perhaps it was true. As Galanis began to speak, his words were like a mist that floated over the room.

"At ease, please take your seats. In a few hours, you will embark on a mission unlike any the world, or the universe, has ever seen. I know you all agree that in just a few months, we have created an army unlike any other. You all should be very proud of where we stand at this critical hour. Through your strength and determination, we are ready to take the fight to our enemies, Cronus, Adecius and their Dog Soldiers."

The entire group sat straight up with stiffened backs and tight jaws in rapt attention to their commander's words. He continued, "You have trained well and mastered numerous tasks that may still be a mystery to you. Above all, you have instilled discipline and pride in every soldier in your command. And I salute you."

He saluted and turned toward Heleron. "Sir, you are to be commended for your foresight in creating the Legion of Aeneas at a time when there were only rumors of a disturbance in the Underworld. With the skill and tenacity of your commanders, Tanaurus and Arcelium, please stand up, you two." They stood to resounding applause and cheers, "You marched an Army of what we called recruits into the unknown world of Van Lang to become what we now call STRAC troops. Thank you, Sir!" Galanis saluted and turned back to face his audience.

"Sergeant Diggs, Damon, post yourselves up here!" They came forward. The serious expression on Galanis' face had changed to a jovial smile and as he motioned towards the two, "I'm told these two self-appointed morale officers have some activities planned for today. Before they get into the details, let me leave you with this. I've seen the results of yesterday's preparations, which tells me your units are primed and ready to go. So, today should be a day focused on rest and relaxation and whatever these two have cooked up."

Sergeant Travis stood up and moved to the front. "On your feet!" The group stood at attention as Galanis and Heleron exited. When they were gone, Travis shouted, "At ease. One more thing before these two knuckleheads take over. Thanks to my good friends at MAC-V and the 177th Aviation, tonight's meal will feature tiger prawns; if you don't know about them, ask Lieutenant Tran, right, ?"

Tran responded in Vietnamese, "Tốt nhất thế giới!"

Travis Laughed, "Whatever that means!"

Perez shouted out, "He says it's 'world's best!'"

"If I can continue?" Travis interjected, "There will also be steaks, leg of lamb, potatoes, beans, and apple pie. And, in case you thought I forgot, two beers per troop." Given tomorrow's 0200 wake-up, chow will start at 1600."

ᴓ　　ᴓ　　ᴓ　　ᴓ　　ᴓ

Combat is not fun and games, but fun and games might take your mind off the clock's ticking, as Sergeant Diggs put it, "Especially if there are no women around." Sophocles couldn't have said it better! I must admit, Sergeant Diggs and Damon dragged me into their scheme. Well, let's say they tapped into my genius as a master of all forms of fun and games. Our plan was simple. Greeks like games. Americans like games. Why not mix the two together for a day of "healthy" competition? I can assure you, dear reader, there is no such concept for Greeks as healthy competition.

Damon rolled out a drawing of Camp Savage with various boxes and circles scattered about, marking where the fun and games would ostensibly take place. Looking at the labels for each of the identified locations, I recognized some of the games from my travels, some going back to my childhood. *Pankration*, a combination of wrestling and boxing; discus and javelin throwing; *astragalus* (knucklebones) a game of dexterity, and footraces. For indoors, there was *latrunculi*, a strategy board game, which I was told was much like chess and *pente grammai* (5 lines), a table game involving moving stone pieces to a "sacred line". Others, which I assumed to be the American offerings, were unfamiliar to me. There were large areas dedicated to such things as baseball, football, and soccer. Tents were set aside for chess, poker, checkers, and a dice game called "craps." I was most curious about several tents labeled "music" and "poetry."

Damon explained, " A few Legionnaires carried lyres and flutes with them from Elysium; others brought books of poetry and songs. There will be places to relax and remember the ancients."

Sergeant Diggs added, "There are other tents available for those who want to 'get down.'" He assured me it didn't involve lying on the ground. There were guitars and drums for more modern sounds and Armed Forces Radio for dancing to what he called "rock and roll."

Food and drink stations were being set up at each location and would be replenished throughout the day with enough variety that the troops would not have to go find something that they preferred. Both Damon and Sergeant Diggs emphasized that there should be no requirement to participate in these activities since many soldiers may choose to sleep or spend time with friends. Company commanders were tasked with sorting out the preferences of their troops and seeing that they knew where to go. Before the leaders headed back to their unit areas, they were treated to these words from the one I had begun to refer to as *Aristophanes* Diggs, "Well, there you have it. This is going to be the biggest goddamn block party Vietnam has ever seen!"

As the fun and games were getting organized, Athena went to the commanders' tent to speak with Galanis and Heleron. She surprised them with her news about the painting of the Strike Force Alpha parachutes. They were delighted until Athena said, "In the spirit of competition being planned for today, my commanders and I would like the two of you to join me as judges of the best chutes."

After a little sputtering, the two senior commanders agreed they would be "honored" to participate. The three of them sat for a while, drinking coffee and eating the coffee cake the cooks had sent to the commanders' tent that morning. They talked about the preparations for D-Day and Athena's mission for Strike Force Alpha. Heleron inquired about the morale of the Legionnaires, which Athena allowed was the highest she had ever seen on the eve of battle. Quite a pronouncement from the goddess of war.

Galanis offered his view that there could never be a more disparate group of commanders: a goddess, a Legionnaire hero of numerous Greek wars, and a Green Beret captain from Chicago. At the mention of Chicago, Athena looked intently into Galanis' eyes, looked away and asked if the commanders were ready to walk with her to the airfield. Before departing, Galanis went into the TOC, spoke briefly with Sergeant Travis, and returned to the other commanders carrying a small box.

When they arrived at the airfield, things were already at fever pitch. The troops were standing by their chutes while their A-Team jumpmasters and instructors exhorted them with renditions of, "I wanna be an Airborne Ranger! Live that life of blood and danger!" and "C-130 rolling down the strip, Airborne Ranger gonna take a little trip. We gonna stand up, hook up, shuffle to the door. Cronus won't be here no more." As Athena and the senior commanders arrived, the troops began to chant, "Strike Force Alpha! Strike Force Alpha!" Cheers, shouts and whistles were unabated as the three commanders began trooping the line.

This was an astounding sight. One hundred fifty parachutes were on display, and behind each one was a STRAC paratrooper. As the judges passed by, each soldier snapped to attention and saluted along with a shout of "Airborne, Sir!" Later that day, it was Heleron who gave me insight into the contest and its results.

"Alagon, the mysteries of our homeland are nothing compared to what I have seen and experienced since entering Van Lang. I had observed this 'airborne' training and seen our soldiers drop from the sky with weapons even beyond the powers of Zeus. Then, this morning, I saw Strike Force Alpha standing like the marble hills of the *Areopagus*. How proud I was."

"And the contest?" I asked in anticipation.

"Oh, magnificent! There was a genius in their artistry. But so many to choose from." He recounted those that stood out, *Typhon* and *Echidna*, the mother and father of all monsters, awash in blood, and yellow fire streaming from their eyes. There was *Medusa* with menacing snakes on her head; the giant *Argus*, guardian of Hera; dragons, demons, *Scylla* with her fish-like body and dogs' heads protruding from her neck; the *Furies*, and *Hydra*, the sea monster with her head of snakes.

"I tell you," the Legion Commander said. "They were all fierce and lifelike. Athena told Galanis and me that the images were painted on the front of their 'canopies' for maximum impact when landing on the objective."

"So, how did you choose the contest winners?" I said with renewed anticipation.

"After trooping the line twice, we three judges had a unanimous choice. It was painted in fine detail like the frescoes of Akrotiri, with blazing colors showing the monstrous heads of Typhon and Echidna. They were all intertwined and snarling—almost too horrid to look upon."

"And the other two?"

"Next was a fine rendering of the three Furies, with wings spread, teeth projected, and flames of death all around. The third was of Argus, his giant body stretched from the bottom to the top of the canopy. Do you know those 'chutes' are eleven meters in diameter? Yes, and due to what Galanis called parabolic shape, there was sufficient area to add all one hundred eyes to Argus' head, with blood dripping from them all!"

He described the pandemonium (not parrots) that broke out each time a winner was announced. Then, the winners were called up to the front for their awards. Captain Galanis asked Athena to hold the box he had brought from the TOC, courtesy of Sergeant Travis, of course. The first prize was a Zippo lighter and a pack of Top's favorite Panatela cigars. The second prize was a Zippo lighter and a carton of Winston cigarettes. The third prize was a Zippo lighter and a tin of Copenhagen snuff, which was a rare commodity the Legionnaires would barter for. The prizes made me think of something Sergeant Perez had told me. Back in the "States," as he called America, large numbers of people considered smoking and using snuff to be filthy habits–something difficult to comprehend since every single person, Greek or otherwise, including gods and a goddess, smoked. As did I.

𝕺   𝕺   𝕺   𝕺   𝕺

The idea of having fun and games, what Sergeant Travis called "grabass" was a great success. It was a *karnaváli,* as we say in Greek. Units are vying to be champions in boxing and racing, with hundreds cheering on. Hilarious moments when Legionnaires were trying to learn baseball or A-Team members trying to master the discus and javelin. On a more serious note, there was the hand grenade throw. Sergeant Gage was reputed to throw a grenade as far as sixty-five feet, nearly twenty meters–five meters beyond the US Army standard. The Greeks, of course, had no standard, but there were scores of Olympic champion discus and javelin throwers in the ranks. It was the final field challenge of the day. After drawing lots, Sergeant Gage was up first. His opponent, one *Gaetano,* was not only an

385

Olympic champion but bore the looks and physique of Hercules.

Each contestant would get two practice throws, with the third throw being the final. Amazingly, both had practice throws exceeding twenty-one meters. As they prepared for the final throws, the crowd of cheering, stomping troops focused on a yellow stake that had been placed at twenty-three meters (seventy-six feet)–the line to beat. It looked like Gage shocked himself when his grenade fell just beyond the marker. Gaetano had to push his way through the throng to reach the throwing line. Once there, without hesitating, he grasped his grenade and catapulted it somewhere well beyond the marker. The crowd burst onto the throwing range to verify that; indeed, the Greeks had won with a throw of thirty-one meters (one hundred two feet). As the crowd disbanded and carried Gaetano to the mess hall on their shoulders, Damon and Sergeant Diggs were grinning as they shook hands and collapsed into a bear hug after they stepped back and celebrated, "Shiiiit!"

By the time evening chow was being served, Helios had already carried the sun far across the Plain of Reeds. H-hour was just twelve hours away . But, as the troops passed around gravy for their potatoes and lamb and sipped on their warm beer and cold iced tea, those few remaining hours were as distant as the belief they could be returning to the Elysian Fields. There was still time to argue about champions of this or that, who crapped out the most, in dice or otherwise, or to marvel at the sight of Sergeant Travis holding court at a poker table with the Six.

When the last slice of apple pie was served and eaten, the troops began to filter back to their unit areas for one last check of their weapons and gear. There would be an hour before "lights out" for reading poems, making offerings to Zeus and Olympus, and one last cigarette. Things were unusually quiet as I passed through Tent City on my way to the TOC to get my instructions for the next morning.

The ADC was in the TOC when I arrived. He was fussing over some charts and mumbling to himself. "What's up, Tom?" I inquired. Since I was now assigned to the command group, he had asked me to use his first name.

He looked up and said, "Oh, hi, Alagon. I'm just making sure that my time charts are correct. I can never quite get used to the early sunsets here versus back home!" As usual, I wanted to know more–big mistake. He asked me to sit down so he could explain his charts. "See, here," he said as he pointed to some numbers. "We need to fix the time for deploying our two strike forces." My mind probably faded out at that point–nautical twilight, beginning morning nautical twilight, and evening nautical twilight, BMNT, EENT. Could he just simplify what it all meant? "Oh sure," he said without hesitation, "It means it will be dark by 1901 hours tonight, and the sun will rise at 0508 hours in the morning."

Being polite, I said, "Oh, that *is* simpler." All I really needed to know was what time to report to the TOC, at or before BMNT. His answer was at, or before, the 0200 wakeup for the troops.

ම   ම   ම   ම   ම

Lights out was set at 1900 hours. That allowed seven hours of rest for those who could actually sleep. At 2100, the command group was busy in the TOC, *dotting the i's and crossing the t's* as the ADC put it. Sergeant Perez had set up a table for me next to his communications station. On it were a stack of Tactical Green Military Logbooks and several boxes of US Army tactical pencils and pens. All of these were fascinating to me as a scribe only familiar with reed stems for writing on papyrus and parchment. Perez instructed me on how to sharpen the pencils and in the operation of "ballpoint" pens. All of this was in preparation for my D-Day assignment–Logging Specialist, a suitable title created by the ADC. A military version of a scribe, which required me to record incoming and outgoing messages for units in the field, particularly hourly SITREPs. I was reviewing the process with Perez when Captain Galanis stuck his head in the door.

"Top, I'm gonna walk the perimeter and then try for a couple hours of sleep."

Sergeant Travis stubbed out his cigar, ready to light another when he acknowledged Galanis, "Roger, Sir. Good luck on the sleeping part."

More military jargon. Perez had to explain that walking the perimeter meant walking around the edge of a defensive position or tactical camp to check on security and readiness. In this case, Perez explained further, "It's a good way for the Commander to walk off nervous energy."

As Galanis walked around the Ranger and Hammer Force training areas, he stopped to chat briefly with Captain Kellogg and Ares. He urged them both to get some rest, but, as with himself, the prospect seemed unlikely. The Commander's thoughts were focused on an endless stream of checklists–has this been done? Better check with Tom on that detail or with Top on these other items; so much for working off nervous energy. Things were quiet for the most part over in Tent City. Several guards were on their way to the far side of the compound. Galanis spoke with them and confirmed that even with H-hour looming, guards were rotating on two-hour shifts. They were impressed when the Supreme Commander shook hands and thanked them for their courage and dedication.

Moving on, Galanis looked across the airfield and could see that lights were still on in the commander's tent by the jump tower. Looking up at the moon, he felt a sudden chill as he recalled the strange encounter he and Athena had while under the same red moon. She had called it a *blood moon*. Perhaps an omen or a message from the gods. In two days' time, he would find out the true meaning.

Crossing the airstrip, he could see the long shadows being cast by rows of parachutes and gear lining both sides in designated sticks. Nearby guards saluted and intoned, "Airborne, Sir!" He returned their salutes and continued to the jump tower, debating whether to check on Athena. He lit a cigarette and headed back to the airstrip, still wondering if he could get even an hour's worth of sleep.

As he crossed the steel plating of the runway, there was Athena. She came close. "Galanis, why are you not sleeping?"

"I could ask the same of you."

"Sergeant Hopkins and I just completed our final check of weapons and gear. Our Hercs should be on station in about four hours."

Just then, a cloud passed over the moon, and it was pitch dark. He lit his lighter so that he could see her face. He slid her green beret from her head and gently brushed her hair. She took his hand away and said in her paratrooper's voice, "Excuse me, Commander. Don't you think you are violating any number of Army regulations? A Court Martial offense, so I'm told."

"You once said I am your brother, your lover, and your commander. At this moment, which do you prefer?"

The moon reappeared, casting a shadow of their embrace onto the runway. They kissed and separated. Galanis stepped back and let out a long breath before he could speak, "Now, who is violating regulations?"

She looked quizzically at him but said nothing.

"As an A-Team Green Beret, I mean. I'm sure that wasn't meant for your brother."

She halted his speech with a wave of her hand. He stood still as if in a trance. What he could see was the goddess Athena as she appeared in a famous statue he had once admired in the Louvre–flowing robes, stark beauty, crowned with her helmet, her palm reaching toward him. A fragrant mist of frangipani surrounded her as she spoke, "Galanis, I have told you. You are of Olympus. Our coming together affirms this. But you have been sent here for a great purpose. Our passion must not interfere with that purpose. These are fleeting moments that belong to the aither of Mount Olympus."

His trance-like state was gone, and Athena stood before him as a commander eager for battle. The Supreme Commander shook her hand and offered these words,

"Athena, you and your commanders have done a helluva job pulling this together. I'll be here in the morning to help with the sendoff of the strike force. Good night, and get some sleep, dammit!"

She saluted. "Airborne, Sir. Good night."

Chapter 37
Saddle Up!

Like so many others, I didn't get any sleep waiting for D-Day to get underway. I walked around the camp for a while but spent most of the time at my desk in the TOC with an endless supply of cigarettes and coffee. Copies of the maps and schedules for the attack had been distributed, so I thought it best that I study them in detail before the *balloon goes up*. I did my best, but there were so many symbols, names, boxes, and circles on the maps that I began to think I had them upside down. Fortunately, SFC Hermes came into the TOC for some coffee, and he volunteered to "square me away."

"Okay, Alagon, Let's start here," pointing to Camp Savage on the tactical map. "It shows that there are two forward regiments, Pegasus and Sciritae and the Hammer Force, in reserve."

"Yes," I said. "I remember that from the sand table exercise."

"Then there are the two strike forces. Alpha, here and Bravo, over there. They will be the first to deploy in the morning, ah, I should say, in a few hours. From there…" He continued squaring me away until an hour before the troop wake up at 0200. Every so often, I would study him, the movements, his military bearing, the tilting of his green beret. The same things I had noticed when he delivered his SITREP to Hades. Only now I was wondering if he, too, like those rumors I was hearing about others, would think it impossible to return to Olympus? Setting that aside, when we had finished the review, I began making notes in one of my Military Tactical Logbooks, using a ballpoint pen.

<u>NOTES</u>

1. Strike Force Bravo, with 150 troops led by Captain Kellogg, will depart Camp Savage at H-2 (0300), to occupy assembly areas Red, White, and Blue.

2. Strike Force Alpha to the ready line at the airstrip at H-2 (0300). Three C-130s were on the ground to transport three sticks of 50 paratroopers each.

3. Legion assembly (minus two strike forces) at Tent City 0330.

4. 0400 Regimental assemblies. Companies at standby positions in unit areas.

5. Air and artillery prep of all targets, if feasible– 0400. Strike Force Bravo units depart assembly areas Red, White, and Blue to the vicinity of Objective Troy.

6. 0430 Airborne PAX loaded. C-130s "wheels up."

7. H-hour, 0500. Airdrops on Objectives Poseidon and Hera. Mobile Command Post (MCP) drop, Drop Zone Olympus, Strike Force Bravo units begin recon by the fire of Objective Troy.

8. 0530 Pegasus Regiment Main Force, commanded by Tanaurus, to march three companies (150 troops each) to the designated Line of Departure (LD), one kilometer south of Objective Troy, in two up, one back configuration.

9. 0530 Sciritae Regiment, commanded by Arcelium, to march three companies (150 troops each) to the east sector Line of Departure (LD) one kilometer south of Objective Troy, in two up, one back configuration.

10. H+2 When Objectives Poseidon and Hera secured, Hammer Force (600 troops) will move to Assembly Area Gold, awaiting further instructions.

After finishing my notes, I had just enough time to head over to the Sciritae Regiment unit area to witness the departure of Strike Force Bravo. That was the first time I had seen a company-size unit in full battle dress, including steel helmets, what they called "flack vests," and hand grenades dangling from their belts. Some carried radios on their backs. Others had claymore mines in pouches on their belts. All were loaded with large packs called rucksacks. Then there were the weapons. The fire sticks carried by the green and blacks, machine guns, grenade launchers, rocket tubes called LAWs and other tubes they called "torpedoes." Once again, too much Army jargon to comprehend. Suffice it to say this was a human armada ready to release its firepower on the enemy.

At precisely 0300 hours, Captain Kellogg led his troops out of their unit area and out of the main gate with its sign *Camp Savage Home of the Legion of Aeneas* visible in the fading moonlight.

When I returned to the TOC, Perez was just coming out of the door. He looked at me and declared that I was in "deep shit" and just kept moving. I wasn't sure what that meant, so I entered the TOC and headed toward the coffeepot. . I never made it. "Son, get your ass over here! Now!" Sergeant Travis bellowed out.

He couldn't have been talking to me; I'm several thousand years his senior. He pointed his cigar in my direction. "Yeah, you, numbnuts." I didn't know what that meant either, so I went over to where he was seated behind his desk. I thought, here comes the "deep shit" part, and I was right. I presumed I should stand at attention. Then, his inquiries began. "Alagon, are you a member of this command group?"

"Yes, Top." No first name this time.

"And what is your duty assignment?"

"Logging Specialist, Top."

"Uh huh, and were you here performing those duties at 0300?"

"No, Top, I went over to see…"

"I don't give a shit where you went; you weren't here to log the radio reports we've received for the last hour, were you?"

"No, but I"

He blew a ring of cigar smoke in my direction as he interrupted my response. "Don't bother. Your only excuse is that you have no excuse."

"Yes, Top."

"So, get over there and get your coffee, plant yourself behind that desk, and get to work!" Except for two short breaks, I never left my desk for the next twelve hours. During those twelve hours, the fate of the Underworld and Olympus hung in the balance, and I recorded it all.

🌀   🌀   🌀   🌀   🌀

When Captain Kellogg and his company-size force were proceeding to Assembly Area White, Portellis volunteered to go ahead of the main group to recon FSB Cronus. Due to his prior experience, he was the best option for determining the status of things at the base. He raced forward and was back with the main group by the time they reached the assembly area. Captain Kellogg's transmission became the first SITREP of the operation.

OPERATION GOLDEN CHARIOT
RECORD OF D-DAY OPERATIONS

0400 *Captain Kellog reports the results of Portellis' recon of Objective Troy. The activity appears routine. No extra security in place. Some evidence that troops are drinking and gambling in recreation halls. No significant signs that the enemy anticipates an attack. The whereabouts of Cronus and Adecius are unknown.*

Shortly after that transmission, Strike Force Bravo units began their move to Objective Troy, where they would conduct their reconnaissance by fire beginning at H-hour (0500).

0430 *LT Tran and 50 troops in position 400 yards from the west side of Objective Troy.*

Forward Air Controller Alexander calling in TACAIR and artillery prep for any visible targets. Results unknown.

Strike Force Alpha was the next unit to deploy. They had been on the ready line at the airfield since 0300. Three

C-130s were on an apron at the south end of the runway with ramps down. Sergeant Hopkins went aboard the lead aircraft and spoke to the captain, "I'm sure you know that this is a *Company* operation. Please instruct your crews that they are to remain on board except for loading operations."

The captain acknowledged the instructions, "Roger, Sarge."

Hopkins added, "And no pictures or recordings allowed."

The captain gave a thumbs up, "Of course."

Back in the TOC, Perez commented to no one in particular, "Well, I guess we're into the 'hurry up and wait' mode now." He explained, "The Airborne troops have been at the airfield since 0300 for a 0500 departure. Right now, they're sitting on their steel pots and packs with nothing to do but wait. We've all had to deal with it before, but we don't bitch any less."

About that time, we could hear the noise from the hercs starting their engines. There was a continuous roaring sound as they prepared to board the troops. Minutes later, Perez's radio came alive, and I logged in the transmission.

__0415__ WO Athena reports three sticks loaded.

Then,

__0430__ Pilot reports, Chalk one-niner, wheels up.

The entire command group stopped what they were doing and walked outside. The lead aircraft banked to the left in a wide arc, followed by the other two. They continued to circle as they climbed to a higher altitude. The lights on their tails and wingtips began to fade as they broke out of their circle into a single line and headed north. As they sped away, Tanaurus and Arcelium ordered their main body of troops to "saddle up." As the Pegasus and Sciritae regiments prepared to move forward, nearly 1,000 Legionnaires would be marching toward a line of departure one kilometer from Objective Troy. They were to hold their positions in preparation for the main assault on the objective.

ꙩ   ꙩ   ꙩ   ꙩ   ꙩ

While at my desk, I could listen in on the internal "chatter" of the various units. Sergeant Perez explained to me what I had heard, "Units at all levels operate on communications networks using different frequencies." He could see the quizzical look on my face and said, "Don't ask. It's too complicated."

Without thinking, I responded, "Roger." Zeus save me!

"Here, I'll show you," he said as we walked over to the row of radios being monitored by various members of the command group. He pointed down the row, "This one is the Command net. If units in the field want to talk to us, they need to switch their radio to this frequency." He pointed to a dial that read 43.95. Moving along the row, there were radios monitoring Regimental, Company, and Strike Force frequencies.

While we were talking, Captain Galanis entered the TOC. Everyone said good morning, and he responded, "Let's make sure it is."

Perez was winding up his tutorial, "And, this one is on the Air Force frequency; see, we can communicate with the FAC and the pilots."

I said, "Many thanks," to Perez as I started walking back to my desk.

Captain Galanis poured a cup of coffee and looked toward Perez, "Manny, check your watch. You've got five minutes."

Looking at his watch, Perez nodded. "Roger, Sir." He took a seat at the Command radio console. When five minutes had passed, he broadcast a message to all units in the field:

0500 (H-hour) Perez confirmed that all commanders and leaders were on the network, including those in the C-130s, and sent this message: "Legion of Aeneas, as you enter today's battle, recall the words of Alexander the Great, "Heaven cannot brook two suns, nor earth two masters." I say good luck and godspeed. —Galanis.

D-Day had begun!

Chapter 38
The Revenge of Cronus

About the time the lead pilot of Chalk One-Niner reported wheels up, Cronus and Adecius were perched on the north tower of the fire support base, looking in the direction of their two secret enclaves–known by their enemies as Objectives Poseidon and Hera. With binoculars stolen from the warehouses of Dong Tam, both Objectives were becoming visible in the early morning rays of the sun. Adecius was examining a large map as Cronus peered over his shoulder. "This, my god, is the battle plan for what they call D-Day," Adecius explained as he began pointing to the various unit locations and then to the top of the map.

Cronus spoke, "And they call this Operation Golden Chariot? What good is a chariot without wheels?" They both laughed, a laugh with the most sinister overtones.

Adecius had stationed spotters on the towers around the sprawling complex. They had been observing the movements of Strike Force Bravo as they approached the perimeter from three sides. Those movements were being reported by radio to the Dog Soldier command center within

405

the compound, as well as directly to Adecius in the north tower.

Chalk One-Niner could be heard approaching from the south. Cronus and Adecius were tracking their progress when the lead pilot reported to the TOC.

0455 Two km east of Objective Troy. Spotted three drop zones, turning west at six hundred feet. Drop zone conditions are favorable.

Then,

0500 Message from Regimental Commander Athena, "Geronimo!"

Perez looked over at me. "I'll tell you later."

As Athena had arranged, she was the first to jump just ahead of the other sticks. As she descended, she could see the lead aircraft disgorging stick number one, led by Sergeant Hopkins. Looking to her left, she did not see Sergeant Taylor's aircraft following. Her attention shifted to the drop zone below. It took just thirty seconds for her to reach the ground and execute a near-perfect PLF, which sent her steel helmet careening down the drop zone. Castor had landed about twenty meters away with his body and radio intact. With chute unharnessed, he sped over to join Athena, carrying her steel helmet.

The drop zone was soon covered with a patchwork of parachute canopies, white interspersed with the black, red and gold of the painted monsters—the head of Augus, the Furies with white teeth dripping blood, the menacing snakes on Medusa's head. Sometime later, Sergeant Castor described the scene as "lotus flowers floating on a dark pond." The command group began to rally at Athena's location. Sergeant Hopkins reported that there were a number of injuries being attended to by Sergeant Santini. After dropping their chutes, the troops began forming a defensive perimeter—a movement they had rehearsed over and over again back at Camp Savage.

Athena walked to the center of the perimeter where Sergeant Santini was triaging a half dozen soldiers, some with sprained or broken ankles, others with symptoms of concussion. Off to one side lay several lifeless Strike Force paratroopers still harnessed to their chutes, displaying the dragons and demons they had painted just the day before. One of them lay face up on his chute, appearing to be clutched between Typhon and Echidna. The fire streaming from their eyes looked all too real as the rising sun played across the drop zone. There was pain written on Athena's face as she looked down on the young paratrooper, the proud winner of the painting contest. Santini reached down and gently removed the Zippo lighter and the unopened pack of Travis' Panatelas. Santini was no stranger to death scenes, yet there were tears in his eyes as he turned to Castor and handed him the items. "Make goddam sure these get back to Camp Savage."

0525 SITREP Drop Zone Athena: Perimeter secure, six injured, four KIA. Stick Three aircraft missing, no drop executed. Assessing the situation at Objective Poseidon.

0532 pilot of Third Stick aircraft reports, "Mayday, Mayday." Returning to Camp Savage, fifty PAX onboard. Prepare runway for possible crash landing."

I didn't know what *Mayday* meant, but "crash landing" didn't sound good. The ADC shouted, "Hermes, you're the fastest guy; get over to the airfield and make sure things are squared away!"

Hermes had already exited the TOC as he called out over his shoulder, "Roger, Sir!"

Castor was trying to contact Sergeant Hopkins or anyone at Objective Poseidon without success. Athena took the handset. "Hoppy, this is Athena, over!" Silence. "Hoppy, this is Athena. I need your SITREP, over." More silence. Then, there was the sound of chaos coming over the net. All of which we heard back at the TOC; yelling, screaming, animal noises, commands being shouted. All this punctuated by bursts of M-16 and machine gun fire and numerous explosions.

Finally, the voice of Sergeant Hopkins could be heard above the din, "Under attack, repeat, under attack. Heavy casualties. Spartoi and strange beasts. Hold one." One of the Legionnaire leaders came on the line to explain that in addition to an ambush at the drop zone by Spartoi soldiers, numerous monsters and demons had emerged from underground at Objective Poseidon. Several Cyclopes crushed paratroopers as they descended to the drop zone. There were lion-headed Chimera, Eurynomos demons and more, ranging about the battlefield causing panic among some of the troops.

Sergeant Hopkins came back on the horn. "Athena, we're asshole deep in alligators over here. We are regrouping on the east side of the objective. We'll hold on, but we need every swinging Richard you can spare to double time over hear."

0545 SITREP from Captain Kellogg, Conducting recon by fire on three sides of Objective Troy when attacked by an estimated 100 Spartoi with whirling explosive devices. Executed simultaneous counterattacks from all positions, with moderate casualties. Spartoi returned to base. Holding at original firing positions.

Athena had dispatched a patrol of six paratroopers to scout what was going on at Objective Hera. Sergeant Hopkins' request for reinforcements would have to wait until her left flank was secure. The mobile command post had been established at the center of the drop zone, with multiple radios turned to Regimental and Camp Savage frequencies. Word was passed to troops on the perimeter to remain on full alert and maintain noise and light discipline, including no smoking. Athena was discussing strategy with her troop leaders when three members of the recon patrol came sprinting toward the drop zone, firing their weapons as they ran. When they got to the security perimeter, Athena and the assembled leaders heard one shouting, "Run! Hurry, run!" Another screamed in terror, "Python, Ladon. Athena, save us!"

Python and Laden were ferocious snake-like dragons within the universe of Olympus. Even considering the power of Cronus, Athena found it hard to believe they could be in Van Lang. Her greatest fear was that the troops would panic and begin to run away. She instructed the troop leaders to walk the perimeter and calm the troops. Next, she asked Castor and Santini to bring the patrol members to the command post to explain what had taken place.

"When we approached Objective Hera, those horrible creatures attacked us." one of them said. Another who was shaking uncontrollably and stammering reported, "We fired our weapons and threw grenades as they tried to wrap around us. There was blood everywhere, but they didn't stop. That's when we ran." When asked what happened to the other three members of the patrol, none of them could say.

0835 Castor provided SITREP for Strike Force Alpha. Recon of Objective Hera resulted in attacks of patrol by Python and Ladon-type creatures. Leaving a rear guard and proceeding to assist Hopkins and troops at Objective Poseidon. Three members of patrol MIA (missing in action).

***0839** Pilot reports landing approach to Camp Savage of Stick Number Three aircraft after dumping fuel. Hermes confirms the airfield is prepared for an emergency landing. Landing accomplished without incident. Sergeant Taylor enroute to TOC for debrief.*

Captain Kellogg and his Rangers continued to have problems of their own. Company-size units of Dog Soldiers exited the base and began marching in line toward all three of the Rangers' firing positions. Their progress was slowed by Legionnaire machinegun fire, claymores, and hand grenades. But as scores of enemy troops were being killed, others would take their places. Lieutenant Tran's defensive perimeter was the hardest hit.

***0930** Sergeant Osbourne reported to Captain Kellogg, Still receiving heavy fire. Running low on ammo. Count seven KIA, nineteen WIA (wounded in action). Lieutenant Tran was lightly wounded. The situation in doubt.*

There were similar reports from the other Ranger positions, generally with fewer casualties, although Sergeant Gage was reported "down" with a head wound. After consulting with Captain Galanis and the command staff, Captain Kellogg issued this order.

1020   All Strike Force Bravo units return to your assembly areas. I say again, Strike Force Bravo units return to your assembly areas. Report your arrival to Sergeant Pollux.

Also reported, *Sergeant Alexander requested artillery support as covering fire for unit withdrawals.*

I did learn that LAW stood for Light Anti-Tank Weapon. Now, if I only knew what a tank was. It happened that LAWs and grenade launchers were the most effective weapons for battling the Cyclopes and other monstrosities that emerged from Objective Poseidon. The Spartoi were using their whirling explosive weapons to some effect. But they stood in the open at close range to deploy them against the Strike Force Alpha troops and became easy targets for machine gunners, in particular. Indeed, the Legionnaires fought valiantly. Some even attacked Spartoi soldiers with their bayonets—jumping on their backs and slitting their throats. Despite their valor and heroism, the number of troops still standing had dwindled to thirty-eight, with many of them already wounded.

Athena and her replacements arrived none too soon. Fortunately, since they were approaching the battle scene from the east, they surprised the enemy soldiers and their menagerie of beasts and goblins from the rear. The eight paratroopers carrying LAWs and six with grenade launchers were positioned at the front of the oncoming Legionnaires. Against the strong objections of both Santini and Castor, Athena traded her AR-15 for a LAW and joined the troops in the front ranks. The slaughter that ensued as Athena gave the command to commence firing was beyond anything ever experienced in the Peloponnese, at Thermopile or Marathon and perhaps the Titanomachy itself. The Cyclopes were felled like the giant trees of *Kavousi.* Chimera and Eurynomos were reduced to smoldering piles of flesh, teeth, and hair. Countless others were incinerated when LAWs were fired into the opening of the underground camp. More than 100 Spartoi lay dead from machine guns and small arms fire. Gaetano, the winner of the grenade-throwing contest, continued to thwart the advance of enemy troops with record-breaking distance and accuracy. After several hours, the situation was stabilized. But Athena and her leaders agreed it was time to move to a safer location.

1250 SITREP from Strike Force Alpha Objective Poseidon secured. The threat of counterattacks is high.

Recommend moving to alternate location Sergeant Hopkins identifies as the Wagon Wheel. Requested air and artillery strikes on Objective Hera to support withdrawal. Coordinates sent to FAC. Results of action: eighteen KIA, twelve WIA, and two MIA. Standing by for approval to relocate.

Tanaurus and Arcelium had completed their movement of Pegasus and Sciritae main body troops to the designated line of departure. While holding their positions, the two Deputy Commanders could listen in on the reports from Strike Forces Alpha and Bravo. Similarly, Ares had led the 600 troops of Hammer Force Regiment to Assembly Area Gold to await further orders. As RTO, Sergeant Rogers kept the command group and leaders informed of ongoing radio traffic. Hearing what was going on at Objective Poseidon, Ares kept his concern for Athena to himself. Instead, he told his senior advisor, Sergeant Santini, "I know my sister. She will bend but never break. She dares, and she will win!"

1305 *Captain Galanis authorized Athena to relocate from the vicinity of Objective Poseidon. In the area known as the Wagon Wheel.*

***1320** Sergeant Diggs reports the condition of Sergeant Gage is critical. Evacuating to Hammer Force at Assembly Area Gold. Sergeant Salinas to arrange further evac to Camp Savage.*

***1327** SITREP Sergeant Diggs assumed command of Gage's strike force company. Enroute from Assembly Area Blue spotted an estimated company-size unit of Dog Soldiers marching in the direction of the portal. Requested artillery fire mission.*

𝕺　𝕺　𝕺　𝕺　𝕺

Even with stolen maps and ops plan documents, Adecius and his Dog Soldier commanders were surprised when TACAIR bombs and artillery rounds began disrupting their troop movements. Cronus was maintaining the shrouded conditions surrounding the Fire Support Base. As operations moved further away from the base, there was little or no protection for their troops. In the base command center, Adecius was railing on his commanders, "We know the full plans of the enemy, down to their every move. Yet, you, you *gráson*! All smelling like the goats of *Polyaigos* have failed me and your master, Cronus. A puny force of so-called Legionnaires attacked us this morning, and you did nothing to crush them!" He began pointing at the ops plan map. "Here, and here, if Cronus and I had not sent monsters and demons to Objectives Poseidon and Hera..." He tossed the map onto the floor and screamed in a demonic voice, "Poseidon, Hera!" as he stomped on the objectives.

As I later learned from one who was there, Adecius' venting went on for hours. After receiving the casualty report of 380 killed, six hundred wounded and forty-eight missing, he became so apoplectic that fire blazed in his eyes. With a violent waving of his arms, he caused the disappearance of his three top commanders, apparently in the same fashion as with Warrant Officer Savage. "We will attack again, and I will not accept any further..." His diatribe was interrupted as Cronus entered the room. Everyone stood, not sure of what would happen next.

Cronus waved his hand, signaling all to sit. The remaining leaders had looks of astonishment on their faces, mixed with fear. Cronus had never before addressed his troops directly—always through Adecius. He clutched his beard as he began speaking in a subdued but forceful voice, "I have brought you here and all these souls to help me establish New Elysium. I have given you firesticks and magical weapons that spew fire and shake the earth like the volcano of Methana." He turned to Adecius, who had remained standing by his side and placed a hand on his Commander's shoulder. "Adecius, it was you who built our fortress in the Elysian Fields." Adecius nodded with a notable look of pleasure on his face. Cronus continued, "And it was you who kidnapped Princess Lethe and gained control of the waters to build a magnificent army of Dog Soldiers."

Adecius chortled his response, "It is true, my god and master."

It almost appeared that Cronus' face had turned to stone as he upended the table where a dozen leaders were seated. "Why then have we failed on such a grand scale in the battles of this morning?" His was a rhetorical question but one that was discussed and debated for the next several hours to formulate a battle plan for going forward. At one point, there was shock and gasping among the leaders when Cronus shouted in a shrill, penetrating voice, "I must ensure that you do not fail again." He threw his arms in the air, with palms facing upward. The room began to shake violently. The leaders sat frozen in their chairs as Adecius stood next to Cronus, seemingly in anticipation of what was to come.

Suddenly, the roof of the command center disappeared, exposing the scene above. The grayish shroud that Cronus had placed over the base had turned black. The leaders looked upward and could see that the "sky" above was a moving, churning mass of dragons—some snakelike and some catlike. Their hissing and screeching was deafening—enough so that the leaders placed their hands over their ears.

Cronus raised his arms again, and the roof of the building reappeared. He scanned the room and stared at each of his leaders with blood-red eyes; then, he spoke his final words before departing, "I have brought these creatures here from the ancient realm of Van Lang. They are now under my control. They will accompany you and your men yet today. Now it is we who will drop from the sky and attack our own objectives while the Dog Soldiers crush them on the ground."

Chapter 39
On the Defensive

I could tell by the doom and gloom around the TOC that things had not progressed well in the first eight hours of Operation Golden Chariot. Even the normally coolheaded Captain Galanis was in an angry mood. At one point, I could hear him shouting at the ADC from just outside the TOC. "Goddammit, Tom! somethings fucked up here. The Spartoi and Dog Soldiers, not to mention that monsters' ball at Objective Poseidon, seemed to know our every move. On top of that, they managed to completely conceal their plans from us. What about the recons we sent up there?"

Though barely audible, I heard Fredricks say, "Sir, we can't have missed the mark that badly. Either we have a mole somewhere in the ranks, or as Heleron speculated, it might be Cronus' trickery."

1348 SITREP All field units report holding in assembly areas. No enemy activity reported.

1400 Captain Galais convened a meeting of the command group, plus Sergeant Taylor.

420

Sergeant Perez and I were only a few feet away from the briefing area, which allowed us to monitor and record incoming transmissions throughout the meeting. I was also able to record the decisions being made by Captain Galanis as he received input from the team. Here's what my scribbled notes reveal:

1. There was consensus that there was a "mole" (spy) within the ranks of the Legion. ADC Fredricks and Heleron were tasked with the analysis of possible individuals.

2. Sergeant Taylor reported the jump on Objective Hera had to be aborted due to blinding flashes of light aimed at the aircraft cockpit. Presumed work of Cronus.

3. All units except Hammer Force would be directed to establish night defensive positions (NDPs) with maximum security and ambush patrols.

4. Main body troops of Pegasus and Sciritae Regiments to extend east and west along LD, establish firing positions and act as blocking force. Prepare to RON (Remain Over Night).

5. Resupply of ammo, rations and water arrived at Camp Savage. Hammer Force was released from

Assembly Area Gold to establish supply trains from Camp Savage to forward units.

6. FAC to continue TACAIR and artillery on targets of opportunity. Establish preplanned targets for all Strike Force positions for use in the event of enemy assaults.

7. Hermes decided to run to the portal to check on security and any enemy activity. ADC and ops staff to prepare revised operations plan for D-Day+1.

As the meeting was breaking up, Perez leaned over to me and said, "Well, that was pretty much a 'come to Jesus' meeting."

My response was, "I don't know who this Jesus is, but he must be important. People around here use his name all the time."

Perez got a very serious look on his face and said, "Goddam right!"

1552 Six Rangers from Strike Force Bravo arrived at Camp Savage carrying badly sounded Sergeant Gage. ADC and Sergeant Travis treating Gage in the Commander's tent.

Then,

1559 SITREP Captain Kellogg reports sending three recon patrols from Assembly Areas Red, White and Blue to assess the situation at Objective Troy. Hermes departed for recon of the portal, wearing Hades Helmet and carrying a radio.

The ADC and Sergeant Travis returned to the TOC and went over to the briefing area where Galanis and Heleron were discussing the "lessons learned" from the morning battles. Fredricks interrupted, "Gage is in bad shape. Bobby and I did what we could for now. The prognosis is critical but stable."

Galanis looked up at Fredricks with obvious concern on his face. "What are the options, Tom?"

"We've got him sedated and comfortable, but if he doesn't improve, our best bet would be to get Santini back here. He would know what to do."

"Okay, keep us posted. Perez!"

Perez nearly jumped out of his chair, spilling his tenth cup of coffee since lunch onto his lap. "Yes, Sir!"

Bobby Travis jumped in, "Perez, if you weren't around here, what, dear god, would we do for entertainment?"

Galanis was laughing when he called over to Perez, "Get on the horn with Athena. We need her SITREP in case we want to get Santini back here."

Perez recovered from his embarrassment. "Roger, Sir."

Fredricks broke in, "After that, check to see what's up with Hermes."

"Roger that, Sir."

Perez didn't even have time to reach for his handset when every network radio in the TOC came alive at once. Strike Force unit recon patrols were reporting large troop movements heading south on a kilometer-wide front. Captain Kellogg requested to talk with Galanis. There was obvious tension in Kellogg's voice as Galanis took the handset from Perez. "This is Galanis. What's up, Gordie? Over."

"There could be at least a thousand Dog Soldiers headed our way. I'm recommending we pull back from our assembly areas and collapse back into the main body of my regiment at the LD. Over."

"Good idea. Make sure you guard your rear when you are pulling out. Over."

"Roger. What have you heard from Athena? Over."

"Hold one." Galanis turned to Perez. "Any report from Strike Force Alpha?"

Perez shook his head. "No, Sir, I can't raise them on the network. I'll keep trying." He turned to look at me, shook his head and said, "Write this down: '**1621** ain't looking good'."

Meanwhile, Galanis was back on the radio. "Gordie, Galanis here. No word yet from Strike Force Alpha. Over."

"Roger, if possible, I'd have her move down here with us. Over."

"I'll let you know if we make contact. Meanwhile, good luck with the move. Galanis, out."

Perez was right. Another hour went by, and things still weren't looking good. Things got worse when Perez radioed to ask Hermes for an update. He had arrived at the portal to find the bodies of at least 100 Spartoi and Dog Soldiers piled at the portal entrance. Using the helmet of invisibility, Hermes entered the portal. After exiting the portal, he called in his SITREP.

1740 SITREP Estimate 100+ enemy KIA at portal entrance and 50+ inside portal. All Legionnaire guards were killed. Encountered 40-50 Spartoi and Dog Soldiers battling with Legionnaire forces at Lethe. Enemy progress halted. Indications are a large contingent of Adecius' troops are on the way to force their way into the Underworld. Returning to Camp Savage.

Then,

1749 Sergeant Damon arrived at Camp Savage with one company of troops from Hammer Force prepared to establish resupply trains for forward units. Sergeant Travis led the group to the airfield where supplies of M-16 and M-

60 machine gun ammunition, LAWs, grenades, food, and water were stacked.

For once, I knew what the Army-types were talking about. Supply trains were commonly used by Phillip of Macedonia and his son Alexander the Great. They had soldiers and servants who carried supplies before and during battles. Before long, a snaking line of Hammer Force troops came past the TOC carrying bundles of LAWs, packs filled with grenades and claymores, cases of C-rations and jugs of water. Others carried green metal boxes of ammunition, cases of radio batteries, medical packs with white crosses painted on them, crates of grenades marked CS-Gas and White Phosphorus (Willie Peter), and critical items for tired and hungry troops, large boxes of cigarettes. Standing at the door of the TOC with my own cigarette sending smoke into the afternoon air, I could imagine myself in the Zagros Mountain pass as General Parmenion led the trains for Alexander's army to help win the battle of the Persian Gates.

The ADC estimated that Ares' troops could carry as much as 10,000 kilos (20,000 pounds) of supplies during each trip to the front. That seemed like a lot to me. Top was outside the TOC enjoying his cigar, so I asked him why more than one trip would be needed.

"Good question, Alagon. I've always said this 'modern' army carries too much shit, but I just requisition what the units ask for."

"So, how much is that?" I asked, hoping Top didn't think I was a dufus for asking. Forgive me, Dionysus, my language skills are going to hell in a handbasket. As we talked, the phalanx of troops heading north continued passing by.

A few more puffs on his cigar and Top answered my question, "The average grunt…"

Here we go again. "The average what, Top?" I asked, confused as always.

Travis replied, "Oh, I forgot, Alagon, you're just a straphanger. Grunts are Infantry troops. Back in the old days, we were called ground pounders. Anyhow. The Legionnaires are each carrying fifty pounds of gear, ammo, rations and water, not counting their flack vests, weapons, uniforms and boots. So, fifty pounds times 1,800 troops equals 90,000 pounds. Like I said, that's a lotta shit!"

It was time for both of us to get back to our desks. Perez had been monitoring the internal chatter of the field units with no news to report. After putting the fourth packet of sugar into my cup of coffee, I asked Perez, "Why did Top call me a straphanger?"

Perez chuckled and said, "Don't worry, it's not a bad thing. In the Airborne, a straphanger is a paratrooper from another unit riding along for the jump with your unit's stick. But Rangers and Green Berets who consider you a trusted friend, make a straphanger an honorary member of the group. So, you are officially a straphanger of the A-Team."

I smiled broadly at the notion and was expressing my delight to Perez when the Strike Force Alpha network radio came alive. We all stopped to listen. The transmission was garbled. The sounds of small arms fire and grenades in the background made matters worse. What we did eventually hear was, "This is Hoppy (broken) we are (broken). Athena, over here. Stay down! (multiple explosions) This is Hoppy, over."

Galanis grabbed the handset. "Hoppy, this is Galanis. You're coming in broken, over."

Hoppy came back on; he was breathing heavily as weapons fire grew fainter. "Roger. I'm moving to a better location. Hold one."

There was dead silence in the TOC, then, "This is Athena. We are under heavy attack. I say again, under heavy attack. Adecius is here!" A shock wave coursed through the TOC.

"Athena, this is Galanis, acknowledge." Silence. "I repeat, this is Galanis, acknowledge!"

Minutes went by. The TOC was filled with a thick haze of smoke as everyone nervously lit one cigarette after another. The only sound was the snapping shut of their Zippos. Castor came on the network and gave a brief SITREP.

1438 SITREP Sergeant Castor reported, Heavy attack by estimated 300 Spartoi and Dog Soldiers being led by Adecius. Security perimeter holding with good cover and concealment. Sky turning black to the south. Athena and Hoppy investigating. Several monsters and demons approaching from direction of Objectives Poseidon and

Hera. Low on ammo and water. Request resupply and reinforcements. Out.

Galanis started pacing and began issuing orders.

"Tom, get on the horn to Ton Son Nhut. We need two hercs here now!"

"Bobby, get Sergeant Taylor over here ASAP."

"Perez, inform all Regimental Commanders, Deputy Commanders and senior leaders of the current situation."

"Anyone know what's up with Hermes? Top, see if you can make contact. I want to talk with him."

"Heleron, as you and I discussed, you need to collect up the Aegis and various weapons belonging to the Six and get them over to the airfield."

"Alagon, head over to the Strike Force Alpha training area and get me a parachute, harness, and steel helmet. And make sure Sergeant Taylor is on his way."

His voice was resounding through the TOC like so many *trebuchets* being fired one after another. When Hermes came on the radio, Sergeant Taylor was in the TOC.

It was then that we all learned what Galanis had in mind. Everyone was seated in the briefing area. Galanis shouted, "Perez, bring that radio over here. Alagon, sit over here and make sure you get this all down." I did, of course!

1510 Commander's meeting regarding relief efforts for Strike Force Alpha.

1. Two C-130s are scheduled to arrive at Camp Savage NLT 1600 hours. Stick Three from the previous mission prepared for the jump at DZ Tiger at approximately 1700 hours. Sergeant Taylor, jumpmaster, Captain Galanis assault commander.

2. Stick Three personnel to load the second C-130 with full resupply for two days of operations. Sergeant Travis to supervise the loading of pallets and cargo nets. Sergeant Taylor to supervise rigging.

3. Selected leaders to carry "special weapons" for airborne drop, along with assigned security detail.

4. Heleron to radio Commander Tanaurus with Pegasus' main body and brief him on the situation and plans for relief. One company to begin movement to the vicinity of Strike Force Alpha's position.

5. Perez to contact regimental command groups and set up a staggered schedule of SITREPs every thirty minutes.

6. Hermes to run to Strike Force alpha location. Use Hades Helmet to make contact with Athena. Brief their command group on plans for relief. Provide updates to ADC.

7. ADC to contact Sergeant Alexander. Have him establish preplanned targets at Athena's location, including close-in. Highest priority.

1540 *Briefing ended.*

As soon as the meeting ended, the command group descended on Galanis. Fredricks spoke first, "Sir, you are needed here. Leading the drop should be my responsibility."

Travis growls "Goddammit, Sir, don't make me pull rank on you. Remember, I'm a Colonel in the reserves!"

Perez made his pitch "You're gonna need an RTO out there. I'd better get a chute ready."

Galanis was having none of it. The issue was settled when Heleron spoke with a soothing voice, "In Elysium, stories are often told of the great Alexander. He always led his troops from the front. When his troops went hungry or thirsty, he went hungry or thirsty; when their horses died beneath them, and they had to walk, he did the same; and now Galanis, *you* must do the same.”

ʚ   ʚ   ʚ   ʚ   ʚ

“The next few hours are going to be critical,” Fredricks was speaking to the ops team. “Each of us will need to monitor the command networks.”

Galanis cut in, “Don’t forget the FAC. I want Alexander’s full attention. When I get on the ground, I’ll take full responsibility for coordinating TACAIR and arty.”

“Roger,” Fredricks responded as he continued to assign monitoring responsibilities, “I’ll stay with Gordie Kellogg and Sciritae. Top, take Pegasus’ main body with Tanaurus. Heleron, Sir, would you get up with Ares and let him know you’ll be his contact?”

Heleron placed his closed fist over his heart in the traditional Legionnaire salute, smiled broadly and said, “As your Sergeant Diggs would say, ‘I’m on it,’” providing a bit of relief from the tense situation.

The ADC continued, "Perez, stick with Strike Force Alpha and report any updates directly to Captain Galanis."

The Supreme Commander had just finished strapping on his parachute and donning his steel helmet, when Sargeant Travis came into the TOC with a strange look on his face. Galanis looked at Travis and said, "I gotta get going, what's up, Top?"

The old soldier seemed to be holding back tears when he responded, "Sir, we just lost Sargeant Gage."

"Perez banged on his desk and erupted, "Fuck no, goddammit, we've come too far for this!"

Galanis looked over to Fredricks and then back to Travis, "I know you two did everything you could. When this is all over, we'll give him a proper send-off." Galanis grabbed his AR-15. Choking up, he said, "Sorry guys, I've got to get over to the airfield. Exiting the TOC he looked back, "Tom, you're in charge. Stay with it."

Fredricks responded, "Roger. Airborne, Sir!" as Galanis headed out of the TOC—a case of the air being sucked out of the room. The ADC broke the silence, "That's one stubborn Greek. No offense, Heleron. Okay, Perez, get the FAC on the line. I'll get him pooped up."

No comment.

1622 *Hermes arrived at the Strike Force Alpha location. No sign of Athena or paratroopers. Reconned one kilometer in all directions but unable to locate. Request further instructions. Situation reported to Captain Galanis on board C-130 ready for takeoff.*

Then,

1628 *Hercs shut down. Galanis is returning to TOC.*

By the time Galanis got back to the TOC, every network radio, except for Strike Force Alpha, was blaring out reports of an attack by Spartoi and Dog Soldier forces. There were heavy casualties all along the LD. I feverously scribbled notes as the reports poured in.

> — Pollux reports from the Sciritae command group. Captain Kellogg was wounded but still in command. Lieutenant Tran and twelve Rangers KIA. Sergeant Osbourne and two

company commanders, MIA. Approximately twenty WIA. Fighting continues.

- Ares, "trains under attack, moderate casualties. Resupply impossible. Enemy forces are approaching my location. Request air support."
- Tanaurus and Arcelium both report losses estimated at ten percent. Breaches by the enemy in three locations. Need resupply immediately.
- Hermes observed a large black mass in the sky, headed south toward Legion troop locations. No further details.
- No further communication from Strike Force Alpha.

Galanis was listening in and pacing. He went to the coffeepot and poured a cup. Suddenly he swung around, slammed the cup down and yelled, "What the fuck's going on here, guys? We've been screwing the pooch all goddam day!" I cringed at the thought.

Then Heleron spoke up, "Galanis, surely you know this is Cronus' work. Strike Force Alpha has gone missing, just as the tower and green and blacks disappeared at the portal entrance. It is a trick of time."

Galanis had calmed down and sat at his desk, musing. "You're right, Heleron. We know he used the same tricks to steal weapons and supplies from Dong Tam."

Heleron walked to the center of the TOC, and his demeanor became that of Demosthenes or Socrates as he spoke, "We are confronted with a two-headed serpent. Adecius is one of those heads. He has used the powers of Cronus, some of which he possesses, and the disturbance in the Underworld to create an army capable of fighting the way you fight. The other head is Cronus, with all the powers of the Titan he once was. You do not have a way to counter his powers. Only Zeus, and through him, the Six, can do that."

Galanis was pacing again. This time, smoking one of Travis' cigars. Stopping, he turned to Heleron. "So that is why you insisted I take the Aegis and other weapons to Athena?"

"Quite so," Heleron replied.

Chapter 40
Counterattack

It didn't take long for Galanis to react to Heleron's words. A speech I would hope to one day repeat on stage back in Plaka. Galanis strode over to the easel in the briefing area and began sketching out his plan. In large letters at the top, he wrote–*COUNTERATTACK*. He turned and motioned for everyone to take seats. He began, "We have no choice but to counterattack and to do so before another thousand troops descend on what now has become our line of defense." He drew a dark line across the page and labeled it LDEF. Two circles below that line indicated the positions of Pegasus and Sciritae main force units. Off to the right side (east) of the drawing was a third circle labeled Hammer Force. At the bottom was Camp Savage.

He explained that the counterattack could not succeed unless the Legion massed its forces. He drew an arrow signifying that Hammer Force would be moved from Assembly Area Gold and come online at the LDEF, linking up with the eastern flank of Arcelium's Legionnaires. They were to attempt a relief of the resupply trains in their sectors.

There were more arrows and lines–flight path, the direction of advance, commitment of reserve forces, drop zone. I was trying to keep up when, thankfully, the commander summarized the plan, "We need to switch gears. As Heleron said, we need to fight both heads of the serpent. First, all units are desperate for resupply. Top, when we get done here, get over to the airfield and make sure we have max cargo on that second Herc."

Travis' adrenalin was up. He boomed out, "Roger, Sir!"

Galanis continued, "And, Bobby, reconfigure the load for three drops, one to each regiment."

"Will do. Unless you need me here for now, I'd better get over there."

"Drive on. And Sergeant Taylor…"

Taylor was as pumped as all of us. He stood up as if ready to run through the wall of the TOC. "Yes, Sir!"

"You need to go with Top and get your troopers squared away for our jump. Before you go." Galanis looked at his watch. "Let's synchronize. On my mark, it will be

1720. Mark. We need to be wheels up at 1750. That will get us over the drop zone at EENT." Turning to Travis and Taylor, he said, "Okay, you two can take off. Vince, I'll be over there shortly for a mission briefing."

The last part of the plan involved the Six. Heeding Heleron's advice, Galanis wanted to deploy the weapons the Six had brought with them to Van Lang. He needed the warrior-gods with him at the front. Once Hammer Force had relocated to the LDEF, Ares and Damon were to make their way to Captain Kellogg's command post (CP) at the center of the line. There, they would join up with Pollux, Captain Kellogg's RTO, and Hermes, who would race to the CP, using Hades Helmet to spy on the enemy on his way there. Having four of the Six at one location was the best option until Athena and Castor returned. Of course, having the four warrior-gods together wouldn't be sufficient unless they had their special weapons. The delivery of which was a critical element of the upcoming jump.

☙ ☙ ☙ ☙ ☙

Once again, Galanis was on the lead C-130 preparing for takeoff. The second aircraft was loaded with 50,000 pounds of resupply, 8,000 pounds above the maximum payload. Bobby Travis "convinced" the crew to ignore the standard limits. The lead pilot contacted the TOC, "Chalk One-Niner, Stick Three, ready for takeoff."

The ADC responded, "Chalk One-Niner, hold, Sir."

The pilot replied, "Roger, One-Niner holding."

1743 Tanaurus, Captain Kellogg, Arcelium and Ares all report black sky has reached their locations. Identified as swarming dragons. Attack appears imminent. Localized attacks from ground forces continue. Casualties are estimated as a combined thirty percent.

1745 message, "This is Galanis. Our mission is a go. I say again, the mission is a go. Out."

As planned, the Hercs were wheels up at 1750. Off to the west, Helios was driving his chariot low across the sky, signaling another sunset. My friends, the ibis were settling into the banyan trees off in the distance. Under different circumstances, I would transform, take flight, and join them. Why not? Transform, I mean. Like it or not, I had become part of the story I was telling. No longer just an observer and scribe. "Tom," I shouted as I sprinted from my desk to the briefing area, "I should be out there!" The ADC was so fixed on reviewing maps for the counterattack that he didn't even look up. Instead, he lit another cigarette as he crushed out the last one. I got his attention. "Tom, listen, Heleron is right; we need to fight magic with magic. Zeus didn't give me extraordinary powers just to be a messenger."

Fredricks looked up. "Alagon, what are you talking about?"

"I'm not a warrior-god, but I can use my special powers to help Galanis and the Legion." I turned back to Travis and Perez. "Top, can you and Perez keep the logbooks while I'm gone?"

Travis and Perez looked at one another, and Travis said in his most sarcastic tone, "Sure, Alagon, and we'll fluff the pillow on your cot for when you get back. Do you mind telling us what the hell you're up to?"

"I'm going to the front. If everything goes okay, I'll call Perez with a SITREP." I stepped through the door of the TOC, spun around twice and transformed into a golden falcon, since what I needed was speed. The speed that would take me to Captain Kellogg's CP even before the airborne drop.

The following messages were entered into the logbooks by Sergeants Travis and Perez:

1815 Lead pilot reports turning east on the designated flight path. Eight minutes to drop. Altitude 300 feet.

Then,

1838 Lead pilot confirms all PAX and cargo away. Returning to Tan Son Nhut Base.

I arrived at the LDEF sometime before the scheduled jump and resupply. I was astonished at the range of my vision while in the air. I could see individual leaves on the trees, a rat running through the tall grass, and a steel helmet with holes in the side. Lying next to it was a dead Ranger. Without noticing, I was about to fly into that dark sky the units had reported seeing. The squawking and hissing ahead caught my attention, but too soon, I was surrounded by hundreds of dragon-like creatures. They took no notice of me. Their focus was on the activity below.

Like the cranes that decimated the pygmaioi, these black demons plunged from the sky and began attacking regimental units all along the front. The scene was one of pure carnage and mayhem. I started searching for Captain Kellogg's CP when I saw two giant birds flying straight at me. I guess my eyesight was not that helpful after all. Those were the two C-130s from Camp Savage. I swooped toward the ground to prevent a collision. Before I could land, I had to perform a number of aerial movements to avoid paratroopers and large pallets and nets containing the resupply. I landed in a large banyan tree and looked up. Sergeant Taylor's paratroopers were firing their weapons at the dragons who began attacking them. Ironically, the menacing creatures were staring at the dragons and monsters painted on the parachute canopies.

I continued to watch as paratroopers fell to the ground when their canopies collapsed. Dozens more of the attackers began to land on the resupply pallets and nets, using their catlike claws to sever the ropes (I think the troopers call them risers). One by one, the cargo bundles slammed into the ground, scattering the contents well short of the intended drop area. I had to do something to stop the rampage. I had never really tested my special powers beyond transforming into small, harmless animals and birds. Think, Alagon, think, I kept repeating in my feathered head. Just then, my eyesight came into play once again. Even in the last moments of a blinding sunset, I saw a paratrooper slipping past the vicious dragon predators and ready to "hit the ground running," according to his training. I saw his canopy as if it were silhouetted in a sunrise over Santorini. Staring at me was the twisted face of Typhon. If my transformation were possible, I would turn the father of all monsters against the evil of Cronus and Adecius in the form of personal revenge. Typhon had once tried to overthrow Zeus for supremacy of the cosmos but lost. Now, perhaps, he (I) could help to defeat Cronus.

In his Theogony, Hesiod described Typhon as "Terrible, outrageous and lawless." To help the readers of this story understand the horror that Typhon presents to his victims, I consulted my copy of the Theogony and read this about Typhon:

"Strength was in his hands… From his shoulders grew a hundred heads of a snake, a fearful dragon, with dark, flickering tongues, and from under the brows of his eyes in his marvelous heads flashed fire, and the fire burned from his heads as he glared. And there were voices in all his dreadful heads which uttered every kind of sound unspeakable… he would hiss so that the high mountains re-echoed."

As I turned around on my perch, I would need all the strength of Zeus to transform. Suddenly, my body (the body of Typhon) grew up to a great height, so huge that the massive banyan tree collapsed beneath me. My first instinct was to kill the dragons that were attacking the paratroopers and resupply cargo. I began bellowing and hissing as flames projected from my eyes and from the snakes on my head. This was a strange and uncomfortable sensation, but I charged straight ahead. Reaching the site of the carnage, I began plucking dragons from the air below me. They screeched and hissed while being crushed by giant hands or being incinerated by the flames from my head. The ground below me turned black with the carcasses of those demons. Any that were still alive were crushed under my feet as I began carrying the pallets and bundles of resupply to the units in the LDEF. Several troops began firing their M-16s at me, to no effect, as their bullets bounced off my leathery skin. However, when the Legionnaires realized what I was doing, cheers, shouts and hoorahs echoed all along the front line.

Swarms of dragons were still attacking units in several locations. I could see they were inflicting great harm on all three regiments. I strode to the western end of the LDEF and began scooping up handfuls of demons and crushing them while stomping on others who were attempting to enter Legionnaire firing positions. By the time I reached the eastern end of the front line and turned around, the ground from the LDEF to a distance of several kilometers was solid black as from a great conflagration. Yet, it was the crushed and burned bodies of Cronus' dragons.

⊘   ⊘   ⊘   ⊘   ⊘

After creating mayhem and chaos as Typhon, I was praying to Zeus and all the gods of Olympus to once again be the trickster, actor, and messenger, Alagon. I went back to the location of Captain Kellogg and his Ranger CP. As I walked, I could see hundreds of Spartoi and Dog Soldiers fleeing in the direction of their fire support base. At least for the moment, the battlefield fell eerily silent. At my height, I could spot the Ranger CP. In the center of the security perimeter stood Captains Kellogg and Galanis. Beside them were the four warrior-gods, Ares, Hermes, Damon, and Pollux. It was time to make my presence known.

⊘   ⊘   ⊘   ⊘   ⊘

Adecius was standing on the south-facing tower of the fire support base, peering through his binoculars. He was

448

unable to see as far as the LDEF positions of the Legion forces, but he knew something had gone wrong by the absence of Cronus' dragons at the battle scene. He was about to dispatch several Spartoi troops to investigate when a mass of several hundred Spartoi and Dog Soldiers could be seen racing toward the base. At that point, Cronus appeared beside his troop commander and inquired, "What has happened? Why are your soldiers running this way instead of crushing the enemy?"

Adecius' face seemed unusually twisted. His eyes were black instead of glowing red. As he turned to respond to Cronus' questions it was clear that he was worried. "We should shoot these cowards for deserting the battlefield, my god, but we should hear their reasons first. We may need them later."

"And what of my dragons?" Cronus asked as he showed extreme displeasure.

"By some trickery or magic, they are gone!"

He handed the binoculars to Cronus. The all-powerful ruler of Elysium scanned the horizon. Flocks of ibis were transiting the Plain of Reeds. Otherwise, the sky was clear as far as he could see. "What do you have planned now, Commander?" Cronus said as he returned the binoculars to Adecius.

"Now, my god and master, we fight to the death!" Adecius was in a frenzy as he once again faced his commanders in the command center. They were joined by senior leaders of Spartoi and Dog Soldiers, who explained what had taken place at the battle scene.

In their view, if they had not retreated, all would have suffered the same fate as the dragons. Even those who were not in the battle were shocked at the mention of Typhon. Adecius bristled at what he was hearing. He began screaming at his command group, "I shouldn't care if Zeus himself were there flinging his murderous thunderbolts! Don't worry. You and all those who ran away will have a chance to redeem yourselves. And, this time, I will lead the attack myself. I am told there are nearly 500 Spartoi and 3,000 Dog Soldiers who are combat-ready. Now return to your units and prepare to march, every last man." No shouts or foot stomping, as the leaders somberly left the command center. They were to have their troops heavily armed and ready to march out in one hour.

ᔕ   ᔕ   ᔕ   ᔕ   ᔕ

Reversing my transformation as Typhon worked well. I was able to pass through the lines on my way to the CP amidst cheers and backslapping. If only it was my adoring fans back at Dionysius' Theatre. Even though I was an honorary Green Beret, I didn't feel I deserved any praise for what Zeus had empowered me to do. Upon entering the Command CP, the first thing that caught my attention was Captain Kellogg smoking a cigarette and talking on his command radio. The yellow in his Ranger tab was crimson, as was the entire sleeve of his Tiger fatigues from his bloody wound. He was receiving SITREPs reporting that the distribution of resupply had been accomplished. The troops were digging into their C-rations and LRRPs. No one needed to say smoke 'em if you got 'em.

Although I enjoyed the warm welcome and being reunited with the four warrior-gods, my attention was constantly drawn to the CP radio traffic, as if I were back at Camp Savage with my logbooks. Any sense of celebration or relief was quickly overshadowed as I heard Captain Galanis calling in the SITREPs for all of the forward units. Sergent Perez recorded the message.

1014 SITREP from Captain Galanis: Airborne drop interdicted by swarms of dragons, heavy casualties and loss of resupply. Made it through the night thanks to Alagon, who is here with me now (explain later). Majority of resupply recovered and distributed along the line. Finalizing plans for the counterattack, but troop strength may not be sufficient. Total losses for two days of operations are as follows:

	KIA	WIA	MIA	TOTAL
PEGASUS*	27	51	112	190
SCIRITAE	68	89	19	176
HAMMER FORCE[+]	59	62	1158	279
TOTAL	154	202	289	645

**Pegasus MIAs include Athena's strike force of 100.*

[+]Hammer Force MIAs include 142 members of resupply trains not recovered.

Even without my abacus, I calculated the losses at thirty-six percent–very high. I recall some of the great hoplite battles, which were brutal, often resulting in hand-to-hand combat, had losses of less than fifteen percent.

Regardless, Galanis' report of casualties sent shockwaves up and down the ranks. His plan for a counterattack seemed to be dashed. He was forced to consolidate his units to strengthen the LDEF perimeter, making sure that gaps were closed, and the resupply was adequately distributed to all units.

I was discussing the situation with Ares and the other warrior-gods. Ares spoke in anger, "We haven't come all this way to be defeated. We are Greeks in the traditions of Hercules, Jason and the namesake of our Legion, Aeneas!"

Damon jumped in, "Goddamn right, and we are Green Berets, the best soldiers in the universe. We will all stand and die if it comes to that!"

Hermes changed the subject, "We need to prepare for the next attack. Pollux, has Captain Galanis gotten a report on our special weapons?"

"Units are still searching. They were scattered during the attack on the drop. Recovery parties have been sent out, but they must deal with the thousands of dragon carcasses covering the area."

While our discourse continued, a thunderous sound enveloped the entire battlefield, and the earth trembled. Units all along the front were in their firing positions, anticipating another attack from the north. Minutes passed. There were no enemy forces to be seen or heard. No black beasts in the sky. Then, with a blinding flash of light, Adecius appeared in the distance. Behind him stood a collection of Legionnaires, presumably those captured in battle. The order rang out along the front. "Hold your fire! Hold your fire!"

This was the mystical Adecius, perhaps twenty feet tall, as he once appeared to the Six on their way to Delphi. As then, his eyes were burning from red to white hot, and the rumbling sound of his voice was the same. "Listen to me! Galanis, your mission here has failed. Ares, the quest that Zeus has demanded of you is at an end. If you surrender now, you will all be welcomed into New Elysium to serve your true god and master, Cronus."

There were shouts and hisses from the ranks. Some shouted *Hestika*. Others, *Putanha Cronus*. There were others even more graphic.

Captain Kellogg ran over to where the warrior-gods and I were standing. "What are they saying?"

Damon laughed and said, "As Sergeant Diggs would put it, 'We don't give a shit, you whore of Cronus.'"

"I'm not sure that's a good thing to be saying right now," replied Captain Kellogg.

"Captain," Hermes responded, "if our troops didn't use these words, they wouldn't be Greeks."

Adecius himself began to laugh and bellow. "Say what you will, but the true god Cronus is a magnanimous god." He stretched out his arms and twisted around, "See," he said, "he has even returned your beloved goddess Athena, although she looks more like one of my Dog Soldiers." The group of soldiers behind Adecius began moving forward. It was true, Athena and her strike force (what was left of it) was being released to rejoin their regiment. The cursing changed to cheers and stomping feet as Athena and her unit passed through the line and proceeded to the Command CP.

Adecius looked directly at Galanis and his command group. "What should I tell my god and master? Will you join us in the building of New Elysium, or has Athena been returned merely to die like the rest?"

Galanis walked over to me and curiously asked me how to say nuts in Greek, which I guessed was a way to say "go to hell." I thought for a moment and offered *Papária,* an insult that means testicles. The Supreme Commander stepped through the security perimeter and looked up at Adecius. In his loudest voice, he shouted, "Tell your true god, *Papária.*"

A roar went up from the Legionnaires behind Galanis, which spread all along the line. The voices of all three regiments repeated, *"Papária! Papária! Papária!"*

Adecius reached down and picked up two handfuls of dragons, scorched and mutilated. "You think you can defeat us like this?" He threw the carcasses to the ground, "Let me show you." He turned and faced in the direction of his fire support base and let out a screech so loud the Legionnaires covered their ears. Then, the army of Spartoi and Dog Soldiers, some 3,500 strong, appeared on the horizon. Adecius strode back to meet them and then reverted to his normal size. They began to march steadily toward the regimental unit positions.

𝓼　𝓼　𝓼　𝓼　𝓼

Galanis summoned all unit commanders to the CP. There was no time to waste. Athena announced that she had returned with sixty-two paratroopers, including Castor and Sergeants Hopkins and Santini. Seven were wounded but fit for duty. Galanis polled the commanders once again to confirm total fighting strength. With the return of Strike Force Alpha, and more than 150 wounded volunteering to return to duty (the remaining WIAs were critically injured and unable to volunteer), the losses had been reduced to 430. Ares came to the briefing later and reported the recovery of thirty-four troops from the resupply trains, adding those and the fourteen Green Berets of the Augmented A-Team still left them nearly thirty percent short of their original strength.

1345 Captain Galanis reported the return of Athena and sixty-two members of Strike Force Alpha. Attack by Adecius forces eminent; 1,418 officers and men preparing to repel. FAC controlling TACAIR and artillery on preplanned targets this sector. Close-in fires on call. Thanks to the TOC staff for resupply and ongoing support.

That was the last message received in the TOC before all unit networks went silent. Travis and Perez spent the next three hours attempting to reestablish communication, to no avail. Fredricks radioed his contact at Dong Tam and MAC-V to find out if there was an atmospheric disturbance or other phenomenon disrupting their communications. Answer all around: negative.

Back in the CP, we learned that the disruption of communications was no work of nature. Galanis' meeting with his commanders was ongoing when every radio network in the CP and along the entire LDEF came to life with the sounding of bugles, followed by the threatening voice of Cronus!

"You have tested my powers and failed to overcome them. My army stands ready to liquidate your forces and bring Zeus' audacious quest to an end. And for you, the gods and soldiers of your pitiful A-Team, special fate awaits you in Tartarus when I sit on the throne of the usurper Hades. You have until the moon is at its zenith to surrender and prepare to march to New Elysium. I will wait no longer."

Fredricks walked outside the TOC, lit a cigarette and took a long drag. The sun would be setting in half an hour.

Already, the yellow, red and orange hues were dancing across Camp Savage. The steel plating of the runway glowed like burnished bronze. Close by, the jump tower stood as a silent reminder of Athena and Strike Force Alpha. He turned to look northward; Tent City looked somehow derelict now that the Legionnaires were gone. Just beyond was the main gate with its sign proclaiming this place as the home of the Legion of Aeneas. He thought of his beloved A-Team and the Six out there in the hastening darkness.

Sergeant Travis came out to join the ADC and offered him a sip of brandy. The cigar in his mouth couldn't conceal the worry on his face. It was fully dark by that time, and Fredricks was looking up at the night sky. "Waddaya think, Sir?" Travis asked between puffs.

Fredricks took another sip of brandy, "Ever since I was a kid, I studied the night sky back in Oklahoma. Even here, I can see the heroes of mythology that I used to think of as my friends. There's one over there, Hercules, and over there, Pegasus, next to Aries. Somehow, we are now one with them. But we are left with one burning question. If we are all children of Zeus, where is our father now?"

Silently, they watched the moon until it was straight overhead. Heleron burst through the door of the TOC, shouting, "Tom, Sergeant Travis, Perez is gone! He has disappeared. What…" He stopped in midsentence and looked from side to side. No one was there, only the haze of Sergeant Travis' panatela.

Before Heleron could react further, Perez' radio came to life with the startled voice of Captain Kellogg, "Tom, this Gordie. Over." Heleron hurried to the radio, "Tom, this is Gordie, urgent. Over!"

Heleron grabbed the handset. "Captain Kellogg, this is Commander Heleron. Over."

"Let me talk to the ADC. We've got big trouble here. Over."

"He is gone. They are gone. Just disappeared. Over."

"Fuck, what's going on? Cronus came on our networks and demanded we surrender. Hold one, have you found them? Found anyone? Goddammit, get back out there and find them! Sorry Heleron, but the entire A-Team warrior-gods and all have gone missing. Over."

"Captain, you won't find them unless Cronus wants you to, as he did with Athena and Strike Force Alpha. Over."

"I was afraid of that. I'm taking command as of now. Stay by the radio; we may need your help. We'll keep you informed. Out."

Chapter 41
A Common Course

As a member of Ong Troi's imperial court, Trang Quỳnh was present for the meeting between Ong Troi and Zeus and all that followed thereafter. This part of my story is as it was told to me by Trang Quỳnh.

Zeus arrived at Ong Troi's palace in the golden chariot of Helios. The Sun God was making his way from the east to his nightly destination beyond the western horizon. A guard stood rigidly at the palace entrance. He was more than ten feet tall with a muscular build that reminded Zeus of his son Hercules. The guard struck his staff of gold twice on the floor of polished imperial jade. When he opened the golden door, a beautiful goddess appeared and beckoned Zeus to enter the palace. His escort was the Princess God Lieu Hanh, the Mother Goddess to the mortals of Van Lang. She is one of four immortals, counterparts, I suppose, to the twelve immortals of Olympus. Her name means Four Palaces, denoting heaven, earth, mountains, and water, which she guards on behalf of the people of Van Lang. Undoubtedly, Zeus took note of her great beauty, as was his custom back in Olympus. They passed through a grand corridor and came upon a vast garden. There were waterfalls and ponds surrounded by bougainvillea and jacaranda trees. Almond and tamarind trees stood among blankets of vividly colored flowers emitting exotic fragrances.

Overhead, birds flitted about, some chirping, others squawking. The large cranes, parrots and bluebirds were familiar to the All-Father, but many more were exotic and unfamiliar. Observing the resplendency of all he was seeing; Zeus' attention was drawn to a menagerie of both familiar and strange animals. Tigers, bears, and leopards ranged throughout the tropical setting. Turtles, otters, and crocodiles lounged on the shores of the great pond. Most exotic were the elephants, rhinoceros, multi-colored monkeys and dragons of all sorts.

The Mother Goddess stretched out her arms and said, "This is the realm of Ong Troi, who rules <u>all</u> of the Universe." Zeus thought her emphasis on the word "all" might not bode well for his efforts to enlist the aid of Ong Troi. He nodded but said nothing. The Princess led him along a gilded path that wound through the garden. When they reached the end, there was a golden door where another guard stood watch. She clapped her hands, and the guard opened the door. A gong was sounded three times, and a cloud of incense wafted forth. Through the haze, Zeus could see a most beautiful goddess with three bluebirds circling above her head.

Trang Quỳnh described her to me. She is Tây Vương Mẫu, the wife of Ong Troi. "She is a woman of outstanding beauty. Surrounding her head is an aura of brightness. Her hair sits high on her head with a bejeweled golden comb, giving the appearance of a crown. Her face is albus white with a small mouth painted red. She wears robes of gold and red with overlapping silk garments of orange, blue and green. A band of gold surrounds her waist, with chains of gold, pearls, and jade falling to her feet. She is always accompanied by three bluebirds, which transform into a flock of beautiful and graceful maids that provide her with food."

Queen Mẫu nodded her head, a signal for the Princess God Lieu Hanh to escort Zeus to her. Zeus spoke first, "Dear Queen Mẫu, it is my honor to be here. I sense we already know each other, as we both know the sun and the moon."

She smiled and replied inscrutably, "The wind and the rain also surround the universe of Ong Troi."

Zeus looked at her face, with its aura of light and said in an unusually soft tone to reassure her of his intentions, "Queen Mẫu, I can sense that our two realms of the Universe are of the same nature. As gods in the realm of Olympus, we protect the earth with its mountains and waters for the benefit of our people."

"Yes," she rejoined, "we know, like us, you believe in upholding virtue, living a moral life and honoring the gods." Zeus was perplexed; how *could* she know?

As they approached the golden door entrance to the palace, the Queen's bluebirds flew away. When the Queen and Zeus entered the great hall, they were surrounded by a herd of fairies flitting about and guiding them to the throne room. It was time to meet the God of Heaven, Ong Troi.

When we later talked, Trang Quỳnh referred to Ong Troi as a Mandarin, meaning a person or, in his case, a god of the highest order. That title provides the God of Heaven further connection to the earth below, where mandarins are an important part of government and society.

He sees everything and knows everything that happens in the world. No one escapes the net of heaven; heaven determines everything. When he is angry with mortals, he can cause disasters like storms, floods and droughts. As to his appearance, his imperial garments are embroidered with a golden dragon. He wears a hat with red tassels down to his cheeks of golden hue. His eyes are dark and piercing, and a mustache extends from his upper lip to his chin. Five colors of pearls accent his robes and his golden slippers. He sits on a throne of gold and holds the sacred Hõt (dragon), which he touches each time he has to deal with things on heaven and earth. Since there are nine levels of heaven, various gods of heaven stand to the left and right of the throne to receive his commands.

Zeus approached the throne and held out his oakleaf crown to Ong Troi as a symbol of peace. The God of Heaven placed his hands in front of his chest in prayer-like fashion and bowed slightly, then reached out and touched the crown. He turned abruptly and sat on his throne. Zeus was left with no choice but to return the crown to his head. While doing so, he could see that Ong Troi was not pleased. He placed his hands inside the large *ao tac* sleeves of his royal robe and spoke,

"You have entered the realm of Ong Troi from beyond the sun that brought you here. You have come at a very troubled time. My people are suffering greatly; some have become slaves to your invaders. You have stolen our lands to build fortresses for your army. And now thousands of our sacred dragons have been slaughtered at the hands of evil forces led by your Adecius. King Hung Vuong has entreated me to rid Van Lang of the invaders from your realm. Before I visit the powers of heaven and earth and our mighty gods upon them, you must confess the purpose of this invasion." He nodded to the visitor, signifying *the God of Heaven had spoken.*

Zeus started to make his case for getting Ong Troi's assistance. "I come from Olympus, where I am the God of Heaven and Earth, as are you. I am here…"

Ong Troi stood up from his throne and shouted, "Enough! We will talk no further until you see the powerful army I will unleash against your invaders if they do not leave Van Lang." Ong Troi was in no mood for dialogue. Zeus would have to bide his time in hopes that an opportunity would present itself.

A thick cloud began to form in the throne room. It began to swirl into a funnel shape, and when it dissipated, Ong Troi and Zeus were in a different place. Trang Quỳnh explained. There are nine levels in Ong Troi's heaven. Zeus was taken to the second level, where there was a broad field representative of the land below in Van Lang.

There were twelve deities and heroes arranged in a single line that stretched from one end of the field to the other. The two gods walked down the line, stopping at each leader. Ong Troi introduced them and briefly described their powers.

- *Lac Long Quan* – the Thunder God.

- *Lý* Ong Trong – Twenty-three-foot-tall giant warrior.

- *Lac Long Quàn* – Dragon Lord.

- *Hung Vuong* – Son of the Dragon Lord, ruler of Van Lang and the tattooed people.

- *Trung Sisters* – Heroic warriors sitting upon their elephants, leaders of the Trung Army.

- *Phung Huńg* – General, leader of the rebellion against invaders of Van Lang.

- *Trong Thúy* – Wielder of the Magic Crossbow able to kill 100 soldiers per shot.

- *Giong* – Heavenly genie with a sword and shield and riding an iron horse with a white tiger at his side.

- *Li Tran* – Dragon (Rong), creator of the people of Van Lang, fierce protector.

- *Thành Gióng and Tràn Hung Dao* – Two gods of war known for their triumphs over invaders.

Ong Troi turned to Zeus. "You see, these forces and many more will rain down on your invaders and kill them where they stand." A cacophony of cheers, horns, gongs, and drums ensued, along with shouts of "Vinh Danh Thān Trói!" –*Honor to the God of Heaven.* "Now, Olympian Zeus, we will talk, and you will tell me when your invaders will leave Van Lang and not return." The God of Heaven clapped his hands, and Zeus found himself in a large banquet hall along with Ong Troi and his council of leaders. Beautiful maidens began serving food and drinks to the assemblage. There were trays of exotic meats and fruits, such as Zeus had never seen. Those, along with fragrant pots of tea and a potent wine made from rice. They continued their repast as Ong Troi signaled it was time to talk,

As one of the assembled heroes and deities, King Hung Vuong was able to convey the situation in the Plain of Reeds to all those present. It was clear that the Legion of Aeneas was doomed to failure, allowing Adecius to marshal his troops to retake control of the portal. Zeus informed them of Cronus' grand plan to take control of the Underworld and, from there, Olympus. Ong Troi and his leaders clearly understood allowing that to happen raised the specter of Cronus seeking control of both realms of the Universe.

King Vuong urged caution, "This Adecius and his army possess weapons of destruction more powerful than any we can imagine, and Cronus has unleashed a hoard of demons and monsters from Zeus' Underworld."

Lac Long Quàn, the dragon lord, spoke up next, "Yes, and because of this, our sacred dragons have been slaughtered. Someone must pay!" Vuong was quick to point out that hundreds of tattooed people had been kidnapped from his kingdom and sent into slavery. "They must be returned!" he demanded.

The God of Heaven was openly distressed to hear about the disturbance in the Underworld, Cronus' discovery of the lost portal, and his plans to establish New Elysium in Van Lang. Zeus learned that Ong Troi was aware of the battles going on below and even the existence of FSB Cronus and Camp Savage, which he learned from Hang Nga, the goddess of the moon. Until Zeus presented the facts of the situation, Ong Troi did not know about the quest of the Six that Zeus had set in motion. Nor did he know that they had joined with the Green Berets to train the Legionnaires for the battle against Cronus. Zeus finished his discussion with a persuasive argument that Ong Troi's army should join with the Legion of Aeneas to pursue a "common course" of destroying Adecius' army and returning Cronus to the Underworld.

By the time they had finished their meal, and the maids were serving sweet cakes of mung beans and rice, Ong Troi had been convinced. He banged a small gong and got everyone's attention. "I have heard enough!" He turned to Zeus and offered up his decision, "For the sake of Van Lang and Olympus and the entire Universe which we both occupy, we will follow the common course that you propose. Now, let us drink to the success of that course and begin to plan our attack."

Chapter 42
Fight to the Death

"We were goddam lucky to get outta this with our asses intact."

Galanis approached Athena, placing his hand on her shoulder. "Well, I speak for us all," he said. "Without these Six, the outcome would have been very different."

Around them, the team reacted with more hooahs.

Athena motioned to Ares to come forward. "This is my brother and the leader of our quest, Ares, the God of War."

The two leaders shook hands, and Ares spoke up, "Captain, greetings from our father Zeus, and you have my personal gratitude. Without your assistance, the outcome for me would surely have been different."

Galanis smiled broadly. "I appreciate that, Ares. Now, we need to wrap this up and hightail it to our base camp. Both teams have questions to be answered. That will have to wait. Until then, Bobby."

"Yes, Sir."

"I need two 'volunteers' to do a quick recon of the enemy position so we can notify Dong Tam."

"Roger, Sir!, Gage, you and Kit just volunteered."

Galanis addressed the two 'volunteers,' "I want you to get as close as you can to their command group but not too close, get in, get out. We need to move out of here in thirty minutes. Okay, you two, move it on out…"

"Galanis," Ares interrupted. "I think we can help… show him Athena."

"We have a way to secretly spy on the enemy." She held out Hades Helmet. "Let me show you its power." Then she placed the helmet on Pollux's head, and he instantly disappeared.

"What the fuck?" Kit Rogers blurted out.

Sergeant Travis gave him the look. "Cool it, Rogers! Excuse me, Ma'am, but what does it mean?"

"It means one of you can become invisible and walk right into this 'command group' of the enemy and not be detected. Would you like to use it?"

"I'll answer that," Galanis broke in, "Yes. I don't care how or why it works. Let's get this done. Gage, you're our best language specialist for eavesdropping. You okay with a little magic to help out?"

"Damn right, Sir!"

Pollux removed the helmet from his head and placed it on Gage's head. Heard but not seen, Gage departed. "See y'all on the flipside."

Before Gage could reach the edge of the clearing, a flash of light burst forth from the medallion given to Athena by Hera. The A-Team brandished their weapons in preparation for another attack. Ares moved next to Athena and put up his hands. "No, Galanis, there is no danger!" Galanis shouted for the team to hold up as the surrounding light was drawn back into the medallion. Then, an image came into view and spoke to Athena, "How are you, my dear Athena?"

Athena replied in a somewhat worried tone, "We are all fine, Goddess Hera, but I fear we are in peril after meeting with green and blacks who call themselves the A-Team."

Hera took on a stern look as she inquired, "But why are you not in the battle with Adecius and his Dog Soldiers? Zeus has met with Ong Troi, the God of Heaven and Van Lang, preparing to join the battle. What will they make of your absence?"

Ares and Athena looked at one another quizzically, and then Ares spoke to his mother, "We know nothing of this Ong Troi or a battle with Adecius. We have just now entered Van Lang."

Now frustrated, Hera intoned forcefully, "But it was you and Galanis who identified the need for Zeus to engage with Ong Troi!"

Ares was incredulous and spoke out, "But we have just now met this Galanis."

Sergeant Travis turned to Galanis, astonished at what they heard. "Sir, this sounds spooky as hell to me, and if we don't get outta here now, our asses will be in the wringer."

"Spooky for sure," Galanis said, "how the hell does this Hera know my name?"

Hermes stepped forward and spoke on behalf of the Six, "Something is very wrong here. It was but a day ago that we confirmed that Cronus was behind the disturbance in the Underworld. And what did we say at the time?"

Damon responded, "The Oracle's prophecy that time is our enemy referred to Cronus, the god of time."

"Exactly so," exclaimed Athena, "Cronus has reversed time and brought us back here from the future."

Just then, explosions could be heard nearby, which the A-Team knew was from enemy mortar fire. "Athena, Ares!" Galanis yelled, "We have to leave now, or there won't be any future." He mumbled to himself, "Whatever that means?"

"Ares, Galanis," it was Hera. "You must carry on until I can get word to Zeus about this trickery of Cronus. When the sun rises over Van Lang tomorrow, you will know that Helios has delivered my message to Zeus. He will know what to do." With those words, Hera's image vanished.

Galanis spoke with a notable sense of urgency in his voice, "Okay, let's head out. We need to get back to the base before dark. Bobby, you lead the way. Let's move at a fast pace but observe normal security procedures. Ares, have your folks mix in with ours and just follow what they do. Sound okay? I mean, is that acceptable?"

Ares was quick to respond, "Roger."

Hermes approached Ares then, and they had a short conversation. Thereafter, Hermes turned to address Captain Galanis. "Sir, Captain, I must return to the Elysian Fields. Ares and Athena can explain the urgency. All of you can go on, and I will join you as soon as possible. I bid you a temporary farewell and look forward to rejoining the team." Then he sped away, without pause, in the direction of the portal.

As the team departed the battlefield, Ares and Athena joined up with Galanis and his ADC. Athena spoke first, "Galanis, you must understand. We do not know who the enemy is that we fought today, but there is a much more pernicious enemy at work here in Van Lang."

ᔕ   ᔕ   ᔕ   ᔕ   ᔕ

Heleron was correct. Search parties failed to find any sign of the missing A-Team. Captain Kellogg, Tanaurus and Arcelium were the only senior officers left in the CP. With radio comms restored, Kellogg tried contacting Sergeant Alexander to check the status of TACAIR and arty. There was no response until a Pegasus Regiment Company Commander came online.

"This is Lieutenant Granus. Over."

"This is Kellogg. I need to speak with the FAC. Over."

"Sir, both my company commander and Sergeant Alexander were killed in this morning's attack. As the senior officer, I have taken command. Over."

"Shit! Hang in there, Ranger and I'll get back to you. Over."

"Roger, Rangers lead the way! Out."

As Kellogg was getting things organized for the battle to come, bugles sounded once again, but not on the radio net. We all exited the CP and looked out across the battle zone. There were hundreds of fires burning at the Dog

Soldiers' encampment. In addition, the trumpeting, drums, and gongs added to the raucous scene. Kellogg retrieved his nightscope from the CP and scanned the horizon. The news wasn't good. "Well, guys, looks like they're loaded for bear." This was not an appropriate time to ask questions.

"It's the same shitload of Spartoi and Dog Soldiers, but I can see, hold on." He continued scanning for several more minutes and then lowered the scope. "There are weird creatures interspersed with the troops–giants, writhing snakes or dragons, maybe both, many I didn't recognize. I lost count at around a hundred."

I spoke up, "These are the same as Hoppy and Athena reported at the drop zone. Nasty creatures summoned by Cronus. And I recall making a note that LAWs were the most effective weapons for killing them." Kellogg turned to his fellow commanders and told them to make sure the Legionnaires were well dug in with fields of fire identified. If possible, every third firing position should have a LAW or grenade launcher. LPs and OPs were to be established for each company. Every available claymore was deployed. Maximum noise and light discipline was to be observed.

After walking the perimeter several times, the commanders gathered back at the CP for what could be the last time. Time for one more cold cup of coffee and a couple of cigarettes before returning to the line. Their faces were stolid. Their eyes projected a certain clarity of purpose. They exchanged salutes and departed as if they were off to a dinner party or a night at the taverna.

Before joining his troops on the line, Kellogg sent this SITREP to Heleron

0420 SITREP Since the last report, twelve soldiers died of wounds, eighteen members of 43[d] A-Team MIA, companies dug in along the entire LDEF, 1,388 officers and men of the Legion of Aeneas to repel the attack. Alagon manning the CP. Kellogg.

ⵐ   ⵐ   ⵐ   ⵐ   ⵐ

I was standing just outside the entrance to the CP as the first piercing rays of the sun could be seen far off to the east. Helios was about to make his appearance, having hours ago spread the warmth and glow over the Acropolis and the streets of Plaka. Those were my thoughts as a series of explosions rippled across the LDEF. It was the sound of hundreds of claymores being detonated, spewing out sparks and flames that lit up the battlefield. The attackers were at the gates!

Enemy troops ran headlong into the wall of steel and fire created by the detonated mines. Scores of attackers were shredded with each blast, only to be replaced by those following behind. Those who made it past the barrage could expect to be in the killing zone of the Legionnaire units– interlocking fires of machine guns, grazing fire from automatic weapons and a second tier of claymore mines. In the midst of blaring bugles, beating drums, and screaming enemy troops, Captain Kellogg radioed to all units. "Hold your fire, I repeat. Hold your fire! The bad guys are starting to retreat. Looks like these are probing actions. They'll be back. Commanders initiate fire only when under direct attack. Kellogg, out."

He was right. When the sun was fully above the horizon, the main attack began. Leading the charge were Cyclopes and the dragon monsters Chimera and Eurynomos. Then came waves of Spartoi with their whirling explosive devices. Behind them, heavily armed Dog Soldiers with machine guns and automatic weapons – perhaps 1,000 in number, and another thousand arrived with M-16s, bringing up the rear.

Heleron was monitoring the radio nets back in the TOC and took over my duties as a Logging Specialist. As the battle commenced, he logged the following transmissions.

0610 Message from Kellogg to all units. If attacked by "strange creatures" use LAWs at 20 feet distance from your position.

Then,

0622 Message from Tanaurus to Kellogg. Several monsters breached my sector, multiple KIAs, using my reserve to repel.

By 0845, Heleron had logged dozens of similar messages. There were multiple penetrations along the LDEF by monstrosities and Dog Soldiers. Captain Kellogg shifted his forces and used Regimental reserves to kill or wound the intruders, but more kept coming. Casualties along the line were mounting rapidly, and without the A-Team, there were no trained medical personnel to treat them.

I was still standing by the CP when a Cyclops broke through the perimeter and came close to crushing Captain Kellogg before one of the Legionnaires turned and fired a LAW into its head. Things were getting close enough to me that I went into the CP and secured an AR-15 –disregarding the fact that I didn't know how to use it.

0912 *Company Commander from Pegasus Airborne reports Commander Taranis KIA, along with seven others.*

There were reports of Spartoi inside the perimeter engaged in hand-to-hand combat. Grenades and ammunition were running out fast. All of the LAWs had been expended except for a few held back by the Regimental Reserve. The reserve itself had been reduced to just twenty-nine troops out of the original seventy-five. The only good news was that Hammer Force had repelled a major assault and caused several hundred Dog Soldiers and Spartoi to retreat.

1044 *Captain Kellogg reports the collapse of the Pegasus Sector of the LDEF. Reserve committed to holding the left flank. Preparing to regroup remaining forces in the perimeter surrounding CP. Water supplies are depleted.*

Captain Kellogg came running back to the CP along with his RTO. I heard him say to all units. "Prepare to fold back from the LDEF and set up a perimeter at the CP. My green flare is the signal for max ordinance downrange to cover the withdrawal. Kellogg, out."

The sun was almost overhead when Kellogg fired his flare. Every weapon on the line opened up on the attacking forces. A broad swath of troops and their supporting monsters were cut down. With a measure of precision, the units began to pull back toward the CP. After thirty minutes, the CP was encircled by the remaining Legionnaires. Once the perimeter was secured, Kellogg requested a headcount. I recorded the numbers so I could call them into Heleron:

KIA	WIA	MIA	Remaining Fighting Force
387	89	72	840

A forty percent casualty rate certainly presented a grim picture. Yet, the commanders and their troops were focused on redistributing ammunition and digging in. Supplies of water were brought in from a nearby stream–not the healthiest source, but in a few hours, our thirst might be quenched for good. I radioed Heleron back at the TOC to report the casualty figures. There was no response. I tried several more times without success. I assumed there was a problem with Heleron's radio, so I gave up and decided to try again later.

Captain Kellogg and Commander Arcelium were huddled outside the CP. Kellogg was using his binoculars to assess the situation on the battlefield. He continued watching as he spoke to the commanders, "I'll be goddammed if it isn't Commander Adecius himself! I'd say he is repositioning his forces for an encirclement of our position. Arcelium, any estimate of enemy casualties?"

"As we withdrew from the LDEF, I had a few of my Legionnaires walk the line to surveil enemy losses. A rough estimate of 1,400 were killed and 325 wounded. All the monstrosities were eliminated."

Kellogg turned to me. "Alagon, you're the numbers guy. What's the bottom line?" I assumed he meant to calculate friendly and enemy strengths. Easy enough to do in my head.

"Sir, based on those estimates and counting earlier losses, total enemy casualties would be approximately 2,700. The total forces available to Adecius were estimated at 5,000. That's a 54 percent loss of troop strength." I was starting to sound like a briefing officer back at Camp Savage, with AR-15 and all! I continued, "With those estimated losses, Adecius can still field at least 2,300 Spartoi and Dog Soldiers for the next assault. Based on our reported current strength of 840, we will still be outnumbered at 2.7 to 1."

Arcelium added, "And that does not count any additional monstrosities that might join the fight."

Kellogg was still using his binoculars to observe the troop movements out to his front. He turned abruptly and called to his RTO, "Georgios, message to all units: enemy troops are on the move. ETA: twenty minutes. Stand ready. Kellogg."

Georgios passed the message and then called back to Kellogg, "Sir, Ranger Lieutenant Drako requests you meet him at the southern sector of the perimeter."

Kellogg headed that way, but before he could get there, shouts and cheers rang out so loud the enemy could likely hear. Kellogg and his two regimental commanders picked up the pace to see what was happening. Every troop on the perimeter was standing up in their firing positions and facing to the south. They were looking at the reflection of the sun on a golden object moving in their direction. The chorus of shouts and the stomping of feet grew louder as someone shouted above the din, "It's Commander Heleron. Our Commander is here!" And indeed, he was. He wore his golden breastplate and carried his shield and sword, accentuated by the AR-15 slung over one shoulder. As Heleron passed through the perimeter, he was surrounded by his troops, many of whom were openly crying. As he approached the commanders, they saluted and thanked him for making his way to the battlefield. Congratulations were short-lived. Kellogg gave Heleron a quick rundown on the situation and asked him to take command of the Pegasus Regiment. Everyone was out on the line with the enemy closing in.

🌀 🌀 🌀 🌀 🌀

The attack was blistering. And it came from all sides: Spartoi, monstrosities, Dog Soldiers in the hundreds converging on the perimeter. The Legionnaires deployed every weapon, claymore and hand grenade they had. Once again, the LAWs, as few as they were, took out the most threatening Cyclopes and dragons, but it appeared that nothing could stop the hordes of Adecius' troops or of Adecius himself.

On the north side of the perimeter, perhaps 100 Dog Soldiers and Spartoi assumed a wedge formation pointing toward the center of the perimeter. In the center of the wedge stood Adecius in his black armor, carrying his sword and shield of crimson. On his head was the Crown of Cronus, there to give him the power and strength to deal the final blows to the Legion and its commanders. Arcelium shifted some of his forces to help slow the progress of the attackers, but it was no use. Trumpets blared, signaling that the enemy reserve force, one thousand strong, should move up for the kill.

Chapter 43

A Roiling Sky

Spartoi in the wedge formation were pelting the defenders with their exploding discs and beginning to open a gap between the Legionnaires' fighting positions. Adecius raised his voice above the din, "Legionnaires, death is the punishment for your disobedience of the true god Cronus."

Then, his troops made a thrust through the perimeter and marched toward the CP at the center. The only occupants at that time were Captain Kellogg, his RTO Georgios and me. Kellogg was continuing to get reports from the perimeter and directing efforts to hold the line. I fumbled with my AR-15 and somehow fired two rounds toward the advancing Spartoi. I thought, *I may be a trickster and an actor, but I will go down as a warrior of Olympus.* Those thoughts were interrupted by a deafening war cry so loud that it halted the advance of the Spartoi and all the Dog Soldiers attacking the perimeter. After removing my hands from my ears, I turned around, and there stood Ares and the entire missing A-Team. The warrior-gods, dressed and armed as if they had never left, were also carrying their special weapons.

489

Galanis motioned to Captain Kellogg. "Gordie, follow me." Everyone exited the CP, and Galinis did a quick survey of the situation. Hoping to reverse the tide, he dispatched the team members to rejoin their units. Ares let out another war cry as they sprinted away. This time, there were no complaints from Sergeant Diggs. After several minutes, the enemy troops were on the move again. Fredricks, Travis and Perez were now at the CP along with Hermes. Pollux resumed duties as Captain Kellogg's RTO. In good Ranger fashion, Georgios requested to return to his company on the line. Permission granted, he ran from the CP, shouting, "Rangers lead the way, Sir!"

Fredricks and Travis organized us into a security perimeter surrounding the CP. Hermes stood by the door of the CP with the Caduceus and an M-16, hoping he could halt the advancing wedge of troops, now only 75 meters from the CP, by putting them to sleep.

Unfortunately, the return of the A-Team and the use of special weapons made little difference. Every unit in the perimeter was engaged in hand-to-hand fighting and was about to be overrun. Ares, Athena and Heleron stood behind their brave Legionnaires, exhorting them on, but knowing that all was lost. Sergeant Travis and Perez were facing north in the direction of Camp Savage. Travis took a half-smoked panatela from his shirt pocket, lit it, and turned to Perez, "Well, Manny, it was fun while it lasted." They looked at one another, bumped their fists together and let go with a long "shiiiit!"

Suddenly, there were dark clouds roiling overhead. A fierce wind blew across the battlefield as the ground began to pitch and roll. Commanders and troops on both sides stood in awe and amazement at the jarring events. The battle scene grew eerily quiet. Athena ran over to Ares and said, "This must be the work of Cronus. Hold on, and we will get through this. Our quest is not done!"

Ares replied, "Dear sister, let us gather the Six together and continue our quest to whatever end." As the Six were assembling, the dark clouds parted, and the sun shone brighter than any of them had ever seen in a clear blue sky. Then the sky parted, and a golden pathway, like the stone ramps of *Epidaurus*, extended down to the ground north of the battlefield. Two golden chariots appeared in the sky above, one carrying Zeus and the other, Ong Troi and Queen Mẫu. Zeus began to throw down deadly thunderbolts, which struck the ground and exploded like an artillery barrage. Ong

Troi spoke to the heavens, "Come forward and kill these enemies of Van Lang."

Thus began a parade of forces down the golden ramp. General Phung Huńg was at the head, followed by the Trung Sisters, with 100 warriors, all perched on giant elephants. Next, Li Tran, the Dragon King, led a contingent of snarling dragons. On they came, Giong on his iron horse with his white tiger and Trong Thúy with the magic crossbow. The gods of war, Thành Gióng and Tràn Hung Dao were leading an army of 500 martial arts soldiers with swords of magic jade and vests of woven gold. Hung Vuong, the ruler of Van Lang, walked alone in his imperial robes, swinging a censor burning incense. Finally, there was Lac Long Quàn, the creator of myths and enemy of demons and dragons, accompanied by Lý Ong Trong, the giant warrior beating a six-foot tall dông son drum.

Zeus was himself a seasoned warrior, even beyond the ten years of fighting Cronus and the Titans in the Titanomachy. However, in this case, the battle was taking place in another world with a unique mix of combatants. General Phung Hung was best suited to command what might euphemistically be called the *Van Lang Irregulars*. The general got right to the task, shouting commands to the arriving "troops" as they exited the ramp. "Trung army over here. Prepare to move out. Giong, you and Trong Thuy take the center. Speed up! Speed up! We need to move out!"

The giant warrior continued to beat his drum as he took his place in the battle formation along with Lac Long Quàn, the slayer of dragons and demons. Their role would be to eliminate any monstrosities within the ranks of the enemy forces. But first, a relief force would have to break through to the Legionnaires' perimeter. The Trung army was divided into two relief columns. The Sisters would lead flanking movements to the east and west of the enemy reserve. Twenty-five elephant warriors and one hundred martial arts soldiers on each side. Their weapons were a mixture of swords, sabers, ji (polearm weapons with slashing blades), spears, and crossbows. Many of these possessed magical powers, like Trong Thúy's magic crossbow. Their mission was to break through the enemy troops attacking the Legionnaires' perimeter and secure the southern portion of the perimeter as a blocking force.

Li Tran began releasing his wing of dragons to fly over the enemy reserve units and attack the enemy forces, assaulting the Legion's firing positions. Li Tran wanted revenge for the thousands of sacred dragons stolen by

Cronus and forced into the battle with the Legion of Aeneas. General Phung Hung began organizing his remaining forces on a broad front, preparing an all-out attack on the rear of the enemy reserve units.

ϭ   ϭ   ϭ   ϭ   ϭ

Adecius' thrust into the center of the perimeter was temporarily stalled as Captain Galanis directed the Rangers to pull back once again and tighten the perimeter. This was a short-term solution since the troops were fast running out of ammunition, and there were no more grenades or LAWs. Then things got worse; the sky over the battle area darkened, and a familiar cacophony of screeches and hisses grew nearer. Everyone at the CP and on the line knew what it meant. I ran out of the CP, preparing to transform into Typhon as before, when there were shouts and cheers from every firing position. The enraged dragons began attacking Spartoi and Dog Soldiers with vengeance. Severed heads and body parts flew in every direction. Yet, the enemy troops continued their assault without regard for their mounting losses.

Adecius' wedge formation had collapsed. The Spartoi surrounded Adecius in hopes of fending off Li

Tran's dragons. Adecius lifted his binoculars and scanned the battlefield to the north. His 1,000 reserve troops should have reached the Legion perimeter by then. What he saw instead was that the reserve units had stopped their advance and turned to the north and were staring at General Hung's disparate army. Some Dog Soldiers were firing their weapons, but the opposing force was too far away.

At that moment, Adecius spotted the Trung Sisters' flanking maneuvers and decided to withdraw in the direction of his reserve forces to the north. It was too late. The troops attacking the Legion position began to panic as Li Tran's dragons decimated their ranks. The Trung sisters spoke to the elephants their troops were riding, "Tôc dô cúa ban sẽ cừu dúóc Văn Lang." *Your speed will save Van Lang.* The exhortation was understood, and the giant creatures jerked forward at great speed. They reached the area south of the Legion perimeter and began setting up in their blocking position. General Huńg was ready to proceed with his plan to relieve the Legion forces while eliminating Cronus' remaining forces. Zeus, in his chariot overhead, provided the opening salvos–thunderbolts that struck the center of the enemy's reserve, creating a large gap that split their ranks in two. That was the signal for the Van Lang Irregulars (a sobriquet I am proud to have originated) to move out. The giant warrior began beating his drum, the sound of which reverberated across the entire battlefield.

𝕺   𝕺   𝕺   𝕺   𝕺

I should inform the readers of this story that my description of the pandemonium that followed the initiation of the attack on the reserve forces is predicated on details told to me by others. Once again, I am only the scribe. However, I was present at the LDEF and CP until the very end.

Three hundred martial arts warriors escorted Lac Long Quàn and the giant warrior to a position where they could observe the enemy lines, looking for any monsters or demons in the ranks. They spotted several Cyclopes and a handful of snarling dragons. They waited there for the main thrust of the attack to begin. The martial arts warriors joined the remainder of the Irregulars forming a battleline facing the enemy to their front. Their crossbows, spears, swords, and sabers were at the ready. General Huńg gave the signal to stand fast. Then Ong Troi and Queen Mẫu appeared overhead in their golden chariot. Ong Troi spread his arms wide as they approached the remainder of Cronus' army. Wind, rain and hail in torrents were let loose and pummeled the enemy units. Elsewhere, the sky was blue, and the sun shone brightly as the General and his forces looked on.

σ   σ   σ   σ   σ

The situation at the CP and around the entire perimeter had improved greatly. Fewer Dog Soldiers were available to sustain the attack, as their attention was on the dragons above. Those who tried to escape to the south were crushed and gored by the giant elephants or slashed to death by the jade swords of the martial arts soldiers. Many more, including Adecius and his Spartoi security force, began to flee northward in hopes of joining up with the reserve forces. That option was about to be foreclosed.

The command group stood outside the CP, watching the action to the north. Galanis and Kellogg were both observing through their binoculars and updating everyone on what they were seeing. Galanis lowered his binoculars and grabbed the handset to Perez's radio. "To all units, if your sectors are under control, I need all A-Team members to report to the CP on the double. Galanis, out." As we waited for the A-Team members to arrive at the CP, the fierce storm over the enemy reserve force ceased and there were clear skies and sunshine across the battlefield.

Ares and Athena arrived at the CP, followed by the remainder of the A-Team. Ares saluted and spoke, "Sir, the A-Team reports, ready to kick some more Dog Soldier ass, Sir!"

Galanis responded, "Hey guys, Athena, we're not out of the woods yet, but I thought you should see the final round up close."

Damon burst out, "Goddam right, Sir. We'll teach them not to fuck with the Green Berets!"

Sergeant Travis called out, "Sergeant Damon."

Damon turned to face Travis. "Yes, Top?" Silence. Damon had just gotten the Travis "look."

Captain Kellogg continued scanning the battlefield with his binoculars when he said, "Holy shit, I don't believe it! Captain Galanis, tell me I'm not hallucinating."

Galanis raised his binoculars and looked to the area just behind General Huńg and his forces. "No, Gordie," Galanis replied, "You're not seeing things." He turned and spoke to his team, "There are what I would estimate to be four or five hundred tattooed people joining the party, carrying an assortment of weapons, farming tools and fishing nets, ready for a fight."

Later, I learned from King Vuong that he had informed the surrounding villagers of what was taking place in the Plain of Reeds. It was clear they had not forgotten Cronus' kidnapping of their families and friends. As farmers and fishermen, they brought whatever they could find to use as weapons and traveled a great distance to the battlefield. Kellogg spoke again, "Okay, they're all moving out, headed this way!"

The Dog Soldiers were still trying to recover from Ong Troi's "gift" from heaven when the Irregulars descended upon them, starting with a murderous rampage by Lac Long Quàn and the giant warrior against the Cyclopes and dragons they had spotted. Enemy troops were trying to fire their weapons without success, thanks to the pounding weather and the mud and water left behind. Many of them panicked and began running in the direction of the Legion perimeter. Their fate was sealed when Giong rode his iron horse, carrying his white tiger and Trong Thúy with his magic crossbow. As they raced toward the Legion perimeter, hundreds of fleeing Dog Soldiers were killed by the arrows from Trong Thúy's crossbow.

At the same time, General Huńg's army waded into enemy positions using their swords, spears and sabers to mercilessly hack away at the enemy. As many of the enemy troops struggled in the mud and water of their positions, they were set upon by the tattooed people and bludgeoned and beaten until they lay face down, half buried in the muck. We were all watching in horror and delight when Arcelium radioed a message to Perez, which was passed on to Galanis. "Sir, Arcelium reports that the entire southern sector has been cleared. The Trung Sisters and their army have left their blocking position and are proceeding north to join the battle against the reserve forces." That would mean the last remnants of Adecius' and Cronus' army would be encircled, with Adecius somewhere in the middle.

෧ ෧ ෧ ෧ ෧

Adecius had no idea that the forces involved in the assault on the Legionnaires were dead or dying. Watching the destruction of his reserve forces, the all-powerful Commander of the Spartoi and Dog Soldier Army was out of options. Giong was fast approaching and Adecius pleaded with his Spartoi guards to protect him, but they began running toward the Legion perimeter. Adecius had no choice but to join them. Trong let fly with arrows from his crossbow and the guards fell one after another.

Adecius ran to within twenty meters of the Ranger fighting positions as if he intended to surrender. It was too late. Giong caught up to him.

By that time, the surviving Legionnaires were leaving their firing positions and assembling around the CP to witness the capture of their evil nemesis, but that was not to be. We watched with surprise and fascination as Giong's white tiger leaped on Adecius' back and began biting and clawing the defeated commander. Adecius struggled with the raging deity of Van Lang. His only defense was to project himself up to a height of twenty feet, as he had done many months before when the Six landed in Itea on their way to Delphi. With the strength of one arm, he was able to wrest the tiger from his back and throw it to the ground. It wasn't until then that I noticed that Hermes was standing among the Legionnaires, holding his bow armed with a golden arrow. Adecius surveyed the scene, knowing that the quest of the Six had succeeded. He bellowed and projected red-hot flames from his eyes. Without hesitation, Hermes released his golden arrow, hitting his target, the heart of the enemy of Olympus and Van Lang. The once all-powerful servant of

Cronus fell dead in the blood-soaked grass of the Plain of Reeds. With him went Cronus' hopes for a New Elysium and regaining his glory of the past.

Chapter 44
Chaos and the Aftermath

Chaos is a Greek word. I know it well as the period of nothingness before the creation of the universe (cosmos) by Gaia and Uranus. The *Abyss* was created at the same time, which became the Underworld. After that, Chaos referred to the confusion and disarray associated with the creation, so it is appropriate to describe what took place over two days in the Plain of Reeds as chaos in its broadest sense. Ironically, however, chaos also refers to the abyss in the Underworld–Tartarus. As the battle was ending, attention began to focus on the god most familiar with Tartarus, Cronus.

General Huńg's Irregulars were sweeping the battlefield after all resistance from the Dog Soldiers had ended. Looking out from the CP, I could see the Trung Sisters perched on their elephants. Their troops were using the giant beasts to herd enemy survivors into the center of the battlefield. Through his binoculars, ADC Fredricks estimated there were less than 500 Dog Soldiers and no Spartoi in a large holding area. That meant there was a ten percent survival rate for Adecius' army. The question arose as to what to do with them.

Heleron answered the question, "We must dispatch Legionnaires to take control of the survivors. I will see that they are returned to Elysium to await judgment by Minos, Rhadamanthus and Aeacus, the judges of the dead. As for the rest of the Legion, I would like to see them return to Camp Savage before we, too, depart from Van Lang."

Galanis turned to Fredricks. "Tom, what's our headcount?" The numbers were appalling but a necessary price for stopping Cronus and Adecius.

KIA	WIA	MIA
1,208	196	51

Legion losses totaled 1,208, a rate of 67 percent. Survivors, including WIAs, eleven members of the A-Team and Captain Kellogg, totaled 611.

"How many troops do you need for prisoner control?" Galanis asked Heleron.

"Forty will be sufficient if they have weapons and ammunition."

Travis broke in, "No problem, Sir. I've scrounged plenty from dead Dog Soldiers."

Heleron put his hand on Travis' shoulder and smiled broadly. "Thank you, Sergeant Travis. We have much to thank you for." He looked around the CP. "All of you, we thank all of you."

As the Legionnaires, led by Arcelium , started off toward the prisoner holding area, the golden ramp descended from the sky as before. General Huńg signaled to the Irregulars to prepare for departure. Athena spoke to Galanis, "Sir." He looked at her wistfully, knowing they had both survived and that she would have to leave. "Sir?" She got his attention. "We, I mean the Six, must thank them before they depart. And then we must continue our quest."

He looked away and said in a soft tone, "You mean Cronus."

"Yes, Sir. Yes, Galanis."

He turned back and she gazed into his eyes as if to say goodbye. "I know what you must do, but I expect to see you all back at Camp Savage before the Legion heads back to Elysium. And that's an order. I told Pollux to keep his radio in case you get in trouble."

As he spoke, she was replacing her steel helmet with her prized green beret. She touched her jump wings, came to attention and saluted. "Airborne, Sir!" Then it was about-face, and she strode away to join Ares and the others as they moved out with the Legionnaires toward the prisoner holding area.

Ares let out his war cry and turned to see if there was a reaction from Sergeant Diggs. Diggs shook his head up and down to signal his approval and then flashed a thumbs up.

For the rest, it was back to business. "Tom," Galanis shouted to the ADC. Fredricks walked over to where Galanis was watching the Six picking their way through hundreds of dead Spartoi and Dog Soldiers and pausing to view the body of Adecius.

"Yes, Sir?"

Galanis broke away from his reverie. "Tom, get on the horn and contact Dong Tam and Ton Sa Nuit and tell them Operation Golden Chariot has succeeded and we are returning to Camp Savage."

Fredricks did not need further guidance. "Roger, Sir, we will need a full resupply of rations, water, beer and cigarettes."

Sergeant Travis overheard the conversation and interjected, "And don't forget my panatelas and a case of brandy. This *is* a company operation, isn't it? Oh, and Hoppy, pass these around." He held out a carton of cigarettes. "That ought to hold until we get back to camp." Fredricks and Galanis laughed and shook their heads, then looked over at Perez.

"Don't ask me. I don't know how he does it," Perez rejoined. Old Top was never going to change, not that he needed to! Next, the Supreme Commander called Heleron, Captain Kellogg and the remaining A-Team members together and instructed them to prepare their troops for the march back to Camp Savage. Looking them over, he noticed that in addition to Captain Kellogg, several had been lightly wounded.

In a jovial tone, he said, "Well, guys, I guess you're out of luck. I doubt the Legion can present you with Purple Hearts." After explaining to Heleron what he was talking about, Heleron offered the answer, "Our tradition is to provide the returning soldiers with massages–we call it anointing with oil to soothe their muscles and their minds."

Guess who piped up. "Hey Tom, can you order up some of those massagers from Saigon as part of the resupply?" Sergeant Diggs said in all seriousness.

To which Fredricks responded, "They're called masseuses, and the answer is, get back to your unit and move out."

In short order, the troops were organized and set out for Camp Savage. They took up a familiar cadence as they marched, which I can translate,

Glory to Greece and glory to Olympus,

Hail Zeus (foot stomp),

Hail Athena (foot stomp)

Your sons are coming home. (loud cheers)

I trailed along behind with the command group and found that I was anxious to get back to my logbooks at the camp. Much of what you have read and will yet read was set down in the logs upon my return to the TOC at Camp Savage.

𝓸   𝓸   𝓸   𝓸   𝓸

The Six reached the golden ramp just as General Huńg was giving the command for his units to move out. He called a halt as he saw the Six approaching. The warrior-gods were profusely thanking the General, the Trung Sisters and all of those in the line ready for their return to the Kingdom of Ong Troi. The General expressed his appreciation for the valiant efforts of the Legionnaires. He noted that his forces were carrying their dead and wounded with them so they could take their place in Ong Troi's heaven. Then he asked Ares, "What of this Cronus? We never saw him or felt his presence."

Ares responded, "We are on our way to his base. Whether he is there or not, we must find him and return him to our Underworld to complete the quest."

The General looked to the sky and gestured. The golden chariots of the two gods had returned to heaven. The General intoned, "May the strength of both gods go with you." He bowed, turned, and gave the order for his units to depart the battlefield.

The Six carried their special weapons and their Green Beret weapons and gear. Their target was FSB Cronus. Along the way, they encountered some 200 tattooed people and their leader, Ti Dong. He spoke to the Six, "We go to find our families and friends that the monster Cronus stole from us. We have helped to kill his soldiers. Now we will kill him!"

Athena pointed out that they had special weapons needed to confront Cronus, but even those might not be enough. Besides, they intended to return Cronus to the Underworld to receive his punishment from the Olympians. The tattooed people were not dissuaded. "We will follow behind you." Ti Dong said as he bowed to Athena, "Perhaps we can help you, but we must free our people."

As the Six continued their march, Damon commented, "Them's some weird people."

Castor joined in, "I can dig it."

Ares halted the group and turned to his two troops. "You still want to be Green Berets, then get to attention and lock your heels." They snapped to, not knowing what was coming. Ares continued, "Then listen up, shitbirds. I'm both your superior officer and the leader of this quest. We're on our way to the most dangerous encounter of our mission, so you'd better get your heads screwed on right. Understood?"

Both replied, "Yes, Sir, yes, Ares!"

Not yet finished, Ares used his best DI voice, "Now get down and give me twenty pushups." When they were done, Ares had one more command. "Now, as your buddy Sergeant Diggs would say, 'let's go kick some Cronus ass.'"

x x x x x

We arrived at Camp Savage in the late afternoon. Two hercs s were already at the airstrip unloading the pallets of resupplies the ADC had ordered. Less than six hundred of the original 1,800 Legionnaires marched through the gate, back at the home of the Legion of Aeneas. The first priority was the triage and treatment of more than 150 wounded. As Senior Medical Sergeant, Sergeant Santini took charge.

Sergeants Taylor and Rogers took 20 Legionnaires and double-timed over to Tent City to set up triage tents. Sergeant Travis, along with Hoppy and Brick Osbourne organized a detail of one hundred Legionnaires and headed directly to the airfield. Once there, they began breaking down the pallets in search of the medical supplies Fredricks had ordered. The Legionnaires set up a supply train between the airfield and Tent City. The remainder of the troops marched to their unit areas to receive the supplies and set up the camp before the sun went down.

Galanis, Kellogg and Heleron led the command group over to the TOC, where all was as we had left it the day before, without the frenetic radio traffic from the battlefield. Shortly after, a runner came to the TOC with coffee supplies, C-rations and a carton of cigarettes, compliments of Sergeant Travis. Perez made coffee as the group chowed down and took long drags on cigarettes called Salems. The package read, "Take a puff–it's springtime." I smoked several, but it was still summer in Van Lang. We all sat around the briefing table. Galanis and Heleron began discussing plans for the Legion's return to Elysium. I would, of course, be returning with them, but I had some concerns. "What will happen to the A-Team after we leave?" I asked Galanis, "Is it possible you can return to your former status?"

Galanis' response was rather deadpan as he stubbed out his third cigarette. "Well, Alagon, we'll just have to cross that bridge when we get there." After that, Fredricks went to the briefing boards and began to outline a schedule for the Legion's departure.

As darkness set in over the camp, the moon (with its beautiful Princess) was traversing the sky, casting shadows over at Tent City, such as I had seen just before D-Day. I walked over to see how things were progressing with the Legionnaires and their wounded comrades. It was going to be a long night. Before it was over, a dozen more Legionnaires had succumbed to their wounds and many more were hanging on. The Legionnaire companies, what was left of them, set up chow lines and distributed the rewards for their efforts: cigarettes, beer and a significant supply of snuff! So it went through the night. I returned to the TOC for some coffee and to resume work on updating my logbooks. Eventually, I fell asleep at my desk.

𝕾　𝕾　𝕾　𝕾　𝕾

The Six approached FSB Cronus with caution. As planned, Athena donned the Hades Helmet, grasped the Aegis and used her invisibility to walk through the wide-open main gate. All was quiet. Some cooking fires still burned, awaiting the return of Adecius and his army. In the drinking halls and game rooms, cards and games were laid out on the tables, along with half-empty goblets of wine. She walked through the command center, where maps and documents were strewn about. Tributes to Cronus were scrawled on the walls. Athena stopped and listened. There were sounds of talking and shouting coming from the other end of the compound. She proceeded in that direction and came upon a group of Spartoi guards. Walking past them into what appeared to be troop quarters, she was surprised to see a hundred or more tattooed people–slaves of Adecius and his commanders.

Exiting the building, she raised the Aegis and turned the Spartoi guards into gargoyle-like statues. A quick walk through the rest of the camp revealed that there were no other enemy troops left. Returning to the captives, she removed her helmet and asked several of them if they knew where Cronus had gone. They did not know, but the guards had begun to talk about something called a portal. She asked if they knew the name Ti Dong. There was murmuring and some crying at the mention of his name. Athena told them Ti Dong was close by and they should follow her out of the compound.

The 300-plus freed captives followed Athena out the main gate. They were chanting and singing, some banging cymbals and gongs. The other warrior-gods welcomed them just as Ti Dong and his contingent of village fighters arrived. Great cheers and shouts erupted as the captives were reunited with families and friends they thought they would never see again. As they celebrated, Athena hurriedly gathered the warrior-gods together. She spoke with excitement in her voice, "Cronus has left for the portal. My guess is that he and his Spartoi guards will try to force their way into the portal and take their chances in the Underworld. Hermes, use your cloak and run to the portal to assess the situation. The rest of us will follow as fast as we can, using our Airborne and Ranger skills, of course."

Castor let go with an "hooah" as Hermes rapidly disappeared in the direction of the portal.

Hermes was less than a kilometer from the portal entrance when he spotted what looked like a company-size unit of Spartoi and Dog Soldiers escorting Cronus to the portal. Although invisible, Hermes reverted to his Green Beret training and sped back to link up with his fellow soldiers and report the results of his reconnaissance. Ares listened and then spoke to his team, "This is our last chance to stop Cronus and fulfill the purpose of our quest. And it is our last mission as Green Berets, so let's make it count! Pollux, I need to use your radio."

"Roger," Pollux replied as he moved next to Ares and gave him the handset.

"Galanis, this is Lieutenant Ares, over."

No response.

"I repeat, Galanis, this is Lieutenant Ares, over."

Another pause and Galanis finally replied, "Ares, this is Galanis. Go ahead."

"We Six, Green Berets, are within one and a half kilometers from the portal entrance. Sent Hermes to recon the area and he reports spotting Cronus and a company of soldiers within a kilometer of the portal."

"Roger, Whaddaya need Lieutenant?"

"We could use some arty to take out the enemy guards."

"Roger, hold one." He continued, "The ADC says we can have a fire mission cranked up in about ten minutes. Where do you want it?"

"Wait, one." Ares gave the handset to Hermes.

"Galanis, this is Sergeant Hermes. Do you remember the time I was returning to Elysium, and we saw a platoon of Dog Soldiers headed to FSB Cronus?"

"Roger, and I called in a fire mission that took out the entire platoon."

"Yes, Sir. I estimate the enemy troops will be at that location in fifteen minutes or less. Can you hurry up the fire mission to catch them in the open?"

"We'll pull out the stops. What about Cronus?"

Hermes gave the handset back to Ares, who replied to Galanis with true Green Beret bravado, "Sir, you crank up the arty and we'll take care of the rest. Ares, out."

1120 D-Day+3 WO Fredricks requested a fire mission, troops in the open, target 179335, urgent.

Then,

***1126** Message from Dong Tam arty, fire mission ready.*

Fredricks was back on the radio with Dong Tam. "Roger, give me max H-E and willie peter. Our FO will adjust. Standby, out."

Next, he contacted Pollux with a request to speak to Hermes. "Okay, Hermes, let everyone know the arty will be on the way in five. You need to race up forward and get as close as you can to the target area. Take Pollux's radio and be prepared to adjust fire, like we taught you in boot camp, over."

"Roger, out." Hermes followed the instructions and arrived near the portal as the first rounds began to fall on the enemy troops. He radioed in several adjustments to make sure the rounds were hitting the mark. Then he gave the command, "fire for effect," which I later learned from Perez meant "give 'em everything you've got!" And they did.

***1142** SFC Hermes reports enemy forces destroyed, Cronus captured.*

ʘ   ʘ   ʘ   ʘ   ʘ

All hell broke loose at Camp Savage. Everyone in the TOC jumped up. There were shouts of "They did it! They did it!" There was dancing in circles, bear hugs and a few tears. Heleron embraced Galanis, kissed him on both cheeks and said, "*We* did it, my friend. We did it, the Legion and the A-Team!"

Perez ran from the TOC and sprinted toward Tent City, screaming, "Cronus is captured! Cronus is captured!" By the time Perez reached the area, Legionnaires were streaming out of their tents, shouting, stomping, singing, embracing, and crying tears of joy. Many of the wounded left the medical tents and joined the celebration. Then came the A-Team–Salinas, Taylor, Rogers, Santini, Diggs, Hopkins, and Osbourne. They ran into the center of the tumultuous crowd, shouting and embracing their Legionnaire comrades. Immediately, they were snatched onto the shoulders of the troops they had trained and fought with. They were carried from one end of Tent City to the other and back again. Perez started crying, sure that this was how his parents felt when World War II ended, and his father came home.

In the TOC, things had settled down to a roar when Travis opened a fresh bottle of brandy and began passing out panatelas. Heleron went to the commanders' tent and brought back a bottle of Metaxa, the famous Greek brandy. Travis chomped down on his cigar and looked at Heleron standing there holding the bottle. "Sir, I'm afraid you've got me there," Travis exclaimed. "I've scrounged up a helluva lot in my day, but never a bottle of brandy from the Underworld."

Chapter 45
Return to the Portal

As I recall, it was November 1968 when I received the order for our A-Team to proceed to the Plain of Reeds, our Area of Operations (AO), as part of a B-52 bombing mission at a site identified as Camp Savage. This was an unusual mission order to begin with and as things unfolded, it proved to be a mysterious and somewhat haunting event for me personally. It all began when we reached the target area, and I reported our arrival to a Senior Operations Officer at Dong Tam with the call sign of Scorpion 6.

"Scorpion 6, this is Orion 6, over."

"This is Scorpion 6. Go ahead."

"This is Orion 6. We've reached the camp and it's completely deserted. Whatever it was for it had to be some massive operation, over."

"Roger, do a thorough sweep and confirm the coordinates for tonight's ARC Light run, and Galanis, make sure your team knows this is Top-Secret, over."

"Roger Sir, Galanis, out."

I turned to my ADC, Tom Fredricks and asked him to call the team together. When they were assembled, I briefed them on our mission. "Okay, listen up. I have no idea what the fuck this is all about, but we need to conduct a complete sweep of this complex and report what we find to Scorpion 6 at Dong Tam."

Sergeant Diggs interrupted, "Alright, guys, I've got dibs on any flags we find to add to my collection."

Sergeant Travis wasn't amused. "Diggs, get your head out of your ass and pay attention to the CO!"

"Thanks, Top," Galanis replied, "Tom, take charge. Get 'um spread out and let's go. We need to be outta here before 0-dark thirty. There's a B-52 ARC Light mission scheduled to turn this place into a swamp. Perez, come with me. I want to check out what looks like a CP over there."

That began my strange journey into the mythical worlds of Zeus and Ong Troi. Perez and I entered the command tent and looked around. This was a first-rate Tactical Operations Center by the looks of the radio gear, briefing charts, desks and tables. Perez quickly pointed out,

"Hey, Sir, there's a coffeepot over here and a can of Maxwell House. Okay, if I fire up the stove?"

While Perez was measuring out scoops of coffee grounds and searching for cups, I looked around what was probably a briefing area and saw maps and documents relating to Operation Golden Chariot.

Then I noticed a table nearby with a stack of standard-issue logbooks. I counted 23 in all, with a supply of Army-issue pens and pencils. I picked a book off the top and flipped through the pages. It became clear that these were the logs of a military operation, but the combatants had strange names like Adecius, Trung Sisters, Athena, and Heleron. As I read on, there were references to dragons, demons, golden chariots, and troops called Spartoi, Dog Soldiers and Legionnaires.

Perez brought me a cup of coffee and I sat down at the desk, jumped a few pages ahead and began to laugh. Perez looked at me and asked what was so funny. "You won't believe this, but whoever was at this desk was writing a novel about Zeus and the gods of Olympus being here in Vietnam. This should make interesting reading when we get back to Dong Tam," I said as I stuck all of the "logs" into my rucksack.

As Perez and I left the command center, his radio squawked to life. "Orion 6, this is Condor 6, over." It was Captain Gordie Kellogg, a Ranger School classmate of mine.

"Orion 6, over."

"Hey, Galanis, I heard you were up here. How's it hangin?"

We talked briefly since our A-Team needed to di di mau before dark. I learned that he and his LRRP team were twenty kilometers north of my position at another camp, which he described as a typical fire support base. It, too, was unoccupied. Strangely, his team's mission was the same as mine: an ARC Light sortie was scheduled in a matter of hours. We both had to move out, so we agreed to meet and compare notes back at Dong Tam.

Before Perez and I could rejoin the rest of the team, Sergeant Gage came running over. "Sir, there's something you gotta see before we leave." He pointed to the north side of the compound. "It's over there." We walked toward a large gate with a sign overhead. I walked through the gate and looked up. "What does it mean, Sir?" Sergeant Gage asked, "Camp Savage, Home of the Legion of Aeneas?"

"I don't know, but I found some logs that might answer your question. Now let's get going." Tom Fredricks had the team formed up at the point where we entered the camp, and we took off for Dong Tam.

When we reached Dong Tam the next morning, we got some chow and hot showers. Then, we had to prepare for a debrief with Scorpion 6, the G-2 head of intelligence. It was hard to believe, but our unit barracks had a day room–a recreation area with a pool table, a small library and a bar. The team sat in lounge chairs and on several green paisley-covered couches (paisley?). As I waited for the meeting, I thought of what I had read. The details began to pour out of the logbooks–airborne and ranger training areas, a jump tower, sleeping tents for 2,000 troops, mess halls, medical tents, an obstacle course and more. It all sounded like some clandestine operation, but what was the Legion of Aeneas?

We had our debrief with the G-2 and not much was said other than, "There's some rumors floating around that this was a CIA operation. If so, those B-52 missions might be the way to make the 'evidence' disappear."

Our team would be on stand-down for the next few days, so it gave me time to read the logbooks I had salvaged. First, based on the little I had already read, I went to the base library and checked out the books they had on mythology. (Yes, Dong Tam was a base of 40,000 personnel with gyms, ballfields, beer halls, a pizza parlor, a miniature golf course, swimming pools and much more.) Before I dove into the logs, I refreshed my memory of what I had learned in high school and college. There they were, names like Aeneas, Zeus, Athena, and Hades, along with Hercules, Jason and Achilles. It didn't take much to recall what I knew about Greek mythology. I was ready to enjoy what looked like a good read.

It was past midnight when I was done with my daily duties, preparing for our next operation, and tackling the usual mound of paperwork. I grabbed a bottle of Jack Daniels from my quarters and wandered into the dayroom. It was empty, so I found a cushy chair, settled in and started reading logbook number one. It was the beginning of a fascinating story set down, in my view, by a master storyteller.

It was immediately clear that the author had a superior grasp of Greek mythology. Characters seemed to leap off the pages. Zeus, Poseidon, Ares, and Hades caught up in a disturbance in the Underworld. Zeus selected six gods and demigods to embark on a quest to fix the problem. It was soon discovered that a portal from the Underworld to the ancient land of Van Lang had been located by the god Cronus and his henchman, Adecius. I read through books two and three which described battles with strange enemies called pygmaioi and Spartoi. There were fierce dragons and a collection of demons and monsters.

I couldn't stop there, knowing there were twenty more books to go. I kept reading for several more hours until my lack of sleep and Jack Daniels caught up with me. I went to my quarters and crashed, sleeping through the sounds of reveille, which blared throughout the base, and I was told later, through two enemy rocket attacks! I woke up, performed my ablutions, and had chow at the Officers Mess. Hard to beat their eggs benedict! I had an off day since the ADC had taken the team into Saigon for a little R&R. God help To Dõ Street. I went back to my quarters and, returned with a dozen logbooks and headed to the dayroom.

So, Van Lang is an ancient name for Vietnam. Somehow, the author learned a great deal about Vietnam mythology. Quite a scholar. What's he doing manning a radio at Camp Savage? Everything changed when I got to book eleven, where the 'Six,' as he calls the warrior-gods, use the portal to enter what they believe is Van Lang. By that time, they knew that Cronus and Adecius were behind the disturbance in the Underworld and in Van Lang. There it was, an impossible segue into the Vietnam War with the 43^d Special Forces A-Team thrown into action. I lit a cigarette and sat there staring at the words. "Perez grasped his handset and contacted the team leader, Captain Galanis. Orion 6, This is Orion one six Romeo, over."

"This is Orion 6, over."

"Orion 6, one six requests that you proceed to our location. This is an alpha-level urgent message. Out."

This had to be a joke, so I kept reading to see if I could get to the punchline. If there was one, I couldn't find it. The story moved on. Our team apparently joined forces with the Six to help them with their quest to save the Underworld and Olympus. We even put these warrior-gods through Green Beret training and accepted them as members of the 43^d Special Forces A-Team (Augmented). There were references to Fire Support Base Cronus and New Elysium and, finally, the story behind the Legion of Aeneas. I was starting to get a clearer picture of the Six and the purpose of their quest, but who, other than the members of my team, would have known enough about our operations, the locations of our hidden base camps, or that Sergeant Diggs is the team's jester? That's when Gordie Kellogg and Lieutenant Tran walked into the dayroom.

"There you are," Kellogg said as he stood by my chair. "We've been looking all over for you. Did you forget we agreed to meet up? What's with all the logbooks?"

My answer was, "No, I didn't forget, ah, I just had to catch up on my after-action reports. Speaking of which, did you find anything interesting at that base camp?"

"Not much," Kellogg replied. "A bunch of maps and charts for Operation Golden Chariot. Never heard of it, did you?"

Ignoring what I had been reading, I answered, "No."

Lieutenant Tran interjected, "There were references to someone called Adecius and units with names like Spartoi and Dog Soldiers. Guess those are some sort of code names."

"What about you?" Kellogg asked, "Find anything at your location?"

"Nothing to speak of. Some maps and papers show it was a training camp," I lied. "No telling for what purpose."

"Roger. We're headed over to the club. It's prime rib night and some hot dancing girls are here with the USO. That ought to be enough to drag you away from your after-action reports."

"Say no more."

As we were leaving the dayroom, I asked Gordie about Savage and Alexander. "They're fine, why do you ask?"

Another lie. "No reason."

☙ ☙ ☙ ☙ ☙

After returning from the club, I had another long night of reading ahead. The following morning it would be back to work with the team, planning our upcoming mission. My bottle of Jack Daniels was half empty, so I poured two fingers instead of three. As I resumed reading, I finally got an answer to two of my biggest questions. How had Camp Savage come to be? Could the CIA, as squirrelly as I considered them to be, really have had a hand in it?

I learned why it was called Camp Savage, what role the Legion of Aeneas was to play in a coming battle with enemy forces, and why there was a jump tower and obstacle course being constructed. I guess there was no real surprise when Gordie Kellogg entered the story. Maybe it was the Jack Daniels, but my head was spinning.

Shocked is too mild a word for what I felt when I read these words spoken by Athena. "You are a god like me. You have but one name, like all the gods and goddesses. You are Galanis. You deliver us from harm and ruin." And later, "You must accept that you are my brother, my lover and my commander."

I was drained. I poured one more whiskey and grabbed the book on mythology from a side table. I paged through until I found a likeness of the goddess Athena. I stared at the picture and started imagining, or at least I thought so, that I somehow had a connection to the beautiful daughter of Olympus. I dozed off and woke up the next morning when the loudspeaker in our unit area blasted out reveille.

ᔕ   ᔕ   ᔕ   ᔕ   ᔕ

Our team meeting went well in between stories of conquests on To Dõ Street. The ADC outlined the mission for the next day. "We're headed back to the Plain of Reeds for a BDA of the campsite we visited the other day."

There were several "oh, shits" from the team. BDA stood for Bomb Damage Assessment, which every troop in Vietnam hated. It meant stumbling and tripping over huge clods of earth, bomb craters, and broken and twisted trees. The goal was to confirm that the target had been destroyed and to count the bodies or parts thereof.

Hoppy spoke up, "Jesus Christ, Tom, can't they get some grunt unit to do that?"

Kit Rogers jumped in, "Besides, the whole fucking place was a ghost town."

Travis interrupted the carping, "Put a lid on it. We're gonna do what the green machine in Saigon wants us to do!"

532

Fredricks finished his mission brief and asked me if I had anything to add. I was undecided about whether I should inform the team about what I was finding in the logbooks. When I got to the front of the briefing room, I decided the answer was 'no.' Well, not until I read the remaining eight logs. What I did say was, "Tom, mark out the best route to these coordinates. I want us to head over there after the BDA." I printed them on the briefing board. "After comparing notes with Captain Kellogg, it looks like there's a tunnel complex at that location–somehow connected to the two camps that were destroyed."

Perhaps I was getting in too deep, but the maps both Gordie and I saw at the camps identified that location as the portal described in the logs. No harm in checking it out, I told myself. What I really wanted to do was to go back to the place where the story in the logbooks began. To prove what, I didn't know.

The team looked puzzled. Sergeant Diggs just shrugged shoulders. Travis flicked ashes from his cigar and looked over at the team as if to say, "Don't ask me." There was no further discussion, so the ADC dismissed the team and told them to be formed up at our unit helipad at 0700, ready to move out.

I went back to my quarters and packed my gear for the move-out in the morning. I had some leftovers from my prime rib dinner in my room and what was left of the Jack Daniels. I chowed down and began to plow through the rest of the logbooks. There came a point in the story where I, meaning whoever had taken my name, became the Supreme Commander of the Legion of Aeneas, along with the A-Team. There were great descriptions of Airborne and Ranger training, operations planning, recon patrols, and a complete intelligence assessment by, of course, Tom Fredricks. There were 1,800 Legionnaire troops divided into three Regiments being trained for a D-Day attack of FSB Cronus and there was one more encounter with Athena as she was preparing for an Airborne operation the next morning. She uttered these words, "Galanis, I have told you. You are of Olympus. Our coming together affirms this. But you have been sent here for a great purpose. Our passion must not interfere with that purpose. These are fleeting moments that belong to the aither of Mount Olympus."

The last three logs continued with the telling of the story but were mostly devoted to what was labeled *Operation Golden Chariot Record of D-Day Operations*. It was late. I crawled into my bunk but couldn't sleep. It was as if I *was* the Supreme Commander awaiting the H-hour that was sure to come.

I tossed about, then got up and sat at my desk, staring at the stacks of logbooks. Before I returned to my bunk, I had reached two conclusions. First, there was no one in the A-Team or anyone I knew who could create the story I had just read. No one person knew about Camp Savage, and FSB Cronus that had just been obliterated by B-52 strikes, nor the separate missions of the A-Team and Captain Kellogg's LRRP team. Who would know how to coopt the CIA and MAC-V into participating? This was all a weird fantasy.

My second conclusion, fantasy or not, someone had to have written it down. Perhaps there was something at the supposed entrance to the "lost portal" that could help to answer my questions and resolve my confusion. I went back to bed around 0300 and immediately fell asleep. At 0500, Sergeant Travis banged on my door. "Okay, Sleeping Beauty, Sir. Choppers are on the pad; two hours to take off."

"Thanks, Top."

As I was shaving, I realized I had been dreaming about Athena. Her image was the same as the photo in the mythology book. We stood face to face in a lush garden. She looked into my eyes. When she spoke, I immediately recognized her voice. "Galanis, I know that someday you will return to Olympus. When you are ready, I will guide you there with the help of Hera, our great queen." That's all I could remember. I replayed those words over again as I grabbed some coffee and a sweet roll from the mess hall on my way to the helipad.

Tom Fredricks had briefed the crews of the three Hueys that were already cranked up. The team was dropped off at a landing zone a hundred yards from the bombing site. Sergeant Travis barked out orders when we got to the site, "Okay, you three take the east. Hoppy, get 'em spread out. Hey, numbnuts, didn't I say spread out? Manny, you stay back there with the CO and the ADC. Alright, girls, move out smartly if you wanna get back to the base in time for all-you-can-eat lobster night!"

After six hours of assessing the damage, we were done. Our legs felt like rubber after clunking our way over two kilometers of rubble and muck. We broke for lunch amidst the usual banter of whose walk was the toughest or longest or a "ballbuster." Tom Fredricks and I made small talk, but my mind kept going back to my dream about Athena.

I called Perez over, "Manny, call Dong Tam operations control and let 'em know we're done here and moving on to the portal, ah, I mean the suspected tunnel complex." That little slip was a sure sign that I was losing all perspective. Perez made the call, and we saddled up. Tom Fredricks called out the direction of march and we were off. Once we left the stench of the bomb site behind, the mixed smells of bougainvillea, jacaranda and frangipani wafted across our path, just as described by Alagon while at Camp Savage.

We stopped for a quick smoke break, and I surveyed the ground around us. There were no signs that a fierce battle had taken place there. We pressed on and arrived at a large clearing. Suddenly, Rob Salinas called out, "There it is. I'll be goddammed. Sir, it's right where you said it would be." The team assumed security positions around the entrance and waited for instructions.

I walked over to Sergeant Travis. "Top, let's get three or four guys to recon what's in there."

"Roger, Sir."

Minutes later, Gage, Rogers, and Osbourne proceeded into the tunnel with flashlights and weapons at the ready. Twenty minutes later, Rogers radioed from inside. "All clear. You all might want to see this, over."

I replied, "We're on our way." Once again, what I observed matched the story told in the logbooks. There were light strings on both sides of the massive tunnel. What looked like fox holes and firing positions were cut into the sides. M-16 casings were strewn about along with C-ration cans, empty cigarette packages and excrement. It looked like a bivouac area at an ROTC summer training camp.

At the far end was a cavernous room of solid stone. Someone shined a flashlight on the wall to our front. Sergeant Diggs burst out with, "Fuckin' Airborne. I wonder how they find time to fight the war?"

Sergeant Taylor rejoined, "I don't know, but they must've brought a fuckin' platoon of engineers with them!"

What we were looking at was a six-foot high parachute with an airborne tab above and jump wings below etched into the stone. I knew instantly why it was there. I felt my heart begin to pound in my chest and my vision began to blur as if I were going to black out. I took several deep breaths. I approached the wall, placed my hands on the jump wings and was mesmerized.

"Sir, Captain Galanis, Sir." It was Tom Fredricks breaking into my reverie. "Sir, there's nothing else here. Should we take off?"

"Ah, what, ah, yes, okay. I'll see you out there in a few minutes."

"Everything alright, Sir?"

"Sure, Tom. I, ah, just wanna make certain we didn't miss anything. I'll be right out."

Finally, I would have to leave, wondering if the etching was a clue or some bizarre pastime of an airborne unit. As I turned to go, I noticed something shiny in the far corner. I walked over and waved my flashlight back and forth until I found an object half-buried in the dirt. I scraped the dirt away and picked it up. It was a round stone surrounded by gold. As I pulled it up to get a closer look, I saw that it was attached to a gold chain. I held it in one hand

and shined my flashlight directly on the object. It was a medallion, <u>the</u> medallion.

I didn't know what to make of it–another practical joke or some god somewhere playing tricks with my mind. I walked somberly back through the tunnel and rejoined the team involved in their usual smokin' and jokin', waiting for their commander to say it was time to di di mau. "Hey, Sir," Sergeant Santini called out. "Find any buried treasure in there?" There was laughter all around. I didn't respond. I looked at my team and thought about all that we had been through together. Did that include some mythological battle to save the Underworld and Olympus? I was convinced that we would never know the answer to that question.

The sun was beginning to go down. Was that Helios and his chariot up there passing over Ong Troi's heaven? The ADC called Dong Tam and arranged our extraction. Soon, I would be back in my quarters, staring at the stacks of logbooks, as confused as when I left Dong Tam that morning. I needed time to think. Was it time to throw the logbooks in the base landfill? Could I ever reveal their existence to anyone else? I started pacing just like the night before D-Day. The night that other Galanis embraced Athena in the moonlight shining over Camp Savage.

There, at the tunnel or the portal, I resigned myself to the fact that I would never know the true story. I lit a Salem and walked a short distance away from the rest of the team. I was looking north, toward the battlefield, the place where I had last seen Athena. I finished my smoke and started back to join the team.

After a few steps, I was startled when light began to flash from the medallion. I stood there waiting in disbelief. A few more seconds passed, and the sky grew dark. I looked up and saw menacing storm clouds passing overhead. I watched its swirling motion with anticipation. The sky was nearly black. I was buffeted by a strong wind as the clouds began blocking out the sun. The light in the medallion began to flicker and then went out. There was intense thunder and lightning followed by torrential rain. I lifted my face toward the sky and let the monsoon rain pelt my face. I knew then that the light coming from the medallion was merely a reflection of the sun. I tucked the mysterious necklace into my pocket and continued walking toward the portal. For a moment there . . .

EPILOGUE

I departed Vietnam in January 1969. My time at Dong Tam and the Plain of Reeds came at the end of my second tour. After being promoted to Major, I spent two years as a senior instructor at the Kennedy Special Warfare Center back at Bragg, helping to churn out A-Team leaders for assignments in Vietnam. On occasion, I would slip during a training session and refer to this or that location as being in Van Lang. I simply told the class that after two tours, I had gained extensive knowledge of the history of Vietnam and gave them assignments to research Van Lang.

Those weren't the only times the story of the Legion and its battle against Cronus entered my subconscious. I might be at a party at the O-Club or at a family gathering and find myself starting to describe this certain big battle that took place in the Plain of Reeds. At this point, I would need to make an excuse for abruptly changing the subject. I say these things were in my subconscious because I never spent time ruminating about what it all meant. True, I had brought the logbooks and the medallion back to the States. But they were in a footlocker in my room at the Bachelor Officers

Quarters, which had never been opened since I moved in a year earlier.

One weekend, two of my fellow instructors and I headed down to Myrtle Beach for a little R&R. Translated, drinking and chasing women. I went for a walk through town and discovered a genuine Greek taverna on one of the side streets. I could smell the souvlaki and moussaka cooking from half a block away. When I entered, I was greeted by the most beautiful woman I had ever seen, Greek or otherwise. Of course, she *was* Greek. Her name was Cassandra, "Cassie" for short. That night and the next I met her when she got off work. We walked on the beach, played miniature golf, and sat in the park talking for hours. Those days were all it took. I had met the woman I was going to marry.

I made the two-hour drive from Bragg to Myrtle Beach every weekend for the next three months. I thought her parents, Greek immigrants from post-WWII, would tire of seeing me, but they welcomed me into the family and approved of their daughter's marriage to what they called a *warrior for freedom*. When we married the following June, my assignment to the JFK Center was extended for another year. We bought a house in Fayetteville and settled in. When I received orders for a third tour in Vietnam, Cassie and I agreed it was time to file for a medical retirement based on my collection of wounds and injuries from fourteen years in what Sergeant Travis liked to call the "green machine."

Our decision was made easier by the fact that Cassie was pregnant. We were expecting a daughter, so Cassie began her search for a "proper" Greek name. At dinner one night, she announced her choice–Athena! I tried to put my wineglass down gently, but it tipped over. I wiped up the mess, and all I could say was, "I'm sure your parents will approve."

My retirement came through; I got a job as a consultant at the Warfare Center; we bought a bigger house, and little Athena arrived two days before Christmas. The story in the logbooks and my personal quest to determine how it came to be were now in the distant past, or so I thought.

Our new house had a nice-sized den, which I turned into a home office. There were shelves and bookcases for my military memorabilia, plaques, mugs, and the like. One wall was covered with framed citations, diplomas, team photos, my commission and retirement orders. I hate to say it, but I had created what military types call an "I love me" room.

Despite that, when Athena came into my office, I enjoyed explaining what this or that plaque or photo meant and where it was from.

There was one shelf she almost always went to and asked, "Daddy, where are all those green books and that necklace from?" After the passage of time, nearly ten years since I stuffed the logbooks into my rucksack at Camp Savage and found the medallion inside the portal, I had decided it was okay to take them out of my footlocker. The medallion was perched on a small brass tripod on a table below the shelves.

I would always answer Athena by saying, "Oh, Daddy got those in Vietnam in the war. When you get older, I will tell you a story about them."

After that she was satisfied to just look at the medallion and smile. Not long after, Cassie was in the kitchen when she heard Athena talking to someone in the den. I was out mowing the lawn, so Cassie went to the den to investigate. When I came into the house, Cassie called for me to come into the den. Athena was standing by the table with the medallion on it. Cassie spoke to Athena, "Tell Daddy who you were talking to just now."

Athena replied, "The lady in the stone."

I asked her, "Do you mean the stone on the necklace?"

"Yes, Daddy, her name is Athena, too."